TH
SHARDS
OF
OPHELIA

NICOLE PLATANIA

Stars Inked Press, Inc.
6320 Topanga Cyn Blvd. Ste. 1630 *1033
Woodland Hills, CA 91367

First paperback edition August 2023

© Cover design: FranziskaStern - www.coverdungeon.com - Instagram: @coverdungeonrabbit

Edited by Kelley Frodel
Proofread by Megan Sanders
Interior design by Lorna Reid
Map design by Abigail Hair

ISBN 979-8-9862704-2-5 (paperback)
ISBN 979-8-9862704-3-2 (ebook)

www.nicoleplatania.com

PRAISE FOR *THE SHARDS OF OPHELIA*

"A stunning addition to the TCOO series! TSOO will leave readers thoroughly satisfied and craving more from these characters. Nicole's writing is immersive, romantic, exciting, and healing. The plot twists had me on the edge of my seat and my eyes glued to every word. I absolutely adored this novel and can't wait to devour all that follow!"

-Olivia Rose Darling, author of the *Fear the Flames* series

"Nicole takes Ophelia and her family to the next level. SHARDS is all about everything that bookstagram and tiktok love in new adult romantasy. The next stage of Ophelia's journey is heartbreaking as it is both romantically exciting. Tolek fans will be screaming all the way from the Mystique territory."

-L.B. Divine, author of *The Prince of Snow* series

"The Shards of Ophelia is a breathtaking follow up to The Curse of Ophelia. While the fantastical world is still the core, Nicole has weaved painful character growth, melancholy realizations, and lessons worth learning throughout every character's story. You will cheer for your favorites and you will cry with them as they navigate the paths their lives have taken and the expanding world around them. This is a must read series and it is only the beginning."

-K. Jamila, author of *Mine Would Be You* and *Golden Hour of You and Me*

"Nicole Platania has crafted an exquisite sequel to the The Curse of Ophelia series - one filled with intrigue, action, and passion. She explores the complexities of the heart and mind while providing eloquent storytelling, unforgettable characters, and a unique world of magic and power. A gripping, heartrending read that will have fantasy romance readers clamoring for more."

-Jessica Ayala, author of *Of Fangs and Shadows*

To anyone who has ever needed permission
to choose yourself: here it is.

Author's Note

This book contains depictions of violence, PTSD, blood/gore, discussed death of a child, death of loved ones, drug/alcohol dependency, and some sexual content.
If any of these may be harmful to you, please read carefully.

PRONUNCIATION GUIDE

CHARACTERS AND CREATURES

Aimee: *Ay-me*
Aird: *Air-d*
Akalain Blastwood: *Ah-kuh-lane Blast-wood*
Alvaron: *Al-vuh-ron*
Annellius Alabath: *Uh-nell-ee-us Al-uh-bath*
Astania: *Uh-ston-ya*
Bacaran Alabath: *Bah-kuh-ron Al-uh-bath*
Barrett: *Bair-it*
Brigiet: *Bri-jeet*
Calista: *Kuh-liss-tuh*
Collins: *Call-ins*
Cypherion Kastroff: *Sci-fear-ee-on Cast-Rahf*
Danya: *Dawn-yuh*
Dax: *Dax*
Divina Delantin: *De-vee-nuh Dell-in-tin*
Elektra: *Ill-ectra*
Erini: *Ih-ree-nee*
Erista: *Eh-ris-tuh*
Esmond: *Ez-min-d*
Ezalia: *Eh-zale-ee-uh*
Gerad: *Jer-ahd*
Glawandin: *Gluh-wahn-din*
Hectatios: *Hehk-tay-shus*
Hylia: *Hi-lee-uh*
Jezebel Alabath: *Jez-uh-bell Al-uh-bath*
Kakias: *Kuh-kye-yus*
Lancaster: *Lan-kaster*
Larcen: *Lare-sen*
Lessel: *Less-il*
Lucidius Blastwood: *Loo-sid-ee-yus* Blast-wood

Lyria: *Leer-ee-uh*
Malakai Augustus Blastwood: *Mal-uh-kye Uh-gus-tus Blast-wood*
Marxian: *Mark-shen*
Meridat: *Mare-ih-daat*
Mila: *Mee-lah*
Missyneth: *Mis-sin-ith*
Mora: *Mor-uh*
Ophelia Tavania Alabath: *Oh-feel-eeya Tuh-vahn-yuh Al-uh-bath*
Santorina Cordelian: *San-tor-ee-nuh Kor-dee-lee-in*
Sapphire: *Sah-fire*
Tavania Alabath: *Tuh-vahn-yuh Al-uh-bath*
Titus: *Tie-tuhs*
Tolek Vincienzo: *Tole-ick Vin-chin-zoh*
Vale: *Vale*
Victious: *Vik-shuss*

PLACES

Ambrisk: *Am-brisk*
Banix: *Ban-ix*
Caprecion: *Kuh-pree-shun*
Damenal: *Dom-in-all*
Gallantia: *Guh-lawn-shuh*
Gaveral: *Gav-er-all*
Palerman: *Powl-er-min*
Pthole: *Tholl*
Thorentil: *Thor-in-till*
Turren: *Tur-in*
Valyn: *Val-in*
Vercuella: *Vair-kwella*
Xenovia: *Zin-oh-vee-yuh*

ANGELS OF THE GALLANTIAN WARRIORS

Bant, Prime Engrossian Warrior: *Bant*
Damien, Prime Mystique Warrior: *Day-mee-in*

Gaveny, Prime Seawatcher: *Gav-in-ee*
Ptholenix, Prime Bodymelder: *Tholl-en-icks*
Thorn, Prime Mindshaper: *Thorn*
Valyrie, Prime Starsearcher: *Val-er-ee*
Xenique, Prime Soulguider: *Zen-eek*

GODS OF AMBRISK'S PANTHEON

Aoiflyn, The Fae Goddess: *Eef-lyn*
Artale, The Goddess of Death: *Are-tall*
Gerenth, The God of Nature: *Gair-inth*
Lynxenon, The God of Mythical Beasts: *Leen-zih-non*
Moirenna, The Goddess of Fate & Celestial Movements: *Moy-ren-uh*
Thallia, The Witch Goddess of Sorcia: *Thall-ee-uh*

-PART ONE-
CLOTHO

CHAPTER ONE

OPHELIA

THERE WAS SOMETHING TO be said for standing up when, internally, you were shattered. When your flesh was a case for broken bones and your heart beat tainted blood, but you slipped a mask over your features and became what was expected of you. Only the strongest survived the wounds dug into their souls.

Walking into the Rapture Chamber, I'd imagined what I would face from the five chancellors of the minor clans. They would see me as too young, too brash for the role of Revered—the warrior who, as the leader of the Mystiques, singularly held the most power on the continent.

So, I'd entered with the confidence I'd seen from warriors before me and the pulsing reminder of the power in my own blood, using that to meld my broken pieces shoddily together for the duration of the meeting.

Twelve hours later, facing down a different battle entirely, my resolve was buckling. I squeezed my sister's and Malakai's hands on either side of me, seeking their strength.

"Are you sure you don't want me to come with you?"

My cheeks flushed where Malakai's stare burned into them, but it was nothing lustful. It was the third time he'd asked me, and I'd denied him for as many.

Instead of meeting his gaze, I tracked the shadows dancing across the marble floors. Night swept further over the mountains, orbs of mystlight popping into existence along the ceiling's center. Buried as we were in the lower level of the palace, one wall built directly into rock, the stars and moon were hardly visible. Dull light shone through the arched windows, gold-trimmed panes peeking between thick velvet curtains.

The Revered's Palace was nothing if not a center of opulence, despite the fact that only Lucidius—our corrupt former leader and Malakai's father—had occupied it in recent years. Even this level, the holding cell, was built to symbolize power.

Ice filled my veins, curling around my stomach at the reminder of the lies Lucidius Blastwood had bathed in while his people suffered. How he'd schemed with Queen Kakias of the Engrossians for decades to ignite a false war between our two clans in order to place their bastard son in the Revered's seat as a sign of peace. The revelation sent shock waves through the continent as strong as the Spirit Volcano erupting. Thousands of Mystiques had been devastated by those actions. Yet he had been here, hidden away in his marble tower, doing Damien knew what with his days.

"Ophelia?" Malakai asked, his whisper slithering down the stone walls.

Shaking my head and blinking back to reality, I dropped Malakai's hand and met his worry-worn eyes. "We'll be okay."

"I won't utter a word." The crease between his dark brows deepened, mystlight casting shadows on the planes of his face.

I opened my mouth to argue but stopped at the bob of his throat. The fidgeting of his stare. Perhaps he didn't want to accompany us to protect me, but to avoid his own ghosts and the memories drawn to the surface by these cells. After signing a treaty to end the war and handing himself over to his father and the queen, spending two years as their prisoner, it made sense why this would haunt him.

I'd seen the pale scars marring his chest and torso, contorting the skin across his back. Though my stomach turned, I'd committed them to memory. This new map of his body outlined my own path to vengeance.

Setting aside my frustration for him, I stretched onto my toes to kiss his cheek, hoping that gentle touch could siphon away his pain as it once had.

"We'll be fine, Malakai." My voice softened with the words I left unsaid.

He stiffened, hand fisting against the bare skin above the skirt of my leathers, nails grazing softly against my spine, longing to keep me there.

"Besides," I added, stepping out of his hold. If I didn't, neither of us would get through tonight. "You have your own matters to attend to."

Bricks fortified a wall between us at the reminder.

"Good luck." I brushed my thumb across the scar his father had left on his jaw. *The father I killed*, I thought, dropping my hand.

He recoiled. Turned.

I almost pulled him back to me, almost indulged the desperate need flaring around my ribs, expanding with every breath. But I stayed still.

Without responding, he strode down the corridor. Each echo of boots against stone inflated the bubble around my ribs until it popped. Silence ricocheted inside of me, cementing that wall between us. Shrouding me in its shadow.

He paused before the farthest door, collecting his breaths. An echo of a pulse flashed through the Bind, the North Star tattoo we'd illegally received before he disappeared. Our jolted emotions bounced back and forth haphazardly along that sliver of threaded soul.

Over time, the bond should've deepened until the ink formed a bridge between us. Our own personal reality, through which we could pass thought and feeling.

But it hadn't.

Malakai left so shortly after we'd received the Bind, our tattoos had barely settled into our skin. After being apart for years—growing and shrinking and coping—everything within the magical ink was convoluted.

Now, there was a brief sweep of knee-shaking nerves, then the connection fell silent, as if he'd brushed aside all feeling. Without another look, he knocked. A dull voice welcomed him in, and the man I loved disappeared to confront his past.

Jezebel squeezed my hand. When I looked at her, her brows were raised.

"What?"

"Is everything okay?" She jerked her head toward the door Malakai had walked through.

"Everything's fine." At least, everything I had space in my mind to consider right now was. "Are you ready?"

For a moment, she looked so young, with wide eyes and a slight frame. The need to shield her from pain snapped like a whip inside me, but the time for that had long passed. She may still be seventeen, but she was as much a warrior as I was—the first underage Mystique to complete the Undertaking.

She closed her eyes, and I could see her build a steel frame around her emotions. When she opened them again, the tawny depths were a void.

Together, we stepped to the closest door, the reddish-brown wood reflecting mystlight on our skin and weapons. Gathering strength from the spear, Angelborn, at my back and dismissing my thundering heart behind my ribs, I rapped my knuckles against the wood.

After a beat of strained silence during which I swore I could hear both my sister's and my own blood rushing, a familiar voice called, "Come in."

We stepped across the threshold of our father's chamber, locked palms sweating. A tense rope knotted between us, each party observing the other.

A month. That's all it had been, but an eternity of experiences spread across the stone floor like spilled oil, leaving a sheen behind even once cleaned. It was clear, there in the thickening of the air—we were not the same girls who left Palerman.

The expression on my father's face stopped my voice in my throat, his eyes dull and cheeks hollowed out. His unbound golden hair fell in wild waves past his shoulders.

"Girls," he whispered, pushing back from his untouched plate and standing to his full, intimidating height.

A piece of my old self crumpled at his cracked voice, and we ran forward, each fitting beneath one of our father's arms as we had as children.

When I left on my quest, I didn't intend to ever see my father again. I said goodbye to Palerman and my entire life, ready to greet my death at the hands of the Curse. But when the Spirit Volcano leached it from my body, I was gifted a second chance. And when

Damien confirmed the Curse was a ruse, I no longer knew what to believe. As I stood there with my sister and father, all of those emotions came crashing down on me.

Reluctantly, I stifled that impending flood and pushed out of his arms. Jezebel followed my lead.

"You look…" he began, taking in the official leathers we wore. A grimace twisted his lips. My eyes drifted over my body, stopping on the Curse webbing on my wrist. The fresh white scars across my waist and arm. "The *lupine daimons*," he whispered.

"The what?"

His eyes focused back on mine. "The scars are from the tundra wolves, aren't they? The *lupine daimons*." I nodded, tucking away the name for the creatures we'd battled during the first step of the Undertaking. My father's shoulders drooped. "I'm sorry I couldn't warn you about them. I'm sorry they—" His words faded into a guilt-laden silence as my scars caught his stare again.

"I'm not. I'll never forget the pain those wolves—the *lupine daimons*—caused me, but I'm proud to bear these scars." He couldn't have prepared me any better without sharing secrets of the Undertaking. "You gave us everything we needed to succeed."

I looked over at my sister in her own leathers. The boots to her knees, with their thick soles. The gold plates around her shoulders and wrists. The fitted dress brushing mid-thigh with a tight corset up the back, made of the imbued brown leather from which Divina Delantin crafted all Mystique Warrior garb.

Together, we looked formidable. To my father, we must've looked—

"You look like true Mystique Warriors," he finished, a silver sheen gathering in the corners of his eyes.

Jezebel cleared her throat beside me, and I swallowed my own emotion.

"Father, take a seat." He snapped to attention at my stoic tone, but listened, returning to the table set for one. The room felt more like a bedchamber than a cell. An empty armoire stood in the corner, doors gaping, and a single bed waited across from the fire.

"How was your journey?" I began easily.

"Plagued with concerns after learning my daughters fled with no indication of where they were going." He ran a hand through his hair, muscles tensing as if trying not to yell.

"I'm sure it didn't take you long to figure it out," Jezebel said.

"I guessed within the day. Your mother practically had to restrain me from coming after you."

"We were fine," I assured him, fighting against images of the many times on that journey when I thought we might *not* be fine.

"What you attempted was illegal—"

"For no good reason." His brows rose at my interruption. I crossed my arms. "The Undertaking never should have been forbidden."

We explained everything we'd learned of Lucidius—one of his oldest and most trusted friends—and watched him crumble. Another casualty of the former Revered's deceit. First my father was silent, eyes bulging. Finally, he stood, knocking his chair out behind him and sending his plate flying against the wall. The china shattered, shards raining to the floor, food dripping down the wall.

Jezebel flinched.

"We need to know, Father." I tried to balance my tone somewhere between gentle and firm. "Did you have any indication of his plans? His betrayals?"

Hurt bloomed in his eyes. "Is this why I've been kept in here? You suspect me?"

"No, we don't," Jezebel said.

"But we have to follow protocols for *everyone* who may have known. Things have not been easy in claiming my place as Revered." Striding to the fire, I averted my gaze, hiding the self-doubt I hated feeling. "Everyone must be formally investigated in order to convince the chancellors of the minor clans I'm fit to rule. The rest of the Mystique Council is being questioned tonight, too."

This dynamic—this demanding of my father—was unnatural, but I supposed I had to adjust to it.

"He lied to us all." The pain in his tone was that of betrayal. "Tricked even me."

"Spirits, how did we end up here?" I thought aloud.

Was Lucidius truly so adept at secrets and lies? I guessed no one really knew him. Not his son, not his wife, not his oldest friend and most trusted advisor.

"That's the question I'm asking myself, *sorrida*."

At the nickname, I turned back to him. "I believe you, Father—I want you to know that. But I'm worried others won't be as easily convinced."

"You can dismiss the current council," he suggested reluctantly.

Part of me knew he was right. Ousting every member following their interrogations would be the quickest way to convince the chancellors that no corruption remained. But that felt like a lazy way to an end.

I was asserting myself as a leader, but I needed to *show* others I understood what that meant. It was not flipping a coin on someone's fate or turning my back on problems.

"We won't be banishing anyone," I stated. "The former Mystique Council will stay here."

"And why is that?" He was leading me, a lesson like all the years he trained me to one day take his role as Second.

"It would be rash to dismiss experienced advisors when I'm new to rule." A bit of that doubt in myself crept into my voice, but I turned it away. "You can resume your stay in the Second's suite. The others can have their rooms, as well. We've all taken empty apartments." Ones we could make our own. "There will be changes to our governing system, but those who are willing will help with reconstruction."

He contemplated for a moment, finally stepping to me, a hand at my shoulder. "Be sure you take rule as your own, *sorrida*. It will not be handed to you."

"I'm taking it now." I gripped Starfire's hilt, swearing, "I'm leading by example, working with the former generation to rebuild a Mystique legacy that was crushed under the last regime and uplifting the next age of warriors. I'll restore my people—our people—back to a greatness we rightfully deserve, but that is not to say I can do it on my own. Leaders must work with those they hope to rule, must listen in order to do right by them."

Things Lucidius never did.

A mixture of pride and wariness swept across my father's face, but his shoulders slackened.

"Are you against this?" My voice cracked.

"I'm not against your rule, Ophelia." He ran a hand down his face. "My daughters—one of whom is still underage—disappeared in the night. You have to understand the fear that overtook your mother and I when we realized where you'd gone. Now, those same girls—the ones I had to teach repeatedly to hang up their weapons as children rather than leave them strewn across the yard—are claiming rule. One is stepping into the position of the most powerful warrior on Ambrisk... I am not denying you deserve it." He looked between us. "I am not denying either of you are meant for greatness, but I wouldn't be a good father if I didn't say I'm terrified for you. It seems we are on the brink of war, and I don't want you at the heart of it."

Did he not understand I already was? I had a personal vendetta against Kakias for the rubble she had turned my life into.

"Some battles are inevitable. We can only prepare ourselves to face them." I crossed the room, pouring a glass of water from the silver pitcher in the corner. The cool liquid washed over my tongue and down my throat, calming my racing thoughts. Spirits, I wished it was rum—or anything a little stronger to cloud my worries—but I'd promised myself I wouldn't drink for those reasons anymore.

"Besides, you fail to acknowledge that while we may have been irresponsible as children, your daughters have been cleaning up their own messes for years now." I drained the rest of my water and faced my father again, a smile on both our faces.

"Tell me of the Rapture, then." He righted his chair and eased into it, ready to hear of the day-long convention we'd had with the leaders of the five minor clans.

"To begin, Aird is a bigot." Jezebel scooted onto the bed and crossed her ankles as she insulted the Mindshaper chancellor.

"He's—" I gritted my teeth, taking a breath. "He's made it clear that he doesn't support my appointment to Revered." The matter had taken up the majority of today's meeting.

"And who would he rather?" There was an unspoken question in my father's voice—*Malakai?*

I shook my head. "He suggested you take the position."

"That's not possible. The Spirits demand the role pass from one generation to the next. The balance—"

"It appears he's selectively remembering what the balance of power demands." Jezebel was right. The chancellor had warped the pillar of our magic in his memory, referencing it only when it suited him.

"And what of the others?" my father asked, tone serious as he resumed his role as Second, picking apart details for a strategy.

"The Soulguiders will vote in my favor." Their chancellor, Meridat, had all but confirmed it today.

"To be expected based on the quarter of your Soulguider heritage. It would be beneficial politically and demonstrate loyalty."

"The other three are uncertain." I worried my lip, my mind replaying every moment of that meeting. "We're reconvening tomorrow, and I need two more votes."

"Titus will likely vote your way," Jezebel chimed in, then looked at my father. "He requested time to conduct a reading tonight, but that is a Starsearcher's way of not appearing easily swayed."

"*Assuming* the stars show him I'm the right choice, that's still only three."

"Seawatchers and Bodymelders." My father contemplated. "The Seawatchers are the most thinly spread."

"Ezalia will be careful, then." With their minor clan split between the Eastern Territory and Western Outposts, guarding the coasts of Gallantia, they were always under threat. "It will have to be Brigiet," I decided, picturing the Bodymelder's wine-red hair and closed-off expression. "I didn't know how she'd vote.

"Jez, when we're done here, we have to tell the others she's our goal." If anyone could persuade an alliance, it was my brigade of reckless and charmingly hopeful friends.

My sister nodded, and I released a breath of relief. But I couldn't allow myself to sink into it. "There are some other matters we must discuss. During the Undertaking—"

"What you experienced is to be kept private, Ophelia," my father scolded.

"Listen to her." It was odd to hear Jezebel's voice overpower him, but he turned attentive—wary—eyes back to me. While we couldn't discuss the ritual in full, small details were allowed.

"What can you tell us of Annellius Alabath?" Nerves fluttered through my stomach.

"Annellius?" Understanding lit his eyes. "You saw him in the volcano."

"Yes," I responded, at the same time Jezebel said, "No." I looked to her, but she avoided my gaze. I realized I knew nothing of her experience. Though she tried to hide it, something had changed within my sister on the journey to the Undertaking, a shadow hovering over her shoulders now.

"Why are you asking?" My father's eyes narrowed, mystlight highlighting steely suspicion.

"I need you to tell me what you know of him."

He braced his forearms on his knees; the air swelled with anticipation.

"Everything I know of Annellius is lore, girls. You have to understand that. Whatever I tell you—there's no way for any of us to know whether or not it's true."

"Understood," I said, but my second pulse—the one that had emerged when I found Angelborn—pounded.

"Take a seat, then." He waited for me to remove my weapons and join Jezebel on the bed. I was unable to escape the feeling that we were children once again, being told a story before bed. "According to legends passed down our line, Annellius Alabath was the first and only warrior in history to reveal he had Angelblood in his veins."

"How is that possible?" Jezebel propped her chin in her hand. "Shouldn't all Alabaths have it, as well?"

"It was removed after him," I answered.

"And it was dormant before him," my father added.

"Angelblood can be dormant?" Jezebel and I exchanged a weighted glance.

"It needs an agent to activate it. Supposedly, Annellius discovered the Alabath secret and created the agent in order to birth the effects within himself." Disapproval twisted my father's lips.

"What were they?" I leaned forward, wrapping my arms around myself to ward off the eerie chill spreading through my body. "The effects?"

"Accounts differ. Some say he was gifted strength and speed even greater than that of the fae. Some say he ascended as an Angel when he died. My father told me when the blood was activated, Annellius was visited by an Angel. Given a task."

Breath lodged in my throat. "What was it?"

"I don't know. Whatever it was, he died before completing it."

So, Annellius grew greedy in his pursuit of this task. The Angelblood was removed from his body and from those who came after him.

Until me, Damien had implied. If only I could call on the damn Angel when I needed him.

In the shadows of the room, I swore I heard a soft chuckle. Jezebel's spine straightened, but before she could say anything, I pushed myself off the edge of the bed, boots thudding to the floor as I stood.

"And that's the end of the tale?"

"Yes, but as I said, it's all lore. Who's to say my father's account is any more accurate than the other tales? There are barely any detailed ledgers."

Theories careened through my head quicker than an Angel's wings. There was order to be found in the chaos—I knew it. "Can I see the records that do exist?"

Suspicious eyes held mine. Then he stood and said, "I'll see what I can find."

I thanked the Spirits my father had always been a fastidious record keeper, housing copies of documents both in the Second's suite here and in Palerman.

"Thank you." I stepped forward, wrapped my arms around him, and pressed my ear to his chest to listen to the steady beat of his heart. "I'm glad you made it here."

For the first time since stepping foot in this room, I allowed the relief of seeing my father to crash over me, grateful for being given a second chance at life.

I didn't know why the Spirits had told me of the Angelblood. I wasn't sure why Damien had referenced it again in the mountains. But I would find out.

"I'm happy you're okay." My father kissed the top of my head. "Both of you." He held out an arm for Jezebel to join us. "And I'll do whatever I can to ease this transition with the Rapture and council."

Only the tightness of his voice told me how pained he was by

Lucidius's betrayal. A stark reminder of how deep this deceit went. Not only in my own life, but across all of Gallantia.

We couldn't escape the pain that man and Kakias had brought into our lives, but I swore to every Angel above I'd get my revenge.

"I'm proud of you both." His eyes settled on the gleaming spear leaning against the wall. "This is your time."

CHAPTER TWO

MALAKAI

EVERY LIE I'D BEEN fed over the past two years hung over my heart, poised to pierce, when I saw my mother and the *fucking wrecked* look in her eyes.

For so long I'd been the only one to feel the effects of Lucidius's decisions. His lies and betrayals—fucking Spirits, the beatings, even— it had all only affected me.

Or that was what I'd thought. I hadn't considered how far his wrath would stretch when I'd disappeared.

The marks were upon my skin—I'd ensured that—but it was becoming clearer every day how far the impacts reached. While I was the only one physically under his thumb, my mother, my friends, Ophelia…they were the ones who felt it.

Looking at my mother now, those fragmented lies threatened to dig into me until my sorrow was an ugly crimson mess upon the floor.

"Mali." My nickname was a sob up her throat. Then, she was across the room, hugging me, tears staining my shirt.

Something thick lodged itself in my throat, but I couldn't cry. I *wouldn't* cry when she was already so distraught.

She pulled back to look at me and ran soothing hands over my hair and down my face, carefully tracing the scar across my jawbone. The new one, left by my father's ring in some of our last days together.

I flinched when she touched it, hating that thick white line every time I looked in the mirror. It was a blatant reminder of everything I'd faced—of every way he'd hurt me. One I couldn't avoid. One everyone's eyes went to the second they looked at me and the world became a crushing weight on my chest.

"Did he…" Her voice trailed off.

My heart sped like it was going to leap out of my throat. My voice was rough when I spoke. "I don't—I can't—"

"Shh, shh. We don't have to talk about it." She stretched up to kiss my forehead like I was a child again. "You're safe," she whispered against my skin, reassuring us both: *You're alive.*

I wasn't sure what she already knew, but I was certain from the tears lining her cheeks that a piece of her had assumed I was dead—there was a dim light of relief in her eyes.

"Let's sit," she said. "Let's talk."

I followed her across the stone floor; my footsteps softened as we stepped onto the thick carpet in front of the hearth. We settled on one of the three settees in the sitting area. Why were these even here? This room was meant for sequestering prisoners. But the gray velvet couches matched the linens on the bed and the curtains hanging from its posts. A dining table was laid with gold-etched dishware, a pitcher of wine in the center.

"Mali?" my mother asked, blue eyes hollow.

The flames warmed my back, siphoning out the chill I hadn't noticed. Bracing my forearms on my knees, I sagged forward, indulging the heat, head hanging limply between my shoulders.

"I stayed a night in Turren on my journey here, and the rumors—they're horrific." She rubbed a hand in circles between my shoulder blades. I prayed she couldn't feel the raised edges of my scars through the fabric.

But she could—I knew she could. Yet, she soothed me anyway.

Why was she the one comforting me? I was the one who had caused the hurt in her eyes; my disappearance had done that. As my father had told me again and again, this was all my fault.

And it was only about to get worse when I shattered my mother's world. Lately, it seemed like breaking others was the sole purpose of my existence.

"He—" I couldn't bear to say his name. "Father and Kakias—they were working together." Forcing the words out was difficult. Each tasted burnt against my tongue, but I kept going. Partly because my mother deserved the truth, partly because I needed to admit it.

When I finished explaining everything, I met her gaze. Silent tears streaked down her cheeks, giving life to her pain in thin rivers that wanted to drown me.

"I'm sorry, Mother. I'm so sorry." Why in the fucking Angels did I have to be the one to do this? Hadn't I suffered enough? Perhaps Damien enjoyed my pain.

"No, Mali, it's all right." She looked at the ceiling until her tears slowed. "I already knew some of it, but hearing you say it. Hearing what he did to you...It's all so much more real than before."

My heart skipped a beat at her confession. "What did you know?"

"I knew of your father's...loyalties." She leaned against the cushions, one hand toying with the tassels on the nearest pillow.

I pushed up from the couch, a fire roaring to life in my chest. "You knew about Kakias? And their son? Did you know what they were planning, as well?" Had she been aware I signed that Spirit-damned treaty? Was she unsurprised when I didn't return from the Undertaking?

"Malakai, shh." She held out a hand to me. "Take a seat, and I'll explain."

I remained standing, the crackling in the hearth accenting my panting breaths, but she clearly wasn't going to elaborate until I listened. So I took a seat, staring at the flames instead of her, trying to process it all.

"To answer your questions—no. I didn't know any of those things. But women are rather smart, if you have not learned that yet. I always felt your father didn't love me as he claimed."

"But you were his partner. You—you—" The tattoo on my chest throbbed, and my head whipped to her. "How did you promise your lives to each other with the Bind if he wasn't loyal?"

"Darling," she began in her most soothing tone. "It was a false tattoo."

"What?"

"It's why I always suspected he was lying." She lifted her hand for me to see the plain band of black ink looped twice around her wrist, oddly impersonal for a Bind. "I never felt the connection one should feel within it." Her eyes flickered to my chest, to the star beneath my linen shirt. "I never wanted to admit it to anyone, but I always thought there was something wrong. I only recently realized your father must have had the imbued ink switched with regular dye so no lasting promises would be made between us."

"Why wouldn't you say anything?" I flopped back against the cushions.

"You forget I was no love-struck girl who fell for him. I felt affinity, and I grew to love the man I thought he was, but this entire partnership was an agreement between our parents."

The Deneski family, my mother's line, was a strong Mystique heritage, and that was how these political arrangements worked. A Revered needed a worthy partner at their side, demonstrating unity and commitment. Their proposal had been supported by every party, save for the man himself, apparently.

I used to think myself fortunate that my parents never sought the same control over my life. Though, Ophelia and I made their task easy by choosing each other at such a young age. Should our parents have selected, it would have been us anyway. The son of the Revered and the eldest Alabath daughter—it always made sense.

"But why not demand he at least respect you? If you knew what he was doing…"

"I saw no point in us being unhappy together if we could be happy apart and still hold the image of power." Her shoulders drooped, each confession paining her. "I thought his dalliance was only that—a physical relationship with another. I didn't know who it was or what they planned. I only focused on fulfilling the role I'd stepped into, on being what the Mystiques needed. And that was an example to emulate and an heir born of two powerful bloodlines."

"An heir that was never wanted." Looking at my hands, I counted the scars left on my wrists from my cuffs.

"Don't you dare think that, Malakai. Not for one fateful second." She pulled both of my hands between hers. "I have always wanted you. You were the brightest point of this entire charade." Tears rolled down her cheeks again. "You are the thing that made it worth it."

Her words cushioned the hatred surrounding my heart, if only slightly.

"He had another son. Another family. *He didn't want us.*" And there it was—the earth-shattering truth that hurt me as much as the physical torture I'd endured. The man who was responsible for my existence regretted it.

"If I had been a stronger woman, I would have left him when he was unfaithful, but politics are trickier than that. For years, I convinced myself I was happy, and once I had *you*, I truthfully was. There were so many times I wanted to leave with you, but I figured that with him in Damenal and us in Palerman, it was the best it could be. Then, when you were little, and I lost my brother, my future was cemented. I had to stay with the Revered until you inherited his rule because I needed to provide for my parents. Ensure their health and safety."

I could barely remember what my uncle looked like, but I remembered the way my mother cried when he died. Until today, it was the only time I'd seen her so distraught.

"One thing is certain," I said through a thick throat. "Lucidius may have given me his blood, but I don't want to be his son."

My mother tugged my head to her shoulder, running soothing hands down my back, and repeatedly muttered, "I'm sorry."

"Why are you sorry?" I asked.

"Because I didn't protect you."

Tears stung the back of my eyes, but I forced them away again. "You're not the one at fault."

She smiled softly at me, the small slip of joy brightening the room's fog of despair. "I'm so happy you're okay."

I might never be okay again, I didn't say.

"I have something for you," she continued, wiping her eyes with the back of her hand.

"For me?" I asked, but she was already striding across the room. She cracked the door of the armoire, and dresses and leathers threatened to overflow—

"He gave you these rooms?"

Anger burned through me at the realization that those belongings had been here before she arrived today.

Lucidius had moved her here. Not that she spent much time in Damenal, particularly after I disappeared, but sometime between then and now, he'd cast her out of his suite. Transferred her palace things to the level for prisoners.

She clearly didn't want to discuss the fucked-up treatment, because she shook her head at my mangled expression and crossed back to the settee, a polished wooden box in her hands. She held it out to me, fingers trembling.

Prickling curiosity numbed my anger.

"What is it?" The box was heavy in my lap, but I only stared at it.

"Open it, dear."

When I lifted the lid, my jaw popped open at the gift tucked in its velvet lining.

"It's only two years later than I intended." Her voice was low, but emotion fought to rise within it.

Gently, I slipped my hand beneath the cool leather. It warmed instantly, as if waiting for me. I removed the warrior's sash—my sash—from the box and unfolded it before my eyes, every movement slowed by shock and reverence. Made of a thick brown leather, it would be impenetrable, enhanced by the essence of power we guarded.

The fact that my mother had this made for me before I completed the Undertaking—that she had enough faith in my worth to take this step—twisted my stomach. *Because I had not come back.*

"I can't accept this, Mother." I gripped it tighter. "It's beautiful. It's perfect, but I can't wear it."

"Yet," was all she said.

I looked closer at the engravings on the sash. Stars. *North Stars.*

"Thank you," I whispered, tracing the largest star, thinking of who it represented.

"You deserve it." For the first time since I arrived, a full smile lifted her lips.

I didn't have the heart to wash it away by admitting that while she had guarded this cherished gift for over two years, I wasn't sure I wanted it.

I lost track of how long I sat in that dim chamber, barely daring to accept I was truly with my mother again. We were both hurt, shadows of people we had once been, but in those few hours, a bit of light returned to her. She'd be okay.

When the moon was high in the sky and she was yawning, I took my leave, tucking her gift beneath my arm.

"Good night, Mali. I love you," she said as I gripped the door handle.

"I love you, too, Mother." The words felt good to say, despite the pressure on my chest. Despite the fact that all evening, my bones were weighed down.

I crept through the palace, stopping in shadows of statues and alcoves whenever footsteps echoed on the marble floors and wide staircases. I stared absently at the murals on the ceilings as I fought to steady my breath. I was in no mood to speak to anyone.

When I finally made it back to the suite Ophelia and I shared, I closed the bedchamber door behind me, leaning my back against it. Everything was heavy—my arms, my head, my heart. My bones each weighed a ton. They wanted a break. Time to rest, that was all they asked.

But there was work to be done and ugly realities to accept. So much time to make up for and so many apologies to utter. So much, when I was already *so broken*—

My breathing turned into short gasps against the cracking in my chest. One by one, those fragmented pieces of the innocent boy who had loved his father pierced my heart. Shame over the lies I'd told, guilt for the pain I'd caused, and even sadness for my despicable father's death flooded out of me with each slice.

Darkness dragged me to the ground. The box clattered to the marble, the corner chipping as it snapped open, the sash tumbling out.

It was a symbol I should've been proud to don.

I didn't want it.

Didn't deserve it.

The tears that had been bundled in my chest all night slipped out, burning with pained fury and blurring the stars on the leather. Since Ophelia had found me—since she'd killed my father—I'd been balancing on this precipice. Now, sorrow flowed faster, trickling over my lips, tainted bitter with disgust.

How was I sad over that man's death? After everything he'd done, I still managed to mourn.

I ran my hands through my hair, gripping it. With shuddering breaths, I reminded myself of the truth.

Ambrisk is better off without Lucidius.

Everyone I loved was safer with him gone.

But the sash, the Mystique Warrior I was meant to become…it was a tarnished, hateful reality. As a boy, I'd wanted those things in order to be like my father. As a man, I wanted to be nothing like him. I'd slice open my arm and untangle his blood from mine if possible, if only to be clean. To draw out any lingering connection to him so I could find my own path forward.

But pain couldn't be lifted so easily. That was the thing I was learning about betrayals—they didn't vanish. No bridge could be built to carry the scorned party over it; you had to muddle *through*. Fight through icy waves, weeds tangling around your ankles, current slapping at you.

If I was being honest, I didn't know if I could.

At some point, I crawled to bed. With the box from my mother on the nightstand, I fell asleep atop the covers, a wrung-out shadow of the man everyone expected me to be.

CHAPTER THREE

OPHELIA

As I STOOD BEFORE the doors to the Rapture Chamber the next morning, the weight of millions of lives balanced on my shoulders. I could have sworn unseen eyes were burrowing into my skin, waiting to see what I'd do next and whether a night of rest and persuasive words had succeeded in convincing the chancellors of my worth.

The walls around me wavered. I wanted to hide, to bury my nose in books in the palace's great library and search for convincing arguments.

But solitude would only be avoidance. If I knew anything, it was that fate had a way of finding you, despite your greatest efforts. I had to dig up the answers within myself.

Angelborn's pulse beat through my blood as I looked to Tolek, Cypherion, and Jezebel—my core guard, dressed in official leathers—then to Malakai and Santorina. The former was allowed attendance in the Rapture because he was a warrior, but couldn't participate since he hadn't completed the Undertaking. I didn't think he minded; he'd been quiet since I returned late last night and found him asleep atop the covers, the room in disarray and a box I recognized on his bedside table.

I tried not to think about that now, though.

"The Bodymelders operate on logic," Santorina reminded me, having spent the morning with the healing clan. "Approach from a factual standpoint, and Brigiet should be convinced."

"Logic, right." Rationale as opposed to the faith Mystiques

operated on. I looked to Cyph, the most practical of us all, and he nodded in encouragement.

"You can do this, Ophelia," he said simply.

"Good luck." Santorina hugged me to her, the cotton of her dress soft beneath my shaking hands. As a human, she wasn't granted permission to join the Rapture. I'd never hated that rule more than now.

"She doesn't need luck," Tolek said with one of his charming grins. "She was born for this."

His support shot through me like a lightning bolt, straightening my spine. He was right.

"I'm ready," I told them, confidence flowing stronger.

Tolek and Cypherion opened the large double doors, and Jezebel entered first to announce my arrival, Malakai following last.

Chairs scraped against marble as the chancellors stood, the apprentices and advisors they'd brought taking up positions around the room's three solid walls, between the gilded statues of each Angel. The fourth wall—my favorite view—was open to the air, looking over the mountains. The only place in Damenal where you could see the entire city.

Every clan was dressed in their finest today. From Titus's swaths of silver silk robes adorning his tall frame, to Meridat's chiffon wisp of a lilac gown, and Ezalia's sand-colored leathers, each leader wore what their people deemed honorable garb. Even Brigiet wore a thick dress and sturdy gloves, and Aird donned a straight-shouldered jacket, a heavy fur cloak draped off one shoulder, despite the warm mountain air.

The symbolism didn't escape me, but I didn't let it show. Removing Angelborn from my back and handing her to Cyph, I took my place at the table. Only once I sat did the chancellors do the same.

"I trust you all got some rest since we last spoke," I began. Both the comment of a gracious host and a challenge. If the chancellors were going to force me to play tedious games, then play I would—and I wouldn't settle for less than a victory.

Around the table, they nodded.

"We did, thank you," Titus said, adjusting the shooting star pin holding his robes closed at the sternum. I met his close-set eyes briefly and swore there was a hint of sorrow beneath his straight black brows.

A tight-lipped smile hid under the scruff of a long, square jaw.

"There is no use in stalling with small talk." Aird's voice sliced through the tension in the room, colder than the snowy terrain the Mindshapers hailed from.

"I suppose you're correct." I ground my teeth, refusing to hand over authority. "Would you like to begin with your vote, sir?"

We knew where Aird's vote would land. It was merely a formality that I requested it. Still, my fingers curled against my legs when he said, gray eyes narrowed to slits of icy denial, "I reject the appointment of Miss Alabath as the new Revered of the Mystique Warriors. I instead propose the council rules in her stead until an appropriate candidate is found."

The Mystique Council was composed of five masters of practice, a Second, and a Revered—all of whom the Rapture thought were currently under inspection. It was a calculated slight, this suggestion.

But I chose a stronger argument. "May I remind you we have an empty seat in this room." I didn't look at the spot we'd left open despite knowing the Engrossian queen wouldn't attend the Rapture. Nestled between Aird and Ezalia, the dark wooden chair cut to look like an Angel's wings was a futile symbol of the peace we hoped to one day reach. The real weight of the gesture, though, was how Kakias's manipulation filled the space, her vile actions taking up residence in the room despite her absence. "Remember the threat that is posed to *every* clan, Aird. Should that sway your decision?"

"The Mindshapers have no issue with the Engrossians, Miss Alabath."

As if on cue, a folded piece of parchment flared into existence in the center of the table. The room fell silent, taking in the black wax stamped with the Engrossian sigil: two axes forming a V with a crown in the center.

Chest tightening, I opened it. One delicately scrawled sentence glared up at me, *I do hope my dear Rapture misses me.*

She didn't sign it. Didn't need to.

This was no excuse for her absence, no explanation for her actions. This was a power play—a reminder that while she may not have deigned to attend the Rapture, she was not to be forgotten.

The energy in the room crackled with heightened tension. I

crumpled the paper and tossed it on the table, trying to focus on the challenge before me.

"If you do not stand with us, we will *all* have an issue with the Engrossians." I pointed to the note. "She is only beginning."

"That remains to be seen, Ophelia—"

"It's *Revered*, sir." Tolek's harsh voice echoed between the pillared wall, carrying out over the mountains. "I advise you respect the name of the leader the Angel has chosen."

The Mindshaper looked Tol up and down, eyes narrowed, and I hated something within that stare. "Should I now?"

Aird crossed one knee over the other, leaning back. His thick frame filled the wooden chair as he stroked his beard, platinum hair falling in a curtain around his shoulders.

I gave Tolek a grateful look but shook my head for him to back down.

"Thank you for your opinion in the matter of my appointment, Chancellor." I turned away from Aird, folding my hands atop the table. "Are there any who are in agreement?"

My heartbeat thundered so loudly behind my ribs, I was certain everyone would hear it. At my elbow, the Bind tingled. A hint of encouragement from Malakai that lifted my chin.

"The Soulguiders' position hasn't shifted since yesterday." Meridat stared at the note from the Engrossian queen, eyes as sharp as the scythes of her people. When she looked at me, sweeping her long braids over a dark shoulder, the many rings and fine bronze chains across her body caught the sun. "We stand with you, Revered Alabath."

My chest loosened a fraction.

One vote. Two with my own.

"Thank you." A blush warmed my chilled skin.

I looked to Brigiet and Ezalia—the Bodymelder and Seawatcher I'd told my father would be our most ambiguous opponents—and silently willed every bit of hope into my gaze. It all rested on the shoulders of these two women, and the Starsearcher beside them.

Brigiet's eyes flickered around the room, landing on a map of the continent hung at one end. Her movements were precise as she rose, the fluidity of the Bodymelders marking each step. She didn't say anything, running a finger along the painted white flowers bordering the image, then the gold frame surrounding it.

As the Bodymelder considered, Ezalia lifted her pointed chin, breaking her thoughtful trance with Kakias's note. Dark brown hair framed her sun-tanned face. She looked directly into my eyes with a sea-glass stare, voice as crisp as a breeze off the Neptitian Sea. "I'm not sure if you know this, Ophelia, but my family has always supported the Alabath line. We've led the Seawatchers in a nearly smooth rule dating back to the Angels." I held my breath as she scanned the room. "The Alabaths are the most historically strong, diplomatically fair, and utterly proven bloodline of the Mystique Warriors. That much is not up for debate between us as members of the Rapture."

"No one has argued against the Alabaths, Ezalia," Aird scoffed. The glare she cast him could cut glass.

The Mindshaper withered.

"As I was saying." Ezalia looked back to me. "The Seawatchers cannot offer you much by way of resources. But we can offer you support. You have my vote for appointment."

She rose, coming around the speckled marble table to shake my hand. The bracelets adorning her wrists chimed against each other, coral and sea-green stones matching the ones embedded in her leathers.

Heat bloomed behind my ribs—a tumble of pride, surprise, and joy. I hadn't expected Ezalia to be able to commit, not with how thin her ranks were. It wasn't an alliance that would benefit my people much, but it mattered in this moment. It demonstrated a united front.

That only left Brigiet and Titus. The Bodymelder had been warming to our persuasions since her arrival, and with Santorina worming her way innocently into their hearts—

But her full pink lips turned down, snapping my last stretch of hope.

"I'm sorry, Ophelia," she began. The rest of her words reached me as though from the opposite end of a tunnel. "There doesn't appear to be enough evidence from the logical perspective."

Logic. Rina said present facts. My mind raced to gather them, but the conversation continued over me.

"Must every decision be made from a logical stance?" Meridat asked.

"My people don't worship our Angel in the same way you do, Meridat. Neither do we hold allegiance to the Goddess of Death, like you; though I'm sure Artale appreciates your vote to support Ophelia. Our decisions are practicum fatale, a pillar of our practice." Brigiet swallowed, but fixed her round eyes on me, apology thick in her voice. "I'm sorry about this."

The meeting was slipping away from my control.

"Titus?" I stalled as I gathered arguments for Brigiet. Facts. Proof of my accolades and my ancestors' before me—

But when I turned to the Starsearcher, his grim nod froze my efforts.

"I'm aware many of you don't understand the nature of Starsearching. Our readings are handed to us, much as the Soulguiders' predictions of spirit deliverance are passed down from their Angel and Artale, but we deal in larger fates than one particular soul.

"Envision a map, with routes such as those drawn by a Master of Trade." Titus rose, speaking thoughtfully as he walked to the open wall, his hands behind his back and three-pointed dagger in his belt. "Every possibility—infinite futures—are mapped by celestial hands and turned over to my clan by the Angel Valyrie and the Celestial Goddess through our use of incense and tinctures. We can't choose what we read; it is the path that a warrior's current course puts them on.

"Last night, when I read at the Sacra Temple in the city...I saw destruction."

The word echoed down my bones, shocking my frame, but I tightened my hold on the Revered mask.

"What kind of destruction?" Meridat asked.

Titus met my eyes over his shoulder. "The heavens did not speak of how; they did not deign to share their understandings with me." His lips twisted to the side as if he was unsatisfied with the higher power. "But they showed me we are on the brink of darkness. Gallantia, Ambrisk—all are threatened."

Threats. Darkness. Destruction. My hands clenched. I scratched the Curse scar on my wrist, searching for something to steady my nervous energy.

Control yourself. Do not react. It is a test. I had to remain in one piece, the face of strength and capability.

"And what does this have to do with my appointment?" I asked.

"Because"—he turned now—"when I enacted the power of the Angel Valyrie—when the prime Starsearcher transferred this warning to me—it was your face I saw among the darkness, Ophelia Alabath."

The mountains could have crumbled around me, and I wouldn't have noticed. Not over the deafening roar in my ears, the way my bones were splintering under the weight of his reading.

Annellius's words during the Undertaking came back to me: *Your blood is strong enough to cause and end wars.*

Titus's reading swooped over me, snuffing out every bit of fortitude I'd worked to instill in myself. He took a breath, preparing to drop the final proclamation that would shatter my resolve entirely.

"It is for that reason that I cannot give my support for your appointment as Revered, Miss Alabath."

Vaguely, I was aware of the uproar the chamber erupted into, but I thought I might collapse. Fate said darkness was entwined with my future, and I was useless against it.

Voices rose. Ezalia and Meridat argued with Titus, imploring him to read again, but their words were a dull buzzing in my ears. Aird was straightening his cloak, ready to flee the chamber. Brigiet still examined that map in her own contemplative silence.

The Starsearchers and Mystiques had a history of amiable relations. Until now. *Until me.* Because whatever the stars wrote for my future—it was a promise of shadows and fury. Defeat gripped my bones, dragging me into the despair I'd barely fought my way out of.

I couldn't even earn alliances.

I'd thought—I'd hoped having this position would brighten the stain of betrayals I'd suffered. Would give me a purpose after being aimless for years, but perhaps Aird and the stars were correct. I was barely an ascended warrior—

Not fit for rule.

Just as I had the thought, my core guard surrounded me. Chocolate-brown eyes swam before my own, Tolek stooping to catch my gaze.

"Compose yourself, Alabath." He slipped a length of rope I

hadn't realized he carried into my hands and nodded pointedly at it. Standing before me, he blocked my hands from view so I could ground myself and my breathing through the repetitive action of tying knots.

"Don't let them see you falter," Cyph said, and I lifted my chin.

Jezebel pinned Titus with a glare. By the door, Malakai remained stoic.

I siphoned off their steady calm, gathered the pieces of my mask, and slipped them back into place. With my energy stifled, I could think straight, approach this from the opposition's point of view.

It was outlandish of the chancellors to think youth and strength were mutually exclusive; damn what the fates may say of my undoing. I may not have had as much experience as the rest of them, but I had overcome just as much. I'd been trained as my father's heir, for Damien's sake. And I had room to grow, to evolve into the ruler the Mystiques needed.

The chancellors didn't know me. They saw a young woman who claimed to have proven herself through a sacred ritual they didn't understand. My journey to the Undertaking—though it revealed Lucidius's secrets—had been illegal. It would look *rash and immature* if one hoped to see it that way.

But it wasn't one-sided.

I'd make them see the other side: the undeniable traits that drove me into that quest and landed me here.

But I'd also open up my heart and show the honorable, raw side of me. I'd peel back the mask of Revered and bleed from those mangled pieces if need be.

If they wanted to see a young woman when they looked at me, so be it. Instead of pretending to be otherwise, I would take that image and forge her into a leader through her accomplishments. One with passion and grace and ferocity.

They'd see their error. For this was a game—and it was one I'd win.

Handing the rope back to Tol with a small *thank you*, and picking up Kakias's note, I stood before the Rapture.

"I'm certain you're all aware this has been a tumultuous time for our continent. The battles are only beginning. In the coming years, months, maybe even weeks, we will all be challenged. We won't survive if we don't band together. Not as six different clans, but as one warrior people, each with different rituals, values, and strengths." I dropped the mask of Revered, allowed a bit of vulnerability to slip through. "*Please*, for the sake of all of our territories and the people we are responsible for, reconsider."

My words went out over the mountains, turning over on the breeze for a stretching silence.

"If I may suggest an alternative?" Every eye in the Rapture Chamber went to Titus. "Since many of us are uncertain how much trust we place in this decision, I suggest we operate on a trial basis."

"And that is?" I asked.

"We leave delegates here for an observation period." He gestured around the room to where the apprentices who had come with their chancellors waited, still as the statues beside them.

"How long?" Brigiet pursed her lips, striding back to the table and settling her hands on the back of her winged chair. The Bodymelder's green eyes lit up at the proposal.

"Until Daminius," Titus suggested.

I calculated quickly. Daminius, the holiday dedicated to the Mystique Angel, took place in the height of summer. That gave me around two months to demonstrate my strength. It should have been plenty of time, but with Kakias's note burning a hole in our future, I wasn't sure.

"They can study the potential new Revered and report back to us on her progress. Then, we'll reassess." A smirk lifted Titus's lips—a scheming one. *This* was his plan all along. Why?

The reins of this meeting continued to slip through my fingers, but I pulled tighter.

"We will host any delegates who choose to stay," I declared. "They will be treated as members of an advisory council, allowing them access to Mystique training—on one condition."

Titus raised his thick eyebrows, interest gleaming in his starry eyes.

"More Mystiques are returning to Damenal by the day. An entire generation has been kept at bay for years, not training, not preparing ourselves for whatever comes next. Assign delegates to remain in my residence, as my guests, and we will learn from them, as well."

"You cannot suggest we share the secrets of our ancestors among all clans," Aird said.

"Did I say such?"

He didn't respond.

"Rituals and customs should be kept to each clan as deemed by the Angels. But we all have knowledge to share. Mystiques won't learn to read the stars or guide souls to their final resting place, but we can learn the unique histories of the celestial powers and the honors of death. We can learn the weapons of a Seawatcher, the healing techniques of the Bodymelders, or even the art of meditative connection among your people, Aird."

I looked over my shoulder, finding Tol, remembering the now-healed wound hidden beneath his leathers and the scar marking his powerful thigh for eternity. My gaze traveled up his body, and when I met his eyes, he inclined his head and winked.

"You have all heard the story of my journey to the mountains. Due to the severance our former Revered instilled among us, we'd never been taught proper battle healing." I turned back to the table, finding Brigiet. "But my friend's mother had. Without the Bodymelder knowledge she passed on to her daughter, I would have lost someone very important to me." My heart clenched, but I pushed my shoulders back and forced myself to continue. "It is time we come together as one people, sharing the power born and honed through the ages. For centuries, we have held each other at arm's length, even where alliances were strong. But it is time we unite."

I took a breath, lowering my mask to further expose the heart guiding my words. The soul of a warrior. "Teach us. Work with us. Please."

And in that time, they would see how capable I was of my position.

If proof of my worth was what they demanded, then prove myself I would.

"My apprentice, Vale, will remain with the Mystiques until Daminius." Titus gestured to the woman standing behind his chair. She couldn't be more than a few years older than myself, but wild light brown waves of hair and wide olive-green eyes gave her a rattled appearance. There was a strength in her stance, though. Until she ducked her head, and it vanished.

Meridat stood next. "One of the twins will remain, as well." She looked over her shoulder to where the two apprentices she'd brought waited. One had sleek black hair, the other a beautiful cascade of tightly coiled curls. They were otherwise identical with dark skin and catlike eyes alert for mischief. "I will allow them to decide which. The rest of my party will depart tonight."

"Are you sure you wouldn't like to stay until the morning?" I asked.

She flashed me a perfect white grin. "We prefer to travel by night. The Spirits are the loudest then."

I shivered at the flare in her amber eyes but said, "Thank you."

Ezalia confirmed she would try to send someone from her council when she returned to the coast, but she could make no promises, having attended the Rapture alone. Brigiet agreed to confer with the host she brought and select the best fit.

Then, it was only the mistrustful, icy chancellor of the Mindshapers remaining.

Aird stood with one elbow perched on the arm crossing his body, his hand tugging at his platinum beard. "I will consider."

He swept from the room, fur cloak turning him into a wolf stalking away. Doubtless, he would be hastily saddling his horse and returning to his territory at the southern tip of the Mystique Mountains.

Once his heavy footsteps had faded down the corridor, I turned to the remaining Rapture. This force of possible alliances that represented the promise of survival amid an uncertain future.

"Thank you for extending this chance. I will not disappoint."

With the meeting officially adjourned and the members of minor clans filing out, I didn't sag under the pressure of Revered as I had yesterday. A fire heated within my veins, the taste of success fueling me. It wasn't the outcome I wanted, but four chancellors at least agreeing to my tentative rule was better than the alternative. It was a tether of hope thrown into the darkness. I'd survived for so long on only my own faith that I had to believe in it.

Until I looked at my friends, grinning, and found Malakai's green eyes narrowed.

The smile vanished from my face.

"This is a horrible idea."

Chapter Four

Malakai

THE MOMENT THOSE WORDS left my mouth, I wished I could have taken them back. Spirits, I'd barely paid attention to the majority of the meeting, too tired and honestly uncaring after last night. Suddenly, voices were raised, Ophelia was drowning, and my hackles snapped up. The last thing I wanted was strangers in our home.

"Malakai." Ophelia approached, steps slowed with uncertainty. "You are more than welcome to disagree with my decisions, but would you at least show me the courtesy of doing so in private?"

Courtesy?

I looked toward the corridor, where the minor clans had disappeared. Only Tolek, Cypherion, and Jezebel had been close enough to hear, and they were now sneaking out, letting the door close quietly behind them.

"No one heard, and I don't know if I'd care if they did." I was too wrung out to care, and her accusation only stoked my fire.

"Do you not take these alliances seriously?" Anger reddened her cheeks. She didn't seem to want to let it explode, though. She'd been fighting it lately, biting her tongue and pleading with me. She stepped closer, only inches away. "You're jeopardizing everything I'm working so hard for."

Fucking Spirits, what did that mean? Of course, I didn't want these alliances. Why should we need them? Even considering it had my chest tightening, that fire bubbling, but I tried to fight it back to show her reason.

"What if that hard work is directed toward the wrong goal? You're being reckless by letting threats in." I looked down at her. "We can't trust them."

How could she think otherwise? Relations had been fine between all clans until Kakias and my father launched a false war against the Mystiques. A false war with very real repercussions—the likes of which our people were still recovering from.

"Who's to say the minor clans aren't going to revolt against us the same way Kakias did? Who's to say they aren't already scheming? Working with her?"

"Why are you so quick to believe ill of them? They haven't acted against us." Ophelia's eyes were round with hurt, like my mistrust of this plan was a personal insult to her. Ridiculous.

The real reason burned through my memories. I clenched my jaw, swallowing a whip cracking through the air, bile stinging the back of my throat. For a flash, I was back in my cell, air heavy with the cloying scent of blood and sweat. Body numb to everything around me. Closing my eyes, I took three deep breaths, forcing the images within the unfeeling place inside of me.

When I spoke again, my voice was low. "I once trusted too easily, Ophelia. I won't be a fool again."

"You think I'm a fool?" She inhaled sharply, her breasts touching my chest, and both of our eyes flicked down to where our bodies connected. This was usually the point when one of us gave in, when we buried our arguments in pleasure.

But neither of us moved. Pain twisted her expression into shock. Fucking Spirits.

Not wanting to fight and worried about what I'd say, I backed down a step. "I think you're hopeful, but faith for a better future is turning you desperate when you need to be strategic."

"Desperate?" She recoiled, my words striking deeper than any physical blow could. "Is it desperate to seek change?"

"That's not what I meant." She was fixating on the accusation without seeing the bigger picture. She wanted alliances and peace, but what we needed was tight borders and tighter leadership.

"That is exactly what you meant, Malakai. Don't try to take it back now." She braced her hands on her hips. "Have you stopped to consider that perhaps I *am* strategizing?"

"You haven't spoken of plans," I scoffed.

"I learned to keep secrets from the best."

The remark hung heavy, widening the space between us, silent except for our breaths and the wild calls of birds soaring above the mountains. I waited, but she didn't crack.

Didn't take back her slight.

It seemed my mistakes still festered between us, turning us away from each other.

"Fine." I sighed, pinching the bridge of my nose and leaning against the table. "I believe you're agreeing to these terms—someone else's terms—rashly. You're not thinking through every possibility. And yes, I do think a desire to achieve stability is driving those decisions rather than logical thought and action." I hated myself for exposing any doubt I had in her decisions, but how did she not see these risks? "Hope can be a weakness wielded against you."

I should know. Hope that my father was not the despicable man I'd suspected him to be was what drove me to keeping secrets all those years. It was why Ophelia and I now stood across this chasm.

"And you're thinking logically by locking *everyone* out?" She was lethally calm, save for the harsh emphasis on that one word. We were both aware the argument had shifted from strictly alliances.

"We don't have to lock them out, but we don't have to let them control us either."

She froze, and when she spoke, her voice was as cold as ice. "I will not be controlled. Never again."

That struck my heart, because I knew that control had become a cliff she clung to. She thought I'd tried to control her future in leaving after we received the Bind. She thought I should have told her my father's plans instead of handing myself over and locking us both into his fate, but I'd done it for a reason. Besides, I wasn't the one trying to control her now.

"By giving in to what the minor clans want, you *are* allowing them to control you. Doing so at the start of your term as Revered will show weakness."

"Kakias is breathing down our necks, Malakai." She grasped the queen's note and flung it at me. "She's waiting for a chance to attack, and we have no idea what that will look like. Working with others will show cooperation, increase our chances of survival."

"We don't need to cooperate!" I roared. Spirits, this was too much. Everything piled on my shoulders—my mother, the sash, the alliances. "We're strong enough on our own."

Here, in the mountains, away from any threats. Away from anyone that could capture and hurt us. My breathing quickened, heart pounding. Whips cracked again in my ears; voices taunted me. *Warrior Prince.* I squeezed my eyes shut against the walls pressing in. Doors slammed, chains clasped around my wrists, cutting into my flesh.

But when I opened my eyes, it was all gone.

Yes, isolation was the only way to ensure we were never betrayed again.

"You're blinded by your own pain," Ophelia breathed, realization widening her eyes. "You didn't see what it was like after the war. Without allies, without trade…We need these things. You say I'm not thinking straight, but neither are you. Shutting people out won't solve anything. These problems—they're so much bigger than one person can handle."

"Shutting people out ensures safety!" I rubbed my wrists, counting those ridged scars. "It is the *only* way to guarantee it."

"It ensures certain death. A hollow, lonely atrophy of the heart."

"Don't let them do this." I nearly fell to my knees under the weight of my memories. "Tell them to leave. Propose a solution the Mystiques come up with—on our terms."

"That will only cost us time and possibly even the tentative agreement we already have. I'm sorry." It was breaking her, to choose this over me—I saw it in each slow blink of her eyes. And dammit if it wasn't breaking me even more. "If I turn them away, they may not come back."

"It's a risk you should take." *It is one I would have taken in order to assert my power.*

She heard the words I didn't say and hesitated a minute before reminding me, "You don't make the decisions here, Malakai."

"Perhaps you shouldn't either," I mumbled.

My words hit her with the force of a star crashing to earth. Her jaw dropped open, but hurt stole her words, glistened in her magenta eyes.

Fuck. I hadn't meant that. As if I could possibly want the position after the way my father had stained it. He had tainted my future, my name, my being. And that taint now warped my mind, making me question everything I thought I knew and damaging it all. Starting with the woman standing before me.

"Well, I suppose it's good you are not in that position of power." The anger she'd been suppressing cracked the surface. "We would be driven into the ground far quicker."

"What does that—"

"You are not the Revered. I am. These are *my* decisions to make for the good of the Mystiques, and though I appreciate your counsel, I won't have your emotions tangled up in your advice."

My emotions? As if she was making decisions out of anything but fear of Kakias and desire to prove herself to the Rapture. Who gave a fuck what those five people thought? She was allowing their vapid opinions to endanger us all.

I opened my mouth to tell her as much, but she held up a hand.

"I'm done arguing. I'm going for a ride."

My heart stuttered as she stormed past me, the shreds of our trust in each other stomped out beneath her boots.

CHAPTER FIVE

OPHELIA

HE FOLLOWED ME.

I knew he had.

And I didn't mind.

Sapphire led us across a path overlooking the northeast of Damenal, the mountains winding their way through the world with sloping sides and jutting peaks, the bones of the continent. We cut between rocks that looked like they had risen from the earth for the sole purpose of hosting this ancient city and the magic beneath. Maybe they had. I'd never given much thought to the formation of the mountains themselves. Whatever being birthed the gods and Angels must have created the land, as well. But there were plenty of conflicting tales on that. The fact that the range had been here for millennia—surviving plagues and wars, outlasting rulers and celebrating them—was a comfort to me, simmering my anger.

As if attune to my attitude, Sapphire didn't stop until my thoughts calmed from a roaring cascade to a trickle. My fury still flared, but under the open skies and the gentle breezes, the urgency subsided. I dismounted, walking to the edge of the trail and sitting in a patch of long grass, swaying in the wind. It was my sign that I was ready to not be alone.

Tolek joined me.

First in silence as I tied knots in a length of rope from Sapphire's saddlebag and Tol wrote in one of his journals, each page embossed with the initials *TV*. He siphoned off those heated emotions that had been warring within me. It was the first time we'd been alone since before the Undertaking, Tol always claiming he had business in the city. At his absence, a hollow ache had followed me. Now, it dulled.

Once my shoulders slackened and I tucked my knees to my chest, arms resting atop them, he reclined on his hands and asked, "What happened?"

"He thinks I'm making a mistake." Unable to stop the flood of words, I recounted the entire conversation to Tol, including the parts that flayed my chest open and exposed my shredded heart within.

"I'll kill him," Tol growled when I finished.

I smirked, knowing he could do no such thing. "He's grieving."

"He's taking it out on you."

I shrugged. "Better me than someone else." An excuse to mask how deeply Malakai's words had cut.

"And where does that end?"

I didn't answer because I wasn't sure. If these fights between Malakai and I didn't end, if we continued to use each other as outlets for rage and cushions for our jagged edges, where would we end up?

Two broken people couldn't hold each other up. At least not two who were as tangled in each other's pain as we were. One of us would crumble. The question was—who would crack first?

I rested my cheek on my arms, looking into Tol's eyes. The sun had risen high into the sky as I rode, the light gilding the highlights in his brown hair and setting the amber flecks in his eyes aflame. That heat burrowed into me, inquiring after my feelings without words, until it hit my soul.

"Do you think he's right?" My voice wavered, each word laced with a vulnerability I wasn't used to.

Tol shot forward, reaching a hand to my shoulder that steadied my rocking world a bit, an emotion I couldn't name twisting his face. "Not in the slightest."

"You don't think allowing the delegates to stay is a bad decision?"

"No, Ophelia, I don't. I think he's being guarded after everything he's been through—and rightfully so." He ducked his head until I was forced to meet his stare. "But I also know that isn't the part of the argument that's worrying you the most."

Damned Spirits, how did he always know? Tolek Vincienzo's all-seeing soul would be the death of me—I swore it.

"You don't think I'm foolish to hope?" My words were small now, hanging in the space between Tol and me like a dying ember.

Since Malakai had thrown out the accusation, it had echoed in my head. Words whispered behind my back in his absence. *Foolish. Desperate.* Words that stuck with me. Maybe he was right.

"Malakai was gone for a long time, Ophelia. Throughout that entire absence, you remained hopeful when none of us could bear to. When we all found it easier to move on rather than dying under hope's fine blade, you allowed that knife to slice your heart to pieces *every single day.*" I didn't know how he understood the feeling so perfectly, but Tol fanned that ember within me until it sparked. "Malakai never saw that side of you or the person you grew into while he was gone."

"I'm not always proud of that person." I shivered as the darkness I'd fallen into threatened to wrap around my shoulders, but Tol's arm did instead.

"You should be proud of what she endured and who she became." He spoke of growth simply, like it was a subject of one of the poems he was always scribbling. "Without you holding on, I think we all would have been crushed by denial. So, no, I don't think remaining hopeful makes you foolish. I think your tendency to hold faith is one of your greatest strengths and just one of the reasons that I believe you're an excellent Revered."

"Thank you, Vincienzo," I whispered, afraid my voice might crack with the tears lining my eyes if I spoke any louder. Tolek wiped them away and scooted closer.

"I admire a lot of things about you, Alabath, and that ability to hope isn't even my favorite one."

"You'll have to tell me the rest of them one day."

"That I will." He smiled, and I couldn't help but return it, promising myself that I'd nurture an unfoolish hope with my every decision. It would be my lighthouse calling me home amid a stormy sea.

Sighing into Tol's embrace, I found the courage to voice what else was bothering me. "I don't like seeing him like this." How hard Malakai's eyes had turned, how distant. "He's slipping away, and I don't know how to reach him. It hurts me to see him hurt and know that I'm causing part of it." But I didn't know how to stop. I was reluctant to fight him, but sometimes I couldn't bite my tongue.

Tol removed his arm from my shoulders and braced his elbows on his knees, twisting a piece of grass between his fingers.

"I don't like it either, but it isn't your doing, so please don't blame yourself. I don't think he's at fault either, but promise me you won't punish yourself, Ophelia."

His earnest eyes burrowed into me, and my lips trembled under the pressure of *everything*. The scars on my flesh and my heart, the darkness looming in my future—all of it. But I looked at Tol and allowed that stare to steady me, then threaded my fingers through his to solidify it.

"I promise. It's not my fault." If I hadn't seen Malakai slipping away before my eyes, I may have believed it. But for Tol, I'd continue to remind myself. I'd continue to hope.

"Good." Relief poured off of him.

We stayed out until the sunset coated Damenal in a wash of soft pinks and lilacs. As we raced each other back toward the palace, I allowed that spark of hope to flourish.

"I was thinking about going into the city tonight," I called over the breeze. I hadn't been, but the closer we got to the palace, the more I realized I wasn't ready to have the fight that waited. "Would you like to come?"

Tolek opened his mouth to answer, then seemed to reconsider. "I shouldn't. I'll see you back to your suite, though."

I wasn't sure what about his response bothered me, but I tried to let it go, riding onto the palace grounds with the warmth of the setting sun instead.

Malakai wasn't in our suite when I returned—thank the Spirits. The wide marble entryway was empty. The art and statues lining the walls watched me like reassuring eyes of the past, high ceilings waiting to catch any aggrieved shouts I threw to the heavens.

Before he left, I hugged Tolek a little longer than necessary, greedily absorbing the steady presence he provided. As we said goodbye, my father came around the corner, striding right into the foyer with a large leather file in hand.

"Tolek." He smiled, extending a hand. "How are you?"

"I'm well, thank you, sir." He gestured to me. "Just making sure your daughter returned home okay from our ride."

"Speaking of my daughter." He faced me, excitement glimmering in his tawny eyes. "I need to have a word with her."

"I'll leave you to it." Tolek nodded to me. "Alabath."

"How was today?" my father asked once the door shut. With his hair in his usual low bun and the flush in his cheeks, I had a bit of him back that I'd missed. The warmth. Comfort.

"We've made negotiations." I chose my words carefully, explaining the situation with the minor clan delegates, my trial period, and Titus's reading. Ignoring the stabbing pain in my heart from Malakai's words.

"Negotiating is good," my father commented. "It will show you intend to have an amicable term as Revered with your people at the top of your mind. Though, Titus's session does concern me."

"It's fine," I lied, waving him off. He'd spent enough time worrying over me lately. "There's an explanation, I'm sure."

Avoiding his gaze, I crossed to the office door. Mystlight lit up the round space as we entered, highlighting the spines of my growing book collection. Since taking over this suite, I'd been slowly lining the tall shelves with my own belongings, letting myself absorb the space, fill every corner.

"What's that?" I pointed to the file my father held as I took a seat in one of the velvet chairs before the fire. He sat opposite me. If I tried hard enough, closed my eyes and envisioned the leather, parchment, and smoke scent, I could pretend we were back in Palerman.

"These are what you asked me for last night." He set them on the small table between us, tapping the cover twice.

Annellius. My heart kicked up, the second pulse speeding with it. Greedily, my fingers curled around the file, unwinding the tie and cracking open the cover to peek at the first yellowed and creased page.

"I'm not sure how useful they'll be," my father apologized.

On the surface, he was right; there were only rudimentary facts. But he hadn't spoken with the Angel or Annellius's Spirit, didn't have that instinct I did.

Flipping to the second page, I read the first line: *Cause of death: blood loss.* I wasn't sure why my skin prickled, but I cleared my throat and steadied my hands. "Thank you for these. It will help."

"You'll be careful, won't you, *sorrida?*" I recognized the concern creasing his brow better than I cared to admit.

"Of course, I will."

"Good." He stood and pressed a kiss to the top of my head. "Now enjoy your evening, and promise not to lose yourself too deeply in those files."

"I promise," I lied.

As he reached the office door, he turned around. One hand rested on the frame, a pensive look in his eye. "Is Malakai here? I've yet to see him."

My fingers tightened on the files. "We're all meeting in the city." Another lie. I'd abandoned the idea the second I learned what was in these files. "I should be off to get ready, actually."

"Damenal is beautiful this time of year." He nodded, but I wasn't sure whether he believed me. "Enjoy it."

"Thank you."

Once he was gone, I locked the office door behind him and put my other worries to the back of my mind. Settling into my chair, I opened the records on my ancestor and lost myself to the story of his fabled, cursed life.

CHAPTER SIX

OPHELIA

MY LOWER ABDOMEN FELT like it was being clawed in half.

I cried out, hunching over in bed, and warmth trickled between my legs.

"What's wrong?" Malakai shot up beside me, placing a hand on my back. Gray dawn light cast a shadow around him, his voice thick with sleep.

"Go *fucking* get Rina," I hissed, clutching my knees to my chest.

"Oh, fuck, okay." He fled the room before I could reply. Malakai had seen me when my cycle arrived plenty of times, and I was willing to bet it was one of the things he didn't miss while he was gone.

We hadn't spoken since our fight. I'd lingered in the office until well into the night. Until I heard the door to the bedchamber close and another hour after that. Because I hadn't known what I'd say to him. With facts and figures of Annellius's life clouding my mind, I didn't trust myself to not let an unintended insult slip.

Now, I curled in a ball until Rina arrived with the tonic her mother had made us since we first bled. Normally, I'd have known my cycle was coming, but I'd been distracted lately. One sip of the cool liquid and it started alleviating the pain. A full dose and I'd barely feel discomfort the rest of the day.

"Twice a day," she instructed, ever the thorough healer.

"I know." I winced, but the sharper pains were already dulling to a manageable pulse in my lower back and a slight headache. "Thank you."

"Of course. I also left your next week's supply of contraceptives in your bathing chamber." She'd been brewing those for me since we took up residence in the palace. Some mornings, I'd hear a gentle knock, and when I opened the door, the next dose was sitting there, Rina having already disappeared down the hallway.

I thanked the Angels for giving me such a doting friend when it came to health and healing. Human or warrior, sometimes there wasn't much difference between us. Or at least, there shouldn't be, despite the distance the world tried to instill.

"Thank you," I repeated.

"Mm-hmm," she hummed. "Keep heat on your back." She headed for the door, probably hoping to get a bit more sleep in.

As Santorina left, Malakai returned, carrying a silver tray. He set it on the table between the fire and the couch I was curled on, then ran a hand over the back of his neck, avoiding my eye.

I hated this.

Hated the jagged spikes of tension separating us. One move and they'd puncture an organ. Anything to make us bleed out all those tainted words we each kept cradled away from the other.

"What's this?" I asked, eyeing the tray, tiptoeing over those spikes. The smell of hibiscus rose to me. He'd found my favorite tea, and those looked like the lemon biscuits I loved.

"I assumed you'd take breakfast in here today if you're in pain." He busied himself striding to the sideboard, organizing the assortment of daggers we'd collected into an orderly line. Including the one he'd taken off his father's body, onyx Engrossian gems and all. He wouldn't tell me why he kept it, but I figured it was his way of grieving, so I didn't prod too much.

His hand hovered over the last weapon—the one I'd carried since Cyph had given it to me for my birthday, the one I'd used on his father—before he shifted that, too, laying it beside the others.

"That's very kind of you," I said, voice small. Timid like I'd never been with him. Afraid of pushing whatever was happening in his mind that I didn't understand. "But it's unnecessary. I won't hide in here all day."

Never mind the fact that my back still hurt and I was utterly exhausted. I wouldn't let the warriors I sought alliances with think me weak or incapable due to my gender. If anything, I'd use this as another strength against them. Show them what I was capable of even while in pain.

"Are you certain?" Malakai asked, giving me every opportunity to change my mind. A sign of support.

"Positive." I sprang to my feet and strode around the table, grabbing a lemon biscuit as I went. "I will take these, though."

"If you insist." Malakai met my eyes over his shoulder for the first time since our fight, the slight lift of his lips at the corners a balm to the bruises between us.

A Starsearcher, a Soulguider, and a Bodymelder. One from each of the three minor clans met us in the palace's training yard for the usual morning circuit, prepared to take up temporary residence with us. Train with us. Dine with us. *Know us.*

"Good morning," Tolek cheered, his voice bouncing off the high stone walls as he descended the staircase from the palace into the sunken dirt arena. Sun coated the space, warm and welcoming. It highlighted the Mystique sigil carved periodically along the facade, as it was throughout the palace and city. An oval with a sword slashing diagonally across it and an outline of three mountains along the bottom.

"He's in a cheerful mood today," Cyph said, eyeing his friend from just over his shoulder.

"And why wouldn't I be, CK? We have guests." Tolek looked over the newcomers, then back to Cyph. "And I'm finally going to beat you in our gamble this morning."

Jezebel barked a laugh. Turning to the delegates, she explained, "Every morning those three"—she pointed to Malakai, Tolek, and Cypherion—"create an obstacle course after training, and every morning Cypherion walks away with his pockets heavier."

"And that isn't about to change today." Cyph walked around the edge of the group, toward the looming armory doorway. The brown leathers covering him neck to boot flexed with each movement, scythe on his back and sword at his hip. "Let's find weapons for you three."

The delegates and Jezebel followed Cypherion, and I observed them. First was Erista, Meridat's apprentice with the wild curls. She had volunteered to stay and represent the Soulguiders over her twin sister. I recognized Titus's apprentice, Vale, too. The quiet Starsearcher with the demure stare. The Bodymelder, though, I'd only just met. Esmond had a broad frame and tall stature that instantly demanded attention, but his demeanor countered it. He remained aloof on the outskirts with keen gazes around our group and arena.

Each delegate brought the weapon of preference of their clan, but as this was to be a show of cooperation, we would also be sharing our specialties with them.

Tol's eyes met mine when he stood with Rina, Malakai, and me.

His blink asked, *How are you?* and my worries eased with the nod I gave him in return.

"It's a shame none of the Seawatchers are here," he pointed out, satisfied that I was okay.

"What is the fascination, anyway?" Rina strapped the dagger I'd given her from my twin set to her thigh.

"He only cares for their weapons," I teased, pressing a hand into a cramp in my lower back.

"Are you all right?" Tolek asked.

"My cycle came," I responded dully.

"Do you need anything?"

"I'm fine." It was a bit more of a snap than I intended.

"That you are." He smirked. "If that's the case, I want to spar with you today."

"Get in line." Malakai swung an arm around my shoulders, pulling me closer.

Tolek eyed his friend, frustrations from our conversation yesterday playing out behind his stare. His need to protect me against any more hurt.

But then, those grievances vanished. He placed a hand to his chest, ducking his chin. "She's all yours."

"It's for the best," I joked to satisfy Tol. "I wouldn't want to have to beat you again, Vincenzo. You might bruise that ego we all adore."

"I think your memory is challenging you, Alabath. My ego is too firm to bruise."

"They're going to kill each other one day," Rina whispered, and Malakai only grunted.

I exhaled a laugh and turned to Santorina. "How are you feeling with your training?"

Her smile brightened. "Excellent, actually. I was thinking…"

"Yes?" I encouraged when she hesitated.

"It's a shame humans are never trained. We're in as much danger as warriors—more so if you consider that you've been around weapons since the day you could walk. I think humans should be given the same chance."

Spirits, Rina's courage was admirable. "You're correct. We'll work on that, as well." I added it to the list of topics to discuss with the Mystique Council. Perhaps they could establish training posts for humans throughout the territories.

It was likely not all would want to train, but it was wrong to not provide the option. If it had been done sooner, perhaps Rina's parents would still be here. When I met her glossy-eyed stare, I knew she was thinking the same.

"We'll give everyone the chance they deserve." I squeezed Rina's hand, promises passing between us.

The delegates, Jezebel, and Cyph reappeared from the armory, the latter holding a menagerie of weapons. My sister and Erista took up a basic sparring pattern, Jezebel showing her a few of the simpler keys of spearwork. Cyph was assisting the Starsearcher, Vale, testing different swords.

Rina sighed, and I followed her line of sight to where Esmond stood alone, a sword in one hand and his rapier in the other. As we watched, he sheathed the former, shirked the top layer of his leathers so he stood in only a thin green tunic, and began a solo warm-up routine with the latter. Warm sepia skin stretched across firm muscles with each motion, and it was clear that while he was quiet, he was skilled.

"He's wary after…everything," Rina explained. After hearing how we'd slayed numerous Engrossians, likely. At least Santorina seemed to have befriended him. "I'll go convince him to join."

"Tol, go with her," I instructed. "Use your charm."

"As you wish." He held out his arm to Santorina and escorted her to Esmond's side. If anyone could convince him Mystiques were to be trusted, Tolek could.

Cyph sliced blades effortlessly through the air, asking Vale to recreate the motions. She did so better than I'd expect of someone who claimed to have no formal training. Cyph observed how she handled each weapon, his gaze serious, a warrior assessing a challenge. He said something that had her bell-like laugh filtering through the arena, and he smiled back at her.

"It's nice to see him in his element," Malakai said, his tone dejected, as it always seemed to be these days. Or perhaps it was jealousy; I couldn't be sure.

"He's good at this," I agreed. Weapons, strategies, and shrewd observation had always been Cyph's strengths. Seeing him use the skills he honed proficiently brought a smile to my face, but knowing Malakai didn't share that sense of belonging dimmed it. I only wished he'd allow me to help.

"Shall we?" I held my hand out to him, waiting for him to slip some reassurance back my way.

"That one's probably too big," Cyph said as we approached, eyeing the sword Vale lifted. They both nodded at us.

She tightened her grip. "Who's to say what's too big for me to handle?"

Malakai exhaled a laugh, but Cyph's jaw hung open for a moment. "I—I wasn't—"

"Relax, I was only teasing." Vale set the long sword down, a satisfied smile on her face, and I decided then—I liked her. Not everyone could easily find their footing in our tight-knit group, but she held her own, with enough spirit to throw Cyph off balance.

Beyond that, the idea of befriending members of other clans was alluring. We couldn't share certain secrets, but there were endless histories and practices we could learn from them. We needed alliances, yes, but did it have to end there? Titus may have been difficult, but Vale seemed open to this arrangement.

Besides, if she could conduct sessions with the stars...well, that was an advantage I'd be foolish to waste in light of her chancellor's reading.

"Men and their sensitivity to *size*," I joked, grabbing a short sword for her instead. "I prefer these." I gestured to Starfire at my hip. "More nimble."

As Vale tested the sword, I surveyed her grip and stance. Both were impeccable, control evident in each swing.

"You're a natural," Cyph said, finally having recovered.

A faint blush colored her cheeks. "I've never held a sword before."

A lie, I thought. When Malakai, Cypherion, and I exchanged a glance, it was clear they agreed. The question was, why?

"What did you spend your training years doing?" I asked. "Have you always been in Titus's employment?"

"I spent most of my life at the Lumin Lake Temple, learning the art of reading the stars and communicating with the Angel and Celestial Goddess. It wasn't until a few years ago that I fell into this position."

"Can you—read as he does, then?" I fidgeted with my sword, working to keep that cool mask of Revered across my features.

Death. Darkness. Destruction. They echoed through my mind, chills peppering my skin.

"I'm practiced." Vale ran a hand down the training leathers we'd loaned her and brushed her braid behind her shoulder. A few pieces slipped free.

"Do you think there's any way his vision was…" *Wrong*, I wanted to say. But those softening olive eyes cut me off.

"I'm sorry, Ophelia." She dropped her gaze. "I don't know what it means, but I'm certain Titus's vision was correct."

As I kept myself from falling into the same pit of panic that tried to swallow me yesterday, I wondered what it could mean. There was a rare substance in my blood—that much I knew. There was also a vengeful queen at my back. For a moment, I felt the chill of Kakias's dagger pressed against my throat, the blade thin and cold. Lethal. Sometimes, I swore the faint line it had imprinted on my skin looked back at me in the mirror, a bead of blood bubbling to the surface.

But when I blinked it was always gone—a figment of my nightmares or a premonition for my future, I wasn't sure.

Our war with Kakias was far from over, but could that be the cause of Titus's reading? Or was it something closer to home? Something within me?

At my back, Angelborn warmed, her pulse beating through me—a comfort and a promise.

"Did your family train at Lumin, too?" Malakai asked. In that moment, he and I were aligned. How had this seemingly ordinary girl come to the side of the leader of their clan?

"Oh, I'm afraid I don't know my family. I haven't seen them in nearly twenty years, since I was only four." Though she said no more, her voice was crystal clear.

"And why is that?" Cypherion pushed gently, focusing on the sword he was polishing for her.

"That's a very personal question." Her brow furrowed. "Where is your family?"

"My father died many years ago." The lie was smooth. For all we knew, his father *had* died. "And my mother didn't handle it well."

Vale's shoulders sank. "I'm sorry. I didn't mean to—"

"It's okay. You didn't know." Cyph extended the sword to her, pulling it back just before her fingers closed around the grip. "But it sounds like there's more to your story."

"Perhaps one day I'll tell you."

Cyph dropped his chin. "I'll hold you to it, Starsearcher."

Malakai and I exchanged a wide-eyed look, but before either of us could say anything, Cyph called for drills to start.

"Holy fucking Spirits," Malakai panted as the tip of my spear landed above his heart, poised to pierce the Bind.

I smirked. "I know, I'm impressive."

"Phel, you've always been talented." He brushed his sweat-soaked hair out of his face. The morning sun caught the drops rolling down his forehead and carving a path around his scarred torso. Something below my stomach fluttered as one slipped down the column of his neck, over his collarbone and tattoo. "With that thing, you're unstoppable."

I looked for any hint of jealousy as he eyed Angelborn—the spear that had been his since birth but was recently passed to me when my right to Revered was exposed—but I found none. He leaned on the spear he'd borrowed from the palace's armory, his eyes sweeping over me.

"What?" I asked.

"Nothing." Now his smirk matched my own.

We were both quiet, eyes locked, arguments past trying to pry their way in. The clashes of sparring around us bounced off the stone walls of the training arena. My workout leathers—cut like my official garb but less ornate—were hot against my skin, though the dawn air was cool. Or perhaps it was Malakai's heated gaze that had my clothes feeling suddenly in the way.

I prowled forward slowly, placing a hand against his chest. And shoved him. "Back to work, warrior."

"Yes, ma'am," he said in a low voice. Heat spread throughout my body.

I stepped back and reset my stance, tightening my grip on Angelborn. I watched for his usual hint of reluctance. Malakai preferred not to train with spears since he'd given his over to me, but we'd decided to work them into our routine. It was a good challenge for him, I thought, but I didn't miss the way he sometimes winced when handling any weapon.

"You were asleep when I returned last night," I said as we began slashing our way around the space.

The tightening of his expression was due to more than the maneuver I made. "You got back late."

True.

"I had work to take care of." A beat, shadows around his eyes deepening. "Are you okay?"

Are we okay?

For a few minutes, he didn't respond. We continued to spar, and only when I had my weapon at his ribs did he ground out, "Just tired is all."

I froze with Angelborn against him, taking in the angular planes of his face that had turned harder each day since we reunited. His sunken cheeks and muted green eyes. Only his skin glowed, training sessions recovering the sun-kissed tan he'd lost in the years he was captured. But it couldn't disguise the pain lingering within him.

"Malakai," I whispered, voice low.

He shook his head. "You win again."

I swallowed the sting of denial. "Are you prepared for this week?" In a few days, he and his mother would officially say goodbye to Lucidius. Twisted as their relationship became, I knew it haunted him.

Again, he shook his head.

"Talk to me." My voice cracked. "Please." My Bind ached for the ease of our prewar life.

But Malakai seared me with an accusatory stare and backed away.

I deserved it. I'd avoided him as much as he had me, but my heart cracked with each inch between us, rejection flooding the space. These clipped responses were all we'd been giving each other, too busy spiraling down into our scars. The communication between us turned stiff and guarded, nothing like what it used to be.

My mind went back to three nights ago, the eve of the Rapture, when we'd been alone in our suite. One moment, his hands had been at my waist, his lips warm against my own. The next, we were shouting at each other. And another moment later, my legs were wrapped around his hips as I tore his clothes off and he buried himself inside me, my back against the wall. We had turned into a riot of fighting and fucking, too much fire between us to handle it in any other way. The latter became my way out.

So when he backed away in the arena, I did the same, and that wall slid up between us. We began our final set of exercises in silence, aggression in every swing. For each lie, I struck. For each secret, I slashed. And for every piece I'd been broken into—I did not hold back.

So that we may always come back to each other.

Come back to me.

No more damn secrets.

We'd sworn that was it, that we were going to move forward and heal, but here he was again, shielding things from me.

And here I was—blaming him.

At some point, the rest of the arena fell away. It was only us, toiling through this dance of steel and unspoken accusations. Going blow for blow, the spear's power pounded through my veins like the second heartbeat I'd come to know.

Malakai met my strikes and got in a few of his own despite having not completed the Undertaking. Neither of us aimed to harm. Neither relented either. The only noise was our heavy breathing and the clash of weapons.

Until a quieter, chiming sound cut through the air.

Confused, we both froze, looking around for the source.

"Did your spear just break?" my sister called. At what point she and the others had stopped training to watch our heated battle, I didn't know.

Jezebel pointed at my feet where a small, jagged piece of gold no bigger than a coin now sat. I bent to pick it up, but when my fingers closed around the metal, it stung.

"Fuck, ouch," I cursed, dropping it.

The tense lines in Malakai's face smoothed as he bent, but he didn't exclaim when he picked up the chip of metal.

"It must have gotten dislodged." In his palm he held the small embellishment from Angelborn that normally sat below the head, inlaid with aquamarine stones outlining the mountains.

"How did that happen?" I asked, looking from the spear to his hand.

"Think of everything that weapon has been through in recent weeks," Cypherion reasoned. "Any one of those battles could have jostled it." The others resumed their work, ignoring Malakai and me.

I held my palm out for him to hand over the piece. When he tilted his hand so it slipped into my own, I cursed again. He gave me a questioning look.

"It wasn't hot for you?" I queried.

Hot was an understatement. The metal was burning, a fire rivaling the Spirit Volcano pressing into my flesh.

"No, it wasn't." Malakai's brows scrunched.

I tucked the scrap into the pocket of my leathers and held out my empty hand. Where it had laid, an uneven red circle was already fading. Malakai inspected my palm, his budding calluses brushing against my older ones.

I pulled my hand out of his, clenching my fingers into a fist. "I'm sure it's nothing."

But the echo of that burn pulsed even as the physical reminder faded into a memory.

Chapter Seven

Malakai

Of the two times I'd stood atop the Spirit Volcano, I wasn't sure which was worse.

Was it the first time, when I'd thought I was handing over my life, only to be betrayed by my father? He'd crushed the hope within me that night, and only continued to drive it out of me over the years following.

Or was tonight the darker of the two?

Tonight, I wasn't alone, but I was more twisted than ever.

I stood with my hand in my mother's. No sound could be heard over the crackle of the volcano's flame, but my heartbeat shook my entire body, roaring in my ears. Across the wide mouth of the volcano, a silhouette was barely visible through the sweetly-scented smoke. The Master of Rites, Missyneth, did not speak; she only watched us, awaiting my nod.

Exchanging a glassy-eyed glance with my mother, I bobbed my head once.

The Master of Rites raised a hand. Two more silhouettes walked to the edge, a box between them. My knees wobbled as they gently opened the lid.

I squeezed my mother's hand tighter as the acolytes removed a long, wrapped form from the box. One held his ankles, the other his shoulders. Each moved with a reverence he didn't deserve, but it wasn't their job to pass judgment. A piece of me was grateful ritual demanded they do this; I wasn't sure I could show the same respect.

I couldn't even blink as they held the body over the fire and released him.

My mother's sob broke my trance, and I wrapped my arm around her. Together, we watched my father's body fall into the Spirit Volcano to meet his final judgment. What happened next, we'd never know—not until we one day joined the afterlife. That would be centuries off, though. Perhaps by then we'd each find peace with his actions.

Part of me—the part of me that had tried to hope—doubted it. There was nothing left to hope for in this bleak world.

I realized I'd been dragging my thumb across my jaw, along the scar my father left there. He may be gone forever, but I'd always have that reminder of what he did, who he truly was.

The last speck of his body disappeared into the luminescent orange abyss, and I turned.

"Let's go," I grunted, fighting the burning behind my eyes.

My mother inhaled shakily but followed. As we wound down the volcano and along the footpath back toward Damenal, some of that pain my father had caused soothed. Not healed but tucked in a cage. Maybe this was what closure felt like. Maybe I'd now be able to seal it away, leave it in the volcano with his doomed body and never have to face it again. Lock it and let the key melt in the flames.

At the edge of Damenal, my mother grabbed my wrist. When I turned to her, her eyes were red but dry.

"It's time for me to go, Mali." She brought a hand to my cheek. I wasn't sure if she even realized she brushed a thumb over my scar.

"Go?" I asked, my voice cracking.

"Back to Palerman. Back to restoring my life." She brushed my hair away from my face. "As you should."

My life? I didn't even know what it looked like. Fuck, my years in chains had practically erased it from my mind. What had I once dreamed of? What did I now desire? No answers came to mind. Instead, I saw darkness. No shining future, no valiant titles. Nothing but an endless path stretching before me. Shadows curled at the edges, threatening to swallow me whole.

Did I want that path? Or did I want something better?

"I'm trying." Or at least, I wanted to, but I didn't know how.

I thought of the harsh accusations Ophelia and I had thrown at each other, the harsher ones we bit back, and how she'd pleaded with me to talk to her these past few days.

Fucking Spirits, it crushed me to see tears in her beautiful eyes, but it was all I knew, this running.

It was easier to turn away from the warring emotions wrapping their hands around my head and heart than it was to do anything about them. Throw up a wall and block it all out. Lock my heart in an iron cage.

"You'll get there. He may have given you your blood, but he does not decide what you do with it. That choice is only yours."

She pulled me in for a hug—the comforting kind only a mother can give, where for a moment you believe everything may actually be okay. But when she released me, the shadows loomed closer, their presence cold and destructive.

She was right, though. My father had given me my blood, but I didn't have to become what he wanted. Spirits, I'd already proved as much by escaping that dreadful future he'd planned.

Some days I wanted to forget about it all completely and disappear. Fall into the volcano after my father's body and let it send me to my fate. Perhaps it would not deem me fit for the Undertaking and the responsibility would be out of my hands completely. The thought was almost soothing.

Choices…I was tired of making the wrong ones. My mother said they were now up to me, but I was scared. Afraid of what I'd chosen before, afraid of the pressure resting on my shoulders.

And I was losing control. Everything I'd once wanted was slipping through my fingers. Me, desperate to hang on to anything familiar. Reality, tearing it away.

With a deep breath, I shoved it all into the cavern within my chest and locked it tight, using the heat of my pain to fortify the barred cage around where my heart belonged. That was where everything would remain. The memories of today, the pain over my father, the guilt over my decisions, and the confusion with Ophelia. It would all stay hidden behind those bars.

"Thank you, Mother." I kissed her cheek. "You go ahead. I'm going to take the long road back."

She hugged me, slipping down the direct route to Damenal.

I sank into the shadows along the path's edge, contemplating the many choices forced upon me. Until a crunch of gravel made my head snap up.

"Jezebel?"

She whirled, eyes wide and shocked for a fraction of a second before they went dull. "I forgot you and your mother were…" Her gaze softened with pity I didn't want. "How are you?"

No way in the Spirit-guarded hell was I talking about this. "What are you doing here? Didn't everyone decide to go into the city tonight?"

"Out for a walk."

Outside of Damenal, near the Spirit Volcano? Sure. But her tone said one thing: end of conversation. She slid her pendant along the chain around her neck, clearly avoiding something, but who was I to judge?

"I was just about to go meet them," I said.

"Me too."

We walked in a silence that hadn't been normal of us before I left. One thick with some tension I couldn't put a name to. But fuck if I didn't know how to talk to anyone now.

CHAPTER EIGHT

OPHELIA

THE CITY ATOP THE peaks was alive with the hopes of the warriors flooding her streets. Dusk faded into a calm violet sky, the full moon rising to bathe us with its promising glow as we descended the winding walkway leading from our home.

With the palace nestled deep in the Northern Quarter, it was a far walk to the taverns in the city center, Angentia Plaza, but after days of exchanging training techniques and meetings with the Mystique Council, my core group and the delegates needed this break. Though, some were more opinionated on *how* we traveled than others.

"No, Tolek, I don't think it's a wise idea for you to stand bareback atop Astania." Cyph's exasperation brought a much-needed smile to my face. I watched my shadow dance across the stone streets ahead of my boots, one arm looped through Santorina's, indulging in the comfort of the bickering.

"I don't know, Cypherion. I'd like to see him try." Erista adjusted the bronze-and-amethyst headband sitting among her curls, dark skin radiant against her matching necklaces.

"Don't encourage him," Rina told her.

"I think she should," Vale chimed.

"Tol, even if you do survive the ride to the tavern, you'd have to take Astania back to the stables by yourself and then join us," Cyph said.

Tolek considered that argument, head tilting to one side. "I'd rather someone ride me instead," he muttered.

Rina and I snickered as we wound through an alley, Esmond smirking on her other side.

This was what I'd wanted to show the minor clans. A family. More than a group of young warriors. More than the hard exteriors and honed muscle we had to offer. We were people, as they were, composed of reckless dreams to fight for and wrenching sorrows to avenge. We were truths buried beneath smiles, secrets masquerading in passion, grief and love tangled in aching bonds forever tying us together. We went deeper than what they saw on the surface, in ability and heart. It was time it was acknowledged.

Spirits, I'd even allowed Jezebel to talk me into a dress for tonight. Though somehow she'd slipped away soon afterward. I hadn't seen her all afternoon.

Regardless, I found I didn't hate the outfit. With a powder-blue silk skirt, thin straps twisting over my shoulders, and a plunging neckline, it was finery I once would have shirked. But I found myself enjoying the pampering now and then, given that I was allowed my official leathers.

"Has there been progress with the Mystique Council?" Rina asked.

Quickly, my eyes flitted to Esmond on her other side. I didn't want to reveal every detail of my council meetings, but I also didn't want to appear to be hiding anything. I needed his support.

Choose your words carefully.

"They've taken the delegate program well." They'd prodded the plan with questions, actually, wariness blatant on a few of their faces, but they'd agreed. "And none argued with my institution of apprentices."

"How will that work?" Esmond asked with eager eyes, his accent smoothing out his harsher consonants. Laughter rained down from the highest windows, thrown open to the night. Starlight bounced off terra-cotta tile roofs and sandstone walls, the city a beacon of hope that strengthened me.

"We're rebuilding our infrastructure from the ground up, planting roots to give a larger representation power. I asked the councilors to get to know the young Mystiques migrating to Damenal to prepare for their own Undertakings and form branches."

To avoid dissent. To stop the uprisings mumbled about across the territory. To distribute the weight of work so more were directly involved.

"We have a similar structure in our territory." Esmond's deep voice rolled into the night as we crossed through narrow alleys. I pictured the lush land of the Bodymelders, sprawling hills sprouting every herb and flower imaginable for their healing practice. "A leader of each small village who reports to the government in the capital."

"Larcen, our Master of Trade, proposed something similar. He's hoping to establish councils in every major city to manage imports and exports."

To repair the damage Lucidius had sown throughout our territory—and others. Though, we no longer had a Master of Communication responsible for ensuring external trade among clans. The last to hold the position had been Malakai's uncle, Akalain's brother, before his death over a decade ago. Larcen had shouldered the responsibility since, the strain of two titles evident in the dark circles always framing his eyes.

"He's eager for the assistance." An understatement. "Missyneth, the Master of Rites, already has a team of temple acolytes. And the Master of Weapons and Warfare thought it a wonderful idea."

Danya, the warrior who had trained Malakai and I often on trips to Damenal as children, offered steadfast support. The eager glint in her eye had told me she already had an idea of who to appoint.

"And Alvaron?" Santorina asked. Bulbs of mystlight hovered above front doors, throwing her profile into a medley of shadow and light as we passed between them. Cheerful voices and rowdy music grew louder as we got closer to the plaza.

"He agreed, surprisingly."

"Why is that surprising?" Esmond asked, sidestepping a small boy running down the street with a wooden sword in hand and the girl who followed.

"Alvaron is the most traditional member of our council. Besides Missyneth, he's held his title the longest." I didn't add that I'd feared the same complaints about my age and experience that I'd faced in the Rapture.

From his tight-lipped nod, I guessed Esmond understood. "It seems you're already earning the support for your title, Ophelia."

My heart swelled with the sentiment, the subtle hint that he might be recommending that support to Brigiet, as well. It bolstered me as we crossed the crowded Angentia Plaza, approaching the Winged Horse, our favorite tavern.

Shouts bounced off the stone walls, the wooden tables and bar packed to bursting. Warm mystlights hung in iron chandeliers, a crackling fire and string instruments filling any lulls. The sights, the sounds, even the smell of spilled ale and liquor—it filled me with the kind of promise I missed. The one that meant our world was repairing itself, our people flourishing once again.

Hours after we settled around a long table in the Winged Horse, Jezebel and Malakai arrived. He slid into place beside me, quiet solitude wrapped around him, an aura telling anyone who approached that he wasn't prepared to discuss what he'd done tonight.

We'd wanted to go with him, or to wait for him in the palace upon his return.

He'd said no. Lucidius's burial was something he and his mother had to face alone.

And we'd understood, but I didn't miss the sidelong glances our friends cast him or the tension prickling off his skin, raising the hair on the back of my neck.

There were enough warriors in the tavern tonight, though, that Malakai could sink into the background. A group of familiar faces from our training and school years in Palerman took the table beside ours, and older warriors started up a dance in the middle of the floor, pushing chairs out of their way as they went.

At some point, Tolek and Cypherion disappeared among the crowd.

"Will the Renaiss celebration be in the city this year?" Erista asked, successfully calling my attention away from the man next to me. I slid my hand into his beneath the table, though.

"We'll be opening the palace gates for the festival actually. And it will spill into the city from there."

The action was symbolic. It wasn't common for a head of rule's home to be opened to any and all on a festival day, but Renaiss was celebrated across Gallantia, by all seven clans. And this was the first we'd truly enjoy since the shadow of the past war was lifted.

It was a holiday of promises and hope, wild debauchery and rebirth. Things Mystiques needed. In two months, Daminius would be a reverent day of worship and accomplishment, but Renaiss was a celebration of what it was to live.

"I'm looking forward to seeing how Mystiques celebrate the festival day." Vale's voice was a low ring amid the rowdy tavern.

I met the Starsearcher's olive eyes that saw so much more than we Mystiques ever could and exchanged an understanding smile despite the fact that every time I looked at her, Titus's reading chilled me.

"Alabath!"

I was pulled from the bench.

"Vincienzo!" I laughed as he spun me, throwing my head back and forgetting any worries. Cypherion was behind him, towing Jezebel along. "Where had you gone off to?"

Tol and Cyph exchanged a gleeful glance. I wasn't sure if I should be excited or terrified.

"What's going on?"

"These two won't tell me." Jezebel crossed her arms, head tilted.

"Did you lovely Alabath sisters know that the tattoo shop in the Ascended Quarter has reopened?" Tolek asked, rocking onto the balls of his feet.

"It has?" My eyebrows shot upward. Jezebel's arms fell to her sides, her jaw dropping.

"Recently," Cyph explained.

"We checked, and they're open tonight," Tolek added.

"Open is a loose term," Cyph corrected. "But they're willing."

"Practically begging." Tol grinned.

"Well, what are we waiting for?" my sister gushed, exchanging an eager glance with me. "Let's go!"

"Go where?" Santorina came to stand with us, Malakai just behind her.

"The party is relocating," Tolek announced, draining the liquor in his hand and placing the glass on the table. "Anyone who wishes to watch is welcome."

"Watch what?" Vale asked, eyes wide.

Excitement buzzed through my veins. "It appears the four of us have a tattoo appointment."

"Marxian, what are you doing here?" I burst through the door of the parlor, the acid scent of paint mingling with earthy wood shavings. Cyph hadn't been joking when he said they'd *recently* reopened.

"I figured you would need your victories etched," the artist answered. The night he'd inked the Bind between me and Malakai seemed like an eternity ago.

"Is the shop in Palerman closed?"

The bearded Mystique shrugged. "I'll keep both, but there's more need of me here now. With so many of our next generation migrating to Damenal to train for their Undertakings, it only makes sense." His eyes swept over the room, taking in the crowd who had come to see the legendary tattoos inked for the first time in years. His gaze froze on someone tucked in the corner. "Malakai."

His head snapped up. Malakai plastered a smile on his face, the group parting so he could approach Marxian.

"It's good to see you," Marxian said, voice thick.

Malakai's shoulders tightened as they clasped hands. "And you."

How painful was this for Malakai? Watching his friends receive the tattoo solidifying a fate taken from him. Was it too much? Was I being horribly selfish in coming here tonight?

But I needed to do this for myself.

Still, I placed a hand on Malakai's arm and squeezed once, to tell him I was there. He gave me a tight-lipped smile before stepping back and fading into the crowd.

"The four of you then?" Marxian whispered.

"That's right." I smiled.

He directed us to the table we'd lie on. "Who's first?"

"I'll go." Cyph stepped up, untying the linen shirt he wore tonight instead of his leathers. I rolled my eyes when warriors behind me muttered appreciations of his body. Cyph had probably just earned himself a dozen new admirers.

"What's the purpose of it?" Esmond asked, watching Marxian prepare the needle.

I was surprised he hadn't been taught our customs; Mystiques studied most clans' public practices and declarations of loyalty, and the Bond, the Band, and the Bind were no secret. But I explained the purpose of the three tattoos. When I mentioned the Bind was to be received last, his eyes dropped to my arm, then flitted to Malakai, full lips pursed.

"I like to break rules sometimes."

A hint of appreciation swept through the Bodymelder's eyes.

"Will you be receiving the other two tonight, then?" Vale asked, watching Cyph settle face down on the table, the muscles in his back flexing.

I hadn't thought past the Bond, the thin outline of mountains we'd receive on the back of our necks to mark our success in the Undertaking and tie us unbreakably to our cause. I supposed we could receive the Band, too, solidifying our ranks within the Mystiques.

"Can't do both," Marxian said. He tested the needle on a scrap of paper. "The magic is too strong. I condone rule-breaking *sometimes*, but I won't do that."

I nodded, understanding.

"What does it feel like?" Esmond asked.

Erista's sharp voice answered, "If it's anything like mine, it's very personal."

I didn't know the purpose of the Soulguider tattoos—theirs being more private than ours—but Erista had a gold band around her forearm with a crescent moon in the center. I imagined the sensation was similar to what I'd experienced, given that all ink was fueled by the same magic, even if it took different shapes.

"It floods your entire body. It's…all-encompassing and instills purpose," Vale added. She rubbed a hand over her shoulder, pulling her hair across it.

"That's a beautiful way to explain it," Cyph said, propping himself on one elbow to survey the Starsearcher. His stare was inquisitive, searing.

"What did yours feel like?" Tol asked, leaning against the wall beside me, eyes tracing the North Star on my arm. The room quieted.

"It was intimate. The most intimate thing I've experienced." The sensation of unknown power working its way through my blood and rooting itself within me was a promise I'd never forget. "Like a thread pulling through every facet of my body, driving into my bones. Then, it stopped. And it waited for the other half." My eyes found Malakai's across the room. "And they tangled together. Two slips of soul becoming one."

"Can you feel each other through them?" Esmond sounded clinical, a scholar gathering research on the body.

I flushed, unable to look him in the eye. I didn't know how to explain the disjointed feeling our Bind had always given us and was reluctant to share a flaw or weakness with the crowd whose eyes burrowed into me. I looked at my feet, my thumb stroking over the tattoo.

"Did it hurt?" Tol asked loudly. His eyes remained on my star, jaw ticking.

"Scared, Vincienzo?" Jezebel smirked, sipping from a bottle of ale she'd brought with her.

Tol flipped her off. "Terrified, Jezzie," he drawled.

"Careful not to scream when the needle hits your skin." She kicked her feet up on an empty table, leaning back in her chair.

I flashed them each a tight-lipped smile, grateful for the distraction.

"I guess we'll see now who's got the strongest tolerance," Marxian interrupted. "Face down, Cypherion."

Cyph did as he was told, brushing aside the auburn curls at the back of his neck so the artist would have a clean surface. Marxian dragged a razor over the skin, removing any hair, and cleaned it.

"Don't move," he instructed.

Buzzing echoed from the needle, and the room held its breath. All eyes were on Cyph, waiting to see the legendary event take shape. Like a dream imprinting itself over the present, I was transported back to the night, two and a half years ago, when I'd first experienced this. The buzzing wrapped itself around me, teasing out my excitement and restoring that same purpose.

Slowly, the ink bled into Cyph's skin. He didn't flinch, didn't say he was in pain at all. As the mountains took shape against his neck, I could practically feel the needled magic pressing into my bones. I tried to catch Malakai's eye, but he faced the window, ignoring the scene.

It was over quickly. The room erupted into conversation, the buzzing needle releasing its hypnotic hold on them once fate sealed itself within Cyph.

Marxian applied the soothing ointment, which Esmond and Santorina asked many questions about, then Cyph rose from the table. With the shorter haircut Jezebel had given him after the Undertaking, his curls brushed the tops of the mountains, a burnt sun teasing the peaks.

"Next." Marxian patted the bench, turning to his workstation to switch out the supplies.

"Jezzie?" Tol asked.

My sister bit her lip, watching the needle with narrowed eyes.

"Scared?" Tol teased. I elbowed him in the ribs. "Ouch," he muttered.

"It's not that," Jez said. "I—oh, never mind."

She untied the straps of her dress where they were knotted behind her neck and lay face down on the surface. Marxian repeated the ritual as he had with Cyph. The crowd trickled out, losing interest after the first tattoo. A few lingered, talking, dancing, and drinking. Cyph and Vale were in conversation with a pair of warriors we knew from Palerman—the Bristol sisters—and a blonde man from Turren.

Malakai sat silently in the corner. Hands clenched, elbows braced against his knees, gaze out the window.

Tolek took his place after Jezebel, removing his dark shirt to reveal defined muscles. A group of Mystiques moved closer, eyes lingering across his sculpted back. Cyph wouldn't be the only one with his options, then. I narrowed my eyes at them, wondering what plans they were concocting in hushed tones. One girl I recognized from Palerman—Hylia, I recalled—certainly had a hungry look in her eye—

"Damien's balls!" Tol yelped when the needle touched his skin.

"Oh for the love of the Angels, Tolek!" I laughed, Cypherion and Jezebel joining me. "It's not that bad."

"It feels like my damn bones are being shredded."

"Interesting," Marxian hummed.

"What is?" Tolek asked, face buried in a pillow.

"Nothing, don't move, kid."

Tol grumbled but bit his tongue as Marxian finished the tattoo. The artist's gaze stayed narrowed.

When Tolek sat up, his cheeks were red. "Jezebel, give me your fucking drink." She handed it to him, and he finished it in one swallow. "You're all sadists if you think that didn't hurt," he panted, his bare chest rising and falling. One drop of ale dripped down his chin, carving a path along his neck and settling in the dip of his collarbone.

"Get out of my way, Vincenzo. I'll show you how it's done." I piled my hair atop my head, tying it with a leather band from Rina, and settled onto the table. Tolek whispered something I couldn't make out.

The razor smoothed along my skin, the cleanser cool in its wake. I held my arms carefully at my sides and closed my eyes.

"Welcome back, Revered," Marxian whispered, and I smiled into the pillow.

Buzzing filled the air, and when the needle met my skin, I almost gasped. Not from pain—it was nothing like the Bind, when the ink seemed to be rooting itself into my bones, twisting through my blood.

This was everything I experienced during the Undertaking slamming into me at once. The shock of the fall melding with the vindication of solving the riddles. The pain of being torn apart in the Spirit Fire tempered by all of my loose ends being forged back together. All of my senses heightened. All of my dreams fulfilled.

The ink bolstered everything the Undertaking had planted in me and pushed it to the surface. I was a canvas for the memories, the tattoo painting an image of my future.

And when the buzzing ceased, when the mountains were forever printed on my skin, those feelings rooted in me for eternity.

I rose from the table, finding Cyph, Jez, and Tol staring at me expectantly. We didn't have to say anything.

We felt it, too, the gazes confirmed. *We made it.*

Vale nodded in silent understanding.

The twisting fluttered along my bones, the magic adjusting to its new home. I was curious to see how it differed from the magic in my Bind. Biting my lip, I shoved away the worry that this promise, too, would malfunction, and indulged in the empowering ink.

The high faded, though, when a bell above the shop door cut through the noise.

Malakai rushed by the window, disappearing into the night.

I tore from the parlor, cool night air tickling the back of my neck where the ink was still settling. Selfish guilt trickled down my spine with the magic.

"Malakai!" I called, but the city soaked up my voice.

Why had I thought this was a good idea? Of course, it would be hard for him to watch us receive the Bond. I'd known that—known he wouldn't voice that pain—and yet I'd done it anyway.

Tolek and Cypherion appeared behind me. "Where did he go?" the latter asked.

"There." Tol pointed as Malakai rounded a corner down an alley, and they started after him.

"No." I put a hand on both their chests, a defeated sigh coating my voice. "Let me."

Taking off down the cobbled streets, I followed the direction Malakai disappeared. A subtle scent of honeysuckle and leather clung to the air, the only way I knew he was heading back toward the palace.

As I crossed into our grounds, I was so homed in on that familiar aura and the sound of his distant steps, I didn't notice another broad chest until I smacked into it.

I bounced back, hand immediately reaching for a weapon—until I saw—

"Aird?"

The Mindshaper chancellor stood on my soil, looking down at me. Platinum hair braided back, thick beard reaching his chest, all attempting intimidation.

"What are you doing here?" Danger seeped into my voice, hand within reach of the dagger at my thigh.

"Evening, Miss Alabath." There was condescension in the way his lips curled around my name, I was certain of it. His wolf's cloak bristled with the rise and fall of his shoulders. "Lovely to run into you."

"In my home. I can imagine the surprise." I waited for him to respond. When he didn't, I added, "You were supposed to have returned to your territory days ago."

"I had business to resolve here." A casual shrug. "But I've found what I needed, and I'll be on my way."

I didn't like it. Didn't like him being in my city without my knowledge. Didn't like the entitlement in the lift of his chin or the way he eyed me, begging for an outburst. A reaction that would justify all of his beliefs about my hotheaded actions and subsequent inability to rule.

Uncurling my fingers from the dagger, I blinked up at him, unaware I'd even grabbed it. I deliberately coated my voice in saccharine sweet mockery. "I do hope you enjoyed your stay. The path through the Merchant Quarter will be the most direct for your exit."

"Thank you for the advice," he bit out. "I'll be seeing you soon."

He left then, cloak dragging across the dirt and stones. With each step, my anger bubbled beneath the surface, uncertainty fueling it, until he was nothing but a silhouette, and the force of the Spirit Volcano roared within me.

Groaning, I stomped up the path to the palace, nearly forgetting the other battle that awaited me inside.

CHAPTER NINE

OPHELIA

I NEVER STOOD ACROSS A chasm from Malakai before he left, but entering our suite to find him in the foyer, hands braced against the wooden table, knuckles turning white with the force, that was how I felt.

"I'm sorry," I started, voice trembling with restraint. "We shouldn't have insisted on the tattoos tonight."

Malakai shook his head and released a dark laugh. "That's not it." For a moment, he could barely hold himself together: arms locked, eyes closed, words he wasn't sure he should share bursting his seams.

"What's going on, then?"

"What's going on?" he echoed, squeezing his hands tighter before pushing back, striding toward me. "What's going on is that I have no fucking clue *what's going on*. No idea what I'm supposed to be doing. Why am I here? What's the point of any of this? These strategies you're constantly speaking of, these meetings, this entire life? I don't want any of it."

His anger barreled down at me, and I snapped. "I'm not forcing you to do anything."

"You're making choices I don't understand." It wasn't what was bothering him—not entirely. I could tell that much from his frantic search for something—anything—to say. But it gave us something to latch on to. So, I did.

"Why do you need to?" I roared.

Seeing Aird had rattled me, and that fury bled into this fight now, but I couldn't stop it. I unleashed all the fear and uncertainty I'd bottled up as the fight we'd been suppressing for days sprang back open, a force stronger than the both of us.

"Why can't you just believe in me, Malakai? You always used to."

"A lot has changed since then, hasn't it?"

We were across that chasm, screaming to each other, voices adrift in the wind. On entirely different drafts. His arguments carried north and mine south, neither destined to reach the other, and that burned me up.

"Can't you simply have faith in me?" I asked, palms open to catch the accusations hurled between us. "Can't you see all I've done without you and believe I know what I'm doing?"

Once, we wouldn't have had to explain ourselves. Support had been a pillar of us, but we'd changed. I shut out the possibilities of what that meant.

"Like you did with me?"

"Don't you dare," I snapped. "Don't you *dare* compare our actions right now." He'd hidden a world of betrayals from me, allowed me to break beneath the sharpened points of their blades again and again. And I was trying to balance healing and proving myself, crumpling under the combined weight, fighting to reach him.

"No, I will compare it. Because you seem to forget that everything I suffered and every lie I told was for a reason. It was to save lives, to save *you*." A ripple of agitation rolled through him, but he shook his shoulders out, stifling his memories.

"I never asked you to save me, Malakai. If you truly saw me, you'd understand that." I stalked toward him, anger slowing my steps to a prowl. "You'd know I'd rather have suffered beside you, knowing the truth, than lived in ignorance forever."

Malakai ran a hand along his chin, palm scraping across that scar from his father. "You're so focused on what *you* want—are you even grateful for the sacrifices I made?"

That accusation slammed into me with the force of the Angels descending.

You don't make the decisions here, Malakai.

Perhaps you shouldn't either.

Was that truly how he saw me? Incompetent, unworthy,

71

ungrateful. Impossible to compromise with, perhaps not deserving of the effort. The implications buried me like a snowstorm, shame washing in with them.

I'd been ungrateful. Selfish. Perhaps he was right, and I was the problem. I should be more understanding.

His narrowed stare shrank me, my faults piling up between us. He'd been broken by Lucidius and Kakias, his trust in anyone beaten so thoroughly it might never heal. In my anger, I pushed him away. Punished him for the choices he made about my life, our relationship.

But he'd pushed me away, too. He thought I didn't notice, but he'd guarded his emotions as fiercely as I had, and neither one of us was willing to relent.

I wished we could revert back to our former selves, where ignorant bliss was all we knew, but that wasn't real life. Reality was a shattered glass waiting for you to slice your hand open against it and pour your deepest desires on its surface.

No, Malakai didn't understand my decisions, and I didn't understand his either. But, Spirits, my fight was dying, my soul weighed down.

Instead of replying to his slights—because truthfully, I didn't know what to say—I leaned across that chasm, meeting his lips in a slow sweep, asking if this was all right. If we could put our problems on hold and get lost in each other.

He hesitated at first, but when I teased the seam of his lips with my tongue, he relented, sighing into my mouth. One hand surged to the back of my head, tangling in my hair as he commanded all of me.

I leaned into the competition for control, forcing him back. Our mouths became a violent clash of stifled emotions as I ripped his shirt free of his pants, undoing the buttons and shoving it from his shoulders. He gripped my hips with one hand, tugging my head back with the other.

My nails left indents in his flesh, red lines clawing down his chest. He growled at the sting, the noise rumbling down my throat, spurring me on. But I was gentler when my hands explored his back, each raised stretch of flesh a stab to my own gut.

Sensing my reluctance, Malakai wrapped his arm around my waist, pressing me into him. *Fucking Spirits*, I nearly gasped when his hard length ground against me. It certainly wasn't the first time, but when I was lost to this crazed anger, it always seemed different.

Malakai broke the kiss, breath hot between us.

"Why can't you stop fighting me?" Malakai panted but watched my hand inch down the plane of his stomach.

I hooked my fingers in the waistband of his pants and tugged, walking backward.

"I think we're on the same side right now."

Domineering and smug, taking my words as a win, he pressed me into the cold marble. I inhaled, arching into him. Bracing one hand against the wall beside my head, he kissed me roughly, his other hand trailing down my body.

We could have been anywhere in that moment. Back in our clearing, in the Cub's Tavern, atop the mountains themselves. We could have been anyone, rather than two damaged lovers avoiding their pain through each other's bodies.

But dammit if it didn't feel good to forget.

Malakai tipped my head farther back, lips moving to my jaw, down my neck, and across my collarbone, goosebumps following in his wake. I stroked him through his pants as heat gathered between my legs.

"Do you care about this dress?" he murmured against the pounding of my heart.

I could barely even remember what dress I wore. I looked down, seeing my nipples peaked against the light blue fabric, and while I did actually like this one, I shook my head. Who cared about a dress when it was standing in our way?

With a lust-drunk smile, he reached for the straps.

But an all-too-familiar glow bathed the room, freezing us.

"Bad timing?" The Angel chuckled.

"Damien!" I shouted.

"By the fucking Angels," Malakai gaped.

"Must you all swear on my kind as such?" Damien shook his head. "Pleasure to meet you."

Malakai remained frozen. The Angel lounged above the table, legs crossed, hands tucked behind his head. His imposing Angellight bathed the foyer like a sunset, coating every piece of artwork and inch of marble floor.

"You truthfully have the poorest timing of any reverent being I've ever met," I snapped, bracing my hands on Malakai's chest. His heart hammered beneath my palm.

"And how many have you met, Chosen Child?" The damned Angel smirked.

"First you appear when I'm drunk and in my undergarments." Malakai mumbled a curse. "Then, after Malakai and I had just been together, and now this? Have you no decency?"

"It is not my fault you are always indecent when time demands I confer with you." Damien waved one hand at where Malakai and I were half-clothed.

"As if you have no control over the matter."

"On that you are correct." Damien's throat bobbed as he sat up, hovering in the air with gentle flaps of his golden wings. And there was something in his purple eyes—something that tugged at my gut and sent my second pulse pounding.

Something that made me turn to Malakai and say, "I'll see you shortly."

"You don't want me to stay?" The disbelief in his voice twisted my heart, but Damien shook his head, and my fate was sealed.

"I'll meet you in the bedroom," I whispered.

Bringing him into this would only spark more questions, more arguments, and we had too much to work out between us as it was. We'd said no more secrets, but Malakai had enough on his shoulders without me making it worse.

Hurt flashing behind his eyes, he left. I banished the ache in my Bind and stormed across the foyer into my office. A fire flared to life, flames reflecting orange and yellow against the white marble mantel.

"Your timing is truly horrendous."

"Your manners have certainly seen better days," Damien observed, following me.

"I'm very sorry, most honored Prime Warrior." I bent in a mocking curtsey, but there was little heat to our banter. "A lot has changed since we first met. I fear I have become a new woman, and perhaps the grace has become selective."

He tilted his head, the most human gesture I'd ever seen of him. "Why do you fear that?"

I pondered his question. "I don't fear the woman I have become. She has endured more than I thought possible. But I fear the things that shaped her and what she has yet to do." Because I didn't know where this path would lead, but every day, the world was slowly caving in on me.

Damien's eyes flashed with an unnamed emotion. "Do not fear what is beyond your control."

The Angel floated to the shelves, plucking a book at random. It was one I hadn't even read yet, a tale about ancient trials that seemed fascinating.

"Make yourself at home, why don't you?" I snatched the volume from his hands and tucked it back into place, but his eyes lingered on the green spine.

"It was my home first if you recall." His light spilled around the room as he floated to the window, illuminating the corners and nooks like they were made for it. He was far more vibrant than the first time we met, even more so than when we spoke outside the mountains just weeks ago.

"The palace has passed through many hands since your time." I leaned against the mantel's cool surface and fixed him with a stare.

"Never forget the one who built it, though. Never forget where you came from." An echo of something I couldn't name flashed across his sculpted features.

I uncrossed my arms, walking closer and propping myself on the couch. "Do you miss it?"

Damien was silent. For a moment, I thought he wouldn't answer me. Then, he whispered, "More than you know."

It was a sentiment meant more for the night stretching beyond the peaks than it was for me, but I tucked it away. Damien and I may joke, I may push him, but an understanding rested between us.

"Cherish your time here, Chosen Child."

The name stiffened my spine. "You were such lovely company until you called me that."

He chuckled. "You were such lovely company when you were more respectful."

"Oh, dear Damien, don't you know I'm made of fire and jagged edges?" The Angel's lips clamped together at the claim. "Will you ever explain why you call me that?"

"In time." There was a hollowness to his eyes I hadn't noticed the last time we'd spoken, a preoccupation worrying his purple irises.

"I painted those, you know?" He gestured to the mural decorating the ceiling, one of pink flowers spilling down long branches, a lone person beneath, stringed instrument in hand. From down here, it was hard to make out any more detail than that, the colors fading over the centuries.

I could picture it, though. The Angel, alive and mortal as any warrior, spending his days in this empty palace. Building our city from the ground up and leaving the tales of his life to look down on future generations.

His melancholy reached out to me, but though I recognized it, I also saw the reluctance. Those few statements had been enough of an ache to share. So instead of prodding his past, I softened my voice. "They're lovely. Now, do you have a cryptic message, or shall I ask questions first?"

"Questions?"

"Last time you visited, you left with the confession that I carried a curse." My fingers scratched at the black scars on my wrist. "You implied it was deadly. My previous affliction was false." *You were never at risk of suffering from* that *Curse.* Those words had plagued my waking and sleeping hours ever since. "I know this has to do with Annellius Alabath."

His flustered blink was barely perceptible. "You have learned more about Annellius?"

Satisfaction spread through me because until this moment, it had remained a theory. I recounted the tale my father had told me, barely having finished when Damien visibly swelled, became that ancient being I'd first met, consuming all space and sound.

He spoke in that archaic voice, dripping with power.

"Born again through the shade of heart,
the Angelcurse claims its start.
Seek the seven of ancient promise.
Blood of fate, spilled in sacrifice.
Strive, yield, unite,

Or follow the last's lost fight."

The proclamation crawled down my throat, taking root in my blood. Became one with my flesh...*strive, yield, unite*...until those words were all I knew, all I heard.

They pounded, consumed, became every facet of me. A shrieking command shuddered down my bones, its roar excruciating, my body seizing. Vaguely, I was aware of gripping my head. Of falling to the floor. Heat barreled through my body.

And as suddenly as Damien had transformed before me, it was over. I was left shuddering and sweating on the rug of my office. Angellight pierced my eyelids, dried the moisture beading on my skin.

"What the *fuck* was that?"

"I'm sorry." There was a faint hint of genuine emotion in that apology, but not enough. "Unite them."

"What?" I choked out, vision blurred.

"Only you can know—" His words were strained. "Fate will fight back—"

A command. There were legends about these things. Back when the Angels roamed Gallantia, before they'd even officially been *Angels*, an explicit command—threat—from a being with their level of power was lethal. If it was broken...it killed its target.

There was a pained intake of breath, one that said so much more than his words ever could—and the light faded.

Damien vanished, voice echoing in my ears. As I stumbled to my feet, another night came back to me: the last time I'd visited my clearing and found the spear waiting for me.

"Fucking Damien," I breathed, staggering to the side table to pour a glass of water. Fingers curling around the wood, my shoulders rounded, the weight of Gallantia weighing on me. *Follow the last's lost fight.*

Annellius. It had to be about him. There was lore that he'd been given a task; my father said it himself. Whatever it was—whatever he failed—was left to me.

Seek the seven. Unite them.

Only you can know—

Fucking Spirits, I was done with the secrets. I'd promised no more lies after the Undertaking. Forgiveness and trust, those were the pillars of who I was trying to be moving forward, and for the most part, I'd stuck to them.

But those were regarding secrets about myself. If I went against a command from an Angel and shared this prophecy, the repercussions could take the lives of *others*.

Fate will fight back. My stomach clenched.

I couldn't let anyone else suffer fate's wrath. And that meant that no matter how much I wanted to tell them, I couldn't.

One lingering pulse of heat flared through me—familiar. The same as that broken piece of Angelborn, burning like the prophecy's power. Was it connected?

"Spirits of all hells," I cursed, wandering to the window.

Damien's last words haunted me. *I'm sorry.*

Whatever this Angelcurse was, it was dangerous. The shaking tenor of the ancient prime's voice grating against my bones confirmed as much.

And it was intended for me.

"Why did you ask me to leave?" Malakai's voice was heavy—with accusation or hurt, I couldn't tell. My head still swam.

I stalled with one hand against the door to our bedroom, facing away from him, fingers curled against the wood.

Three seconds. That was all I allowed myself. With my eyes closed, I dragged a breath slowly through my lungs, channeling every bit of strength left in my drained body. Then, hating it, I slipped into the mask I'd grown accustomed to wearing.

Only you can know—fate will fight back—

I looked over my shoulder. Malakai sat on the bench at the foot of our bed, elbows braced on his knees. Defeated. That was the word that came to mind from his drooped head, hair wild as if he'd run his fingers through it repeatedly.

"What do you mean?" I asked.

Cowardice twisted my gut, cool and slicing as a blade. I was unable to give this broken man one sliver of the truth. One tiny step that might help him toward healing. Help us. But I wasn't willing to reveal Damien's words. Not when I didn't understand that warning myself, and not when there was already overwhelming pain between us. Sharing would only add one more thing we needed to reconcile while trying to heal.

And if I was honest, I was still hurt by the way Malakai had allowed me to bind myself to him without knowing. By the secrets he had kept.

Maybe I wanted some of my own.

Moving forward was a challenge, trying to navigate our hurt yet shrinking in loneliness. If I could, I'd remove the weight of the world from his shoulders. He'd carried it for too long. But then, I'd crumble beneath it—neither outcome was fair.

"You didn't want me to hear what he said." When his gaze lifted, lashed anger burned me. Malakai was pulling back the curtain I'd drawn over our problems.

"It was about the Rapture." I tugged that curtain tighter, striding across the room on legs much sturdier than I felt.

Mystlight flared along the dressing chamber as I entered and headed straight for the vanity. The scent of honeysuckle and leather wrapped itself around me.

Dammit.

"Talk to me," he commanded.

I didn't answer, but a warm hand rested on my shoulder. My Bind heated and a twinge of sorrow clanged through my still-broken heart.

"That one worked," I told him, brushing my lips over his knuckles.

"I think it's easier when we're closer." Physically and emotionally. The latter was the one we'd been struggling with.

"I'm sure we'll figure it out." My voice was hollow. I looked in the mirror and found my eyes matching it.

"It would help if you told me what's going on." Gently, Malakai turned me to face him. "Talk to me," he repeated.

Talk to him. The words echoed through my ears, bouncing around my head and filled the cavernous space between us. The suite, the palace, the entire Spirit-forsaken city itself. *Talk to him.* As if he showed me the same consideration.

It was petty. It was cowardly. It was weak and childish and certainly *not* the behavior of the Revered I claimed to be, but fuck them all, this was not a matter of weapons and strategies. This was a battle of the heart, and it proved to be as brutal as warfare.

It was with cruel satisfaction that I looked into Malakai's eyes, his accusations from earlier still swirling between us, and said, "I'm taking a bath."

He was silent, but his pupils enlarged, giving away his anger.

We refused to break eye contact as I slid the straps of my gown off my shoulders and let it pool at my ankles, my undergarments following.

Malakai didn't give in to the bait, and I didn't invite him to join me as I strode to the bathing chamber, shut the door behind me, and turned on the tap. Over the water rushing into the sunken tub, I heard a door slam.

Once the room was full with enough steam that I could no longer see my wan reflection in the mirror, I sank into the tub. Thank the Spirits that the magic of our mountains provided an endless supply of deliciously hot water.

I scrubbed at my skin, needing to wipe away more than the sweat sticking to me. The taint of my atrocious behavior, the gross satisfaction coating me, and the fear gripping me with Damien's prophecy—I needed to do away with it all.

With floral-scented soap and a rough brush, I scrubbed. I scrubbed and scrubbed, as if that would cleanse me of thoughts of curses and sacrifices.

But a part of me knew—those things were unavoidable.

The water had grown cold, my skin raw, but my temper had barely simmered. And my thoughts—those had not calmed at all. But I had yet to hear Malakai return, so I rose from the tub, used one of the fluffy towels to dry off, and spent an exorbitant amount of time applying lotions to my skin and oils to my hair.

Rarely had I given in to such beauty routines before the war. After the treaty, we'd stopped spending on luxuries, but my body had been so worn after the journey across the territory and the Undertaking, it couldn't hurt to pamper myself.

Moving forward, I wanted to employ all of my tactics. If my

opponents saw youth and beauty as a fault, I'd turn them into strengths. Use them to get beneath their skin. Beauty could be a weapon sharper than the finest blade, and I was fighting battles at every turn. Much like showing my core guard as a family, these other sides of me made me whole, a person rather than an emotionless figure.

Unfortunately for my opponents, my arsenal just became much more expansive.

After combing my hair longer than was necessary and still not hearing any movement outside the door, I emerged from the bathroom. Selfishly, I was glad Malakai had yet to return. While bathing, I'd turned Damien's prophecy over in my head carefully, picking it apart for hints as to what was being asked of me.

No—demanded. This was not a request.

Blood of fate, spilled in sacrifice. The words chilled my very bones.

As if carried on a wind, I drifted across the room to the sideboard bearing our weapons.

It was there—that haunted dagger with the Engrossian gems. The one that belonged to Lucidius. Malakai had cleaned it, wiping away the visible stains of its cursed past, but they lingered.

Firelight bounced off the blade as I lifted it, the volcano flashing through my mind. Veins of lava bathing the battle in an orange glow as warriors fell one by one. Sparks and shouts. Lucidius's weight pressing against my chest, hands around my throat. My blade dragging across his flesh, blood claiming the end of that life.

But not all threats were thwarted that day.

The Engrossian dagger swallowed up the light as I brought the sharpened edge against my palm. The metal was cool, biting into my skin, but I barely felt the sting; it wasn't deep, just enough for a stream of red blood to bubble to the surface. Crimson beads slowly filled my palm, running down my wrist.

The blood caught the light. It was…ordinary. I had seen plenty of bloodshed—much more than I wished to see in my short life. This was nothing special. Why then—

The door opened. "Ophelia…" His voice trailed off as he took in the scarlet staining my arm, soaking into my silk robe.

"Ophelia, *what in the fucking Spirits?*" Malakai rushed to me, using his shirt to apply pressure to my wound. He retrieved the blade from my hand, wiping it off on his pants, and placed it back on the dresser.

Within minutes, the cut healed over thanks to our quick healing made even quicker while in the mountains. My palm and arm were left crusted in streaks of crimson.

"Ophelia…" he hedged. He dropped his shirt to the floor, lifting my chin with one hand and holding my wound with the other. "What's going on?"

I didn't answer. I couldn't. Because when I saw my blood dripping down my arm, only one word came to my mind. One word that I had no fucking clue how to explain. Removed centuries ago, yet alive in me.

Never at risk of suffering from that *Curse.*

Your blood is strong enough to cause and end wars.

Destruction.

What in the name of the Spirits did it all mean?

I had no answer, but that word echoed through my mind, ominous and cautionary all at once.

Angelblood.

CHAPTER TEN

OPHELIA

"Is THAT NEW?" JEZEBEL asked, eyeing the necklace I clutched.

Head snapping up from the tome I was reading on Damien's life, I uncurled my fingers from the metal charm.

"It's the piece that fell off Angelborn." As I lifted the token, it caught the early summer sun streaming through the palace library windows. Santorina and Erista looked up from their own work, observing the piece.

Jezebel cocked her head. "You didn't have it fixed?"

Only you can know— Fate will fight back—

"It didn't need to be there." I shrugged, letting the chain fall against my chest. How could I tell her that something in the way this piece of metal heated reminded me of the Angel's presence two nights ago without testing his command? It was in the familiar warmth and presence that settled within me.

But it was a secret I had to keep because it kept my friends safe. Even as I told myself that, though, something I didn't want to acknowledge squirmed in my gut.

"Erista," I said, searching for a way to distract myself. The Soulguider delegate's catlike eyes flashed to mine. "When you journeyed to Damenal, did your party encounter any aberrant creatures?"

"Aberrant?" She propped her chin in her hand, the gold ink around her forearm glinting in the light. "Not in the desert, no. The streams have been clear, too." The Soulguiders' sand dunes stretched from the western coast of Gallantia to the base of the mountains. Thin rivulets ran through the dust, used to deliver Spirits home. Hearing all was well in that sacred land calmed my nerves a bit.

"There was one night, though," Erista continued, her brows pulling together. "When we stopped in a small mountain town to eat…there was a roar. No one knew what it came from, but it shook the walls of the inn."

Jezebel stiffened, flipping through the pages of the book she read on the Spirit Volcano's history.

"Interesting," I mused. Watching my sister, I shrunk at the memory of that winged beast attacking in the forest. Then, I thought of Santorina beside me, a knife to her throat. "And no other creatures?"

"What should I have seen, Ophelia?" Erista asked.

"Fae?" I breathed. Rina's hand clenched atop the table.

"Fae," Erista repeated. "How in the name of Xenique would a faerie be in Gallantia?"

"We encountered one on our way here," Jezebel explained.

"He tried to kill me," Santorina ground out. Taking a breath, she finally uncurled her fingers. "But he realized I was under warrior protection."

"Why was he here?" Erista gaped.

"To put forth a warning," I explained. "He said that threats to fae magic are looming. He was sent to see how far they spread."

"Sent by the queen?" The Soulguider looked between my sister and me now.

"I believe so." I clutched my necklace again, its heat steadying. "Lancaster—the fae—agreed not to harm anyone in our lands and to keep us notified of developments in this looming power."

"I don't think we can trust him to hold to that." Jezebel's voice was dull. "But it doesn't sound like we have a choice."

"The fae queen has a bloodied history," Erista said. "Composed of secrets, tricks, and bargains normally ending worse for the other party. Rumors say she can read bloodlines."

We all shivered at that. Prejudices ran deep between warriors and fae, but it was hard to deny the stories we'd been warned against. Legends of their queen were slick with blood. The lives shackled to hers due to naivety. The secrets she wielded

And if Lancaster was here on her order…

"We don't trust Lancaster, but we can't discount his information. Not until we know what's waiting for us." I shivered at the thought of him being out there somewhere, doing Spirits knew what on our continent. What threatened fae magic would surely threaten our own. "Besides, fae can't lie. They may be bred to play with words and calculated tricks, but that earns him a certain degree of trust. Theirs isn't the queen I'm the most concerned with, anyway…"

Twisting my necklace around my finger, I contemplated Kakias. We hadn't heard a word of her since the Rapture. What was she planning?

Jezebel slammed a book shut, pulling me from my thoughts. "Come on, we'll be late for training."

As Rina and I followed Erista and my sister down the wide open-air corridors of the palace, the mountain breeze helped me organize my thoughts. I'd been picking apart Damien's prophecy, but had gotten nowhere, circling back repeatedly to this Angelcurse and what in the Spirits it could mean.

The windows we passed looked over the Sacred Quarter, the Sacra Temple's golden spires shining in the distance. Perhaps I needed to extend my research outside of the palace walls.

And maybe…just because I couldn't tell anyone what exactly Damien said, didn't mean I couldn't ask for help in other ways.

Gripping Rina's wrist, I pulled her back a step and lowered my voice. "I need your healing expertise."

"Are you okay?" Rina's piercing stare assessed me.

"Yes," I said quickly, but was I? "I'm wondering about curses."

Her eyes narrowed on the dark webbing on my wrist. "I thought it was gone."

"It is, but I'm curious." I fought to keep my voice level, choosing words vague enough to not draw suspicion or fate's wrath. "Are there any common curses you've learned of?"

Rina lifted her eyes to the sky as we descended wide steps to enter the training arena. "I've studied some, but I'd have to think. I left all my books in Palerman."

"Take your time." Impatience clawed at my gut, though. I didn't know how long I had to *unite them*, but if there was a chance Rina could help decipher what threat the Angelcurse carried, I'd give her time.

"What I can tell you," Rina said as we began Cypherion's warm-up routine, "is that there are practically thousands of curses in existence, but most are not deadly as yours was. Not unless they come from a higher power."

"And how do those afflictions work?" *One, two, three*, I counted out the lunges, hoping steady movement hid my burning interest. An Angelcurse was certainly born of a higher power.

"From what I recall, those kinds of curses are extreme, Ophelia." Worry creased Rina's brow as she stopped working, turning to me. "They're rare and dangerous, almost always connected to someone's being at a deeper level."

"And can they be healed?" I didn't even know if healing was what I needed, not with Damien's words being so vague.

"I'll see what I can find. Perhaps Esmond knows something."

I nodded. "Don't say it comes from me."

She leveled a harsh look at me, but I didn't have a chance to argue because Cypherion and Malakai both shouted, "No!" at Tolek.

"You barely even know how to use the damned weapon," Cyph said, taking the bow and arrow Tol was lifting. Where had he even gotten those?

"You wound me, CK. I happen to be very skilled with a bow."

"I've never seen you use one." Cyph crossed his arms.

"And you've never seen me in bed, but I can assure you I'm far from incapable there, too."

"Oh, Gods," Santorina commented, both of us snickering.

"I suppose they got tired of waiting for us," I added as Tol set up their gamble for the day.

"Why don't you take them on, Ophelia?" Erista said, loud enough to be heard by the boys. Challenge sparked in the Soulguider's eyes. Jezebel looked between the two of us, a knowing smirk dancing on her lips. "I'd love to see the Revered truly fight."

I assessed the girl, from her curls to the sturdy boots on her feet. There wasn't a hint of malice in her posture. No, the feline smile splitting her full lips was a promise. It was faith. She truly *wanted* to see me take down the boys.

"That sounds like fun." I grinned, retrieving Angelborn from where she leaned against the wall.

"Excellent." The devilish flash of Tol's smile shone across the arena.

"Are you sure?" Malakai asked.

"Unless you're afraid," I teased. Malakai's eyes hardened. Cypherion only shrugged.

"Spears, boys," I demanded, swirling my own in one hand. "What order do you wish to lose in?"

They exchanged a look, silent communication passing through the trio that had trained together for nearly a decade. "I'll go first," Cypherion offered. "Mali, then Tol."

I instantly latched on to his strategy. Cyph—the largest and strongest fighter—would tire me out, and if he didn't win, Malakai would be second, in the middle, as he hadn't completed the Undertaking and was the weakest. Tol, nearly as strong as Cyph, would be last, to take out any reserves I saved.

If only I made it that easy for them.

"Show no mercy, CK," Tol cheered from the sideline.

"Thanks, Vincienzo," I retorted.

"I'm only trying to get you riled up before it's my turn." He winked, and I couldn't help but laugh.

Turning to Cyph, I tilted my head. "We've never truly fought, have we?" When we were in formal training, our instructors had always paired Cyph with the largest, oldest warriors, underestimating my size. After training was suspended, I'd only worked with Jezebel.

"I suppose not." Cyph grinned and slid into that lethal side that lived within him. "Time to find out who truly is the best."

It was an even fight, leaving us both panting halfway through. Cypherion fought with precision, noting my every weakness, but I fought with cunning. I favored my left leg when there was no reason to at all, and he fell into my trap. When he swung his spear at my left, I dodged, sweeping under his arm to bring the tip of Angelborn's blade beneath his chin.

"You knew I'd mark that," he observed. "That I would attack based on your faults, so you faked them."

I shrugged. "Know thy opponent."

"A great reminder, Revered."

The fight with Malakai was barely a battle at all. I wasn't sure if he was holding back or if I had truly grown that much stronger than him. Regardless, we had trained together our entire lives, and I knew his tactics better than anyone else's.

With only a few swipes, his weapon was on the floor, and Angelborn was poised above his heart, hovering over the Bind.

"That was much easier than usual," I joked.

He shook his head. "Having an off day." He avoided my eyes as he bent to grab his spear, leaving me in the middle of the arena with a furrowed brow. But I didn't have time to ask, because Tolek slid into his position. I was breathing heavily, my cheeks flushed, but I squared my shoulders.

"Let's see what you've got, Alabath." Tol set his stance.

I struck first, the adrenaline from my last two wins coursing through my veins. He met the attack, forcing me back a step. I growled, lunging again, but he met that strike, too. Like he was predicting everything I would do.

Because he was, I realized with hints of both admiration for his work and frustration for not having noticed.

"You've been paying attention?" I quipped. Our spears sparked.

"I wasn't going to lose to you again."

I ducked his next attack, sweeping my weapon out, but he dodged it. "No more cheater's shots?"

He laughed, the sound spurring me on for another strike. And another. Each one was well met.

"There's no forest creatures here to distract us," he taunted.

"Don't need them," I panted, tiring from the combined force of three consecutive fights, "to beat you."

I brought my spear around my body as if performing a flamboyant attack. If Tol had been watching me, he should have known the move wasn't my style. I was a direct fighter, not a showy one. The distraction was quicker than he anticipated. Tolek had barely moved before my weapon was aimed at his throat.

"Yield?" I whispered, so low it was almost seductive.

He raised his brows and dropped his weapon. "I yield," he barked, but then his lips split into a grin. "Well done, Alabath. Next time, I'll get you."

"Good luck with that, Tolek," Malakai said, glaring at his friend, and Tol's expression fell.

Malakai took my chin in his hand, kissing me softly.

"You were spectacular, Phel." But the words were as stiff as the walls between us. He placed another kiss to my lips, and my heart stuttered in time with my shoulders tensing. Did I sink into it or turn away? These days, I never knew. His fingers flexed against me as if fighting the same battle.

We were so torn, the two of us. Walking through the footsteps of strangers. When Malakai pulled back, my lungs were tight. I shifted my chin from his grasp, sucking in a deep breath.

When I looked back, Tol had been replaced by the delegates, impressed with the skill of the Revered. Erista winked, and I smiled despite the conflict roaring through me.

"I want to learn to do that," Vale whispered.

"That was impressive," Esmond said. "I understand how you've made it to where you are today."

I thanked him, warmth spreading through me at the compliment, but my attention was elsewhere. Cutting around the trio, I looked toward the staircase leading to the palace, but Tol was gone.

CHAPTER ELEVEN

OPHELIA

"COULD THIS MEAN SOMETHING?"

I peered over Malakai's shoulder, a fresh cup of herbal tea balanced atop the stack of Sacra Temple books I'd said I'd dig through that afternoon. The top volume was on historical battles, a few beneath it on ritual law, some on Angel appearances, but tucked between them was my true interest—the files on Annellius Alabath.

They'd been taunting me all morning—every day, truly, since my father had given them to me three weeks ago. I was certain Annellius had something to do with this mess the Angel had delivered to me, but I had yet to uncover anything helpful. And Damien had been suspiciously quiet.

The papers practically burned through the books as I set them on the table, tucked away in a corner of the temple archives, swiping up my tea before it could stain the cover. I leaned over Malakai's shoulder, his honeysuckle scent filling my senses, and read what he pointed to.

Prophecies made by the third minor clan of the warriors of Gallantia—the Starsearchers—are subject to interpretation. If made within one of the sacred temples on their land, they are believed infallible. Readings taken outside of these spaces fluctuate on their reliability.

"Maybe…" I mused. "We know Titus didn't read in a Starsearcher temple. He may be believed stronger due to his status as chancellor, though." I shook my head. "It feels like speculation." Malakai had taken on the task of researching every facet of the Starsearchers to interpret Titus's vision, but I was reluctant to rely on unconfirmed theories when it came to the darkness he read.

"There's no evidence to prove him right either, though," Malakai argued.

I cupped his cheek, turning his face to mine. "Thank you for trying." With the pressure mounting, I was grateful for Malakai's steadfast shouldering of this topic.

We hadn't fought since the night Damien appeared, but we hadn't talked much deeper than this either. At times, Malakai seemed like he was returning to his old self, but then I'd catch the shadows behind his eyes and realize it was a mask—one he held up even in front of me—and he was further than ever.

We were like a silk scarf slipping between my fingers, unraveling to the floor between us. As it went, we'd reached an amicable plateau of peace, and I was okay to settle there. To set up my camp on that flat surface and sit beside him in a friendly silence, telling myself the love story I thought was written in the stars rather than living it. We were better this way.

Still, having his help with this search was important to me.

"We'll figure it out."

"Maybe we should approach Vale again," I offered, falling into a seat beside him.

Malakai shook his head. "She won't talk."

I drummed my fingers on the table, its dark wood pristine. Light streamed through the various shades of blue stained glass in the windows, casting the image of Damien as a warrior onto the table's surface.

The temples throughout Damenal were littered with different portrayals of the Angel's life. I'd spent a lot of time observing them these weeks as Malakai and I made our way through sacred texts that could tie back to Titus's readings.

Malakai was right. We'd approached Vale twice, and both times she'd sworn she knew nothing. We'd even considered writing to Titus himself, but I didn't want to expose just how concerned I was yet.

I huffed, falling into my seat and picking the top book off my stack.

My muscles ached with every movement. Cypherion's training was more thorough than anything I'd ever undergone. Even with my full strength from the Undertaking, he had me crawling to the sidelines after every circuit.

He'd taken charge of not only our workouts, but all Mystiques who had shown up in recent weeks. One positive of our generation being withheld from the war was we now had a surplus of warriors who wanted to train. Many were unskilled, rusty at best, and some malnourished thanks to Lucidius's shredding of the trade system, but all longed to return to what we once were.

Hope—that was what our foundation had become.

We opened the training arena to them as they migrated to Damenal. It was not only the palace yard—not any longer. For daily sessions with Cypherion, any Mystique who wished to train was welcome.

Seeing the numbers grow…it made my heart swell. A piece long ago broken, restored.

My abdomen tightened when I leaned forward, the sore muscles barking. I rubbed a hand across the gap in my leathers, fingers lingering on my scars.

"Cyph is a sadist," Malakai joked, tracking my movement.

"I swear a part of him enjoys it." I laughed.

"At least you don't whine like some of the others."

Tolek and Jezebel had taken to being *very* vocal about their displeasure with Cypherion's workout routines. Though, the former still managed to complete every set quicker than most, with my sister on his heels. Jezebel charged to the dining hall immediately after every session to consume more food than any other warrior. Even Malakai was resuming his previous skill.

"I think they just enjoy teasing him."

I didn't care who complained or what they said. Not with the improvements we were seeing. My own muscles had never been as firm as they now were. I wasn't sure what we trained for, why these sessions felt so imperative, but we were doing what we were born to do. For now, that was enough.

Tipping the book in my hand toward me, I opened to the first hidden document on Annellius, careful to keep the book tilted away from Malakai.

Annellius was believed to be the most powerful warrior of his time, the strongest since the First Warrior, Damien himself, who ascended as an

Angel during the cataclysmic event that memorialized the seven primes into eternal existence.

Damien's prophecy haunted my dreams. I reviewed what I was sure of so far: An Angelcurse existed, and it plagued me. To resolve the curse, I had to unite seven of *something*.

I'd read through numerous books on historical artifacts in the past weeks, but nothing lined up. They must relate to the Angels, given it was their curse, so I'd been visiting as many temples in the city as time allowed.

The one question I kept coming back to, though, was *why me?* Why not Jezebel? Why wasn't Angelblood active within her when Damien had implied that it was within me?

We'd been discussing it the other day, theorizing how it could have happened. I was grateful Jez and I could at least share that much, though I had to keep the Angelcurse a secret.

The only thing we kept coming back to was my eyes. Why were they magenta, as Annellius's had looked in the Spirit Volcano?

Was it a sign that the blood was active?

The shade of heart, the prophecy said. Did it refer to the pink coloring of eyes? It felt like a loose connection.

I slammed the book shut, exhaling in frustration.

"Nothing helpful?" Malakai looked between me and the book on historical battles skeptically.

I chewed my lip. "I'm tired of reading about warfare."

As far as he knew, that's all I'd been researching these past weeks. Strategies that may help win my position as Revered. Retracing the steps of history.

I pushed back from the table, crossing to the tall shelves that sectioned us off from the rest of the Sacra Temple. The largest in Damenal, it housed a small library within its holy walls.

"I'm tired of the uncertainty we face. Of feeling like everything is stacked against us, and I don't know how to fix it." Admitting that truth made my stomach twist—feeling weak, feeling like I was failing. Despite my platform of hope, fear swirled in the shadows.

"The delegates have warmed to you. The chancellors will, as well," Malakai comforted. He didn't know that was only a piece of my concerns.

"But I have no idea what I'm doing. I'm acting like I do, but I have no fucking clue." My voice rose, but I still didn't look at him.

"Trust your instincts, Phel." He said it like my whole life boiled down to that one notion.

Maybe it does, a voice in my head said as I continued to read the titles lining the shelf. I'd followed my instincts this far, never questioned myself before, so why was I now? *But if that's true, why does my life suddenly feel like I'm an empty library shelf, all of my books out of place?*

I dragged my hand across the spines, searching for anything that called to me. Anything that looked like it spoke of the Angels, curses, or the Prime Mystique. There didn't appear to be any system to this organization. *The Book of Legends, Sanctum Fatale, Temple of Celestial Movements*—

I pulled that one off the shelf and turned to hand it to Malakai, but he was already behind me.

"Here," I breathed.

"What's that?" It was clear from his gravelly tone that he had no interest in the book, but he lifted it from my hand, pretending to read the title before he set it on the waist-high shelf jutting out from the bookcase, then he grabbed my waist and hoisted me up on the shelf beside it.

When I met his eyes, I couldn't read them.

"Do you want to know what I think?" he asked, tracing the hem of my leathers.

"What's that?" His fingers inched higher, disappearing under my skirt.

"You're too stressed." The low sound of his voice had me pressing my thighs together, but he caught the movement and stepped forward so that my legs were around his hips.

"Am I?" I whispered.

"Anything I can do to help?" Malakai outlined the edge of my undergarments, and already my mind was going elsewhere.

"We can't. Not in a temple." My breathy argument lacked conviction, though. I moaned as he swept his thumb down my center lightly. Teasing.

"We can if you're quiet," he whispered, his breath hot against my ear. For a moment, we were teenagers sneaking around once again. I wanted to go back to that time, seal up this distance that had formed between us.

I hadn't realized my eyes had drifted closed, but when I opened them, his were only an inch away, amusement dancing there, and Spirits it was so good to see, I let all the arguments and space fall away in favor of this.

"Can you be quiet?"

"Yes." I gasped.

He brushed slow circles exactly where I wanted him most, rewarding me for answering. My fingers curled around the shelf as he added pressure.

I was fully clothed, he had barely touched me, but I was already burning for release. Like something within me was coiled tightly, begging for it.

I was certain he could feel through my undergarments how badly my body wanted him, but he continued moving slowly. Asking taunting questions I could barely answer. Edging me closer, then drawing me back.

"Malakai…" I breathed his name, begging. We still hadn't kissed—hadn't even moved from our original positions.

He pushed aside my undergarments, slid a finger inside of me, and the world started to fall away. Angels, Raptures, curses—it all faded into the background as my body and mind honed in on that spot.

"Yes?" he purred.

"More" was what I tried to say, but it came out as a moan.

He covered my mouth quickly, laughing. "Don't let the acolytes hear you." He curled his finger, hitting a spot that made my hips buck, the book beside me crashing to the ground.

In that moment, I was completely under his control—and I hated that. Hated it for wrenching up those memories of heartbreak and betrayal alongside the pleasure, but he added a second finger, and I was too far gone to care. Too desperate to get out of a reality full of threats and suffering and death.

I closed my eyes, let my head fall back, and gave into him.

And when he circled his thumb at exactly the right speed, I went over the edge entirely, that tightened thing inside of me releasing in one bout of ecstasy.

I leaned my head against his shoulder, catching my breath as the high started to fade and life returned. We could only hide in pleasure for so long, but I held on for another moment, indulging in the ease we had together even if it was masking hardships. Like raindrops clouding a window, the view blurred beyond the glass. Malakai and I had so many raindrops—wild tempests brewing daily—but in these quiet moments, I allowed the view to be marred and pretended I didn't miss it.

I was still like that when hurried footsteps drifted through the temple, coming toward us.

Collecting myself, I made to hop off the shelf just as Tolek rounded the corner. Malakai's faced turned stony, and his hands tightened on my thighs, holding me in place.

Tolek glanced first to the table where our books were sprawled, then finding us against the shelves, he looked quickly away. "Sorry to interrupt."

"I'm assuming it's important?" Malakai asked, voice icy.

Tol narrowed his eyes. "Actually, yes. Two…visitors just arrived at the palace to request an audience. They attempted to scale the fence when we didn't let them in."

I shoved Malakai's hands off of me, quickly forgetting what we'd been doing, and scrambled to grab my things.

"Have you gotten any information out of them? Their names? Purpose?" It was odd someone would be so brazen, daring to hop the fence with a guard present.

Tolek's shoulders stiffened, hands behind his back.

"It's Barrett, the heir to the Engrossian throne." My heart plummeted to my feet when he looked at Malakai. "Your brother is here."

Chapter Twelve

Malakai

My chest tightened, the bars of the iron cage rattling. But they held.

"I don't have a brother," I spat.

"Malakai…" Ophelia stepped toward me, reaching for my arm, but I shook off her touch, striding for the stained-glass windows of the temple, the blues washing the city streets out with a drowning haze.

I didn't look at Ophelia. I didn't look at Tolek. How were they acting like this was normal? *Your brother is here.* Fucking Tolek. He said it as if it meant nothing, when those few words drove deep into the cracked foundation I'd been rebuilding within myself. They tore it up one shoddily placed brick at a time, until they were weighing down my shoulders, crushing me.

Ophelia and Tolek muttered behind me, but I couldn't hear what they were saying. In truth, I didn't care. They were likely talking about me. About…him. About what he was doing here, what it meant for the Engrossian threat, what it meant for us.

I was curious, but I was more furious than anything. A ray of light reflected off the glass, a blinding white spot on life outside these walls. How often I'd walked these streets in recent weeks, musing over my lingering questions.

Wondering how my father had kept so many secrets.

And now, after I'd decided to force away all my feelings on his actions, one of those secrets was thrown into my path.

Ophelia's and Tol's voices continued in hushed tones. Irritation prickled my skin—I wanted them to *stop*.

"I'll see him," I announced, clenching my fists. Their whispered conversation ceased. "Let's go."

I strode from the temple before they could respond.

Tolek led us through the Sacred Quarter and into the palace, Ophelia a step behind him, but no one dared speak. Our boots echoed against marble floors, down grand staircases, and into the bowels of the building—the cells.

Good, I thought. Barrett and everything he stood for belonged imprisoned.

"Cypherion and Jezebel are standing guard," Tol said, fingers brushing the family dagger at his hip. "We had to send Santorina in."

"Why?" Ophelia asked. Mystlight gilded her profile and slid through the waves of her hair when she looked up at him.

Tolek smirked over his shoulder at me. "He didn't like when we wouldn't grant him an audience. He nearly impaled himself on our fence trying to climb it."

I tried to stifle my laugh at the image. Ophelia narrowed her eyes at me.

"What?" I asked.

"Nothing."

"Listen." Tolek turned at the top of the final staircase into the cells. He clasped his hands behind his back and looked between us, choosing his words carefully. Ophelia nodded, and he focused on me. "I'm not going to pretend I understand how you feel, Mali, but we shouldn't be too hostile."

"*What?*" I seethed. If Tolek Vincienzo thought he could instruct me on how to act—what did he know of these matters? His life wasn't as complex as mine.

"Doesn't it strike you as odd that he's here?" Tolek inclined his head.

I chewed the inside of my cheek to keep from snapping. "It's *suspicious.*"

"Perhaps." He nodded, but there were opinions he was holding back. "But we need to find out why."

"He's right," Ophelia added, gaze flickering between the dagger at my waist and my scowl. "There's a smarter way to approach this than attacking him."

I took a deep breath, looking up at the ceiling. The stone and iron furnishings were oppressive, my scars burning with the memories of my own prison, but there was a familiarity about it.

"We'll see."

That foundation within me crumbled further with each step down the final set of stairs, but I fought it—made an exceptional effort to build up my own base.

Goosebumps rose along my arms. It was a stark difference to the volcanic cell I'd lived in for two years, but the same stain hung in the air, like this place was used to blood and the hands of those who drew it. Like it had seen so much of it that the stench permanently clung to the slick stone walls—forever a reminder.

Rina was exiting the cell as we approached, an apron tied around her waist. Crimson stained the pockets.

"You went in alone?" I whispered once the thin wooden door was closed. It didn't seem to be very sturdy—how careless of whoever selected this room.

"I can take care of myself," she affirmed, but her voice softened when she took in my expression. "He didn't attempt anything."

"He's chained, but he's been cooperative," Cypherion said, and Jezebel nodded.

"Of course, he has." I shrugged. "He's injured and under our jurisdiction. He'd be a fool to attack or attempt escape until he's healed."

Cyph frowned at me. "It doesn't seem he's here to attack at all. He wants to talk."

"And in there?" I dismissed that opinion and flicked my gaze to the second door over Cyph's shoulder.

"His consort," he answered. "They arrived together."

"Though, that one was smart enough not to follow his prince over the fence," Jezebel added.

A consort. A weakness.

"If either of them tries anything, we know where to strike." I secretly wished for the chance.

"We should question them and then decide what actions are

necessary." Cyph spoke diplomatically, but if it came to it, I believed he'd be by my side while giving the heir what he deserved.

"We need to be strategic," Ophelia said, placing a hand on my arm. I raised my brows at her, and she scoffed. "Trust me, Malakai, I'd be the first to get revenge for everything done to you, but we don't know that he's like his mother or father."

"Everything done to *us*," I corrected. "We've all been hurt and that man in there is a symbol of it."

Ophelia nodded. "I'd love nothing more than to run a spear through Kakias's son. But personal vendettas aside, having him as our prisoner gives us leverage against her."

I didn't put it past the queen to shrug off her son's disappearance, the cruel conqueror that she was, but I sighed and grumbled, "I'll behave."

"No *fatal* injuries," Ophelia whispered.

"Nothing I have to stitch up," Santorina corrected. She wiped the last of his blood from her hands. I didn't know why it surprised me that it was as red as ours.

"Minor stabbings, then." Jezebel grinned, looking around at us.

"Whoever gets the best shot in wins," Tolek said.

"Cursed Spirits save us," Cypherion exhaled.

"Only if provoked," Ophelia commanded.

The mask of the Revered slipped over her features, and the energy shifted. The aura of vengeance still hovered, but the light was siphoned from it. Dark desires, vendettas, and strategies twirled behind her magenta eyes. Every step, every breath she took, was laced with power as she lifted a hand to the door and threw it open.

Ophelia was incredible as she strode into the room, every soft side of herself disappearing beneath that mask. I didn't know how she did it.

The others filed in before me. Hands within reach of our weapons, we crammed ourselves inside. Even Rina crowded into the corner, likely to ensure none of us reopened the wound she had stitched.

Despite the fact that the cell held little furniture, it was uncomfortable for four warriors thrumming with power, a healer, a prisoner, and myself. Disposing of the prisoner would free up some space.

He hadn't been allowed great comforts—I smiled at that. The chill from the hallway was worse here. That would be even more uncomfortable for the Engrossian than for us, given that his lands were humid, the air weighing on you with sticky warmth. The tang of blood was rich. Stale, like it was older than just his wounds.

I pressed against the closed door behind Tolek and Cypherion, but Barrett's slimy voice was loud, "A full guard? I'm honored you find me to be *such* a threat."

"Prince Barrett," Ophelia clipped.

"Revered Ophelia Alabath. I only wish to talk."

Her name on his lips had me clenching my fist. It was like he was taking what belonged to me, when his existence had already claimed so much of my life.

My own cell flashed before my eyes, slick with pain and hate. I shrank back against the door, trying to breathe normally. *I am not the prisoner*, I reminded myself. *He cannot take anything else from me.*

"If you only wish to talk," Ophelia said, "why hop the fence?"

"I needed to get your attention somehow after being denied entrance. These dramatics are surely unnecessary."

My fingers grazed the plain dagger on my belt. Perhaps it would finally find a home in the prince's chest. At the thought, I stood to my full height and banished all memories of my own imprisonment.

He would not take anything else from me.

"The *dramatics*," I threw the word back at the prince, "are likely to stop me from killing you immediately." Tol and Cyph shifted, and I locked eyes with the Engrossian heir. "Though I doubt they'll try too hard to hold me back."

My heart nearly stopped when he met my glare. My father's eyes—my eyes—stared back at me.

"Hello, brother," he cooed.

"Don't call me that," I growled.

I stepped forward, standing behind Ophelia, Tol and Cyph close to my sides. It was only their support and pure, undiluted rage keeping me upright. Because the man before me shared more of my father than even I did. He was a warped version, pale skin and a cruel mouth, a slightly pointed jaw and higher cheekbones, but looking into his dark green eyes—Lucidius was there.

The guilt I had been suppressing since my father's death snapped free, rising up in me, threatening to drown me.

He was dead because of my friends.

He was dead, and I missed the man I thought he was.

He had done horrible things, yet I was *sad* because he had not wanted me. A piece of me wished he had. A larger piece of me was so fucking grateful he was gone.

"He was not a good father to me either, you know," Barrett muttered.

I clenched my jaw.

He's dead. He didn't want me. He's dead.

I promised Ophelia no fatal injuries, but dammit, that promise was stretching thin.

"You say another word to him, and I'll slice out your tongue myself, *Your Royal Highness*." It was the voice of the Revered, but it tangled with a saccharine animosity only Ophelia could muster.

Tolek watched her with a smile, adding, "I'll hold down his shoulders for you."

Barrett's eyes swept over my friend twice, and he fucking grinned. "I'd rather enjoy that."

"Flirting, pretty boy?" Tolek quirked a brow.

"Perhaps you should take your chance now, Tol. If he doesn't cut the jokes, he won't be as pretty by the time he leaves this room," Cypherion said. Though they jested, their voices were as lethal as the weapons they carried.

"It's an honor to earn the attention of *royalty*, Tol," Jezebel drawled, mocking the title.

Barrett was unfazed by the threats and jokes. He leaned back against the wall, stretching his legs out on his cot. "You must be the younger Alabath." He observed Jezebel. "We never had the pleasure of being introduced."

"The pleasure is all yours." She smirked.

"I can assure you that in this moment, it's not." The prince raised his wrists, chains clanking against each other. The sound made me flinch. "But I can think of uses for these in which *pleasure* might be shared between us."

Jezebel rolled her eyes, crossing her arms, but Tolek, Cypherion, and I all tensed, a low growl rumbling through me.

"Relax, boys," Barrett said, dropping the act finally. "I truly do wish to talk. Besides, I'm a committed man and would never do anything to jeopardize that." A flash of nerves passed through his eyes at the mention of his consort, likely wondering if harm had already come to him.

"Beyond flirting with my guard, why are you here?" Ophelia asked.

Barrett reclined against the wall, shifting the pillow behind his back, rifling his dark hair. Even that simple movement reminded me of my father. My heart thumped in its cage, but I told it to shut the fuck up.

He cannot take anything else from me.

"Barrett," Ophelia warned when he didn't respond. He was burning toward the end of her patience. I almost felt sorry for the bastard at what he'd find there. "Shall I allow Cypherion to persuade you to talk?"

Cyph angled his body, every blade visible. Whatever this prince had to share must be very valuable if he was toying with us this much.

Barrett sighed. "That won't be necessary. I'm here to share information on my mother."

CHAPTER THIRTEEN

OPHELIA

I ASSESSED THE ENGROSSIAN heir, from the worn tips of his boots, to his black dirt-and-blood-streaked shirt, to the many rings adorning his fingers. From the easy cross of his ankles to the challenging smirk on his lips. From the pale, sickly skin that was Kakias to the eyes that were Lucidius.

There was more to him, though. Subtle tremors of his hands and nervous glances at our weapons I wasn't sure the others noticed.

I did not know what to make of him, but I recognized an act.

"We're to believe you've come to us to share information about your own mother? Your own people? With the enemy?" Speaking the words aloud made them seem even more ridiculous.

Barrett blinked at me, all jokes dropped. "Yes, I am here for precisely that reason." There was a gray tinge to his skin that almost made him look sick, cheeks hollowed.

"And why should we believe you?" Cyph asked.

The prince leaned his head back against the wall, a weight seeming to settle on his shoulders. "Because I don't agree with what she's doing." Lips tightening into a grimace, he pushed himself to the edge of the cot, fingers curling around its metal frame. "My mother is heading toward a fate worse than death, I believe."

"And what could that be?" I tilted my head at him. We locked eyes, each evaluating our opponent—or potential ally?

"Slaughter."

"You think she's going to get herself killed?" Was he here to ask us to help her? Not a shot in the Spirit-guarded hell would that happen. I'd run Angelborn through his chest and send his body back to the Engrossian Valleys before the question left his lips.

But the prince shook his head. "I think she's heading toward the slaughter of *innocents*."

Silence hung over the room, and through it the cries of dying Mystiques clouded my mind. The *slaughter* of my people at the hands of Engrossians after Kakias gave the order to send them into Palerman. Blood across the city center, cobblestones sticky beneath my boots as we moved bodies. My father nearly losing his life. My sister, only fourteen at the time, witnessing such destruction.

"You didn't seem to care last time," I spat.

"Did I not?" His fingers curled tighter around the edge of the cot. He was restraining himself. From what, I wasn't sure. Barrett hadn't fought in the war. He made no public appearance during that time. And—

He made no public appearance.

"You didn't approve of the war, did you?"

Barrett shook his head, sighing. "I saw no point in the loss of Engrossian life."

Malakai scoffed. "And Mystiques? What of our people that fell at the hands of yours?"

"It was a shame for them to die, but they aren't my priority," Barrett shot at him, voice thick with malice. Then, he said to me, throat bobbing, "You would have held the same view."

He was right. If it came down to Mystiques or Engrossians—if it came down to Mystiques or any clan—I would choose Mystiques. Every time.

"My people are not all made in the image of my mother," Barrett pleaded. With the purple shadows beneath his eyes, he looked exhausted. The weight of lives balanced on his shoulders.

"They didn't seem to mind attacking us before," Tolek challenged. He shifted, favoring his scarred leg. For a moment, the scent of his blood surrounded me again.

We couldn't trust the Engrossians.

"I'm not saying they're all innocent. There's rotten fruit in every bunch." Barrett shrugged, running a hand through his curls and bracing his elbows on his knees. The movement was so reminiscent of Malakai. My friends noticed it, too, gazes shifting between the half-brothers.

"How can we believe *you're* innocent?"

Barrett raised his shackles.

"That means nothing," I asserted. "You were injured. You needed our help."

"If I was here for nefarious purposes, don't you think I'd be a little more creative than arriving at the main entrance to your palace in the middle of the day?"

Yes, I did. It hadn't settled right with me when Tolek reported the arrival, but I neither confirmed nor denied that to the prince. The lift of one corner of his lips told me he knew anyway.

I looked over my shoulder at Cyph. He stood with one hand braced on the sword at his hip. With a nod, he scooted around me to stand beside Barrett's cot, curling his hand through the chains like a leash. The prince watched with a curious tilt of his head.

"If I am to believe your claim"—I strode toward him as much as I could in the small space, commanding it—"you need to tell us more."

Cyph drew a dagger, and the Engrossian's eyes widened at the pristine blade.

Barrett swallowed. "Your threats are unnecessary. I've said I'll talk."

I bent down before him, looking directly into those dark green eyes. "Start."

"My mother is moving troops."

My stomach flipped. "Why?"

"I believe she intends to reignite the war."

That made no sense. Kakias lost Lucidius, she lost her cover, she lost her prisoner. Starting another war would only ensure everyone saw her as a conqueror. She could never place her son on the Revered's seat now, despite who his true father was.

What was it she was after?

My mind raced through the reasons why this didn't make sense, but Barrett's voice was sharp enough to slice through them all.

"She's been traveling often. I don't know where she goes—she won't tell me. But she only brings a small guard with her. I think it's a diversion, while the real threat is the armies she's rebuilding. Do not forget, we didn't suffer as your people did in the war. Many survived. Many who still need work, despite the gruesome state of it. My mother knows this and has called on them. They've already started marching eastward."

Not northeast toward the mountains, but east. What lay in the east?

"Do they not march for Damenal?" I asked, crossing my arms to keep my hands from shaking. Tolek and Jezebel pressed closer to me.

"I don't know." Barrett shook his head.

I flicked my gaze to Cypherion. He tugged the prince's chains until they dug into his wrists.

"Ouch! Bant's golden cock, what was that for?"

"Your answers are unsatisfying." I turned away, pacing.

Barrett huffed. "I'm telling you what I know." I stiffened but said nothing, so Barrett barreled on, "The only logical plan was that the army would march to Damenal, yet the last report I intercepted said east."

"When was the report?" Cyph gripped his knife tighter.

The prince watched his fingers curl around the handle, words rushing out. "Two weeks ago. I traveled here immediately. It said—" He cut himself off.

"What did it say, Prince?"

"I truly am horrendous at these matters, aren't I?" He groaned, and I wasn't certain what he meant by that. "There's a small camp of Engrossian Warriors in your Southern Pass."

The Southern Pass, the wide stretch that led directly from Damenal to Bodymelder and Mindshaper Territories—potential allies.

Internally, my spirit was screaming, but I slammed that mask against it. *Gather information. Build a strategy. Demonstrate my capability and protect my people.*

"How many?"

"No more than thirty."

"Why?"

"To cut off access and surround the capital."

Two weeks. For two weeks, they'd been so close, and we'd been oblivious. What else had the queen planned that we didn't know?

Keeping my arms crossed, I assessed the prince with a seething silence.

"It's suspicious that he'd tell us." Jezebel narrowed her eyes at Barrett.

"I'm inclined not to believe him," Tolek said.

"It does seem like a trap," I added as if the heir wasn't even present.

Barrett leveled a harsh stare at us. "I don't wish to see any more bloodshed for my people. If that means selling out my mother to you, it's a risk I'm willing to take."

I raised my brows at him. "Regardless of that fact, if your mother's army is marching, it doesn't matter what you want—there will be bloodshed. The only alternative is us rolling over." Something we would never do.

"Now if that is all…" I turned toward the door, barely able to keep my anger leashed.

But whatever restraint Barrett had on himself snapped. "I don't know what to tell you, *Revered*." He tried to push to his feet, but Cyph yanked him back, chains clanking. "Diplomacy, negotiations, it's all new to me. I have no power under my mother's rule—I—" He took a heavy breath. "I'm merely a pawn. One tired of sitting by while people die."

There it was. The reason I'd maintained my disinterest—to push him. I wanted him poised at the breaking point. Because it was clear the Engrossian prince had more to say, frustrations that needed airing, that might make him a true ally.

"Thank you for the information." I nodded at my friends to file out before me. "There will be a guard at this door night and day. If you wish for us to believe you, I'd advise you not try anything."

He sank down onto his cot, disbelief in his wide eyes and parted lips.

"Get some rest, Prince Barrett." I closed the door behind me with a click.

Chapter Fourteen

Malakai

"Jezebel, call the council," Ophelia instructed the moment we were in the Mystique Council Chamber two floors above the cells. "Cyph, Tolek, start mapping routes. Rina, can you prepare a pack of tonics and ointments?"

They fluttered around me as if I was a statue in the middle of the room.

"What are you doing?" I rounded on Ophelia.

She gaped at me. "What?"

"What is all this?" I waved my hand at the preparations.

"Malakai." A softness lowered her voice. "There's an immediate threat to the city. We have to respond."

"Why are you pretending to believe him? He's obviously lying. We should throw him off the fucking mountain." I paced along the windows, looking out over the courtyard and training arena. After my years being locked up, the view was refreshing, but even so, the memory of chains at my wrists dug deeper. I rubbed the scars, counting the ridges.

The Engrossian deserved at least that much.

"Why would I kill him, Malakai?" She approached slowly and tried to take my hand. I jerked it away.

"Are you fucking kidding me?" I pulled aside the collar of my shirt to remind her of the Engrossian ax I now bore.

Ophelia had the decency to flinch. "I'm sorry," she muttered. She stepped forward, placed a kiss to the scar, and observed it for a long moment, jaw grinding. Then, she swallowed, blinking back her emotion, and righted my collar, hands tightening around the fabric. There was steel in that grip and fury in her eyes, though she spoke with the voice of the Revered. "But this is a political decision. We can't assume his information is a trap because of what his mother did to you."

I stumbled back a step, forcing her hands off of me. *Politics, strategies, alliances.* It seemed every choice she made these days was for those narrow-minded goals.

"Was it a political decision when my father put shackles around my wrists? Was it *political* when Kakias instructed hot blades cut my flesh?" I roared. "Everything claims to be political, but not everything must be." Some things should be innocent choices, not tangled up in the motives of clans and strikes against enemies.

"Those were all matters of strategy, Malakai," she soothed. "They were twisted, decided upon for perverse reasons, but it boils down to powers and policy and pride. I won't make my decisions based on their actions."

"That's what you're doing!"

"Not in the same way. I'm choosing not to punish him for his mother's actions, but I will if he gives us his own reason to. If he's lying to us, he'll—"

"It would punish her, not him," I seethed.

"There might be a better way to enact revenge."

"She's right," Cypherion agreed, placing a hand on my shoulder. "Look at it, Mali. Not hurting Barrett, allowing him to help us—that might strike Kakias even deeper." Ophelia nodded at Cyph. In that one action, I was more isolated than ever.

"So now we're suddenly not only *not* hurting him, we're giving him free rein?"

"No." Ophelia's tone turned harsh. "I never said that."

"You might as well have."

"If what he says is true, we need his insight into the Engrossians. How their armies train, their movements."

"I'll never ally with him."

"You don't have to. But I can't squander what could be a chance to cut off a very real threat before they arrive. A shot at survival."

What did they know of fighting for survival? I'd learned not to rely on others for that.

"I don't trust him," I growled.

"I don't either, yet." But she was considering it. And that was enough to twist my heart. Enough to squeeze the life right out of it.

"He might not be so bad," Tolek offered.

I glowered at him, unsure who I was even looking at.

He raised his hands. "I'm aware of everything he stands for, everything he is a reminder of. But you don't know him."

"Neither do you," I spat.

"No, I don't. We won't ever, though, if we don't consider this information. Think of what we'd be turning away."

"We'd be giving him a chance to *ruin us.*"

"Malakai has a point," Jezebel said. Finally, someone fucking agreed with me. She pushed back her chair. "He could be playing us, loyal to his mother."

"That's a risk," Ophelia agreed. "It's always a risk, and I'm not going to trust him outright."

But she wasn't going to *not trust him* either.

"If it truly is authentic, we need to move on the Southern Pass," Cyph said.

"He seemed genuine when I stitched him up," Santorina said. "He was grateful."

"He has a unique position as heir. Both a bargaining chip and an undeniable wealth of knowledge." Tolek ran a hand over his scruff. "I vote he stays."

"It's not a fucking vote!" I snapped.

They all froze.

"I'm sorry, Malakai," Ophelia whispered. My heart might have stopped beating, I couldn't be sure. Because Ophelia was the one person I was always sure of before I left, and now, I didn't recognize her.

Before anyone could offer another excuse for their misplaced faith, I stormed from the room.

I hadn't even decided where I was headed, but my feet carried me there.

The hallway stretched before me, shadows curling around sconces and statues, foreboding. My chest rose and fell as I stared at the door, darkness separating us.

For weeks I'd avoided this place—this entire section of the palace. Ophelia and the others had come here to search for anything my father may have hidden, but I couldn't. It held too many ghosts I didn't want to address.

But now, they'd sought me out.

Anger churned my blood, heating and warping until I was charging down the corridor, throwing the door wide.

Dull mystlight blinked to life when I entered, as if surprised. Like it knew when the inhabitant of this suite had died and pieces of its energy went with him. There were no reminders of me or my mother in my father's former home. Not an artifact, not an image.

Shoving that disappointment aside, I strode for the office. It was locked, but I threw my shoulder against the wood—once, twice, three times, until the lock snapped, handle clattering to the floor.

It still smelled of his piney cologne. Exactly like the office he'd held in our home in Palerman.

Though carefully rifled through, the room remained *his*. Trinkets, papers, and books were thrown about lazily beneath dull mystlight, as if he'd spent many long hours slumped over the desk, working on whatever despicable plans he concocted. I hadn't expected it to feel so…lived in. Holding his presence despite the weeks since he'd died.

Fuck, there were even bottles of liquor and sticky glasses lining the shelf beneath the window. Like he'd only left briefly and expected to come back. That, more than anything, was a punch to my gut. A stark snap to reality.

He's not coming back. I breathed through the sentence and the roar of guilt it dragged through me.

But his son was here.

I stormed to the shelves and tore down every book I could reach.

The son he wanted more than me was here.

I swept the bottles of liquor from the table. Glass shattered, a mimic of my own world breaking. Shards crunched beneath my boots, filling the room with echoes of broken promises. Sharp cries of a father not protecting his son as he should.

Not wanting his son to exist.

The words on the papers covering his desk blurred before my eyes. It was his handwriting scribbled in cramped lines, his arrows and doodles. They spoke of Angels and tokens and prisons and things I could not give a single fuck about—not in his hand.

Each streak of dark ink ignited the anger inside me. Before I knew what I was doing, the papers were flying through the air. Shredding beneath my hands. Falling into the stains of dark liquor that seeped across the ground.

I collapsed to my knees with them.

It was unfair.

It was *so unfair.*

I'd only wanted to follow in his footsteps. I'd only wanted to make him proud. I'd never known there was no chance.

Liquor seeped through the knees of my pants, glass digging into my skin.

At some point I started crying. I wiped my tears away angrily, at first, but the cascade quickly overwhelmed me, a curse I couldn't outrun. It happened often these days. And no one—not my mother, not my friends, not even Ophelia—understood the torment constantly warring through my body. I was eternally alone.

I need to be alone. The solace of isolation was perhaps the only place I could be free.

CHAPTER FIFTEEN

OPHELIA

IT WOULD BE A two-day journey to the location in the Southern Pass, then possibly another day or night to locate the Engrossian camp and stake it out. I didn't want to waste any more time lingering in Damenal when they already had two weeks on us.

"You have everything?" my father asked for the third time, finishing the loose braid in Sapphire's mane outside the palace stables.

"Yes, we've been over the plan. There's nothing left to do but act."

"I'll watch out for them, sir," Danya, the Master of Weapons and Warfare assured him, and I could feel the relief in my father's exhale. Young by warrior standards—in her early forties—Danya had earned her position on the council prior to the war and proved that she deserved it despite the outcome. She was a small woman who flawlessly wielded a sword greater than my father's, a weapon that should have thrown her solid frame off balance, yet she controlled it. A true master. A reliable source of protection.

My father smiled at her. "Thank you, Danya."

She nodded, cropped black hair swaying, and left to see that the others were ready.

"And thank you, Father, for watching over the city." He'd be staying behind with Larcen, Alvaron, and Missyneth to ensure Damenal was defended. Now that we knew there was an active Engrossian threat, preparations were being made.

"You're sure you want to do this?" His eyes flicked over my shoulder to where the rest of our party was readying the horses. I knew who he was assessing—Barrett. He and his consort, Dax, would be attending the raid with us. Bound in chains.

Between Tolek, Jezebel, Cypherion, the delegates, and the handful of warriors Danya had selected, we'd ensure the Engrossian heir wasn't a threat. Malakai had even decided to attend at the last moment, surprising us all, but I promised him he could keep well away from his half-brother.

"It's a risk," I agreed, watching the prince struggle onto the horse he'd share with a Mystique guard. "But he showed up here. He requested an audience and was desperate enough to hop the fence, despite the guards. He led the man he loves into potential danger for this." That had to mean something. I was wary, but a small piece of me wanted to trust him. Or at least find out what else he hid. "He's supposed to be our enemy, but the pieces aren't aligning."

My father was silent for a moment. Then, quiet and pained, he said, "He looks so much like him." He watched Malakai readying his own horse in solitude. "Be careful, *sorrida*."

The warning felt like it was about more than just Barrett.

"I will, Father. I'll see you in time for the Renaiss festival next week." It would be a day to celebrate the promises and hope we'd been blessed with this year—a day our people needed.

"I'll see you. I love you."

"I love you, too."

We left the city then and set off on the word of a supposed enemy.

Boulders formed tall walls around our camp as I sat beside Jezebel the first evening of the journey. Leaning back, I looked to the sky overhead, dusk creeping slowly toward night. Tall grass tickled the backs of my legs, and for a moment, serenity wrapped around me.

I breathed it in. Breathed it out. Closed my eyes. Wondered about what we'd face in a few days, listening to the crunch of Jezzie's knife through crusty bread. Something about the mundane action of my sister preparing food was soothing amid the unknown.

The others had all taken to their own tasks—surveying the area, planning tomorrow's route, watering the horses. But I was content to do as Jez directed.

"You're buzzing with thought," she said, handing me a block of cheese to slice.

She wasn't wrong.

"You support this plan, right?" I started, not looking up from the work, cutting one chunk after another in my calloused hands. The Curse mark on the inside of my wrist swallowed up the starlight as I watched the darkened veins flex with each motion.

Jezebel didn't pause. "Of course, I do."

"I suppose I'm worried." My cheeks flushed with the confession. "Since I've claimed this role, I've second-guessed my decisions more than usual."

Now Jez set down her knife.

"Ophelia, what you've accomplished so far is extraordinary. Few warriors would have survived what you have, and even fewer would forge ahead. You're rebuilding our lives. Our city."

"It's mainly the Mystiques."

"They may physically be doing the work," she countered, "but I've spent a lot of time in quieter parts of Damenal since we've been there. And do you know what they whisper of?"

"What?"

"Their symbol of hope. The girl who exposed a corrupt regime and put a stop to a conqueror. Your bravery and loyalty and determination, it inspires them."

Tears stung my eyes, and I brushed them away before Jezebel could see them fall.

Hope. It's what I'd promised myself to uphold. I'd been outrunning a fear of failure, but perhaps progress wasn't always loud. Leaps were made in the quiet stretches.

"I'm only doing what has to be done." My necklace heated, a reassurance from Angelborn herself. I pressed my palm to its warmth, and it nudged one of my broken pieces, slipping it back into place. With the comfort of that, I admitted, "I'm worried the chancellors won't be convinced that I'm fit for this role."

They weren't Mystiques. They didn't feel the ripple of healing the way our clan did.

"And would that make you view yourself any differently?"

I considered that. "No, but we need their support. It could change the tide of the war." If Barrett's word was true, that war had already begun.

"Think of it this way." Jezebel rose, rinsing her hands with her canteen. "Use our time out here and the Renaiss festival to show the delegates who you are. You've already begun, but here you'll be the courageous leader and fighter. There, you'll be that symbol of hope. Let them see every side of you, and I'm certain they'll be swayed if they haven't been already."

Show them all of me. Tear down more walls to build my arsenal. I could manage that.

"Thanks, Jez."

She smiled, but there was an opaque sadness to it.

"How are *you*?" I prodded, willing her to open up to me.

"I'm fine." Her eyes flitted away again, searching the clearing we'd settled in for an excuse. They landed on Malakai. "How's he?"

Now I was the one to look away. "About the same."

"Ophelia…"

"Don't start, Jez." I ducked my head, letting my hair fall in my face as I removed berries from her pack.

I wasn't ready to peel back the layers of what was happening between Malakai and me. Because the truth was, I didn't know. I couldn't tell how he felt about anything anymore. His family, Barrett, his own life. He was unhappy—that much was evident. The foundation of our stable plateau had cracked with the prince's arrival. But I couldn't articulate a single explanation beyond that.

"You two used to share everything." She spoke gently.

"It's hard to discuss it all." I didn't tell her he wouldn't talk to me. I didn't want to paint him as the bad guy. "I'm the one who killed his father."

"That man needed to die, and I'm certain he knows that." She sighed, and I thought in that moment she felt the weight of what hovered between me and Malakai. "I'm sure his feelings are complicated."

"As are mine. He lied to me—"

"Oh, believe me, sister, I am as furious about that as you are. He lied to you—he lied to all of us. And though we all understand why he did it, it's not an easy thing to accept. I idolized him growing up, and to learn that he not only hurt you, but left without a real goodbye to any of us—" She inhaled, eyes closing. "Well, it made me question a lot of things." Her eyes eased open. "But what I'm trying to say is that if you want to move forward, you have to do just that. Put it behind you."

I picked stems off berries, watching a small mountain of them pile up like the words I held within me.

"Or…you must do what is best for you." Jezebel watched me; she probably caught the tremble of my lips as I bit them. "But I advise you choose a path forward and allow the Angels to guide you." There was a layer of sinister weight in her tone I chose to ignore. It spoke of searing truths. "Or your heart," she amended. "It will always steer you right."

I wasn't sure I knew how to read the shredded, mangled thing my heart had become. For years, it felt like it lived outside of my body, resting wherever Malakai had been, the synced beats the only way I knew he was alive. I was still learning how to own it, how to piece it back together.

I thought Malakai was doing the same with his, but our paths were unaligned. Where they ended, I didn't know. But even in this conversation, a bit of the edge I'd been living with dulled with my sister's understanding.

"Sometimes the decisions that are best for *you* aren't easy." She collected the sliced bread and cured meats. "It's simply the way of the world. Especially in the position you're in. Those who hold power cannot please everyone."

My head snapped up. "I'm not a people pleaser." I'd never made decisions on the whims of others.

"Then why are you not considering what *you* need now?" She turned toward the group with the prepared meal in hand, taking a step as I mulled her question over in my head.

"How are you so wise, Jez?" I asked, following.

"I've had good examples." She shrugged, a modesty I'd never seen in her flushing her cheeks. "Faced a lot recently."

I wanted to ask what she meant, what she wasn't telling me, but there was that opaque curtain between us again, and I knew my sister. She wouldn't let me find the gap in it until she wanted me to.

"One more piece of advice?" she whispered as we approached the now ravenous group. "Talk to them, too." She nodded in the direction of the Engrossian heir and his consort, then shoved her empty canteen into my hands.

I grabbed the back of the Engrossian prince's jacket and pulled him along behind me, ignoring his outburst of reluctance and the snickers of my friends.

"Couldn't wait until I finished my meal, Revered?" He held up the slice of bread he'd managed to grab, chains on his wrists swinging. The firelight glinted off the manacles then caught on the first finger of his left hand, where he wore a thick silver ring with the Engrossian royal sigil. An emerald in the crown glimmered in the light.

"We're getting water." I pushed empty canteens into his hands, staring at that ring for a moment. Entranced with it.

"Of course, we are." But he followed me around the turn in the path, climbing up a sloping, grassy mountainside toward the stream we'd seen earlier. "You do see the irony of this, don't you, Ophelia?"

"Enlighten me," I drawled.

Barrett caught up to me, lifting his wrists and shaking them so the heavy links cracked against one another, a sharp clang in the still mountains. "Here I am, the son of your enemy, come to *help* you vanquish the woman you blame for every unfortunate fate that has befallen you. And you've chained me."

I opened my mouth, but Barrett raised his brows in challenge. I waved a hand to tell him to carry on.

"Not only am I now essentially your prisoner, but I'm being held in *chains* from my *father's* former residence. The father I *barely knew*, who apparently had plans for my future—plans I was not granted a say in. Just as he and my mother had plans for *your* future, and plans for *my dear brother*." His brows scrunched. "Are you seeing the irony here?"

"That you're not much different than I?" I shrugged, crouching down where the stream flowed thickest. The prince mimicked my movements, uncapping the first canteen.

"Well, there is one stark contrast between us, Revered."

"I suppose you're going to enlighten me."

"*You* saw to it that *I* would receive nothing more from my father." It almost sounded like a threat.

"What are you saying, Your Royal Highness?" I eyed him across the water, the babbling stream filling the silence.

"Nothing." He shook his head. "Only reminding you of what you've done. I don't need that man—I never did—but it was not my *choice.*"

Spirits, how did he know exactly which strings to pull to unravel my facade? I scratched at the Curse's mark to steady myself.

"I am sorry for that, Prince. I truly am. But he left *me* no choice."

"I understand. Still, when I seek to assist you in dealing with my mother, you chain me as they did your beloved Malakai. There is a poetic irony in this circumstance." He tilted his head, moonlight gilding his sharp cheekbones, sunken shadows deepening beneath them. The purple circles framing his eyes darkened.

Barrett reached for the next bottle, his half-open shirt sliding to the side. And I nearly gasped. Above the wound Santorina had stitched up, long purple scars crossed his chest and abdomen. They were stark against his pale skin, like shadows on snow.

They were the scars of the Engrossians that were set with a secret, saltwater ointment before being allowed to heal. *Keeping them* from healing properly. A mark for their warriors when they came of age.

And his—this warrior prince's—were the most brutal I'd ever seen, slashing a jagged X across his body.

When I tore my gaze away, he was watching me. "Did they hurt?" I asked.

"More than anything," he sighed, then straightened. "But it was an honor. Or so I thought at the time. Regardless, I took the pain gladly. Much like yours, I presume."

His eyes dropped to my midriff, then traced my wrist, where the scars of the *lupine daimon's* claws slashed through my skin. But where the prince's were dark against light, my scars were white lines against tan skin. Utter contrasts, both forged through pain.

I straightened. "These are a sign of my strength. Of what I survived." I could practically feel the wolf's warm breath against my body, see the ebony teeth and nails.

"As are mine." *Though not by choice.* Barrett's scars may be the opposite of my own in appearance, but they represented more similarities than I wanted to admit.

Carrying on with the rest of the canteens, trying to appear unfazed, I said, "I want you to tell me everything you know about your mother's plan."

"I already told you."

"Not everything."

Barrett flashed that crooked smirk again. "Ah, Ophelia, you are clever." Spirits, when he ran a hand through his hair, he looked so much like Malakai, it was haunting. But that grin held a fervor Malakai lost during his imprisonment.

I returned the smirk. "I simply understand negotiating, Prince."

"And what have you gleaned from that understanding?" Curiosity brightened his tone.

"I know you want something." I looked over the warrior raised in an environment of malice. "You would not have handed over your information so easily yesterday if it was all you had. You had to give us something in order to gain our trust—to keep us from enacting one sliver of the torture your mother sentenced Malakai to. But I'm willing to bet you retained another bargaining chip."

As he thought over my words, low coos of night-doves and howls of wild dogs drifted to us.

"And why do you think that?" Barrett finally asked.

"Because it's what I would have done."

He considered me with those uncanny green eyes. Then, he said, "You remind me of her, you know."

Any hint of commiseration between us turned to ice.

"What?"

Barrett *laughed.* "She's not all bad. There are some qualities in my mother that are admirable. Or they would be, if not warped as they are in her." I clenched my hands into fists, regretting trying to understand him. "Ophelia, regardless of what she's done, she's ambitious and protective of those she does love. It manifests in despicably twisted ways, but that much is true. Even you would have seen it. You share that fire, even if yours is lighter—the illumination to her darkness."

"I am nothing like her," I hissed.

"Fine, fine. As you say." But that gleeful smirk did not leave his lips.

"Tell me what you know, Barrett, or those chains will never leave your wrists." Twisting the cap back on my final canteen, I rose and picked up the bunch. Instead of heading back to the group, though, I followed the stream around the side of the hill.

"My mother was after more than conquering the Mystiques."

"What was it?" I kept walking, ignoring the quickening of both my pulses.

"I don't know specifics."

"Then what help is this?" I groaned, stopping and staring up at the stars. Did my best to not throttle the prince who I thought might be trying to help.

"Because in battle, understanding your opponent's motivations can be as pivotal as knowing their strategies. And perhaps this war doesn't look at all how we expected."

"What do you mean?"

"While we know the previous war was waged to put me in your seat of power"—he kept walking, leading me now—"my theory is that it was a front for secrets darker than we imagined. My mother always has ulterior motives. I don't think she would share those with anyone." He stopped. "What do we have here?"

As I caught up to him, I saw it. A cave.

Plenty of caverns dug into the rocky faces of the mountain range, but when we stepped into this one, it seemed different. Like it inhaled upon our entrance, exhaled with each step, the thing alive on its own.

"It's just a cave," I said, ignoring the warmth beading in my necklace. "What do you mean with the theory about your mother?"

Waiting for him to speak, I dragged my hand along the cool rock. The walls didn't move, but that sensation of expanding and contracting stayed within me.

"I'm saying she is after something else." Barrett didn't follow me as I walked toward the back of the cave, but I quickly realized there was no end in sight. Odd. "Before I left, I investigated her private quarters and found information on ancient Mystique lore."

My teeth clenched, and I spun toward him. "That's private."

There were legends that we shared between clans, and then there were the personal ones *no one* divulged. The ones guarded by temple acolytes if written down at all. They stretched back to the Angels themselves.

"That's what I thought," Barrett agreed. I searched his moonlit face for any hint of betrayal, of misleading, of anything that might reveal this was all a plot.

There was nothing.

"So, Lucidius betrayed the Mystiques again?" I guessed.

But Barrett was watching me with a worrying crease between his brow.

"There's more?" I asked.

"It wasn't only lore. It was paired with a concerning amount of information about you, Ophelia. I don't know how it ties together, but I think it's *you* she wants. The last war, the coming attack, it's all for you."

"Me?"

Barrett nodded, and that one motion pulled the mountains out from under me.

Was it possible Kakias knew about the Angelblood? The Angelcurse? Was that why she had been after me this entire time and tried to kill me in the volcano?

All of this precious blood wasted in a worthless girl. That's what she'd said to me.

Her blade was at my neck again, her fingers dug into my skin, and that inexplicable power of hers steeled my bones.

Looking the prince over, trying to collect my warring emotions, I asked, "Is that all?" I slipped past him, leaving the cave behind, and fought to pace my steps. But the sad smile he flashed told me he saw through the facade.

"That's everything I know. Let me know if I can help figure it out." He brushed a hand through his hair again, sigil ring catching the light.

"If any of this is a trap, it will be the last regret of your life." His throat bobbed as my threat settled. "Let's go back."

When we returned, I watched Barrett walk to Dax, the two exchanging quiet words on the outskirts of the group.

With dread forming a vise around my stomach, I strode for my pack and pulled out the parchment and Mystique ink I'd thought to pack. It was supposed to be for emergency messages to Damenal. But this—

This *was* important. I couldn't keep waiting for allies to decide they wanted me. I had enough evidence to prove that a threat was building. I needed to act.

Pressing the pen against the parchment, I watched as one bud of black crawled from the tip, staining the paper, as dark as my future was.

I think it's you she wants.

"She can't have me," I growled.

I wrote the letters.

CHAPTER SIXTEEN

OPHELIA

THE NEXT DAY, I cornered Dax while passing through a narrow stretch of craggy mountain peaks, their jagged edges reaching into the clouds. I waited until he'd been switched onto Cypherion's mare, Erini, to ride with him—which was comical considering how large the two of them were—since I didn't want others overhearing.

"We haven't spoken much," I began, inhaling the crisp air and letting Sapphire's easy pace relax me.

"You've been busy with your interrogations." There was heated defense in those words, mirrored in Dax's hooded hazel eyes.

That made me like him more.

"Should I have done otherwise?"

Dax thought for a moment, then ran a hand over his shaved brown hair in defeat. "I suppose not."

Cypherion exchanged a silent smile with me, cataloging every movement of this Engrossian.

"Dax, I'll be honest with you—"

"Why?" he interrupted, and I balked. "I don't mean to discount the offer, but I have to ask. Why be honest with us? Barrett has a wishful heart—hard to believe after the life he's faced—but I'm a skeptic. So I have to know—why bring us with you at all? Why trust us?"

"I don't trust you," I reaffirmed. "But I want to. I want to believe that while a lot of unfair fates have befallen me, there is still good in the world. I want to hope."

"Because she's a good person who has the weight of a clan on her shoulders," Cypherion added. "She's trying to see circumstances from every side before blocking out possibilities." He looked to me, understanding and encouragement bundled in one slight nod. "As a good ruler does."

That had me sitting higher in the saddle as Sapphire ascended an incline between two sloped walls.

"So, Dax, I want to trust you. But I need you to give me some reason that makes you two trustworthy."

Dax's eyes stayed on Barrett, thirty feet ahead. He watched his body sway easily with Elektra's movements as he rode with Jezebel, muttering in her ear the entire time. My sister waved him away like a pesky fly.

"He's good, you know." He adjusted the place where his dark green leather sleeves met his manacles, tucking the metal away. Unlike the prince, who wore loose, casual clothing, Dax dressed like a soldier. Ready for combat. "He's not like his mother."

"How can I believe that just because you say it?" Never mind the affinity gnawing at my gut after my conversation with Barrett last night. Wanting to trust them wasn't enough.

Dax continued tracing the chains around his wrists, grumbling something beneath his breath. Then, in a soft voice, he said, "He had to kill three of our own guards to get here." My hands tightened on the reins. "The queen—I think she knew what he was planning. Or suspected him of something. She had me sequestered."

"Why you?" It was a gasp, almost, but I kept my eyes on the outline of the mountains stretching against blue sky in the distance. The clouds brushing their peaks.

"She thought he was going to run." Dax's eyes narrowed, wary fury breaking through. "And she knew he wouldn't go without me."

"He killed them to get you out," I finished for him. And with that, I saw a bit more of myself in the prince. That inability to leave behind someone you loved. The carnal need to shield. And I realized, just because he was raised under a wicked regime, did not mean he himself was wicked. Barrett's heart beat with hope just as mine yearned to.

If I could crack open all of his actions like this, pick them apart to their barest of bones, the motives were not much different than my own. Protect the one he loved and ensure a peaceful future for his people—one with as little bloodshed as possible.

"Why did she care that he ran?" Cypherion asked. "If she truly only used him as a pawn and didn't share plans with him, why would it matter?"

"She needs an heir," I said, but it didn't sound convincing, even to my own ears.

"Her Majesty does not fare well with loss," Dax said. "The only time we'd tried to leave before, she locked Barrett up for a week. He hadn't seen her in two months before then, but when something disappears from her—or threatens to—she loses any essence of control."

I pondered that, wondering how it tied into her desire for me above all else and what her true motives could be.

Despite that, though, as Dax's story worked its way into my thoughts on the remainder of that afternoon's journey, a small piece of me was growing to understand these two Engrossians.

Stars winked into existence on the second night, and I wanted to imagine they were waving good fortune to us for what waited tomorrow. That they weren't sowing discord along the path of my future.

We'd rest tonight, spend a few hours traveling to the outpost where the Engrossians were rumored to be stationed, assess their camp, and strike at nightfall.

"Any idea what they have in store for us?" I asked Vale as I sat next to her around the mystlight lantern, looking to the heavens. Everyone had gathered to review tomorrow's plan once more.

But it was Erista who answered from across the way. "I bet they're quiet in preparation of the Apex Moon."

"The what?" Tol paused his writing in the journal propped on his knee, turning curious eyes to the Soulguider.

"Starsearchers don't much believe in lunar lore the way Soulguiders do," Vale explained. "The Apex Moon shouldn't affect our sessions."

"Interesting," Erista observed, head cocked with that feline gaze. Whatever she was thinking, though, she didn't say. Instead, she turned to Tolek. "The Apex Moon is the night of the month when the connection with the Goddess of Death, Artale, is the strongest. The souls venturing home that night find it easier to pass through the barriers between life and death, and our predictions are clearer—essentially she pulls back an opaque curtain to us."

"How does the connection with her work?" Collins, one of the warriors Danya had chosen to come with us, asked. He was a large man, twice her age at least, with thick brown hair to his shoulders and an eye-crinkling smile that softened my nerves every time he flashed it to me.

Like right now. Despite the eerie topic of Artale, I was lighter when I grinned back.

"We are mere conduits. Deliverers of her children back home to her, no matter what realm they end up in after ours." The mystlight lantern seemed to glow brighter as Erista spoke. "The network of streams through our deserts carries them to the afterlife."

With that responsibility came the premonitions, I knew from my grandmother. Soulguiders were gifted visions of one's future—particularly feats leading to their demise. Unlike the Starsearchers' readings, they couldn't be spoken of.

"And what of Xenique?" I asked after the First Soulguider, now their Angel.

"Xenique was the first with this connection, born of unique circumstance. But we, like the other warriors, honor her above all else. Without Xenique, we would not be blessed with the responsibility of guiding souls home, despite Artale's power." Erista spoke slowly and chose her words carefully, clearly avoiding the private pieces of lore. "She was the driver behind everything we are today, breaking barriers that were otherwise unchallenged in order to earn her power."

Cyph spoke up, aiding the Soulguider, "I once read that Xenique obtained the goddess's blood and it's been passed down her line since."

Erista nodded, relief sharpening her attention. "It's believed some today even share it."

"But Godsblood is the rarest substance on Gallantia," Esmond said.

Even more rare than the Angelblood twisting through my veins.

"Does your family share it?" Jezebel asked Erista, pointedly avoiding my gaze.

"No." She shook her head, curls bouncing. "My family doesn't lead back to the Angels. But if my father is to be believed—which I advise you take every claim he makes lightly—we have a number of Xenique's artifacts in our trove."

"You don't agree?" I asked.

She shrugged. "Every Soulguider claims their family's heirlooms belonged to the Angel. It's a point of pride."

"That must be a warrior trait." Jezebel laughed, and it warmed my spirit. "I can think of a number of Mystiques who care a bit too much about those things. Or they had before the war."

"Yes, well, the war changed many things, didn't it?" I only muttered it, but just to be safe, I glanced up to ensure Malakai hadn't heard. He was polishing a borrowed sword behind us. Brows drawn low, eyes quiet but thoughts loud.

I tried to tug the Bind, to brush some reassurance against that thread, but it strained. He didn't react.

Sighing, leaving him to his thoughts, I turned back to the circle, heart a bit heavier.

"I don't know why legends differ between the moon and stars," Vale was saying. "It's as if the fates couldn't agree on the two."

"Regardless, Ophelia," Erista said, "you shouldn't expect to hear from Meridat regarding that letter you sent until after the Apex Moon passes."

I'd told them all of the letters I sent to their chancellors last night, begging for alliance in light of the raid. The Engrossians were moving. We were responding. War was looming.

But I hadn't told them what Barrett said about his mother's interest in me. With Damien's ominous warning, I hadn't figured out how to explain that I thought it all wove together.

"Alvaron will love that you went ahead without his counsel," Danya had joked, but she'd given her approval.

The others had all agreed that it had to be done. Now we waited for answers, and I pretended not to worry over them.

As the night wore on, the conversation dissolved into a mess of legends between all clans present. Even a few Engrossian tales from Barrett and Dax, though some were reluctant to listen to those.

When the hour turned late, Erista stood to move to her sleeping mat. "May the Angels and Goddess guard your dreams," she wished us.

"I'm not sure how I feel about the Goddess of Death watching me sleep," Tolek mumbled to me.

"Neither am I." But I couldn't help but laugh at the lighthearted spirit of the evening, despite the gravity of what came next.

CHAPTER SEVENTEEN

OPHELIA

WE LEFT OUR HORSES a mile out from the Engrossian camp at dusk. Barrett and Dax had given us every detail they knew about the warriors there—how many, the weapons we should expect, the tactics—and we'd scouted them earlier. The prince and his consort would be staying behind, though, guarded by two of Danya's warriors and Vale, who said she'd watch the stars.

Before I turned away from Sapphire, Cyph placed a hand on my horse. Reluctance tightened his jaw as he chewed over his words. "I think I trust them," he finally whispered.

Looking over my shoulder, I found Malakai. Alone, buckling on his metal vambraces.

"I'm starting to," I muttered, unsaid fears scraping against my throat. Guilt sliced me as sharply as the sword hanging at my hip, but it was the truth. Silent agreement passed between Cyph and I as we led our small troop into the pass, but that burgeoning trust was the only reason we were able to.

I moved quietly despite the armor I wore. Truthfully, I found it stifling compared to the freedom of my leathers, but when I remembered the deadly slice of the Engrossian axes, the armor welded within Damenal seemed a wise precaution. The blacksmiths and leatherworkers were creating more every day, readying for whatever war awaited us.

The air in the mountains was cool. Crickets chirped and wolves howled and, faintly, I wondered if the *lupine daimons* were awake tonight, but tried not to consider the other beasts roaming the mountain range.

A breeze trickled down from the peaks that should have been calming, with the moon shining its luck down on us, but each step forward was like wading into muddied waters, unsure of what lay in the depths ahead.

Finally, my ears perked up.

Chatter drifted from a valley, so low it barely broke through the pounding of my heart in my ears; I wouldn't have picked it up before the Undertaking. We came to the top of the sloping hill, peering into the shallow canyon below. Dull light was visible, as if smothered by a fog. They'd set up camp at the bottom of a valley? Unwise.

I stopped, looking up at Cyph beside me. He nodded, lips tight.

The rest of the group fanned out along the ridge. Jezebel fell in on my left, Tolek on her other side. Malakai and Danya took spots beside Cypherion, and the others around them. Twelve of us in all. Less than half of who waited below.

We'd solidified our plan before leaving. We didn't need to discuss it again. Didn't want to risk our voices being heard.

But when a wolf howled at our backs, our precautions didn't matter.

The Engrossian voices silenced. The light through the fog vanished.

"Stay true," I muttered. Pulling Angelborn from my back. "*Now!*"

We flew down the hill, forgoing any attempt at silence.

With cries and cheers, our combined force of Mystiques, a Soulguider, and a Bodymelder landed on the Engrossians.

Pale skin and purple scars shone beneath white starlight. With flashes of deep green armor, the scouting party tore from their shadowed cove of a camp. Clashes of blades—axes—struck our menagerie of weapons, but—

There were only twelve.

Twelve Engrossians, instead of the thirty we'd expected.

An ax swung toward me as I tried again to count the collision of limbs and weapons and armor. I blocked it with Angelborn's hilt, swiveling beneath the Engrossian's arm. Quickly, I flipped my weapon, drove it toward his heart—

He ducked it. Floated like a breath of wind at the last second, in a maneuver so smooth I almost missed it.

I nearly froze.

That move never failed me. And how had he moved so silently?

But I couldn't stop to consider it, only grip Angelborn tighter and meet another strike. I danced around the valley with this opponent, meeting attacks fiercely.

My chest pounded as an ax lowered toward my neck, and I lifted my spear to stop it at the last second. Sparks shot up between us.

I staggered, my ankle nearly rolling over a rock. Breath tore through my lungs, scraping up my throat as I braced myself against the Engrossian's weight.

My arms burned as I pushed. And pushed. And pushed.

His face loomed over me, my back bending. His eyes locked on mine—took in their magenta shade—

"Not so unbeatable now, Alabath."

Getting my stance beneath me again, I summoned the strength the Undertaking had given me and shoved the Engrossian back, using his weight against him.

Despite his uncanny swiftness, I ducked out of reach of his swinging ax and rammed Angelborn beneath his rib cage, between the buckles of his armor. He screamed with the impact.

"Challenge accepted," I growled, tugging the spear from his body and shoving him to the ground. He landed with a thud that echoed through my ears.

I spun to see Danya's and Cypherion's opponents fall, too. My chest rose and fell, throat raw already, anticipation heavy between my ribs.

Where were the others?

Thirty. We'd prepared for thirty.

"Ophelia!" Tolek yelled.

I whirled toward him, barely having time to look an Engrossian in his dark, soulless eyes before he tackled me.

We rolled across the dirt, elbows and knees and metal jarring. Gravel burying itself in my skin, slicing.

Angelborn fell from my hand. The warrior pinned me to the ground.

Dammit, how were they that quiet? I should have heard him before Tol shouted.

Hands empty of weapons, I threw an elbow into his face. The mask he wore buckled, snapping back into his nose. Blood seeped beneath its edges, sprinkling around me.

He pinned me. Knees framing my legs, an elbow in my sternum. I wrestled his bruising grip, but he was larger.

The Engrossian swore, grabbing me by the shoulders and slamming me into the ground. The air sped from my lungs, vision spinning as he pulled a fist back, landing a punch to my cheekbone. A crunch echoed in my head.

"Fucking Angels," I hissed over the spinning pain.

I couldn't reach Starfire, not with his weight on my hips and my arms pinned.

Wedging one of my legs between us, I kneed him in the groin. The warrior doubled over. Swifter than he could sense, I tore my dagger from my thigh and drew it across his throat.

Blood spilled over me, hot and sticky and reeking, and he fell.

His weight crushed me for a moment while I regained breath. Then, he was thrown aside.

Tol stared down at me, eyes burning. "Are you all right?" He lifted me to my feet, looking over every inch of my body, wiping drops of blood from my cheeks. I winced when his thumb grazed the blooming bruise—potentially cracked bone—and Tol's eyes turned murderous.

"I'm fine," I assured him.

Swiveling away from me, Tol brought his sword down on the neck of the Engrossian I had killed, severing his head from his body completely.

"That's better."

"How chivalrous of you." I flashed him a brief smile, still panting, as Tol brushed the back of his fingers gently over my bruise.

Then, a roar crested the mountains, severing that moment of peace. At least another dozen Engrossians ran down the hill toward us.

They'd split their ranks at our initial attack, their position in the canyon intentional to stall our chance of escape.

Swiping Angelborn up and sheathing my dagger, I charged.

With the pain still radiating through my skull, I channeled all the strength and every bit of training I'd honed in my life. Used it to predict their movements. To meet blades before the strikes landed true.

Ripping Starfire from my belt, I sliced the back of the knees of one Engrossian.

He roared, tumbling to the ground.

I echoed it, spinning to ram my short sword up through the jaw of another.

For the first time, I dug into the tattoo on the back of my neck. It reached out to the ascended Mystiques in our party as if the mountains were a tree, and us the tangled roots.

It was different than a soul bond in a Bind. This was matted and dizzying, but I found the three connections that were a little shorter than the others—newer—and spun toward them.

Jezebel battled a woman two times her size. Tolek and Cypherion took on three Engrossians between them.

And thirty yards away from them, no Bond connecting us, Malakai—

Two of the moss-armored warriors circled him. Blood dripped down his chin, sword held weakly in his hand.

"You have some fight left," one taunted. His broad chest nearly obscured Malakai from view as they backed him toward a wall.

"Always did." Malakai spat, crimson painting the gravel at their boots.

They snickered. "Are you so certain?"

"He's as much of a coward as his father," the other muttered as she prowled. She spun her ax around her hand lazily.

"That incapable fool," the first responded, reaching out with a toying strike at Malakai that he met easily. "He couldn't even dispose of his greatest mistake."

"We should have killed you both years ago, Warrior Prince."

At the title, Malakai froze, eyes wild and panicked.

His knuckles turned white around his sword, joints locking. And I saw his memory tunneling back to those years he spent under their care. It was barely a moment before he snapped back to himself, but it was all the Engrossians needed.

They launched at him, the female knocking aside his sword, the man pinning his shoulders to the ground. The buckles of his armor snapped beneath their fingers.

Blades rose over his skin.

I ran, but my path was blocked by a wraithlike opponent, long, thin arms each swinging an ax.

He struck out, and I ducked, looking below his arm to see Malakai get kicked in the side. The woman dropped her ax, a small blade appearing in her hand.

I swiveled around my own opponent, barely fighting back, just trying to get past him. I couldn't focus enough to land my own blow—not with their taunts still reaching me.

Every carving on Malakai's skin flashed through my mind. Every scar that I'd mapped these weeks, every shadow, and every wince he fought off in our own training.

These sick bastards knew. They knew what he'd survived, knew what taunts had been wielded at him. Had maybe committed some of the heinous torture themselves.

And they weren't done.

Malakai had never completed the Undertaking. He was likely weaker than either warrior attacking him now, let alone two combined—

A blow struck my chest, winding me.

As maniacal smiles split the faces of the warriors over Malakai, I swore: Whether I used blades or bare hands, no Engrossians would ever hurt Malakai again.

Looking back to my own opponent, I charged. Met one strike. Two. Then, jabbed Angelborn in his thigh.

Wrenching her free, I shoved him away. I didn't stop to finish the job, spinning back toward Malakai—

But someone else was already there.

Barrett.

Dax and the two guards we'd left them with rushed into the fight, too. The prince held a sword in his chained hands, the two Engrossians staring in disbelief.

"Your Highness?" the female asked, her slim blade nearly falling from her fingers.

"The one and only." He looked to Malakai on the ground, then back at his warriors. "I wish I could say it was pleasant to meet two of my own."

"You've been imprisoned?" the other Engrossian asked, eyeing Barrett's chains and taking a step toward the prince.

But Barrett backed away. Guarded Malakai.

"I broke out of one cage." He flexed his fingers around the grip. "I'm earning my way out of the other." With that, Barrett swung his sword at his own man. He stumbled back, confusion and reluctance slowing his response.

"Come with us," he reasoned, ax hanging loosely at his side. "We'll get you home."

Barrett swung again, awkwardly given his cuffed hands. "I no longer have a home."

Malice coated his voice, and I saw the moment realization dawned on the two. As they charged at their prince who no longer claimed the throne. As they raised their weapons against him.

And I ran—sprinted with all the breath left in my body. Lungs tightening.

Pulling my arm back as I closed in, I let Angelborn fly.

She sank through the woman's neck with an echoing squelch and anchored her to the ground.

The man spun to face me, a grotesque grin breaking. "You continue to show your hand."

"What does that mean?" I spat, skidding to a stop near him. I drew my sword but held myself back.

"It means she knows you better than you think." Fear chilled me. I couldn't form a response—just *froze*. Couldn't even summon the strength to react as he lifted his blade, because he had voiced one of the ominous thoughts I feared most.

Being known—understood—by the queen when I still didn't have a damn clue what she wanted.

My eyes locked on that blade as it rose, and I willed myself to move.

To strike.

But I only watched it lower, watched his eyes get wide and gleeful for a moment.

Then, a blade shot through the back of his head, straight through his eye, banishing that ghoulish grin for good. Beads of dark red sprinkled my boots as he fell.

When I looked up, Malakai was there.

"Are you okay?" he asked, voice shaking. He wrapped his arms around me, tremors wracking his muscles.

"Yes," I breathed. I squeezed him tighter, letting him feel the beat of my heart through the Bind. Reassuring and strong, I hoped.

Soon, the sounds of battle faded.

But the pained panic that took him over at the phrase *Warrior Prince* was seared on the inside of my eyelids. Angels, the scars of those memories, the horrors they'd inflicted would never leave him. I shoved aside every ounce of fear the Engrossian's taunt about Kakias had instilled in me and squeezed Malakai tighter, letting him know it was okay.

He was not back in that cell. He was free. He'd never go back there again.

I looked at Barrett, whose eyes fell on the two Engrossian bodies bleeding before us.

"Thank you," I said.

His head snapped up, face paler than usual as he looked at us both. "No. Thank you."

We understood.

He would have killed those warriors if it came to it—but he hadn't wanted to. I was reminded of the volcano, when I'd taken that burden from Malakai's shoulders by killing Lucidius. The blood may stain my hands, but I was okay with that. At least I could keep them from feeling that remorse.

Slowly, the others joined us. I retrieved my weapons and Malakai recovered his armor. He held it at his side and slightly away from his body, like it was poisoned.

"Any injuries?" I asked, sweeping my gaze over each of them briefly, counting those before us. My sister, Cyph and Tol, Erista and Esmond.

One was missing—

"Collins," Danya confirmed, looking behind her. His body lay still, arms folded on his chest, eyes closed. "It was swift."

Her words hollowed out a piece of me. I didn't know him well, but it was the first death of a warrior I was responsible for. It tarnished my heart, darkening the easy presence his smile had gifted. A loss I couldn't prevent, a life that ended trying to help my cause.

My chest caved under that pressure, an echoing pang, despite the fact that I'd barely known the warrior.

"We bring him home," I instructed through the dying piece of me.

Looking up to the stars, I wondered who else would be lost before this war was over. They twinkled down at me, all-knowing Spirits swirling in the mountains beneath my feet and Angels hovering on my shoulders, and I swore I'd carry the memories of those lost with me forever.

First Collins, then whoever came next in this war. I'd remember each face, each heart, each spirit.

"They were better fighters than I expected," Tol said as we started back to the horses.

"Better than the ones from before," Jezebel whispered.

It was possible they had been training harder in the months since I'd killed Lucidius, aware of the threat, but they hadn't moved with the brutality of the Engrossians we fought after the Undertaking. This troop was swifter, like death on a wind. It was...different.

I made sure Malakai was out of earshot before asking, "Did any of them say anything to you?"

They both shook their heads.

When we reached the horses, I dug into Sapphire's saddlebag for the keys I'd hidden there. Bone tired and limbs heavy, I found Barrett and Dax, slipped the iron into their cuffs without a word, and let their chains fall to the floor.

Barrett held my eyes for a moment, and I knew he understood. Saving Malakai had earned my trust, but the claims the Engrossians had taunted me with stayed buried between us.

As I prepared Sapphire for the journey home, I was less victorious than I'd expected. Instead, all I heard were those words: *She knows you better than you think.*

A chill hovered over my spine through the rest of the night, waiting for me to put pieces together.

CHAPTER EIGHTEEN

MALAKAI

HE'S AS MUCH OF a coward as his father.
  We should have killed you both years ago.
  Warrior Prince.

Those last two words had a power over me that I didn't care to admit, beating me down more viciously than any captor ever had.

They were all I heard the entire two days and nights that it took us to get back to Damenal. Every breeze whispered them as I sat upon my mare's back. Ombratta's hooves clapped out the rhythm of them. As I stumbled through the palace now, the squeak of my own boots against marble cried them into the night.

I'd tried—I *swear* I tried. I hadn't wanted to go on the raid. Truthfully, I hadn't wanted anyone to go. Too many risks lurked out there.

But not going was admitting what was wrong with me.

Besides, Ophelia was going, and I'd left her alone before. Not that it had mattered that I was there. Once we got outside these walls, I shrank within myself. Barely spoke to anyone the whole time, even when they tried. Even when I felt her inquiring if I was all right through the Bind.

And once I'd heard those two words—*Warrior Prince*—well, then I became fucking useless.

The entire journey home I was drunk off the pain of my memories. They'd ripped open my past and thrown it back in my fucking face.

And I'd crumbled.

Ophelia had tried to talk to me when we returned to Damenal, but I'd locked myself in the bathroom. Brought my father's dagger in there and just stared at the damn thing.

I didn't know how to talk to her about this. There was nothing she could say anyway. Nothing anyone could say would block out the cracks of whips against flesh or the tearing, burning, sticky blood trailing down my skin. The jeers, the taunts, the unremorseful abandonment of my life—

And that was why I found myself in the lower level of the palace, knocking on Santorina's door.

"Come in," she called. She looked up briefly from the book she was hunched over. "I assume the raid was a success given that none of you are bleeding out on my floor right now?"

"Mm-hmm." I grimaced, but it wasn't technically a lie. The attack was successful despite my failures.

I didn't want to admit that the Engrossian prince had fed us good information. Valuable information, even. Everyone had been right. He'd wanted to help us, apparently.

He'd saved—

No. I wasn't ready to admit that one.

I still didn't trust him. Grinding my teeth together, I pictured his arrogant face. I couldn't help noticing all the things he had in common with my father. Spirits, he may have been right about this raid, but why had Ophelia been so eager to believe him? We didn't know him, didn't understand him.

"Then what can I help you with?" Santorina shut the book, the snap pulling me out of my spiral. I didn't respond for long enough that she turned up the mystlight lantern on her desk and lifted it, white light falling across my face. Her round eyes went rounder still. "Are you all right, Malakai?"

"I need...help." It hurt to say. It was the first time I ever had, and the words scraped through my throat against my will. "Something to distract me. The memories. They..."

I couldn't explain it. Couldn't describe how the torture I'd undergone for two years plagued my waking and sleeping hours. I kept it at bay around the others normally, but it was becoming harder. And in situations like the raid, with the moonlight bouncing off of polished axes, it was impossible.

"I'm not sure what you think I can do for you." Apology weighed the edges of Rina's words.

"Please." It was a stiff plead. Near begging. "Just...anything." Anything to shut up the echoing taunts of the Engrossian Warriors so I could steal a few hours of blissful oblivion.

Santorina searched my face, battling with herself. She wouldn't give me anything that could hurt me, I knew that. But did she worry that helping me avoid my memories would inadvertently cause damage? Spirits, maybe it would. But I didn't care. It was worth it.

Finally, she exhaled.

"You have very dark circles under your eyes," she observed. "I can give you a tonic to help you sleep. But just enough for one night. That's it."

I'll take it, I nearly burst, but I didn't want her to see my desperation. "Thank you."

Rina nodded, lips thin. "Sit while I make it."

While she went to work measuring and mixing ingredients I didn't recognize, I looked around her workshop. Stacks of healing tomes lined the shelves, jars both full and empty scattered throughout. Herbs, liquids, powders, crushed petals and leaves, it was all neatly organized in labeled boxes and drawers. Everything, down to the freshly sharpened daggers hung by the door, was decided with care.

"What are you studying?" I needed to talk, to keep my mind from observing how the light reflected off of those weapons.

Rina looked at me, then back down. "Curses."

"Why curses?"

She looked at me again, considering, then thought better of whatever she was about to say.

"It seems like something one of us should know about, considering the Engrossians employed them before."

"That was the sorcia, though." The dark witch from the Northern Isles whom the Engrossians had somehow recruited to their side, despite the fact that the sorcia usually remained impartial on affairs of the warriors. "And they haven't interfered with us since."

"Still, you never know." Rina kept her gaze on her work, expert hands flying about the table, knowing where everything she needed was without looking up.

"You like it here?"

She nodded, voice more open than before. "I like having a space where I belong and a purpose. The same reason I always liked the Cub's Tavern, but this is better. That never quite felt right." She set her concoction over a mystlight flame and turned to me. "Let that boil and when it cools you can take it."

I nodded. "Do you miss Cub's?" We'd spent many nights at her parents' tavern before the war, and damn if I didn't miss it myself.

Rina contemplated, cleaning up her station. "I miss it because it was my parents' dream to create a haven for us. I miss it like I will always miss home, but I don't miss it beyond that."

"You don't ever wish you could go back to that life?"

"No. I thought I might when we first decided to stay in Damenal. I thought I'd regret it." She dunked a rag into a bucket of water and wiped it across the counter. "But that was my parents' dream, not mine. It was my time to move on."

Time to move on. I swallowed those four words. Why did they twist my heart? Fuck, my chest hurt. I rubbed my palm across my sternum and cleared my throat.

"Are you going to expand here?"

"I'd like to train more to heal, but I have other things I'd like to do, too." She looked around the workshop, lost in thoughts of her own path, her own dreams.

What was it like to have options? I'd never known. My whole life, I was meant for one thing. Until, suddenly, I wasn't. And now there was nothing left for me but the ghosts lurking in my nightmares, crowding my every thought until my vision spotted, my palms sweating.

I needed to get out of here.

A soft bubbling signaled that the tonic was done. Rina removed it from the flame, bottled it, and handed it over. "Be careful, okay?" Worry settled in her eyes, but I ignored it.

"Thanks," I said, leaving her workshop and downing the tonic as I went.

CHAPTER NINETEEN

OPHELIA

MOONLIGHT CAST SHADOWS ON the marble floors. Voices echoed through the open walkways. On the palace grounds and all through the city, warriors were preparing for Renaiss. I breathed in their anticipation, happy to have something to look forward to after the bloodshed of the raid and the weary journey home.

After bathing, I'd been restless. Malakai was distant, holed up in his own mind as he often was these days, and I couldn't find the strength within me to pull him back. Tol and Cyph had left hours ago for a tavern in the city, needing to wash away the battle with ale. Not to mention the flood of company they'd find there with warriors excited for tomorrow's festivities.

I knocked on Jezebel's door, thinking to check on her after the bloodstained journey. She may be the youngest ascended warrior in history, but she was exactly that—*young*. It was a fact she often convinced us to overlook, what with her fiery strength and confidence, but seeing her against fighters with centuries of experience ignited my protective side. It likely always would.

The sight of her beneath that scaled creature all those weeks ago twisted my chest as if it were happening all over again and I remained helpless against it. "Jezzie?" I knocked again, turning the handle. It was unlocked.

Poking my head into the foyer of her suite, I found it empty.

"Jezebel?" I called again.

Still no answer.

Quickly, I checked her office, though I knew it was futile. My sister had barely touched the private room since settling into the palace. She wasn't one for books or paperwork when she didn't have to be; she tended toward action.

I opened the door to her bedchamber but stopped in my tracks when I found my sister in bed—Erista beneath her.

"Ophelia!" Jezebel shouted, looking over her bare shoulder at me.

I crossed my arms, leaning against the door frame. "Lock the door next time, sister."

"As if you ever do," Jezebel scoffed, not bothering to move or cover herself.

I rolled my eyes, gripping the door handle. "As you were, Jez. Erista." I nodded to the Soulguider apprentice as I pushed off the wall, swinging the door shut behind me.

It hadn't been quite the interaction I'd expected, but knowing my sister was with someone soothed a bit of the worry within me. Still, Jezebel had *a lot* of explaining to do.

This year, Renaiss meant more than any in memory. It was the first in years that we would actually *celebrate*. The first where wealth was trickling back into the markets, the cities. A chance at joy trickling back into Mystique hearts, revelers dancing until their feet were sore and senses blurred.

The council had been doing an impressive job of reinstating trade between cities and establishing loans for businesses. Gold, giant bars of it, more wealth than anyone could imagine, had been sent from Damenal in recent weeks.

I was grateful the council was monitoring it for the most part. Truthfully, finances were things I didn't care for. The relationships we built on those agreements and the formation of ruling branches—that was where my strengths lie. Balancing it all was a skill I was still learning.

Today was drawing a symbolic line between us and the past. Even the air seemed lighter when I woke before dawn. Like the world was tilting back toward normal.

Unable to help the smile on my face, I got ready with Jezebel and

Santorina. Glasses of sparkling champagne had been brought to us as we lounged around Jezebel's dressing chamber—she'd schemed her way into having the rooms with the largest ones.

"Where are the delegates this morning?" I asked.

Jezebel wove flowers through the crown of my hair, eyeing me in the mirror. The sharp shake of her head told me enough—*do not mention Erista.* She apparently wasn't ready for anyone else to know—though as the champagne in her many glasses drifted lower and the blush rose to her cheeks, I wondered if her inclinations might shift today.

"I'm sure they're readying themselves," she replied, setting another tiny white bud among the rest. They'd be trashed by nightfall, surely.

"Ensure they know they're welcome at all of our festivities."

"Esmond knows," Rina interjected, digging through Jezebel's abundance of cosmetics. "What color should I be using, anyway?" She was slightly less familiar with the warrior holidays than we were. Though she'd celebrated plenty in Palerman, her fluttering movements betrayed her. Rina wanted to blend in.

Jezebel grabbed a dark purple liner and held it up for her. "Use this on your eyes and a natural color on your lips."

"So, Esmond?" I asked as she drew a flawless line out from her lid that gave her round eyes even more lift than usual.

"Yes, Esmond." Rina didn't look at me as she matched the second eye to the first.

"He seems nice."

"He's broody," Jezebel laughed.

"He's…mysterious," I corrected.

Rina sighed. "He's still a bit wary of us." She dabbed a light, shimmering powder over the liner, making her dark eyes pop. She tried to dump the cosmetics in front of me and turn away, but I snatched her wrist. Jezebel snickered, continuing to style my hair.

"You're with him *every* night," I whispered, brows raised.

"Oh please, Ophelia, I simply enjoy his company. He's smart and kind." She wrenched her wrist from my grasp and turned toward her dress, hanging on a rack in the corner. She slid it up her body, hands arranging the sheer lilac skirts that parted to her thigh.

She twirled before the mirror. Smart and kind were important traits—ones I'd select for any partners for my friends. But for Santorina, it wasn't enough. She needed someone who truly saw her strength and wit. Who understood how she felt out of place at times but didn't judge her for it.

I'd seen her through various breakups over the years, most recently with a female warrior weeks before the war who'd always thought herself better than Santorina due to her blood status.

"Never again," we'd sworn as she'd dried her tears. She'd never again be with someone who saw her as less, who did not appreciate the power she held on her own.

Perhaps we'd find someone for her today. It was Renaiss, after all. A day staked on freedoms and new light.

"Okay, Santorina, your turn," Jezebel instructed, dragging me from my reverie and pushing me off the stool so Rina could take my place.

The dress my sister designed for me was light and crisp white, perfect for the long sunlit day. I slipped it over my body and fastened a trail of three tiny buttons from my hip to my ribs, delicate and made of glass. The thin layer of tulle skirts floated around me, cascading with my every move like my own personal waterfall. The bodice was nothing more than two swaths that connected to the skirt, crossed around my breasts, and reattached at the base of my spine, leaving my torso mostly open.

"You are in charge of dresses from now on, Jezzie," I gasped, watching the gold accents in the skirt catch the light and complement the necklace I wore.

With the white and gold petals—yes, gold, though I didn't know where Jezebel found those—woven into my hair, I looked ethereal. Like an image of myth. Complete with the shimmering dust at the tops of my cheekbones and gold lining my eyes, I was a legend born unto myself.

Renaiss was a day of reveling and taking chances, of unbound freedoms and unspoken promises. Spinning before the mirror, I was the Angel ready to write them.

The main garden of the palace was flooded with warriors young and old, games being played, drinks being passed. Jezebel and Santorina were down there already, but I'd told them I wanted a moment to admire it all from my balcony.

We'd opened the gates at sunrise to anyone who'd wanted to enter. The archway marking the entrance was draped with vines coated in tiny white flowers that sparkled in the sun. Each time a guest passed beneath them, lifting the floral curtain, my heart thumped painfully.

Even with the city stretching beyond, streets packed with revelers, it reminded me of my favorite clearing.

Or my former favorite clearing, given that I'd sworn to never return after finding the spear there.

As I made my way to the front steps of the palace to join the revelry, I put the thought from my head.

I hadn't planned a grand entrance—I didn't want to be presumptuous as Revered—but attention fell like a wave of silence across the crowd. It caught my breath in my throat, but I lifted my chin and threw my shoulders back, descending the stairs with as much of an Angel's grace as I could muster.

Sunlight reflected off my dress, the material shimmering as a breeze gently lifted my hair behind my shoulders. My thin heels echoed on each step in perfect time with bells tolling over the city.

And the smile that split across my face was one of genuine shock.

All of the eyes on me spoke of one thing: hope. I thought of what Jezebel had said the other night. To them, I was guidance through the dark, here to dig our people out of the destitution we'd been plunged into. I was the image of light. A bounty of hope wrapped up in a white gown trailing with promises. The symbol of freedoms only dreamed about.

The realization wound itself through my bones, tangling with my destined blood, until it knotted itself in my soul.

When I reached the last stair, Malakai handed me a glass of champagne, fresh berries floating in it. I could smell them from here, as sweet and decadent as the adoration pulsing around me.

I raised the glass, liquid catching the light. My voice rang out over the crowd, "May the season bring light and promises."

And so much more.

The crowd erupted into an applause that boomed out across the mountains—in my honor.

I looked at my friends gathered around me, eyes drifting from Malakai before me to Jezebel where she whispered to Erista. From Santorina in the corner of the stairway, to Cypherion whistling beside her. Finally, I met Tol's eyes. Leaning against the banister beside a group of girls from Palerman, sleeves rolled to his elbows. He winked, and my grin widened, laughter bubbling up my throat.

This. This was why I fought for my position. To bring this level of levity and stability to a people horribly, unfairly ruined. And this was only the beginning.

After hours of garden games, watching children fling rocks into chalk-drawn patterns and older Mystiques spar with dulled blades, I tucked into a banquet table with my core guard, Erista, and Esmond. Pitchers of red cocktail with fresh fruit slices floating in it lined the table between floral garland. Trays piled high with spring vegetables, rice dishes, and cured meats were passed around.

"Vale!" I called as the Starsearcher wandered past our table alone. I set aside the salad Malakai had been handing me and stood to pull out the last empty seat at our table of nine. "Dine with us." My smile was genuine, but the request wasn't debatable. I wanted all three delegates here today.

"Thank you, Revered," she said, taking the seat between me and Cypherion. In her dove-blue dress with twinkling jewelry, she looked like a vision cut from the earliest hours of dawn, when darkness warred with day.

I grabbed a pitcher and poured both myself and Vale a full serving of the deep red drink, then raised my glass.

"I'd like to thank our guests for celebrating the festival with us." The other hundred tables were filled with chatter, but at mine, eight faces looked at only me.

"As if the five of us are nothing special," Jezebel muttered to Tolek.

"I am grateful for you every day," I chastised. "But today I'd like to honor our friends from different clans and thank them for giving me the opportunity to prove myself. For all of us to prove ourselves."

Directly across from me, Tolek lifted his glass. "Well said."

"And to you, Revered," Malakai added louder, eyes intent.

We all took long sips of the sweet cocktail and began on the feast. The staff of the Revered's Palace had outdone themselves. When I told them I wanted to host a full Renaiss festival, I'd worried they wouldn't be able to pull off one so elaborate.

I'd have to speak with Alvaron and ensure they were being paid accordingly, because the food was exquisite. Everything was fresh and flavorful, spices I hadn't tasted in years dancing across my tongue. Where they got such ripe fruits and vegetables on such short notice, I didn't know, but I didn't care as I slipped each bite between my lips and savored the taste.

"Well, I don't know about you all, but I'm certainly ready for the evening." Tol's lips twitched mischievously as he used two fingers to capture a berry where it floated in his wine and pop it into his mouth, looking me directly in the eye. A challenge.

"Renaiss is often a night to remember," I answered, finishing what was left in my glass in one sip. Malakai's hand snaked around my shoulders.

"Or a night not to remember," Jezebel corrected. I didn't think anyone besides me caught the wink she threw toward Erista.

"If any of you are too inebriated to find your beds, I won't be carrying you," Cyph scolded—as if he didn't celebrate right along with us every year. Well, every year that we *used* to celebrate.

"I feel as if I'm missing the joke," Vale said, pausing with her fork over her dish.

"Every year on Renaiss, the cities in the Mystique Territory throw festivals that last the entire night. Dancing and drinking. Honestly, any excuse for all sorts of raucous behavior," Tolek explained.

"Which is Tolek's favorite kind of behavior," Rina added. He nodded at her, eyes dancing with mirth.

"Damenal used to host the largest celebration of all," I explained to Vale. I briefly wondered how the Starsearchers celebrated the day. "This is the first year the festival will return."

"And rumors say this event will top those in the past," Malakai finished, voice strained. Under the table, I gripped his knee, running my hand up and down his thigh, and a bit of the tension left his body. It was the first holiday in years that he was not locked up. What gruesome memories would that bring to the surface?

"I'm certainly ready to see how Mystiques celebrate." Erista's voice carried across the table.

Everyone fell back into their private conversations, some serving themselves more food or drink. Jezebel and Erista rose and disappeared into the crowd. Tolek was swept away for a game with Hylia, which Rina and Esmond joined.

Soon, Malakai stood, too, kissing my cheek. "I think I'll go challenge some old friends." His eyes were on the sparring ring where a number of men about our age gathered, but his voice was hollow.

"Don't let them win." I winked. That left Cyph, Vale, and me.

When Malakai was out of earshot, the Starsearcher asked, "Are the rumors about what he endured true?"

I breathed a sigh of relief, grateful she hadn't asked in his presence. Malakai was brutally fragile lately, like he could shatter completely at any moment.

"I'm sure the horrors you've heard were accurate. Especially the most unbelievable of them."

Her eyes widened. "I'm so sorry." She laid a hand atop mine on the table, squeezing gently. Her gaze flicked between me and Cyph, who reclined in his chair on her other side. "Truly, what you've all survived—what you're doing each day here—it's admirable. I'm going to recommend Titus votes for your appointment."

"Thank you, Vale." I squeezed her hand in return.

Then, I exchanged a knowing glance with Cypherion.

"Do you have any insight into Titus's premonition? The one that made him suggest this system of delegates in the first place?" Her eyes narrowed slightly, then quickly resumed their wide innocence, but it was a moment too slow. I lowered my voice to ask, "What do you hide, Vale?"

She folded her hands in her lap. "What do you mean?"

"I saw you in the Rapture. Titus defers to you before making decisions. Your opinion is vastly important to him. There's cunning in your smile and kindness in your heart, and apparently a wealth of secrets hidden behind those lovely green eyes of yours. I'd like to know what."

"I am the apprentice of Titus. My purpose is to support him. To collect insights that may help or harm him and the Starsearchers through whatever means necessary." Absently, she ran a hand over the place where her shoulder met her neck, rubbing circles across the skin hidden by her hair. "I find cunning and kindness to be useful tools."

And though it didn't feel like the whole truth, it was enough for now. I liked Vale, and I didn't want to interrogate her. "That is also admirable."

A breeze gusted across the table, rifling the garland and lifting my hair.

Cyph gasped. His eyes were locked on Vale—on that place where her neck met her shoulder—a murderous calm I rarely saw in him slipping over his features.

He dropped his voice, leaning in. "You're a slave?"

I craned my neck to see what he was looking at. The wind had blown Vale's hair back behind her shoulders, revealing a halo of stars pressed into her skin. They were etched over in silver ink, as if to hide the scar, but from this close it was clear it had been *branded* into her.

Vale eyed us both, that cool evaluation seeping back into her sharp-featured face. "I am not."

Cypherion and I exchanged a wary glance. That stamp on her skin meant she belonged to one of the temples of the Starsearchers. Or at least, she *had*. The archaic practice of the temples claiming young girls was supposed to have ended centuries ago, but in some far stretches of the continent it lingered. It was rare but not unheard of to meet a girl with one of the temple symbols branded into her skin.

The sight of it now had my gut churning. It was disgusting and a complete violation of a warrior's power and rights to commit anyone to such a life unwillingly.

Vale's hands shook, but she clasped them in her lap.

"You don't have to talk about it," I soothed.

"I'm not ashamed of where I've been," she snapped. Her usually soft eyes turned brutal. "I did belong to a temple once, yes. Maybe one day I'll tell you of that. But it saved me. And when I fell into Titus's household, he had the scar covered for me. I am not a slave."

"Vale." Cypherion was calm. Hesitant. "You don't have to share it with us. But you can tell us the truth."

A wall snapped up behind her eyes. Though Cypherion's voice dripped with nothing but kindness and she was recommending my appointment to Titus, it didn't mean she trusted us with her personal strife.

"There's nothing to tell," she deadpanned. "I am an employee of Titus and lucky to be so."

Cyph's throat bobbed. "Not all cages look like prisons."

Vale locked her gaze to his. "Not all chains are meant to be escaped." She pushed back from the table before either of us could respond. Cyph shot to his feet, but he didn't go after her. Instead, he tracked her through the crowd and up the stairs into the palace.

Then, he turned the opposite direction and stormed toward the training yard.

Chapter Twenty

Ophelia

THE DAY MELTED INTO night, a pink-streaked sunset fading to deep violet, speckled with stars. The lawn became a collage of dancing bodies, partners floating gracefully as the music slowed to a gentle melody.

A strong arm wrapped around my waist, tugging me close.

"Here," Malakai whispered in my ear, spinning me and placing a delicate wreath of flowers on my head, arranging my hair so it fell perfectly. "Beautiful." He leaned to kiss my cheek, adding in a low voice, "Just like the wildflowers that used to stick in your hair."

Heat coiled within me. "Perhaps we'll find a new clearing tonight."

"Anything can happen on Renaiss." He smiled, and while it appeared genuine, no wave of happiness passed between our Bind. No glimmer of excitement met his eye. While there may be flowers laced through my hair and starlight shining down on us, we were not the same boy and girl who used to spend stolen hours hidden between high grasses in our clearing.

It was an act, but this was the closest we'd felt in weeks.

"Dance with me?" I held out a hand, hoping to savor whatever moments I could.

I must not have hid my concern very well because his brows pulled together the slightest fraction. "Of course."

Malakai locked one hand with my own, the other wrapping around my waist. He held me tightly against him, and for one dance, the rest of the world fell away.

We were just us. Just Malakai and Ophelia. Two promised children sent into each other's path by the stars. There was no war, no curse, and no treaty. No lies, secrets, and pain. My heart had never been broken. He had never been imprisoned.

I hadn't spent the past weeks crawling across the shards of myself. There was nothing to repair, nothing to forgive.

Beneath the bright light of the North Star, we were wrapped in the naive comfort of innocence once again. As I looked into Malakai's eyes, our lips so close we shared breath, the shelter of the past slipped its embrace around us, letting us live in the forgotten peace when we were all that mattered.

But the music faded, the beat livening and bodies quickening, and the spell broke. The pain of each cut filtered back into my consciousness one at a time, each sharper than the last. Standing within Malakai's arms, memories slipped through the cracks in my heart until I existed in only shards again.

It happened behind his own eyes, too. Our warped life grasped control of the present, reminding us of who we had grown to be and all that had occurred. Though my love for Malakai burned fiercely, not even the light of the North Star was able to keep the shadows at bay.

There was a lounge in the palace that was hardly used, nestled in one of the tallest towers. When we were fourteen, Malakai, Tol, Cyph, and I had found this hideaway on a visit to Damenal and spent the weeks here curating a collection of sunken velvet couches and thick rugs softer than the sand on the Seawatchers' beaches, trinkets decorating the shelves. Maroon gauzy curtains rippled in the breeze from the tall windows, moonlight filtering through, casting a red hue on the room.

As teenagers, we snuck bottles of liquor from the Revered's private supply on annual visits to Damenal. Lucidius had been oblivious.

Now, the hideout functioned as our private lounge away from prying eyes. When we settled in for afters past midnight on Renaiss, it was only my immediate circle, the delegates, and a handful of friends.

Everyone fell into the couches and chairs, the dim mystlight falling over the space like a layer of secrets.

"Our dear delegates," Tol started, taking a glass full of a swirling blue liquid from Cyph. "Tell us, what do your Renaiss celebrations typically look like?" He sprawled on one of the red velvet love seats, sleeves rolled to the elbow and his top buttons undone. Hylia sat on one side, a boy from Turren on his other. Each ran a hand up his arm, teasing his hair, leaning in closer.

Erista gave Tolek a feline smile. "I'm afraid you don't want to know what those who commune with the dead do for fun." She sipped her wine.

"No, we probably don't," I laughed, tucking my feet beneath me.

"My people have a way of celebrating." Vale dragged her round chair closer to the center of the group, eyes bright. "If you Mystiques can handle it."

"I'm sure we can." Tol leaned forward.

The Starsearcher pulled a pouch from her side and removed what looked like a very thin piece of parchment. "Searchers use tinctures when conducting sessions." She flattened the paper. "But there are many different forms of herbal remedies." From within the pouch, she removed a pinch of crushed flower petals and creased the paper, pouring a bit in the center. "Some are better for recreational purposes than readings."

The room hung on her every word as she licked the end of the paper and rolled it into a cylinder. "These won't give you predictions"— she swept a gaze across us—"not even if you were a Starsearcher." She twisted the ends and held it at the nearest candle until it caught flame. Then, she lifted it to her lips and inhaled. She held the smoke within her throat for a few seconds, blowing out perfect circles. The air filled with the floral scent of whatever petals she had crushed.

"Anyone?" she asked, lifting a brow.

Cyph took it first, his eyes widening then glazing over as he exhaled. The effects were immediate.

He handed it to me. I only took a little, but the smoke was sweet. The haze filtered through my body, lifting any lingering tension. I reclined against the couch, watching the tincture float from hand to hand, limbs sinking into the cushions.

"It's like the pipes of the Mindshapers," Esmond observed. "Bodymelders use something similar in an oil form to relax muscles."

By the time it had been passed around the room, the effects were lifting from me. It had been brief but euphoric. The only person who didn't try it was Malakai. He sat at my side stoically, shifting his drink between his hands. I squeezed his arm, but he only gave me a half smile.

The room dissolved into clouds of floral smoke and heady liquor, sensual smiles being passed around and low murmurs exchanged. Jezebel and Erista slipped out without anyone's acknowledgment. Soon Esmond followed, Santorina on his heels.

It was the third time the door opened that the room fell still. Two sets of footsteps cut through the silence.

"Now this looks like something I'd enjoy," a resonant voice claimed. Malakai's fingers curled against my shoulder.

I took his hand but spun around. "You got my note?"

"We did." Barrett smiled, genuinely appreciative.

"Thank you for the invitation," Dax said with a nervous glance around the room.

I wanted to say something to welcome them, tell them to enjoy themselves, but Malakai growled, "Invitation?"

My spine straightened. "I invited them to join us given…recent events."

With everyone around, I didn't want to get too involved in explanations, but something had changed during the raid. Barrett hadn't only given us good intel on the Engrossians, he'd interfered in a fight against his own people to save Malakai.

"You what?" Malakai shot to his feet.

Spirits, part of me knew I was making a mistake when I'd sent the note to Barrett's chamber. That Malakai would be angry. But he and I had barely spoken in days, and I was tired of the animosity. Tired of placating Malakai's bias toward the man who did him no wrong. Tired of the Spirits-damned wedge it drove between us, forcing me into complacency. I was ready to be rid of it.

"I invited them here. Tonight is a celebration for all clans. Brokering peace and hope."

I'd been a coward to not even tell Malakai of my plan. I'd hoped he would be more at ease after the festival, more willing to compromise.

Clearly, I'd been wrong.

He scoffed, indignant, and the malice lining his features wiped away any sense I held on to.

Next thing I knew, I was on my feet, too. "They were kept from the celebrations all day; it's only fair."

"How could you?" he whispered low enough that only I could hear, a glower worse than anything he'd ever aimed at me heating the air between us.

But where he was fire, my voice was ice. "How could *I*?"

We were no longer talking about Barrett. The fringe of every argument we'd had was unraveling—*we* were unraveling—pushing through the rubble of my shattered self. I'd shoved it away for too long. Tonight, with my senses opened to the possibilities of the future, actual happiness having danced through my veins, I was tired of putting my feelings aside.

Maybe it was the energy of the holiday finally getting through to me, maybe it was Jezebel's recent encouragement, but I was tired of settling for less than I deserved. I'd pushed aside my own shredded heart long enough, tiptoeing over my broken pieces. Even with the Rapture and the Mystique Council, when I'd grasped at my true fate, I'd done so over the fragments of my heart. Never healing them, only sweeping them aside.

Later, I'd told myself. I'd have time to heal later. But broken glass was meant to draw blood; later was not going to come if I didn't step forward.

Something had awoken within me, and it wanted better than this.

Malakai and I both breathed heavily.

The stare he leveled at me was not only made of fire—it was roiling disappointment tinged with mistrust. It was blooming betrayal and the aftereffects I knew intimately. It was a burning heartbreak piercing through his green irises and the severing of a final strand stretching between us.

The Bind ached as Malakai turned on his heel, slamming the door behind him.

As I followed him down the darkened corridor, I couldn't help but remember another hall we'd walked six weeks ago, when my heart was breaking irreparably and his footsteps filled mine. That night echoed with betrayals. Now, we bathed in the shadows of their damage.

How life had changed so vastly since then and yet we found ourselves in the same undetermined situation, I didn't know. All I knew was the pain I'd seen in his eyes, the echo that ripped through my Bind, and the feeling that I was walking into battle without a hint of armor.

The door to our bedchamber clicked shut behind me, locking us and our tempers in.

"Why would you invite him?" Malakai paced in front of the fire, one hand rubbing circles over his chest. I fought the urge to soothe my Bind in the same manner.

"He's our ally, Malakai." I leaned against the bedpost, crossing my arms.

"He can't be trusted," he spat.

"He's shown that might not be true."

Malakai froze, eyes shooting to mine. "Why do you not believe me on this, yet you believe him? Why don't you trust me?"

And that was the problem we kept facing. The one I had turned my back on again and again. What we'd wrecked so thoroughly, and no matter what way we spun it, how we avoided it, we could not outrun that fact.

We no longer existed on the same page. Spirits, not even in the same realm of understanding. Both too blinded by our own experiences to look at what the other needed. A wall existed that kept us from closing the distance between us.

We no longer trusted each other.

I took a deep breath, fighting the urge to tell him that if anyone had the right to rage over broken trust, it was me. I'd done nothing but trust him with my entire heart and he'd torn it to pieces.

But I didn't want to have *that* fight again.

There was a more important truth lurking here.

"Trust doesn't exist between us." I took a deep breath, biting my lips against the stinging in my eyes. "Not as it once did." My voice shrank with every word. "We're different."

There was no coming back from those words, but I'd thrown them out into the universe, ropes dangling, stretching for a place to tether that didn't exist.

Maybe there hadn't been something to pull us back since the day Malakai turned his back on me over two years ago. When he made that choice, he risked our untainted love. In the years he was gone, we'd both changed.

Grown into different people. Two who didn't fit together as we once had.

His arms fell to his sides, my words battering him with weighted blows. "What are you saying?"

"I'm saying we can't continue to deny it. I cannot *live* in this—this—toxic realm of anger." Tears broke from the corners of my eyes, falling hot and harsh, laced with vulnerability that stained the carpet between us and broke free this bottled-up truth inside of me. Rage settled in its absence—at myself for allowing us to get to this point, at Malakai for hiding from me. Each sparked within my blood. "I'm done. I have to be done because this isn't good anymore."

"You mean—" His eyes widened, and he swallowed, jaw ticking in time with my words echoing between us. "You're leaving me."

"*Leaving?*" I shrieked, embers of fury igniting. "That's rich coming from you."

"You know I didn't want to leave!" Frustration turned his words into a roar.

"This is what I'm talking about!" I yelled, throwing my arms wide. "We always return to *this* fight. The past haunts us like a vengeful ghost, and I am *tired* of it. We don't agree on anything anymore." Exhaustion weighed down my soul, blurring my mind, and I lost track of my words. "I want to be happy—I want to move on."

I hadn't meant to say it, but the moment that confession left my lips, a warmth wrapped around me. *Relief.*

He took a deep breath, realization seeming to settle in it. "Alone."

It wasn't a question.

"I don't know—" The argument died on my tongue because I *did* know. "I can't fall back into this avoidant dance with you. We're being reckless with our hearts, and I'm putting a stop to it."

The words were stronger than I felt. Malakai was all I'd ever known.

But I dug into that relief, wrapped it around me like a comfort blanket. Dulled the pain pulsing off of Malakai now that the truth was out. But that was a coward's move. If I was going to do this, it was only fair to us both that I was honest. I shucked that blanket, let it pool around my feet and bare the ugly reality.

"I've tried to pick up where we left off, but the truth is, we're different people than we once were." We'd both been keeping secrets, burying our pain, and I knew myself. I wouldn't stop doing that, wouldn't start healing, if we remained.

I wiped tears from my cheeks, their stains a reminder that some things weren't meant to be fixed. Some endings weren't meant to be happy.

Malakai swept across the room until he was standing before me, toe to toe. I looked at his shirt. Two buttons were undone, and the third was slipping out of its fastener. I wondered if I should fix it for him. Stretch out and rehook—

A sturdy finger touched my chin, tilting my head up, and I forgot the buttons—remembered I couldn't fix things anymore.

The silver lining his eyes cracked my heart open further. It blurred the heartache and haunting in those irises, but…there was acceptance there, too.

He wasn't fighting what I said because—because he knew I was right. He had probably been denying it as long as I had.

Fucking Spirits, I hated this. I hated the constant pain we both lived in.

My lips trembled. "We're both so broken."

"I know," he muttered, his hand sliding to cup my cheek. I leaned into the warmth that was once my solace but had since become my vice. "And we can't help each other. Not like this."

I nodded, tears blurring my vision. "I'm sorry."

"It's not your fault." I heard the words he didn't say. *It's mine.* A sob slipped out of my lips at the silent acknowledgment of what had started this downward spiral.

And while I appreciated it—it was too late.

"I wish it didn't have to be this way." I needed him to know that. I needed him to know that this was not an act of revenge, not me giving up. I had fought against this, fought to save us, fought to put together both of our broken pieces. But as long as I was focused on him, *I* was only breaking further. Grinding those shards of my heart into dust.

161

Malakai swept a thumb across my cheekbone, but he couldn't catch the tears as quickly as they fell. "Me too." He leaned forward, pressing his lips to my forehead.

"We're only hurting each other more," I whispered against his neck, lips brushing his skin.

"We're no longer good for each other," he exhaled into my hair, like now that we opened this door, we had to keep admitting what we'd denied for weeks. A knife sliced directly into my chest, twisting, shredding, incinerating with each truth.

"We'll never heal together." What had been broken between us had launched us down different paths, and I'd been too scared to accept that until tonight.

Still, reluctant to let him go, I wrapped a hand around his wrist.

Neither of us moved. Neither spoke. We held on to that moment for a bit longer, allowing the truths we'd spoken to settle. His other hand slid around my hip to the small of my back, pressing me closer to him. I placed my palm against his chest. His heart beat a rapid rhythm beneath my fingertips, and I wished I could soothe it.

No, I corrected. *You must fix your own heart.*

When he pulled back, I looked at him from beneath wet lashes. For a brief moment, it all passed before my eyes. Every long night spent tangled in each other's arms in our clearing, the moon reflecting beside our North Star, each innocent laugh echoing from the first day we became friends to the last one when he walked away from me.

So many beautiful, effortless memories of devotion and tenderness buried within the folds of heartbreak. But just because something had once been worth fighting for didn't mean it would be forever. And just because something ended didn't mean it was never beautiful. We'd shared countless smiles and firsts, the purest bond bottled up into a rush, intoxicating and rich, cushioned from the world as we were.

It was for those moments—for the girl I used to be, who fell in love with the strong, kind-hearted boy—that I tilted my face up.

I pressed my lips to his softly.

He hesitated at first.

I thought he'd pull away, but when I pushed up onto my toes, he tangled his hand in my hair, tilting my head back to claim my mouth.

His tongue swept across mine with urgency, as if we both knew we only had so much time left together before we had to face reality.

The whimper that slipped up my throat wasn't passion—it was desperation. The need to have him one last time. My hands fisted in his shirt as I pulled him toward the bed, fighting that voice in my head that said I shouldn't do this, that it would only hurt more. But Malakai and I spoke better with our bodies than our words, and it was through that connection that I needed to say goodbye.

Malakai understood what I needed, moving his hands to my hips, guiding me. His fingers slipped to the side of my dress, but I beat him to it, ripping the seam. Buttons bounced across the floor with dainty echoes so reminiscent of shattering glass, I nearly flinched, a sob catching in my chest.

But the white fabric pooled around my ankles, silencing them.

I kicked it aside, crushing my mouth back to his. My hands reached greedily for his waistband, untucking his shirt, tearing through the buttons.

He lifted me atop the mattress. For a moment we only looked at each other. At our tear-streaked faces and the broken hearts we bore so feverishly.

I lifted a shaking hand, traced the Bind where it shone on his chest, and curled my fingers into a fist over the symbol, biting my swollen lips. Gently, Malakai gripped that hand, smoothing out my fingers and kissing them once.

"It's okay," he whispered.

I dragged my hand through his hair, pulling him on top of me before the mourning lingering in his voice could overwhelm me. It killed me that we both suffered, but dammit, we weren't good for each other. This loop of pain that had sucked us in had to stop.

We'd once burned brightly, but that flame had flickered out. And that was entirely natural—it was the cycle of life. Things died. Our love had died.

And that was okay.

I kissed him in response, telling him without words that he was right. It may not feel like it now, but we'd both be okay.

His lips traveled down my neck, each kiss growing more needy. He braced one hand beside my head, fingers coiling in my hair as his kisses turned to bites against my skin. He cupped my breast, thumb circling, and took the other between his lips. I arched into him, trying not to think of all the other times we had done exactly this.

Instead, I locked that emotion away and focused on carnal need—on the heat building between my thighs and the want surging through my body.

I reached for the buckle of Malakai's pants, demandingly. He held himself on one elbow, sliding them down his legs. The thud of fabric against the floor made me freeze.

Because this was the last time.

He traced the outline of my undergarments, fingers toying with the lace at my waist.

We weren't waiting, weren't stringing this out. He slipped that lace down my thighs, gripped my hips and pulled me to the edge of the bed. He positioned himself against me, waiting for me to say this was what I wanted.

I nodded, because I was ready.

I was ready for what we were about to do, but not what came after. I'd never be ready to lose Malakai, but we'd lost each other long ago, and now we made a choice.

And I loved us both too much to hold on.

He pressed into me slowly, leaning down to kiss me—tenderly at first, a hand cupping my cheek. Then hurriedly.

It was impossible for me to stop the tears rolling down my cheeks, staining the silk comforter below us. Malakai's own mixed with them as he moved, shared sorrow fueling each roll of our hips and gasp of pleasure.

As I dragged kisses across his collarbone, nipping at his shoulder, I knew that young love was wholly over, but a piece of me would always love Malakai. He owned the memories of my heart, but that was the problem. He was holding on to it wrongfully. I'd been caught on a leash.

Still, while I blamed Malakai's actions for allowing us to get here, I didn't find him wholly responsible. The true devil was fate. Her cruel hands had wound our life-strings around her fists until they were hers to snap.

The love that had once burned so brightly it dulled the stars in the sky…it was nothing more than smoke.

I hated fate for it. For taking what was good and twisting it. Warping it. Destroying it. Never mind the fact that this was the right decision, it was still a heartrending one, and I didn't have to be happy for it.

I dragged my nails down his chest, pressing my heels into the small of his back to drive him deeper. I tasted honeysuckle and leather with every inch of my body and rode higher toward my climax, knowing there would only be a few more minutes of us being one.

But I hadn't been his for a long time.

Malakai's hands tightened around my hips. He buried himself in me repeatedly, and these were not the slow, sensuous strokes of the boy I fell in love with, nor were they the passionate, indulgent thrusts of the man he had become. Each one was a confirmation—a promise from both of us. Because as our tears coated our cheeks, salt flavoring our kisses, we said goodbye to what was once beautiful.

For the last time, Malakai and I went over the edge together in a burst of passion that tapered into a spinning black hole.

He collapsed against me. We remained chest to chest, sweat sticking to our bodies and panting breaths filling the room. When he rolled off of me, I almost curled into his side out of habit, but instead we looked at each other until our breathing stilled.

Malakai pushed himself onto his elbow, pressed one kiss to my temple, and whispered, "Until the stars stop shining."

Then, he turned away.

Exactly as we both knew he must.

I didn't look at him as he pulled on his clothes and left the room, but when the door shut, I stumbled to the bathing chamber on legs that could barely support me and slammed into the counter, hands white-knuckled on marble.

That bed—I didn't want to be in that bed any longer. Not the one we had shared. Not the one that would only remind me of every fight, every *distraction*, up until this last time.

I turned on the tap, but I didn't wait for the tub to fill. Instead, I sank to the floor, curling my knees to my chest, and drowned in memories.

Tears came in forceful sobs this time. There was no stopping the howls that wracked my naked, sweat-stained body.

But I didn't only cry for the love I lost. I didn't only cry for the future that now seemed darker than a starless night.

It might be selfish, but I cried for the scraps my heart had become, and the possibility that I'd never repair it.

CHAPTER TWENTY-ONE

DAMIEN

A BROKEN HEART, A trivial mortal fear that had the power to undo them all. Though, I had been mortal at the onset of my existence, so why then did I not feel it?

There were other things I felt. The clawing desperation for our goal, the faint wistfulness for my mountains, the sinking fear when my master lashed out at me after my recent overstep. The fresh golden scar decorating my face from hairline to jawbone, disappearing down my neck, still throbbed with the heat of his power. For having said too much. Risking exposing our hand and losing her.

Second strike, he'd said, and I'd been trapped.

The third—I did feel fear at what that would mean.

But things like heartbreak? I cast my mind to those early years, many millennia ago, now dulled by the shadows of time. A faint ache passed through my chest, unsteadied me. Perhaps I had once suffered that pain, but it was fleeting now, fluttering away before I could recall.

All I knew of it was the pain twisting the face of the girl in the Angelglass. Magenta eyes shining with tears rather left unshed. Fingers gripping the wooden desk as she pulled herself together.

She'd disappeared with the boy, and when they both resurfaced on the fogged glass, there was a different weight upon their shoulders. A different strength, though murky with loss.

"Did the crack in the glass widen?" Xenique asked. Her wings fluttered, personal stake heightening her nerves.

"Yes," I whispered, trying not to call attention to the minuscule length it had stretched. I threw my burgeoning power into it to see if I could feel anything, take any more steps forward. We'd been gathering, conserving, for so long, using only when necessary.

But how would this affect us? The weight of eight stares wondered.

We needed the Chosen Child, and through the tie to her, the boy.

Fate…She was a mist hovering among us, the creator of all futures. Fate was a gilded waltz gliding on the wings of unrepentant choices, each flowing into the next as day did to dusk. And the fates of that girl and boy were intertwined through a greater power than myself—than any of us.

But was there some way one *could* control it?

I wondered, tracing the crack in the Angelglass with my gaze, eyes on the girl who held *my* fate in her veins. Was there any way to bind fate to will and sway it to one's whim?

"These obstacles must stop," our master growled, hair like silver ink floating on the wind of his subdued power.

No one responded. There was nothing to be done or said. Mortal affairs were beyond our control, no matter the cost they put on us. We could do nothing but watch the wars between their kind and hope fate turned in our favor, saving who we needed.

Undoing or salvation, which would she be? And how could I bend the result?

-PART TWO-
LACHESIS

CHAPTER TWENTY-TWO

MALAKAI

"YOU...WHAT?" CYPHERION NEARLY dropped the liquor bottle.

"It's over," I repeated. The words were like an iron brand dragging up my throat. I gripped the mantel in Cyph's office until the wood groaned beneath my hands. It would only be fair to break something as I'd been broken, to destroy—

Cyph removed one of my hands from the wood, shoving a glass in it instead. I didn't know what it was, but it was strong and that was what mattered. I didn't hesitate to down the damn thing.

At first, it only made the burning in my chest worse, but after Cyph refilled the glass and I threw that one back, it soothed.

He fell onto the green velvet couch, his own drink in hand. "Are you okay?"

I paced before the fire, searching the study for an answer. The room was almost entirely warm colors with plush jade couches and dark wood furnishings. Comforting amid the turmoil of my night. The books lining the shelves and maps sprawled across the desk were cozy—worn but not cluttered. Organized, everything having its precise place according to Cyph's astute mind.

My thoughts were nowhere near as orderly. "Yes and no."

Cyph reclined, one arm slung across the back of the couch, waiting for me to continue. Looking like he'd sit there all night if need be.

"Yes, I'm okay because I know it was the right decision."

"You do?" There was a hint of skepticism in his voice.

I nodded. "I've been denying it for weeks now because...just because." I didn't want to crack the bars of my heart open enough to explain how I'd been clinging to the only thing left in my life that resembled the *before*. Everything had changed when I was gone. My friends had grown, my family had fallen apart—I'd wanted one thing to remain.

I'd wanted her to remain.

But that was out of my control.

"I never would have brought it up." I leaned against the back of the couch, watching the flames in the grate burn higher. "I would have kept fighting."

"Maybe you weren't fighting *for* anything," Cyph hedged. "It seems you were fighting against it."

"Fuck." I blew out a breath, stuffing my hands in my pockets and nudging the toe of my boot against the wall. "I hate you sometimes."

He huffed a laugh. "I'm sorry."

"No, you're right." I waved off the apology and grabbed my empty glass, falling onto the couch opposite his, leaning forward and bracing my elbows on my knees. "I know you're right and that's why I'm okay. Partially."

"But the other part?"

"That half of me was always hers. Before I left…well, shit, you know how we were. I lived and breathed for her." And fuck if that half didn't hurt like I'd been flayed open. "I don't know what to do with it now. I gave up everything, sacrificed so much for her."

"So did she. Ophelia was a wreck for two years when you were gone. Constantly fighting with everyone, drowning her sorrows in drinks, or holing up to find answers. She changed. The way you two were…it was unhealthy." He leaned forward, poured a little bit more into my glass. "I'm not trying to be an ass, Mali, but you two both sacrificed a lot for each other. To the point where you couldn't stand on your own." He lifted his glass to me. "That half that was hers…it belongs to you now, brother. You have to live for yourself before you can live for anyone else."

Live for myself. I wasn't sure I knew how to do that. How to identify what I wanted and just…take it. How to outrun my past.

I dragged a hand through my hair. "I guess I'll have to figure it out."

"I have faith in you." That made one of us. Inside, I was so twisted by the torment I'd suffered mentally, physically, and emotionally that I'd lost hope of recovering.

"Can I ask…" Cyph's eyes went to my chest.

"I don't know," I sighed. I placed a hand over the Bind. It had echoed with silence since I left Ophelia. I worried what she was doing now. How she was coping. I hated her being alone, and thanks to the distance in the Bind, I couldn't judge any of her emotions.

"It never worked right," I explained. Cyph lifted a brow. "We always claimed it was because I left so soon after they'd been inked, but we've been together for over a month now and…it still didn't work."

"You've been fighting," Cyph offered, but his voice lacked conviction. He ran a hand over the back of his neck—his Bond.

"It was more than that." Like the magic in the ink knew what was coming. "But I don't really know what we can do about it." Maybe I'd talk to Marxian once I recovered from the shock. The artist might know how to undo the tattoo. Though, I had to admit, I'd never heard of it being done. Mystique tattoos operated at a soul level. They bound those who had them for eternity. Unless we could find a way to undo it, Ophelia and I were forever tethered through the Bind.

"Spirits," I groaned, shoving the heels of my hands into my eyes. "Why the fuck would fate allow us to tie ourselves together like this if only to rip us apart?"

Cypherion considered. "There's a reason for everything."

"Seems cruel," I scoffed.

"I never said it wasn't."

We fell into a contemplative silence. I was grateful—surprised—that Cyph had been alone when I knocked on his door. It appeared the fates did look out for me occasionally.

"Can I ask one more thing?" He fidgeted with his glass, and I sat up straighter, nodding. "Does this decision have anything to do with T—"

"No," I interrupted, my fingers curving around my glass. "No, it doesn't. This was *only* about us."

His lips thinned. "I had to be sure."

"I understand." I sipped my drink. "To be honest, I don't think that could have been farther from her mind."

"She doesn't know?" His brows rose.

"I think—" I shook my head. "I can't be sure." I didn't know if anything had happened while I was gone; it was a distant idea in my mind, but I didn't want to ask Cyph right now. A growl rumbled in my chest at the thought. "But everything between us has been so fucked up—everything in her life really—it's taken every strand of her energy to hold herself together. There hasn't been time for thoughts of…any of that."

I hated that I had a hand in making her that way. We were both to blame.

Cyph blew out a breath, shoulders drooping. Every move was heavy, weighted by the precarious future we faced and the relationships shifting around us.

Ophelia's stare as we lay on the bed after that last time was seared into my brain. I'd seen her furious, I'd seen her distraught, but now she'd been haunted. Uncertain. Things I'd never associated with her. Had that been how she looked the years I was imprisoned? Was that vacancy the person our friends had kept afloat?

Spirits, if that was true, we really didn't belong together. Because that look in her eyes—there was nothing I could do that would undo this mess.

I guess some forevers weren't meant to survive. I threw my head back against the couch, clenching my eyes shut until I saw stars, like that could rid my memory of the imprint of her haunted stare.

But it wouldn't leave.

"I fear this might truly break her," I whispered.

"Look at me," Cyph snapped. "She needed to break."

I nodded, though I didn't know if I understood.

He continued, "Don't worry about her now. She's survived so much, and if this is what breaks her, then it's long overdue. I have no doubt she'll repair herself, and you know that, too. You're using her pain to drive yourself into a deeper hole of despair because it's easier than pulling yourself out of it, but what *you* need to do is heal. Fucking curses, Malakai, you're just as broken as she is." That truth stung. "Focus on that."

I swallowed. "Okay." I hadn't realized that one of my fingers was tracing the Bind over my shirt, but I dropped my hand to my side, searching the room for anything else to say. "Mind if I sleep in here?"

"Anytime." Cyph rose, clapping me on the shoulder, and strolled from the room.

He returned a minute later with a stack of blankets and pillows. Tossing me some, he settled down onto his couch, stretching out.

The mystlights faded. Soon, his breathing evened out into a steady slumber. I laid on my back, eyes on the wood-paneled ceiling as if I could look through it and see the North Star above. I wondered how my North Star was fairing. Although, I guessed it was no longer my right to call her such.

Still, I'd meant what I said before I left. It may not be in the way it once was, but I would love Ophelia *until the stars stopped shining*.

CHAPTER TWENTY-THREE

OPHELIA

THE ONLY THING BETTER than riding Sapphire at sunrise was being beneath the stars, me and her. I got both, taking her out as inky sky faded into lilac, the moon making room for the sun. Even then, the hollowness within my chest lingered.

In the few hours I'd sat on the bathroom floor, I'd begun to sink into a bad place. A darkness that rivaled when Malakai first left. Shadows infringed on me, grasping for every spark of life I held on to.

It was familiar and comfortable to resort to that darkness—but I forced myself out of it. I'd spent years there. I didn't want to go backward.

The decision wasn't all bad. There was the satisfaction of knowing I'd made the right choice for myself, despite how deeply I already missed him. Missed the ease we used to have. The way his scent used to cling to my things after a day together in Palerman, the way he whispered my name in a crowd and I always knew where to look, the light in his eyes when he saw me.

I missed having my world revolve around my North Star.

We've changed, I reminded myself. It was done.

And though I missed what we had, I think a part of me had been preparing for this for a while. Knew it was inevitable with our trajectory. And that made the sting hurt a little less. Made it easier to see a light on the horizon.

Not everything was meant to last forever. That was what I would remind myself as Sapphire galloped steadily beneath me. I'd have to discover the personal motivation within me that got me out of bed each day, that my world revolved around now. I was not foolish enough to think it would be easy—not with the echo of Malakai's footsteps that had walked beside mine our entire lives. I could do it, though.

Reclaim my future, my life.

I wouldn't think about the Bind or how we could even separate those threads of connected soul. Not yet, anyway.

Sapphire crested a rise in the mountains that was perhaps my favorite view, at the southwest of Damenal with a valley behind us, leading away from the city. Cyphers, oaks, and brush decorated the mountainside. If we kept west, we'd find our way into the Starsearchers lush territory. Or if we cut south, we could explore the desert climates of the Soulguiders. And beyond that, the frigid Mindshapers' land wrapped around the base of the mountains.

We could go anywhere. Just me and my warrior horse. Disappear into the dawn, taking the pieces of my shattered heart to sort through, avoid all of the *destruction* awaiting me, hide from the heartbreak and warfare and political schemes, the curses and prophecies and bloodstained futures.

I could rid myself of it all.

A breeze stirred my hair. I turned my face toward it, the subtle aroma of wildflowers wrapping around me, soothing me.

It was a ridiculous thought, as nice as it would be. There would be no running. Not from this. I had hidden from my pain for too long, building up a wall of aggression and snapping at any who tried to knock it down.

I had sworn to myself I would never do that again.

This time, I would collect the shards of myself and build them into something more beautiful than before. Maybe one day, I would give it away again to someone who truly saw me for all my wrecked pieces. Someone who loved the woman I'd become rather than the girl I used to be. But first, I'd learn it as I never had. Understand the hollows and what it took to fill them. Love it as I never knew to.

I would not be broken forever.

"We'll be okay, girl," I whispered to Sapphire, leaning forward to pat her. "We'll find our way."

A tear splashed to her mane. I hadn't even realized I'd been crying, but they dripped one by one from my cheeks as we watched the sun rise fully over the city atop the peaks. Listening to the breeze stirring the grass and the birds calling to their mates, I found a bit of peace within myself.

That sense of understanding threading between me and Sapphire echoed with her reassurance. *It's already okay*, she seemed to say. It didn't mean I didn't hurt, it didn't mean Malakai and I breaking up was easy, but she was right.

So like I'd been needing to, like I'd been avoiding, I released all of those strings of my relationship with Malakai and finally breathed. One big gulp of air that felt unnatural without his scent in it but that whispered against the space left behind, instilling life into it. It was what everyone had hoped would happen when he disappeared. That air would be enough for me to survive on when his life had become my own. It hadn't. It wouldn't ever have because every one of my breaths at that point had been for him.

Now, they were for me.

We didn't run away, but we stayed out for hours longer than I'd planned.

With Renaiss celebrations lasting all night for those whose relationship wasn't crumbling before their eyes, everyone would be in bed until midday. I snuck Sapphire back to the stables and continued through the garden to the palace, scampering up the stairs, thoughts on the heat of the bath I was going to run in solitude.

Where was Malakai? My gut twisted at the chance he would be in our room. We would no longer share it, but I wasn't sure if I wanted it as my own anymore. It had only ever been *ours*.

"Good morning, Ophelia."

I froze on the top stair, hand curling on the railing. "It's afternoon, Tolek," I said without turning. My heart thundered in my chest.

"That it is, yet everyone seems to be sleeping. Where are you coming from?"

I drummed my fingers on the banister. "A ride." I couldn't turn— he'd know from one look at me that something was wrong.

"Lovely day for it." Confusion was clear in his voice.

"It was," I whispered. He was likely only waking, had probably just walked out whatever guests had spent the night in his suite, or maybe he was coming home from wherever he'd been. I didn't want to know.

His steps rang out on the marble stairs, slow and daunting, until he stopped before me. Nerves fluttered in my stomach. My fingers continued their steady drumming, and I kept my stare on them.

Then, Tolek slid a finger beneath my chin and—gently enough that I could have stopped him should I have wanted to—lifted my gaze to his. He searched my face, taking in the red-rimmed eyes, the shadows framing them.

I bit my bottom lip, waiting for his questions.

"Tea?" he asked.

My heartbeat calmed. "Yes, please."

Tol held his arm out, and as I slipped my hand around it, my frame strengthened. By the time we reached the kitchens, a bit of the tightness within me had eased.

"Are you sure no one will care that we're in here?" I asked. Mystlight flared to life above us, illuminating sandstone floors and speckled granite countertops. Wide windows stretched across one wall, sunlight filtering through sheer yellow curtains, and a myriad of herbs grew beneath them.

"Ophelia, you *are* the Revered, did you forget?" Tol swung the pantry open, gathering an assortment of teas. "Besides," he added, boiling water over the mystlight stove. "I come down here all the time."

"You do?" I hopped up on the counter, making myself comfortable. As he'd said, this was my palace.

"I don't sleep well," Tol explained without looking at me.

"Is that new?" I tried to remember a time when he'd mentioned it before.

His shoulders tensed. "Since we've been here," he clipped, then shook his head. When he continued, his voice had returned to normal. "I come down here for tea or liquor at night. It happened so often, the staff started leaving the damned stuff out for me."

I was glad he had made himself at home quickly in the palace, even if it was due to insomnia. Tolek fit well here, with the finery and the abundance of friendly faces, the freedoms and possibilities. Damenal was built for warriors like him.

"It's good to know they're accommodating."

"More than." Tol piled a tray with the pot of tea, two cups, sugar, and a plate of biscuits. He carried it to where I sat and set it beside me, preparing both of our cups. One scoop of sugar in mine, as I preferred, and two in his own.

"Sweet enough?" I quirked a brow.

Tolek made a show of tasting his tea. "No," he decided, adding one more scoop.

I shook my head, but I was laughing, and I hadn't expected that out of today. When I tasted my own drink, it was perfect.

"Okay, I made you tea and I even provided biscuits. Now, tell me the reason for the morning ride."

The smile vanished from my lips, eyes instantly stinging. I looked at the ceiling, the kettle, counted the leaves on the mint plant under the window. Anything to avoid meeting his gaze.

"Malakai and I—umm—" I drew circles around the rim of my cup, the pad of my fingers gathering drops of condensation. Surely Tol could hear my heart pounding. "We broke up."

"What?" Tolek fumbled his cup, catching it before it crashed to the ground. Hot tea poured over our boots and his pants. "Shit."

"Here, let me—" I started to scoot off the counter, but he put a hand on my knee, and I froze.

"I'll deal with that later." His face was grave, a crease forming between his brows as he searched my eyes. "What happened?"

"Only what's been happening since he's been back," I muttered. With Tolek's attention on me, moisture gathered in my eyes. He lifted his hand to wipe one rogue tear away as it slipped down my cheek, catching it before it could fully fall.

"I didn't realize how bad it was," he whispered.

"I was denying it." I shrugged. "I think he was, too."

He leaned against the counter. "And how do you feel about it?"

"I feel..." I chewed my lip. "I feel...not good. But okay. It—it had to happen. We're not right for each other anymore. Every day that we helped each other avoid our problems, we were only hurting ourselves."

Tolek considered, folding his hands behind his back. "I'm sorry it turned into that, Ophelia." The genuine concern deepening his chocolate eyes made the ache in my chest worse, like something was pounding against my sternum.

"It's not your fault." I picked up a biscuit and broke it in half. It tasted like cardboard thanks to the churning in my stomach, but I nibbled on the corner for something to do. "I'm not sure I know what to do now, though. How to move forward." Especially with everything imploding around us. All of the very real threats I couldn't ignore.

Tol sighed. "Do you want my honest opinion?"

"Always."

He swallowed, contemplating. Then, he moved the tray aside and hopped onto the counter beside me. "Malakai is one of my best friends, but when he left us, you changed. For so long, you fought for him—and that was admirable—but now you need to fight for yourself. There's only so long that you can fight for a future that doesn't want to exist. But you're strong and you deserve to be happy. I can guarantee he wants that for you, too. And I'm certain you want it for him. So you move forward like you would any other day. You wake up each morning and you face it. You don't run from it, though. Promise me you won't run from it." He waited for me to nod, desperation burning in his eyes. "If you do that, you'll be okay."

Wake up, move forward, find my own path.

He didn't know I'd already decided to do exactly that. But even having reached that conclusion on my own, Tolek's confidence bolstered me, like it stacked my bones back together until I could stand straight again.

"You're sure about that?" I asked. Sometime during his speech, my tears had dried.

"Positive." He pressed a kiss to my temple. "I don't lie to you, Ophelia."

I leaned my head against his shoulder. "Thank you for never lying."

Tol wrapped his arm around me, and we sat in silence until the tea was gone.

CHAPTER TWENTY-FOUR

OPHELIA

"OUR NUMBERS ARE OFFICIALLY up to a thousand new trainees," Cypherion reported, standing before the council in his brown leathers, scythe resting against the dark wood table.

"That's quick growth." Danya nodded, impressed, her black hair swaying around her chin. She looked up from the map she was positioning troops on. Each clan was marked by a different symbol with the Mystique sigil adorning the top of the map, optimistic and proud. "It's only been a month since the program began?"

"Yes." Cyph's hands were tight at his sides. "And more are traveling to Damenal every day." Since he'd begun training Mystiques to prepare for the Undertaking—and eventually the looming war— we'd seen tremendous improvements in the candidates. And Cyph— he was a natural-born leader.

"There's also smaller groups gathering in the cities," Larcen added. "I've been inquiring after the status of warriors as the communication lines strengthen."

I released a breath of relief. Everything was falling into place.

In the days since Malakai and I broke up, I'd thrown myself into meetings, research, and training. Anything to keep my body and mind busy enough that sleep was unavoidable when my head hit the pillow at night—Jezebel's pillow, actually. I'd been sleeping in her room for a week now, not quite ready to be alone. A hollow sadness ached through my heart each time I was, a pulse of a past life, but I'd need to move into my new suite soon. Large apartments similar to my old one, but without the stains of the past.

Daily war councils didn't allow me a chance to escape Malakai, but he remained stoic in the back of the room. I didn't make eye contact with him, focusing on holding myself together instead.

We may not have had a large army, but we had an expanding force. We had growing trade once again and commerce was flourishing. The council had adopted apprentices as I'd requested. All except Danya, who continued to reassure me she had a plan.

"How many of your warriors have completed the Undertaking?" I asked Cyph. The groups he trained were all seventeen or older, many having been in our predicament of missing their eighteenth birthday. Everyone younger than that was sent to lower training groups, and those who had ascended were in Danya's care.

"Only three hundred."

"Have we lost any to it?" I held my breath—the room held its breath.

"Two," Cyph mumbled. His shoulders curved inward, hands bracing themselves on the table.

"That's an impressively low rate, Cypherion," my father said, gripping Cyph's shoulder. "You should be proud of them all."

Though any loss of Mystique blood was a shame, my father was right. Out of hundreds of warriors, only two had not survived the Undertaking. It was a risky endeavor, and everyone in this room knew that. Most of us had lived it, save for Malakai, Barrett, Dax, and the delegates.

"I'm going to lower it," Cyph swore.

"It's not your fault." I stared at him until he looked back.

His lips forced a smile, but worry dulled his blue eyes. "I know." The words sounded hollow, and he sank into a chair.

I cleared my throat. "Now on to the Engrossians. There's still no indication of what Kakias has planned. Where her end goal is."

"Damenal is what makes sense." Danya's lips twisted. I feared that was precisely why Kakias chose otherwise.

"If she's sweeping toward the Mystique Territories, she could ravage the trade routes we're rebuilding," Larcen hypothesized, running a hand over his auburn scruff.

"Or she could be aiming to cut off communications between us and other clans?" Jezebel pointed to the map unrolled across the table. "If she gets to the western border of the mountains and cuts both north and around the southern base, she'll sever the Mystiques from all other clans, save for the Seawatchers, who can't offer much aid, anyway."

"She knows many Mystiques have returned to Damenal, though," Alvaron claimed.

"Even better," Cypherion said. "She'd be dividing us. Not only would we be unable to amass one army, but Damenal would be without a number of key resources. It's not a bad plan."

"No, it's not. But she'd be positioning her armies at the base of the mountains, then." Danya scanned the map with the precision of a warrior who'd planned countless battles. "It would be easy for us to surround them."

"Assuming we can gather our forces quickly enough," Tolek said. He was right—Kakias was acting swiftly because she knew we were still recovering the army that had fallen to her two years ago.

"It still doesn't explain why," Cyph mumbled.

Barrett was right; understanding your enemy was as transformative as knowing their strategies.

I exchanged a glance with the Engrossian heir and shook my head. We couldn't explain that his mother was after me without me explaining my Angelblood theory, and that would lead to Damien's prophecy and the Angelcurse—and…only I could know.

"What is she after?" Tol mused. "Why ignite a war again?"

The words clawed their way up my throat, nearly bursting from my lips. Spirits, I was close to my breaking point beneath these secrets. *Me. She's after me.*

"Allies," I blurted instead. "It doesn't matter *where* she is. We'll need allies if she cuts off our troops." Shame squirmed within me, but I avoided Barrett's questioning eyes. "The chancellors have yet to respond to my letters."

"It's been over a week since you wrote," Jezebel interjected, lips curling in a threat to storm the territories herself and demand answers.

"I know, but it's a delicate decision, declaring war or not." Perhaps I should have visited each clan rather than written to them. But that would have taken weeks—months, probably, considering how many territories I would have to travel to. That was time we didn't have.

Absently, I ran my fingers over the pin at my chest. The one my grandmother had given me for my twentieth birthday. To guide me, she had said. I had taken to wearing it daily, resting on that reassurance.

"Can the delegates tell us anything?" Vale, Erista, and Esmond sat at one end of the table. "Do you have any idea what your chancellors may be thinking?"

"I haven't spoken to Titus," Vale offered of the Starsearcher chancellor. "But I'll write to him today."

"Thank you." I nodded. "And may I ask how your own readings are?"

Vale straightened, her expression giving nothing away. "They're decent. Titus had the best tutors in our clan on staff."

"Would you be open to conducting one around the coming war? Perhaps seeking Kakias's next steps from the stars?" I'd been mulling over the idea for some time. Vale hid secrets—they were clear in her eyes, riddled by the past. Her connection to the celestial movements was a tool we needed.

"That could be incredibly helpful in knowing where to station our forces," Danya interjected.

"And general strategy overall." Cypherion's mind ticked down his list of preparations.

"Particularly with allies." Jezebel and Erista exchanged a glance.

Barrett toyed with his sigil ring. "If anyone can understand my mother, it will be the stars."

Vale looked from one to the next, imposition clear on her face. "I can try. I can't promise results."

"Thank you." The satisfied snapping of a trap sounded in my head.

"The Apex Moon has passed. I expect you'll hear from Meridat soon." Erista's confidence was reassuring. A bit of the tension in my chest eased.

"And Brigiet?" I faced the Bodymelder apprentice.

Esmond ran a hand over his hair. "To tell you the truth, Ophelia." He paused. "I don't know what to expect from her. Brigiet is a very…private person."

An understatement.

"Please write to her, as well, and see if there is any movement on her decision."

"Of course," he promised. I didn't know what way Esmond would sway the Bodymelder chancellor. Though he appeared to trust us, we couldn't be sure how deep that loyalty ran.

"If we might be moving without the minor clans"—Danya shifted their symbols off the map—"we'll need to fight smart. Brute force and size will go to Kakias."

"We aren't sure what her plans are, though," I added.

"We can assume she'll attack Damenal." The Master of Weapons spoke with years of experience.

But I looked to the Engrossian heir. "Can we?"

Barrett leaned forward, twirling one of his black curls around a finger and studying the map of Gallantia spread over the table. "No." He straightened. "Never assume my mother will do what is obvious."

"In the last war—"

"In the last war her motives were kept secret." Barrett drummed his fingers on the arms of his chair. "She didn't much care how the war was run, so long as she won. She allowed her general control of the armies."

"She won't this time?" my father asked.

"He died," Barrett deadpanned. "Your daughter killed him."

"Victious," I breathed, swallowed by the memory of the rogue Engrossians attacking us on the journey to the Undertaking. Of Tolek's blood staining my cheeks, like sliding a knife between my ribs.

As if sensing my discomfort, Tol stepped to my shoulder. Closing his notebook and setting it on the table, he brushed his arm against mine—a simple assurance that he was here.

"Who will lead her armies now?" Tol asked.

Barrett shook his head, but it was Dax who answered. "She never appointed anyone." His pale cheeks flushed. "I was a lieutenant below Victious. After he died, Kakias…she announced wanting to lead herself."

"Why?" I asked, ignoring how high-ranking the prince's consort had revealed himself to be. Danya moved pins around the map, her pen scraping satisfyingly through Victious.

Barrett shrugged. "Do not be fooled that she'll actually fight. She likely doesn't want to share her strategy with anyone else." *Share what she's actually after*, his pointed stare said. "It would be unwise to underestimate her."

War was a game—a bloody, brutal one but a game like any other. Each side was driven by pride, a desire to conquer or protect, a desperation to survive, but those motivations didn't plant themselves. Even the most shadowed, twisted wants of a person's heart must be tended for roots to sprout.

"What does your mother fear more than anything, Prince?"

He considered. If I wanted to beat Kakias, I had to fully encompass her. Because she was more than any warlord vying for power, she was shaped by complexities. They'd presented their edges in the volcano, but a heart beat in the center, I was sure of it.

"Loss, I'd say." Barrett finally swallowed, looking down at his hands. His words echoed what Dax had implied during the raid. The queen was afraid of losing what she cared about. "My mother had a difficult childhood. Being the sole heir to her father's throne and power made her a target for predators, and it…she was left with scars." I opened my mouth to inquire what he meant, but Barrett quickly continued, "She's afraid of losing anything. It's why she allows so few in." *Including me*, he didn't add, but it weighed the downturn of his lips.

I didn't know how that connected to her current motives, given that she was guaranteeing there would be loss on both sides, but I didn't push Barrett further. I briefly wondered if he was regretting his place here, but he lifted his chin, an unremorseful glint in his eye. Dax grasped his hand atop the table, and the two Engrossians were silent.

"Until we have a response from the chancellors, there isn't much planning that can be done. Danya is right; we scheme—we don't rely on numbers. We plan as if this war will be fought with only Mystique armies." I planted my hands on the table, leaning forward. "Because there is not a future in which we fall prey to whatever Kakias has planned."

I dismissed the meeting. Malakai had not spoken a word the entire time, and when we finally locked eyes as he exited the room, my heart crumpled in my chest, a piece stretching out to him. I slammed a rope around it, tugging it back where it belonged. He would have no more of me, nor I of him, despite the sadness that sank like a rock in my stomach.

My body and mind were being stretched. Spirits, my very soul was. An impossible mountain of pressing needs demanding my attention, and I did not know how to solve any of them.

I had spent every spare moment researching Damien's prophecy. Angelcurses and things once lost. Annellius and sacrifices of strong warriors. Rina had come to me with information on a number of suspicious curses, but nothing sounded like what Damien spoke of.

The shade of heart…seek the seven…blood of fate, spilled in sacrifice…

But even as I sat here now, that second pulse in my body thrummed, and I was certain it was connected. That the Angelblood alive in my veins, but I couldn't figure out how I was supposed to wield it. Was it a weapon or a threat? A sin or a savior?

Recently, I'd been searching for patterns among the seven clans that could be hiding similar tasks or demonstrate what seven items I needed to unite. Nothing stood out.

Threads, that was what I had. A tangled mess of clues and no indication of which ends belonged together. They were pointing toward something, though.

It wasn't the first prophecy the Angel had given me, but the stakes were higher now. Not only did I risk *following the last's lost fight* should I fail, but Mystiques were relying on me, and my future as Revered was being challenged. Alliances were being withheld. I rubbed my hand over my eyes. Spirits, I needed to sleep for four days.

"Tired?" The chair beside mine scraped back.

"You can tell?" I opened one eye to see only Barrett and I were left.

"You look exactly how I felt every day before leaving the Engrossian Valley Palace. I'd been staying up nights to prowl through my mother's plans. Barely slept until I got here."

"You seem to have recovered nicely." His cheeks were still hollow, but he no longer looked ill, instead naturally defined.

"I feel safe here," the prince admitted, toying with the sigil ring on his index finger. I watched it twirl, and the second pulse in me quickened, my own fingers fidgeting.

"I'm glad." I smiled weakly at him, but his face fell. Full lips almost set in a pout.

"I have to ask…"

"No." I shook my head. "Please don't." My voice cracked with the pressure of secrets. "I can't say why, but there's a reason I'm not telling anyone, and I need you to keep it a secret, too."

His eyes—Malakai's eyes—swept over my face, and I felt like they almost saw me as deeply as his brother's used to. "Okay. For now."

I took it.

"I actually wanted to apologize, though." Barrett leaned back in his chair, crossing one ankle over his knee.

"For what?"

"If my arrival caused any…tension between you and Malakai. I can stay away if it's driving you apart."

"Thank you, Barrett, but it's not necessary." I fought the current of pain threatening to swarm me, swam against it until I surfaced. My spirit gasped for breath as I voiced the truth to this man who was so recently an enemy but had become a kindred spirit. "We were already on this path; we just needed to admit it. Besides, you leaving would be hiding from the problem, which is what we'd done for far too long before you arrived."

"He sees it as me or him, doesn't he?"

I gnawed my lip as the question did my heart. "I think part of him feels that I betrayed him by allowing you into our lives, but that's nothing to do with either of us. That's a scar from his father."

"And you won't coddle him."

"I can't make choices based on his pain when the entire continent could be at stake."

Barrett nodded. "Well, I'm glad to hear it's not my fault. I'd hate for my brother to blame me for him losing the woman he loved." He laughed, lips twitching in a pensive smile.

"Give him time." I hesitated, but stretched a hand across the table and held his. Part of me had expected him to recoil, but he didn't. "He'll come around to welcoming you into his life."

He'll heal, I didn't add, but I hoped it was true.

Whatever Meridat saw in the Apex Moon was in my favor. She sent word confirming her earlier sentiment during the Rapture: The Soulguiders would ally with us officially against Kakias in whatever war may come.

After reports of the raid and the clear threat the Engrossians posed, Titus's agreement came a few days later from a tight-lipped Vale, though he made it clear this was an alliance with *the Mystiques*. His approval of my position still hung in the air, and Vale gave no indication as to why.

The Seawatchers gave their allegiance, too, but they couldn't offer much in way of physical troops. Their warriors in the Western Outposts would stay there to fortify the border against the Faelish Waters, and those in the east would be split. Half would defend the coast; half would come to our aid. It was a small help, but it was something. Danya and I spent long afternoons planning where each clan's troops would be stationed, defending the circumference of the mountains.

Esmond's response was not quite as encouraging. Brigiet had passed on the alliance, claiming their territory's location made it too tumultuous of a deal. But she did agree to offer the help of their healers—to both sides of the war, if Kakias requested it. I couldn't fault her reluctance, but I did take out my frustration in the training arena.

"Easy, Alabath," Tol hissed as I came within a hair of slicing his rib cage.

"Watch your left," I clipped.

He tensed for another attack. "Noted."

We danced across the dirt, and I stewed over the one outstanding response: Aird. The Mindshaper chancellor had yet to write back. After his initial refusal to support my appointment and our altercation on palace grounds, I had little hope that he'd come to our aid. Still, I'd included an additional plea in his letter that I hadn't shared with the others. A reminder that while his territory framed the southern tip of the mountains, the range was under *my* jurisdiction as Mystique leader. Should we choose to cut him off from resources, his people would suffer. But should he choose us, we'd offer access to the precious streams of magic within the rock.

The threat was ash on my tongue as I swung at Tol, but Aird had forced me into it. The truth was, the Mindshapers had the largest army of any minor clan, followed by the Bodymelders. If he allied with Kakias, we'd be in trouble.

Tol's sword grazed my thigh, pushing Aird from my mind. Dammit if Vincienzo hadn't actually been working hard these past months. He'd always been skilled—he was infuriatingly good at everything—but he'd gotten better.

"Cypherion's lessons seem to be paying off," I teased.

Tolek raised his brows, dodging my sword. "Surprised?"

"Only because normally," I huffed over the clashing of weapons, "I would have taken you out by now." Around us, the arena was a masquerade of sparring partners. We'd expanded into the garden, taking over part of the lawn for workouts. Younger trainees practiced in arenas in the city rather than the palace grounds.

"What if I was going easy on you?" Tol taunted.

"Were you?"

He laughed at my skepticism. "No. You've always been too good for me." But as he said it, he got his blade under my sword arm and held it against my throat. I'd been wrong to think he wasn't a challenge. Tolek Vincienzo was anything but easy.

"Yielding to me, Alabath?" Our chests rose and fell in unison, faces only an inch apart, his breath hot against my lips, my favorite smirk lifting his.

"Revered," a hesitant voice interrupted from the side of the arena.

I waved the pink-cheeked staff member over and thanked her as she handed me a letter. She turned abruptly and left.

"What is it?" Tol asked, looking over my shoulder.

I stared at the envelope in my hand.

Aird had sent his answer.

"Threats will get you nowhere, Miss Alabath," I read aloud to Danya, my core guard, and the delegates, having pulled them all from the arena into the council chamber.

"And he gave no reasoning for his rejection?" the Master of Weapons growled, sweat on her flushed face.

"He doesn't approve of me. *That* is his reasoning." It was an unsound, ungrounded, unfortunate reason, because now Aird had written himself into my personal list of enemies, and that was a very painful place to find yourself. I held out the parchment, though I could recite the words from memory by now. It was one sentence, but it had intentionally taken him weeks to write.

Danya fumed as she read, then thrust the letter back at me. "He's making this personal."

I crumpled the page in my hand and braced my fists on the table, head drooping. "I even offered to make a deal."

Had it been layered with a threat? Yes, but I couldn't roll over entirely. Aird needed to be given something with parameters. A steel spine to support my position against a man who saw me as dirt beneath his boots. Handing over power to him wasn't the answer, and apparently neither was negotiating.

"What kind of deal?" Tol asked, stiff.

By the time I finished explaining the offer, my father and the rest of the council had arrived, each reading the note and stewing in their own anger.

"You had to try," Jezebel said.

"Yes, but now that I proposed the option, he'll want it. He'll find a way to manipulate me into it." Weakness twisted itself between my ribs, tightening my chest. "There's no way around it—Aird is a problem."

One I wanted to get rid of, though logically I couldn't.

"The chancellors are driving knives into my skull." Danya rubbed her temples, head snapping up a moment later, as if remembering the delegates were present. "Sorry," she sighed. "I do enjoy the three of you."

"No, no." Erista waved off the apology. "I don't want to speak for anyone else, but Aird is a bigot."

"He may be, but his troops are useful." Danya prowled around the room like a cat.

"Are they siding with the Engrossians, then?" Cyph asked.

"He didn't say." Anger curled hot within me, and I slammed my palms on the table. "He's sentencing warriors to death and didn't even provide an explanation. That son of a—"

"It's not over." Malakai spoke for the first time since we'd arrived. Every head swiveled toward him. It was the first time I'd spoken to him in nearly two weeks. The first time I'd truly looked at him. He looked…better than I expected. Like the time he'd been spending in the shadows was soothing.

"This letter doesn't say no. Aird has not rejected your request yet." Malakai cleared his throat, attempted to channel the man raised to be Revered of the Mystique Warriors, schooled in diplomacy. "There's an empty seat on this council for exactly this purpose. The Master of Communications was once responsible for learning the minds of every chancellor and balancing the relationships for these moments." He paused, looking directly at me. I didn't feel any pangs of desire when our eyes met, but a silent understanding between us.

"He didn't say no. So you believe we should send someone to appeal. To find out what he wants."

"Appoint someone to go to the Mindshapers, win over Aird. *Persuade him.*"

I reined in my anger. "I don't know. He didn't have a problem rejecting my claim at the Rapture, denying to send a delegate, or sneaking around Damenal."

"It's worth a shot." Malakai shrugged one shoulder, voice falling flat again.

"Are you volunteering?" Hope seeped into my voice at the thought of him returning to his once-ambitious self.

But he shook his head. "I'm not fit for any such position."

That broke my healing heart a little, knowing how he thought of himself. I shook it off, though. He was right, sending someone to Aird was our last shot. And if we were going to try, it had to be the most persuasive person.

I exhaled, acceptance spreading through me, and my eyes found Tolek.

He stepped forward. "I'll go."

"Are you certain?" I asked, biting my lip.

"Anything you need." He nodded, and Malakai stiffened, eyes narrowing, but I shut out everyone besides Tol.

I was reluctant to let him go, not because I didn't believe in him but because he steadied me. Without him here, I'd be incomplete. But I couldn't put that need first.

I squared my shoulders. "You'll leave in three days. Take three warriors—ascended warriors—with you. No more. We don't want them to know you're coming if we can avoid it."

"As you wish." He bowed slightly, then left the room.

A pit widened in my stomach with each step echoing down the hall. I took a deep breath around it, filling my lungs to the point of bursting, ignoring the sensation of a blade dragging its jagged edge against my heart.

CHAPTER TWENTY-FIVE

OPHELIA

THE ROSE SCENT OF the candle I'd lit brightened the early afternoon and my spirit with it. Propping open my second book of the day, I nestled into a chair in my office. The table was strewn with stacks of books on the Angels and what lore we were allowed to study of the other six clans. From the Mindshapers' meditative therapy to the Seawatchers' Isla Trysva—their version of our Undertaking—I was determined to absorb as much information as possible in order to figure out what I was meant to unite.

Empty dishes dotted the space between my notes, remnants of the past two days. Aside from training and war councils, I'd barely left the room.

I thumbed through the opening pages of *Legacies of Deities*, settling into the introduction. It spoke of the Angels in life and theorized where they may have come from given they were the first warriors. By the time it summarized their ascension to the heavens, the candle was burning low, afternoon fading toward dusk.

They were power solidified within the body, blood threaded with pure ether and bones riddled with bits of magic. The seven former warriors became something other, never before seen, and were gifted beyond imagination. When they ascended, the Angels left pieces of themselves behind, tendrils to be found within their descendants and fossilized—

Glass shattered somewhere outside.

"What in the Spirits?"

I tore from the room.

Voices rose from the second-floor landing, and with a rocketing heart rate, I recognized two of them.

When I rounded the corner, it took me a moment to figure out what I was seeing.

Malakai threw himself at Tolek, who caught him, slamming back into the wall. Frames rattled, and a bust of some warrior—I didn't know who—crashed from its pedestal to the ground.

Tol brought his fist into Malakai's side. It looked like more of an effort to ward him off than to injure him.

"Tell me the truth!" Malakai shouted. He swung a fist into Tolek's jaw, a spray of blood flying from Tol's mouth. The droplets arched through the air, landing at my feet, tainting the white marble.

Through the swelling lip, Tol yelled, "I don't know what the fuck you want me to say!"

Malakai grabbed his shoulders, pulled him forward, then shoved him into the wall. "Tell me what's been going on with you two!"

You two? Who—what?

The only person I'd seen enrage Malakai to anywhere near this level was Barrett, but there couldn't be anything going on between Tolek and the prince.

No, I'd know if something worth *this* was going on. But who could Malakai feel so strongly for that it was worth fighting his oldest friend?

The only possible answer came to me in a crushing wave, drowning out the blows and shouts.

One bout of life-changing shock as I understood.

Cyph ran up the stairs. When he met my gaze, it was clear he already knew what was going on. Maybe he'd known for some time, and I was the only one who had yet to figure it out.

Me. This fight was over *me*.

Malakai pulled his fist back again, but before he could land the blow, Cyph locked both of his arms behind his back. "Knock it the fuck off, Malakai!"

"You're supposed to be my friend!" Malakai raged, voice cracking. "But you can't even tell me the truth."

"There's nothing to fucking tell you." Tolek spat more blood onto the tiles. "Nothing ever happened."

"I'm not an idiot—"

"That's enough!" I shouted.

They ceased, chests heaving. Neither had noticed my arrival. Tol's jaw was crusted with blood, his lip swollen. Malakai's shirt was torn, an angry bruise blooming across his ribs.

But the injuries didn't compare to the looks in their eyes.

Malakai's stare was a rotten mixture of betrayal and fury, pupils blown and crazed. And Tol...Tol's face was etched with shattering vulnerability, slow blinks trying to hide the devastation. It took everything in me to stand still, to not automatically go to him and work away the hopelessness forming.

It was because of those looks that I swallowed my anger and tried to adopt my most level tone. "I don't know what's going on between you two, but you're both being absolute idiots." I clearly didn't do a good job.

In the span of three minutes, my world had been cracked open, the insides swirled about. The truth of why they fought...Spirits, my heart thudded.

Santorina arrived and began wiping the blood from Tol's face with a damp cloth.

"You." I pointed at Tolek. "Go with Rina. I'll speak to you shortly." I turned to Malakai. "You. Follow me."

Blood roared in my ears with each step I took back down the hallway and into a room at random, dust coating the empty table and shelves. Mystlight flared over us, but aside from a small fireplace and sitting area, I barely noticed the furnishings.

I was too busy trying to convince myself not to punch Malakai.

I shut the door behind him, gripping the knob until my bones ground against the metal, counting my breaths, trying to speak as calmly as possible. "Are you going to explain what *that* was?"

Though I was certain of the answer, I wanted him to have to explain his actions.

"Are you?" Malakai snapped from the fireside.

Shock rocked through me. "What?"

"That was over *you*." Twisting to face me, he winced and held a hand to his side where the bruise was getting darker. "Are you going to tell me?"

"You're being an ass, Malakai," I groaned, rubbing my eyes.

"How long has something been going on with you two?"

"What in the Angel-damned hell do you think is going on?" I roared. "And why do you think it would give you *any* right to *attack him*?"

He seethed silently, pacing, feet dragging across the faded rug.

"What do you think is happening?" I repeated calmly, trying to placate the anger simmering off of him.

He worked his jaw back and forth. "What's between you and Tolek?"

His anger was misplaced—so fucking misplaced because I'd never so much as kissed Tolek Vincienzo in my entire life. And even if I had done so in the weeks since we broke up, who was Malakai to say anything of it?

"Nothing," I growled. The irony was that until he'd thrown a fit, I didn't have any hint that anything suspicious *was* happening.

"Truly? Because I've seen the way you look at each other. Even before we broke up, there was always something different about the way you two interacted."

"What are you saying?"

He shoved his hands through his hair with a groan. "You two were—are—like planets. Always rotating in each other's orbits, like it's a natural instinct you can't avoid. It got worse, too, since I was gone. You always turn to him, and you expect me to believe you didn't notice? I'm not stupid."

"Well, you could have fooled me right now."

Tolek and I had always existed like two parts of a whole. Explanations unnecessary, reckless abandon indulged without question, tears shed without embarrassment.

But nothing had ever happened. We had never acted on the charged chemistry thrumming between us, causing an inherent form of communication. I didn't even know if Tolek felt it, too, or if I had made it up.

"Tol and I are close. We understand each other on a deeper level, as you and I have." *Had.*

His entire frame drooped, and I realized too late the implication of that comparison. "What happened when I was gone, Phel?"

"What happened?" Every minute of those two years rushed through me at once, every slice of longing, every shard of heartbreak. And with it my control snapped. "I *broke*—that's what happened. You were the brightest star in my life for eighteen years, the point around which my world revolved, but that's unhealthy for anyone. Because when you lose your polestar, you have nothing left."

"So, it's my fault? Because I signed the treaty and gave myself over, it gives you the right to be with my best friend?"

The fire cast shadows on him, and I briefly wondered if that was how it felt to be in his head. All dark past and dimmed hope.

I tempered my anger a little.

"It's no one's fault." I ran my hands through my hair, calming myself further. Malakai was angry and healing. That's why he lashed out. "I'm not with him, but even if I was—like you said, you left. Had you expected me to live out the rest of my days alone?"

Instinctually, I wrapped my fingers around the Bind, almost willing it to kick back to life to assure me that we *had* had something special when we received it. That passion hadn't just been a figment.

Malakai averted his gaze, toying with the cuff of his sleeve, and that avoidance broke my resolve.

"This is simply how things are, Malakai. For so long, I was blinded by the light you brought into my life, but when you left me— with this tattoo on my arm that couldn't find its home—I was plunged into darkness. It took *every good part of me* with it. You took those parts."

Did he still not comprehend? After how many times I had tried to explain it to him? It seemed like he was purposely ignoring me. And maybe he was; that was his right, but he didn't get to throw it back at me without even attempting to understand.

Angels, matters of the heart were messy.

"What we had was all blinding starlight, then? Nothing real?" He turned away from me, falling onto the couch with a contemptuous huff. The dismissal landed like a blow to my cheek. Were there truly no good pieces left of the man I'd loved?

"No." Not wanting to get too close, I perched on the arm of the couch. "Do *not* put words in my mouth. We were beautiful. We were perfect and innocent and maybe too much so for this world, but every single moment between us was real."

Despite the silence in my tattoo, I knew it was true. I found that strength in myself to not darken our past with sordid beliefs.

"You were the only thing I ever considered for my life, but maybe that was the problem. We were complacent, taking the obvious future as destiny. But look at everything that's happened. Everything we've been through. The easy path is not always what we're given."

I had never seen myself as Revered and yet it was now the title thrumming through my blood. The strings of fate had a way of redirecting us, and I was learning that relinquishing control was okay. Becoming comfortable with the uncomfortable was freeing.

I took a deep breath, exhaling the venom charging through my blood. "When you were gone, I grew. We both did. And this new version of me isn't suited for that new version of you."

"And are you suited for him?" He hunched, elbows against his knees.

"I don't know." I wasn't just sparing his feelings. I had always known something deeper lay between me and Tol, but I had never stopped to pick it apart, decide what I wanted from it. Or ask Tolek what he wanted.

When I admitted I was as lost as he was, a piece of Malakai visibly crumpled, head into his hands, heart bleeding out on his sleeve. Like thinking I was holding it together was somehow holding his world together, too.

"I don't know what to do," he whispered, rubbing the heel of his palm against his chest as if it seized and flopping back against the cushions. He didn't only mean this situation—he meant the rubble his life had become. If I had to bet, I'd say this entire fight had only been fueled by that mess.

"Me neither."

Two and a half years ago, a part of my heart had been ripped from my chest, repeatedly trampled with each injustice I experienced, up until the day we both stopped pretending we would work.

Then, I'd shifted my focus from catering to the delicate scraps of his heart to piecing my own back together. Despite how broken he looked before me, I couldn't let him take that progress. The part of me he had owned may have been warped, but it was finding its way back into place. I was healing. I would always hold some allegiance to Malakai, but my heart no longer belonged to him—it belonged to me.

Malakai's frame shook with a sigh. The stature was one I was very intimate with: When the world was too much and that last scrap falling onto your shoulders turned you to dust.

"I think you at least know where to begin." Malakai grimaced, but the weight on him dulled his edge into resignation.

I nodded, pushing to my feet. "I'm sorry." I didn't know what I was apologizing for.

"Don't be. I—"

"I'll always care about you, Malakai." Maybe he needed to hear those words, because a soft smile cracked his hard exterior. And maybe—judging by the warmth blossoming in my chest—I needed to say them.

"Me too. I don't blame you."

"I blame fate," I said.

Pieces of Malakai's good still existed within him, I knew it. Maybe he'd find those pieces. He'd collect them, nurture them as they demanded, and one day someone deserving would help him put them back together.

Chapter Twenty-Six

Ophelia

My knock was subtle, but I knew he'd be expecting it. Just as I knew he'd be standing on the balcony off his bedroom, glass of dark liquor in hand. It was always like this with us—the predictability. The moving in tandem. The understanding.

"I figured you'd find me when you were ready." Tol didn't look at me when he spoke, and I was afraid to face what I would find in his eyes if he had. The setting sun gilded his frame like my own personal Angel.

I crossed the tidy bedroom, notebooks stacked on every surface, and joined him on the balcony. My fingers were twitching. Absently, I traced circles along the stone.

"If I don't start talking, you'll likely wear a hole in the railing," he joked flatly. "Sorry, I don't have anything to offer for knots."

Stifling the tension within me, I reached over, lifting his glass from his hands and taking a long sip. I didn't recognize the liquor, slightly spicy with a hint of orange. It was how I imagined Tolek tasted.

Passing the drink back to him, I folded my hands to stop their fidgeting.

"I'd rather talk," I said.

"And what is it you'd like to discuss, Alabath?" He slid the glass between his hands, not looking at me. I couldn't remember a time before the Undertaking when Tol had avoided me. That he did so now made my chest feel like it was going to cave in.

"I've already spoken to Malakai." His shoulders tensed. "What *was* that, Tolek?"

He took a long sip of his drink, sucking his lips between his teeth, pursing them as he swallowed. "I'm not sure what you mean. *He* seemed to have an issue with *me*."

Who *had the issue* was irrelevant. Why it had started—that had my heart thumping against my ribs.

I cleared my throat. "And was that *issue* for good cause?" Even to my ears, it sounded like an accusation. His chin dropped, and I quickly corrected myself. "What I mean to say is, is it true? Because whether or not it is, his grievances don't justify his actions."

"Is that what you truly think?"

"I think it's none of his business," I confessed, taking a deep breath. "But it is mine. Was he right?"

Slowly, Tol turned his eyes on me, and the look in them was unlike anything I'd ever seen before. It was deeper, a bottomless hole of emotion that I was on the precipice of falling into. Tol showed more of himself to me than he did to others, shared sides of that scarred soul that he didn't dare expose elsewhere, but this was more.

"And what does it matter if he is?"

My stomach swooped, my heart with it, because that was as good as a confession.

"How long?" I whispered.

"Since the day I first saw you fight." He ducked his head. Bashful—an emotion I never thought I'd see on him. "Not the play things we did as children, but the first summer we *really* trained, when we were thirteen. The fire in you, the inability to back down, and the utter glow about you when you did what you were born to do. You were mesmerizing. My young brain became obsessed. Spirits, I think I noticed it earlier than that, but I didn't understand it then."

The fact that he'd been captured by those things about me and held on to them for all these years caught my breath in my throat. But—

"That was the summer…"

I didn't have to finish the sentence. He knew as well as I did that summer was when Malakai and I first confessed our feelings for each other.

"That was when I decided I would never tell you." He finished his drink, setting the glass aside. "If the feelings never subsided, I decided then that I would keep them to myself as long as I lived."

"Tol…"

"I don't want pity, Ophelia." He looked at me, eyes hard.

"I'm not pitying you." Maybe I was pitying myself for never knowing, for never seeing. "The feelings never subsided."

"What do you want me to say?" He turned toward me, hand pressing to his chest. "Do you want me to say that I've loved you for as long as I can remember? That I woke every day aware you were his and accepted it because you loved him and that was enough for me. Being your friend, walking through life with you, even if in a different sense than I hoped…it was enough. Is that what you want me to admit? That I was allowed to make you laugh, share in those brightest moments, and feel the light you spread to the world. And when that light needed rekindling, I would do that, too. Because if that's what you want to hear, then I'll say it. I'll tell you every hidden truth darkening my heart if it's what you want—it belongs to you anyway."

He clutched the railing, knuckles turning white, and that grip tightened around my heart. It had been him holding it together all these years.

His love was the glue between my broken glass. The fire forging me anew. And I'd never stopped to realize.

"I want the truth, Tol. I want to know why you never told me. When Malakai was gone, you still didn't tell me."

"How could I?" His brows pulled together, but he ran a hand over his face, collecting his thoughts. "You were so hurt, so broken. I watched you fall into that dark space, and I swore I would help you climb back out of it however you'd allow me to. But I also swore I would do nothing to hurt you any more than you'd already suffered."

It was instinct to step toward him, but I stopped myself from unlatching his fingers on the railing. Spirits, I wanted to. I wanted to unburden all of these heavy truths from his heart.

"How could you have hurt me?" I asked instead.

His face nearly crumpled. "If I had told you, it only would have ended one way." When he saw the confused tilt of my head, he continued, "You were so in love with him still, carrying that spark of hope that he would come back to you. If I had told you what was in my heart, you would have rejected me. And I know you—it would have hurt you to do that to me."

A selfless decision, caring only about the pain that rejection would inflict on me. I didn't deny that I would have done it. I'd been so desperate for Malakai, I likely wouldn't have looked at anyone else.

Still, I wished Tol hadn't been so selfless.

"You were never going to tell me?"

"If I could have gotten you over what happened, as nothing more than a friend, I never would have told you." He read the secret-burned scars that made me flinch. "I know that takes away your decision in the matter, and for that I apologize, but I wasn't willing to be the cause of any more damage to your heart."

"And what about your heart?" He'd always been pushed to the side, so much so that he now chose it for himself, sacrificing to put *me* first.

"What about it?" He shrugged.

My blood heated at the casual dismissal. "Tolek Vincienzo, your heart matters as much as anyone else's."

To me, it mattered more than most. It always had—and I was only starting to consider what that might mean.

"But you needed a friend when Malakai was gone. You didn't need…whatever I might be. And once he was back…"

Understanding tapped at the confusion in my mind. "You tried to keep your distance?"

It was why I hardly saw him in those first weeks after the Undertaking. Why he'd seemed to disappear until I needed him most, always attune to those moments like an instinct forced him back to me.

He'd tried to give me the space to heal with Malakai.

"I thought it would help you two if I didn't complicate things further—I tried, I did. But, Spirits damn me, you're hard to stay away from, Alabath." He shook his head, and with each confession, tension melted from his shoulders. The hollows I'd formed at his distance filled.

Tol finally unlatched his fingers from the banister. "I never needed you to love me, Ophelia. Not in the way I love you." One step toward me. "Did I want you to? Of course. More than I wanted to live." Another slow step. "But I never needed it." A third, and he stopped, inches away.

My heart pounded, the Bind inked on my arm pulsing with each beat.

"What I needed was for you *to love*. To allow yourself *to be loved*. To save the girl I fell in love with from succumbing to that brutal darkness so she could grow into the woman—the warrior—she was meant to be. And if you never loved me, but the rest was true, I would've been okay. I would've been happy to be by your side in whatever capacity you needed."

I had loved Malakai—I would always hold love for him. The piece of my heart that had been torn from my chest, warped, and put back together would always carry an echo of the young love that fate had torn apart.

I had thought it all belonged to me now, but I was wrong.

There was another piece, stronger and yet to be shredded, that belonged to Tol. To the friend who was my moonlight on a dark night. Who held me in my bleakest moments and waited for me to come back to myself. Who not only saw my rough edges and loved each one but also found the soft sides hidden beneath.

We had told each other as much before I completed the Undertaking.

You carry a piece of my heart.

And you, mine.

I hadn't understood the gravity of those words at the time. What he truly meant. Even now, with Tol laying his heart bare before me, I still didn't know what *my* heart wanted.

But awareness was stirring inside me—a beast that wanted that happiness Tol spoke of. An instinct that might know how to find it if I could fight my way past the pain I'd suffered so far, avoiding any more slices from the shattered pieces of myself.

"I don't know what capacity I can offer yet," I whispered, hating myself for not having a suitable answer for him.

He released a low laugh, his breath fanning across my skin. "I'm not asking you to know. I'm asking nothing of you."

He meant it, too. If I wished, he would bury this day beneath the mountains and let the beautiful friendship we had built over the past twenty years bloom on its grave. Because Tolek Vincienzo would never ask anything that I could not give.

"I leave tomorrow," he said. "I'll be back in three weeks."

His piece of my heart cried out at the fact that he was leaving so soon after I'd learned his truth, but perhaps it was good. I needed time to be alone, to nurse my own wounds, repair my own heart. To figure out what it wanted.

"Maybe that time will help me—figure this out."

He shook his head. "It doesn't have to."

Yes, it did. He deserved an answer. The fact that he didn't ask for one only made me want to find it more.

"Take this." I unclipped my grandmother's pin from my leathers. "For when you go. So I'll be with you."

The sun slipped behind the mountains, stars popping into the violet sky and the world falling into serenity. As if nature itself had been waiting for Tolek to reveal his secret and was finding some peace in the truth. Tenderly, he wrapped his fingers around the pin.

"I'll see you in three weeks' time, Alabath." Tolek kissed my cheek, the brush there and gone as quickly as a hummingbird's wing, but my breath caught in my throat.

"I'll see you then, Vincienzo."

I backed away, not once breaking eye contact with him as he clipped my pin onto the left breast of his leathers. I could no longer avoid the depth in his stare that begged me to fall over the edge into it.

If I chose to, I knew he'd catch me. Tol would remain my tether if I allowed him to.

I watched him leave the next morning.

He tried to sneak out before the sun rose, but I hadn't slept. Hoods drawn, weapons secured, four figures marched out of the palace grounds on horseback.

From my balcony, crisp twilight air winding its way around my bare feet and lifting my silk robe, I tracked the figure in the front.

My eyes stung, but I told myself it would be okay. I'd see him soon.

CHAPTER TWENTY-SEVEN

OPHELIA

"HOW ARE YOU FEELING?" Santorina asked as we walked the path through the gardens, snapping stems and pulling roots for ointments.

A week had passed since Tolek left, and still my heart seemed to be miles away, speeding toward the Mindshaper capital, while my head was in Damenal, trying to strategize for a war, decode Damien's prophecy, and predict Kakias's next move.

Truly, though, my mind spent the majority of its time trying and failing not to replay Tol's confession. Every hour since he'd left, it had cycled through. And with each repetition, my stomach churned further.

"Fine," I clipped. Rina rolled her eyes, drawing a sigh from me. "Conflicted."

"I still can't believe you didn't know." She added a few flower petals to her basket, their hue as vibrant as the clear sky.

I'd told her about Tol's confession the day he left; not every vulnerable word we'd shared, only that he'd admitted feelings. When I finished, she'd stared at me blankly.

"I know how he feels. I assumed you did, too" was all she said.

Now, helping her clip ingredients, I looked back over my own actions these past two years. It was no secret that I loved Tol, but I'd never given thought to *how* I loved him, too busy stewing in my own heartbreak and reeling from the betrayals it caused.

But a number of different types of love existed. There was the blood-bound familial level I had for Jezebel that couldn't be severed from this planet. Or the pure adoration I held for Rina and Cyph, rooted in their passionate yet gentle hearts. There was the kind Malakai and I had shared, full of breathy innocence and starry-eyed hope, showing each other what it meant to love and be loved in return. That one was dazzling and all-consuming.

Tol had always been different. He'd always been a force I gravitated toward, pulling at different pieces of my soul as the moon did the tide. What I felt for him not only burned through me, but it also flowed at the deepest levels of myself, an intrinsic current, but a slow one, creeping up on us. He was who I called out for when I was breaking, who I let see every part of me.

Those were the undeniable facts I kept returning to as I sorted through the mess of my own heart.

In whatever capacity, I could not live without Tolek Vincienzo.

"I suppose I was blinded by circumstance."

Santorina set her basket down, brushed her hands across her simple gown, and stared me squarely in the eye. "Circumstance has transformed into choice now."

I swallowed the truth, not sure how to respond.

"Come on," Rina encouraged, wrapping her arm through mine and grabbing her basket again. "Let's go prepare these."

We shuffled back up the path leading to the base of the palace, chatting idly about where the Bodymelders Brigiet had promised to send would be stationed and how quickly Daminius was approaching.

The clock was ticking on my time to win over the delegates, only two weeks left now. And Vale had yet to see anything that could expand on Titus's destructive reading, though I figured whether we knew what caused it or not, we had to face darkness. All we could do was prepare.

I thought Esmond was warming to me. If he could convince Brigiet, then I'd have a sure grip on my title heading into Daminius. I only hoped it was enough.

As we walked, I fidgeted with the necklace I'd fashioned from the piece of Angelborn. My fingers missed the feeling of the pin I'd given to Tolek, but they now found an odd comfort in the constant dull heat of the metal. The more I felt it, the more positive I became that it was linked to the Angelcurse. I'd started researching relics, but I'd found no mention of spears linked to Damien yet. There had to be something I was missing, something—

Rina gripped my arm, pulling me to an abrupt halt. I looked over at her and then followed her horrified gaze to the palace steps ahead. A trickle of something crimson was tracing a thin trail toward us, leaking from a polished wooden box set upon the bottom step.

Blood.

A dagger was poised in the lid, pinning a piece of parchment in place. The gentle breeze lifted the corner, and goosebumps rose along my arms.

"What in the realm of hell?" Rina breathed.

The clouds overhead shifted, sunlight catching the hilt of the dagger. My knees weakened as an ornate *V* was illuminated on the handle.

Vincienzo.

CHAPTER TWENTY-EIGHT

OPHELIA

IT HAD A FUCKING ribbon on top of it. Blood soaked into the tattered edges where they trailed to the ground.

A gift.

A cruel vow steeped in blood.

Whose blood was the question. Because that dagger piercing the note—

Holy fucking Angels.

I screamed, vaguely aware of people gathering. That dagger stared at me, taunting me, twisting every shred of my heart.

My knees buckled, but Rina held me up. Cyph stepped forward and braced my elbow.

"Wh-who…what…" I couldn't even get the words out.

My lungs. They couldn't work right. Just clenching in small gasps.

Cyph's face was pale as he barked instructions to search every inch of the grounds, dismissing every lower-rank warrior. My sister rubbed soothing circles across my back, but the pressure burrowed through my spine, around my ribs, into my heart.

All I saw was the ornate *V* etched into the handle of that dagger and the solid grip I'd seen use it countless times. The cocky smirk and wink as he threw it.

All I heard was his voice. *I'll see you in three weeks' time, Alabath.*

Blood leaked red and true, inching toward me. I couldn't escape it. Couldn't look away from it. It wouldn't stop.

Whatever was in that fucking box was damaged, likely beyond

repair. Who was I kidding, with that much blood that box likely held…pieces of someone. Bile climbed up my throat, and I clung to Rina. My nails dug into her arm, leaving crescent marks, but nothing could hurt as badly as the sight of his dagger.

Tolek…

"Ophelia," Jezebel muttered.

My head snapped up. "What?" I breathed.

"Did you hear what we said?" Jezzie's face was pale.

"N-no," I stammered, shaking my head, looking around. Everyone was here, eyes wide and fearful—my friends, the delegates, the council, Barrett and Dax…Malakai. He stood on the third stair, arms crossed, lips a tight line. But there was concern in those narrowed eyes, in his clenched jaw.

"We have to open it," he said.

My heart thundered against my ribs as I stepped forward. Beside the dagger, a smaller item I hadn't noticed before reflected the light: my pin. The world spun, but I breathed over it, taking the gift I'd sent with Tol and tucking it into my pocket.

Trying to pull myself together for those watching, I eased the dagger out of the box. The paper fluttered away, the one word printed on it dancing in the wind: *Ophelia*. A gift for me. When it landed on the stair, face down in the sticky crimson puddle, the faint embossing in the corner caught the light: *TV*.

I curled my fingers tighter around the dagger. They'd taken paper from Tol's personal journal. I slid his weapon beside mine on my thigh, knowing exactly where I'd prefer to plunge it.

With a deep breath I threw off the lid and stumbled back into Cypherion. A metallic tang filled the air, wrenching gasps of disgust from our group.

The box was full—nearly to the brim. Dark, thick blood sloshed within. So much of it. Chunks floated in the center—ice. As if they'd frozen the contents, defrosting it only once it reached us. How they managed that I didn't know, I didn't care, because whoever this blood belonged to…they clearly were no longer alive.

Cypherion grabbed the note, careful to avoid the scarlet stains. I'd never seen his hands shake before, but now they trembled.

"*Ophe*—" He cleared his throat. "*Ophelia, you ferocious, wicked little thing. Remember, sacrifice is a skill we must conquer. Will it be your blood or his that coats the altar?"*

I might have screamed. I couldn't be sure if the sound broke from my lips or echoed through my head.

"P.S.," Cypherion continued. *"The scar on his thigh is lovely. In two weeks, he'll start receiving a matching one each day, unless I see you first."*

Fury rolled through me hotter than the heart of the Spirit Volcano. And I swore—anyone who touched him would die at my hands. I'd revel in watching the life leave their bodies, until darkness swooped in to steal their spirits.

Storming around the box, I hurried up the stairs. Footsteps followed me.

"Where are you going?" It was the only voice that could shock me enough to stop me.

I whirled in the doorway, finding Malakai's face only inches from mine. "Where am I *going*?" I gaped.

"You can't listen to her," he demanded. He looked at me like *I* was the ridiculous one.

"Are you seriously saying I should let her have him?" I panted. "She'll *kill him*, Malakai!" I wanted to shove him, but I fisted my hands at my sides.

"She won't."

"Look at what she did to you."

"But she didn't kill even me." He pivoted to stand in front of me, blocking my way into the foyer. "And I was an outright threat, a symbol of betrayal, while Tolek is only a pawn to her."

"Torturing him is okay, as long as she doesn't kill him?"

"He'll survive it," Malakai said—and it almost sounded like a reassurance for us both.

He was right. Physically, Tolek would survive it, but the damage it would do to his soul wasn't worth it.

"I'm going." I stepped around him.

"Ophelia, stop." Malakai gripped my arm, and the delicate control I had on myself slipped.

"*Let go of me!*" I shouted, voice high and tattered, as I ripped out of his grasp and charged toward the stairs to my suite.

I needed to leave.

The walls were pressing in.

How long had she already had him? How much time did I have?

"If you give yourself to her, she'll kill you both," Malakai called after me, and I froze.

"I'd never allow that," I replied without turning. Spirits, it was hard to draw breath.

"You can't charge in there on your own. Not without a plan."

I had a plan and it involved slaughtering Kakias and everyone who stood with her. I didn't know how I'd find them, how many of them there'd be. The odds weren't good, I'd admit it, but I couldn't leave him. Not without trying.

I gripped Tol's dagger against my thigh, clenched my eyes, and focused on breathing.

Once the world was spinning less, I turned back to my friends scattered throughout the foyer waiting for me.

"It's not what he would want." Malakai's voice had lost its edge.

That argument stuck between my ribs, guilt welling around it. Tolek would certainly not want me putting myself in danger to save him. But he'd do it for me.

"What do you propose then?"

Malakai's jaw opened as he blinked up at me, but he shook off the shock that I'd asked. "Stay here. She won't kill him. You know she won't. We'll get him back eventually."

Eventually. The word was a knife to my heart, carving out the pieces I was realizing I needed most.

"Malakai is right." Barrett stepped beside his brother, who grimaced but didn't protest. "My mother will not kill him unless she gets something out of it. You can't play into her hands."

I'd always been on Barrett's side, but now I wished I hadn't let him stay. I chewed my lip, taking in every expression turned up to me, from defeated to disgusted, and landing on Cyph. "What do you think?"

He dragged a hand over his face, head falling back, utterly crushed. "It goes against every instinct in my body," he sighed, "but they're right. You can't go. We'll make a plan and send a party after him, but we need to be smart about this."

My bones were heavy, holding myself upright becoming harder

with each breath. What was left of my strength leaked away at the realization of what we were doing.

Nothing.

We weren't doing anything to rescue Tol, though he had rescued me in more ways than one.

The dagger was cold in my hand as I pulled it from my thigh. It slipped from my shaking fingers, blade clattering against marble, sliding down the stairs with shattering echoes.

Right there, in front of everyone, I sank to my knees, wrapped my arms around myself, and sobbed.

My temper was still simmering hours later. Unable to settle in my rooms, I wandered the many wide corridors of the palace instead.

He would not want that, they'd decided.

He'd want you safe, they'd insisted.

I hated that they were right. Leaving him to Kakias…it felt wrong. Allowing him to suffer went against every bone-deep instinct. To be her prisoner.

Spirits, the things she could be doing to him. Chains, blades…I shivered, his screams echoing in my ears. I clenched my eyes against the image of his face contorted in pain, the blood dripping down his body. I couldn't—

"Ophelia!" A gentle hand shook my shoulder.

I hadn't even realized I'd fallen to my knees, still gripping the railing. Jezebel slipped a hand beneath my shoulder, hoisting me up.

"Are you all right?" she asked, worry creasing her brow.

"I'm fine." My shaking voice betrayed me, but I turned away, staring out at the dark night sky.

"Mm-hmm," she hummed, crossing her arms.

"What?" I hissed.

Jezebel's eyes swept over me, tucking away details before I could hide them. But I was surprised when she said, "Nothing."

I looked her over, searching for any conversation to grasp on to. Eyes landing on her crescent and amethyst necklace, the symbol seemed somehow familiar.

"The necklace is from Erista, isn't it?" It was an exact replica of the tattoo around her arm, coupled with a classic Soulguider gem.

"She sent it to me when we decided to keep the secret. It's a family heirloom—one her family didn't care for enough to notice it was gone." Jezebel brushed a hand over the emblem.

"That's—wow, that's commitment, Jez." Warriors didn't part with artifacts easily, and Erista had told us how seriously the Soulguiders handled theirs.

She brushed me off, but I caught her blush.

"So this isn't a new tryst, then?"

She shook her head.

"Tell me how it began." I looped my arm through hers. We strolled down the moonlit corridor, and I pretended I was okay.

"The last summer before the war." When she'd attended a summer exchange in the Soulguider Territory. Before the war, Tol, Cyph, Malakai, and I had visited each minor clan for our own exchanges. Combining groups of young warriors was always unpredictable debauchery, and the Soulguiders were a welcome host.

"You hid it for that long?"

"We hadn't intended to. But once the war began, politics wound their way into our relationship. We didn't know how anyone would react to an inter-clan commitment."

"It's never been an issue before." I thought of our own maternal grandparents—a Soulguider and a Mystique.

"But with such unrest…I don't know, it felt easier to keep it to ourselves."

A piece of me envied her for having that option. For her relationship not being on display for every warrior to discuss—and use to their advantage. A larger piece of me was grateful they were not subjected to the pain that publicity caused.

But I supposed the distance was a different kind of pain; the secrets causing their own wounds. It couldn't have been easy. For the thousandth time in my life, I was impressed with my younger sister's strength.

"And you've stayed together all these years?"

"There hasn't been a moment since we first admitted our feelings that we haven't been committed to each other." Jezebel shrugged, as if it was nothing.

That's how love should be, I thought with a pang of sadness that threatened to close my throat. That easy to commit to one another. I'd had that once—remembered the thrill and stability I'd allowed to fade.

"Why didn't you tell me?" She'd always had to watch my relationship be the center of attention, yet she hid her own happiness.

"I wanted to—I wanted to tell you all. When the war broke out, we only kept in touch via letters. I stole father's ink to write to her, but it was the only option." We both laughed at that. He'd been furious about his well of imbued ink being lower, needing it for urgent messages. I should have scolded her, but I'd have done the same. "And then once the war was over and...everything happened—I don't know, life fell apart. It felt wrong to share it."

The darkness that had consumed me had kept us apart.

"You could have told me, just so you know."

"I know," she exhaled. The smile on her face was lighter than I'd seen in years. Jez was a combination of wild force and pure heart, but the gentle lift of her lips was nothing but the latter.

"I'm happy for you, Jez. And you can expect open support, no matter what clans you belong to." I meant every word.

"Thank you," she whispered.

I smiled, pulled her to me, and relaxed slightly, her happiness easing the tension in my shoulders.

"You know, sister," Jezebel pondered. "You used to give away smiles like they were nothing."

"They cost nothing," I agreed.

She stepped back, leveling a serious stare at me. "I know that, but when Malakai disappeared, it seemed you forgot. Smiles became guarded, like each you gifted was a precious jewel. Only the truly freeing moments, when you allowed a glimpse of your old self to slip through, could earn one."

Tendrils of darkness crept around me as she spoke, but I forced them back. "I didn't have many reasons to smile back then."

"You had exactly five."

I raised my brows. "And you know this how?"

"Because I watched you, waiting for each so I wouldn't miss the fleeting moments when the sister I'd lost peeked back into reality."

My breath hitched with the guilt of her pain over me. "And what were these five reasons?"

"The first was Starfire. Training, though illegal, burned off your anger. That was why I agreed to it every morning, though I thought it futile. For the light that returned to your eyes. But when we were done, you'd quickly fade again. I soon realized those smiles weren't happy— they were vengeful. Still, I took them.

"The second reason was Sapphire. The freedom you two shared under the open sky, or feeding off each other's energy in the stables. Those smiles were light. Dreamy." Jezebel stepped to the window, studying the night. "The third was stolen moments of peace. You know I followed you to the tavern many nights. You offered smiles to the starlit sky when you thought no one was looking and you forgot for a brief moment how awful life had become. Those ones were wistful, transporting you to a different time."

I swallowed the vivid memories of those silent moments when I could slip away on the breeze.

"The fourth was that tea you love," she laughed. "And when paired with lemon cookies...the smile glowed. That was my second favorite."

"Why?"

"Because it was the second most innocent. The second most effortless. Satisfied. When you didn't realize you were smiling, but it simply poured out of you."

"And what was your favorite?" She'd saved that for last, I was certain.

"The fifth reason for your unabashed smiles when life had turned dark was Tolek Vincenzo. When he was around, you didn't revert back to the girl you'd been, but you grew into a happier version of who you were born to become. And he was *always* there for you."

I bit my lip against the emotion welling inside of me, my heart ticking away painfully behind my ribs.

"It's late. Everyone went to bed hours ago. Good night, sister." Jezzie turned, striding down the corridor like she hadn't sent my world into shambles and lit a guiding light among the rubble.

Her footsteps echoed on the stone floor, and I was left staring at a moonlit sky, not a star in sight.

"We're going on an adventure, girl," I whispered to Sapphire as I swung myself into the saddle, her whinny an agreement. "We're going to get him back."

Everyone else might have left him on his own, but I wouldn't.

I pulled my hood up, both to fight off the wind as we tore out of the palace grounds and to hide my identity. Sapphire would still be recognizable, but we'd be gone before anyone could sound an alarm. And if they tried...well, I had my weapons on me. The Vincienzo dagger strapped to my thigh.

The night was quiet save for the pounding of Sapphire's hooves on the path and my blood roaring in my ears. I urged her forward with every ounce of energy I held, visions of Kakias's gift imprinted on my memory.

If I didn't get there soon...no, I wouldn't think that. I would get there in time.

With every stride, my heart pounded in a rhythm I hadn't realized had become its new tune.

I raced to rescue the cause of it.

CHAPTER TWENTY-NINE

MALAKAI

"*WHERE THE FUCK DID she go?*" I dug into the Bind, trying to find an inkling of Ophelia, but I couldn't feel a damn thing. Like when I'd first been imprisoned, it was there. But silent.

A frustrated growl rumbled in my throat.

"You know damn well where she went, Malakai, and you better knock off your territorial little games, because while my sister may tolerate them for fear of hurting you further, I have no such qualms." Jezebel's voice was laced with calm fury.

"What are you implying?"

"I'm not *implying* anything. I'm standing up for her when she won't." She crossed her arms, and I almost felt her next words before she said them. "I told her to go." She leveled me a stare that nearly had me withering. Where had the little girl who wistfully begged to train with us gone? Jezebel was fucking terrifying now.

But I could be worse. I pushed to my feet, voice a lethal dare for her to press me. "Why?"

Cypherion and Santorina sat quietly at the breakfast table.

"Because she needed to." And Jezebel sank a little admitting that. Her gaze turned pitying, and that rattled my chest. It was the same look she'd given me that night we ran into each other near the Spirit Volcano. This fight between us had been brewing even then.

Ophelia was gone, run off to rescue Tolek like the damn hero she was, blades sharpened and poised for revenge.

It was idiotic and irresponsible. She was practically handing herself over to Kakias, delivering her seat here to the hands of that bitch queen. The chill I'd gotten the first time I laid eyes on her shot down my spine, and my anger flared with it.

"She just left us?" I growled, rubbing my tongue over my teeth.

Why wasn't Jez angry? Her sister had abandoned her, too, yet her fury was reserved for me.

"She can't do this." Panic clouded my chest, weighing me back down into my seat. We were safe as long as we were here—away from threats. But look at what happened when one warrior left the mountains. Capture. "She can't leave everyone. We're relying on her."

"She didn't leave them alone." Jezebel's eyes swept over me, then Cypherion and Santorina.

"And what do you think of this?" I glared at them.

"The second the threat was read I knew there was no stopping this," Rina claimed. "I wish she'd consulted us, but—"

"We shut her down." Cyph ran a hand down the back of his neck. "Once we said no, she'd seen this as the only way. Am I frustrated she went alone? Yes. But are you really surprised?"

I wasn't. Because this was what Ophelia did. She risked everything for those she cared about, diving headfirst into the battle while we were still planning the war.

And it was Tolek.

But did she consider there was an entire clan relying on her? While she cared for Tol, she cared for the Mystiques, too. And if she were to get caught, she'd be abandoning them.

Jezebel's voice softened. "She's trusting us to take care of the Mystiques in her stead. To continue the plans she's begun."

Pressure mounted on my shoulders with their stares, questions hanging in the silence. And I knew what they wanted.

"She should be the one leading this war." I'd relinquished any claim I'd held. It would only be a farce.

"Don't you dare imply that she's not leading us." Jezebel's anger was a quiet storm again, all sympathy swallowed in her tumbling clouds. "Tolek may be only one warrior in this war, but we won't win it without him."

Did they think I wanted my best friend left to that woman? We may not be on good terms right now, but I didn't want him to endure even a second of what I had. Invisible blades dragged against my skin, goosebumps rising. I fought the urge to shrink into myself, blinked away the memory.

"This is war." I slammed my palms on the table. "It's bloody and conniving and brutal. We've all sacrificed and will continue to do so, but giving in to this threat is exactly what the queen wants, and we don't know why."

"Ophelia won't give in." Jezebel ground her teeth.

She was right; Ophelia was brilliant and not above scheming to get what she wanted. She wouldn't give herself over that easily—I hoped. Unless Tol...

"Why does the queen want her so badly?" I huffed. "She's obviously a threat as Revered, but what's Kakias so desperate for?"

It couldn't only be Mystique power. Not with her son now helping us and her plans with my father exposed. No, there had to be an angle we weren't seeing. That letter had outright demanded Ophelia.

"Knowing that wouldn't have changed Ophelia's decision," Rina comforted.

"It could have given her an edge," I snapped.

"It's done." Jezebel's voice was sharper than a blade. "She's gone now."

"She's right." Cyph pulled back the chair next to mine and clapped a hand on my shoulder. "Advantage or no, we can't keep going in circles over her choices."

"It's so much to risk for one warrior," I mumbled, bracing my elbows on the table and holding my head in my hands.

We were fucked. Truthfully, abysmally, fucked by the Spirits.

"You may think one person doesn't make a difference." Jezebel stepped toward me. I looked at her out of the corner of my eye. "But you're wrong. Because Ophelia is the best shot we have. And if something happens to Tolek, she will be irreparable."

"She can survive anything," I snapped, but even I heard the lack of conviction in my voice.

Jezebel assessed me. If I wasn't so upset, I'd marvel at the ability of the Alabath women to make men larger than them feel so small. "She survived everything you put her through," she spoke slowly, "barely. And in large part, it was thanks to him. If she loses him, it will destroy her. Worse than ever."

Worse than anything I'd done. Worse than Kakias's threats.

I raked my hands through my hair again, squeezing my eyes shut, and tried to release a bit of the hostility clouding my mind. If there was one thing I was certain of, it was that I didn't want to cause anyone any more pain.

"She won't come back from that," I mumbled, understanding.

Jezebel fell into a chair, gripping my arm. "I've always loved you as a brother, Malakai, and you were good to my sister for many years. That's why I'm telling you this now: Let go."

"You love me, huh?" I asked, ignoring the way my pulse raced at the last two words she'd said.

"Of course. And I was devastated when I thought you died. Furious when I found out you left without a proper goodbye." That fucking tore my heart up.

And that was it. The discomfort I couldn't grasp when we'd walked back from the Spirit Volcano. Jezebel was angry with me. I'd apologized to the others, but never to her.

"I'm sorry, Jez," I said.

"Just do better." Her lips twisted to the side, a small shrug. I nodded. "I made the choice to forgive. To move on. You and Ophelia have chosen to do that in your own ways, too. So, figure out what's happening in your head and don't let it hurt her anymore. Because she's trying to choose herself now."

Choices. Spirits, mine had fucked up countless lives, left me in a constant pool of guilt. I deserved it. This payment for the pain I'd caused to those I loved. If I hadn't signed the treaty, if I hadn't given in to my father and disappeared, maybe we could have fought our way out of the war. Maybe, with enough people rallying against him, we could have stopped his plans.

Without him shoving Mystiques into further turmoil for those two years after the treaty, would lives have been saved? Would we be less disjointed if I'd only spoken up?

I'd gotten us here. Though my intentions had been pure, the methods I took were twisted, blinding.

But maybe…I met Cyph's eye…maybe I could help fix it still.

"Tell me everything about where our troops are now." I pushed back from the table and left the room, three sets of boots following me. "Where did Ophelia leave off?"

Cyph's voice was stabilizing as I marched through the palace, asking Rina to send the council and delegates to the chamber. He told me of the placements and advantages of each legion we had gained from our new allies and how the diplomatic relationships were swaying. Jezebel filled in the gaps.

As I settled into a chair beside the Revered's in the council chamber, I dragged a hand over my face. Fuck, how had I allowed myself to become so complacent? Was Ophelia right that that's what we'd done with our relationship, too?

I knew nothing of the plans that had been laid. I'd spent every meeting blocking out the noise, doing my best to appear present without actually listening.

Now, I found myself in the seat I'd relinquished, trying to help until Ophelia returned. Spirits, she'd better return. She hadn't even officially been inducted as Revered, but I'd seen the reaction to her presence at Renaiss; we couldn't afford to lose her.

The council and delegates arrived, and I straightened, summoning the voice I'd learned as a teenager. One of a true leader. With their help, I wouldn't have to make threatening decisions, but I needed to try to be the symbol Ophelia had become. At least in this room.

"Why are the Soulguiders being placed on the southwest border of the mountains?" I asked, tracking Danya's hands across the map. "Does it not make sense to move them east with our troops?"

"We've placed legions at the weakest points of the range, assuming Kakias is after power," Danya explained.

"But we're spreading ourselves thin." There were clusters of Mystique and ally pins across territories, but I could tell by a quick scan that none matched the strength of the Engrossians.

Danya frowned. "Until we can decipher what the queen wants, we're doing our best."

I was unsatisfied with the risk, but I nodded. I didn't want to insult the Master of Weapons and Warfare.

"The closer the Soulguiders are to our land," Erista added, brushing curls out of her face with a ringed hand, "the stronger we are.

We aren't solely fueled by your mountains like you." Did that mean she felt weak, being here all this time?

My eyes flitted to Vale. "Same with the Starsearchers on the northern line?"

She chewed her lip. "That's a safe guess."

"But?" Cyph prodded.

"But we're actually strongest near a temple, if it's readings you're after. Anywhere that there's a connection to the Celestial Goddess so that we can channel her and the Angel Valyrie."

"And if we're after fighters?" Danya asked.

"We'll fight mercilessly wherever we're stationed." She lifted her eyes to Danya, then to Cyph, nothing but steel promise there.

A memory surfaced from one of those many meetings I'd barely attended. "Vale?" I started, waiting for her to meet my eyes. "Did you have any luck with the reading Ophelia requested?"

"Not yet." The Starsearcher's gaze shuttered, slipping back into her subdued act.

I'd watched her these past weeks, always alert and observant until her readings were mentioned. The avoidance drew a trickle up my spine.

Vale wanted to keep secrets, so I'd keep mine, as well. If there was one thing I'd learned since the war, it was that while everyone hoarded truths, they also had something that would expose them.

In my years as a prisoner, I became an expert at picking apart tells, deciphering the hidden meanings beneath their words even as I buried my own. Secrets and broken promises were a currency I now dealt in.

And that made the fact that Vale was lying much more intriguing.

Sitting back in my chair, I dropped my shoulders and sank into the wood. "Please, keep trying. We need anything we can get about Titus's reading or Kakias's plan." I scrubbed my hands over my face, barely catching her nod through the cracks between my fingers.

Internally, I grinned. *I'll figure you out, Starsearcher.*

CHAPTER THIRTY

OPHELIA

"WHAT ARE YOU STARING at?" I murmured to the chitara perched atop a flat rock.

Squatting down, I looked into its beady eyes. One of the many magical beasts that scampered among the forests and plains of Gallantia, it was a docile critter—at least today. Legends said chitaras once held powerful abilities. Shifting and venomous bites that only existed in stories now.

It tilted its head from one side to the other, tiny hands fiddling with a blackberry, bushy tail swishing and curling up behind it.

Though it didn't appear harmful, its gaze had been locked on me for minutes, from the second I had stopped here for a brief rest. I tried to follow its line of sight but was afraid to look away for too long. Nothing seemed out of place on my leathers, though they were streaked with dirt after two days of travel.

I lifted my hand. It didn't move.

I touched my necklace.

Its head tilted again.

"This, then?" I mused.

It released a small squeak, eyes flitting to my face. Its stare was communicative, but what it was trying to tell me, I couldn't parse out.

My voice dropped to barely a whisper, smooth and welcoming. "You can show me." I stretched a hand out, fingertips an inch from its tiny paw.

But the chitara only released another small squeak, twitched its nose in what seemed ominously like a warning, and scurried away through the piles of dead leaves toward the mountains. Sapphire whinnied as it fled, a trickle of discomfort dancing down my spine.

Sighing, I shook it off. Wild Gallantian creatures were odd, the mythical ones more so.

Still, if I hadn't already believed there was something mystical about the heated emblem on my necklace, I would have now.

Leaves crunched beneath my boots as I walked back to Sapphire, coating the forest floor even during the height of summer—odd. My warrior horse had ridden relentlessly through the mountains. We stopped only for quick food and water and for me to relieve myself, but each time I tried to sleep, my mind raced. Adrenaline forced me up quickly.

As I crouched beside the river, cupping water to rinse my face and neck, my eyelids were heavy, but my body buzzed with desperation to continue.

In my reflection, there was hardly any of the girl I used to be. Carefree, young, and unafraid.

Grief, rage, and heartbreak replaced her.

My soul worn, it shone through the harsh set of my lips and sharp stare.

Sighing a quick goodbye to that innocent girl, I sat back on the dirt, counting the moonlit spots in the branches crossing above my head and imagined what was happening in Damenal right now. Malakai…he was likely furious.

But he and I were done.

We had to be—there was no piece of me that could love him in the way I once had.

In leaving, in choosing to go after my best friend, the person I needed more than anyone, I wasn't choosing between two men.

I was choosing myself.

I breathed in the crisp night air, allowed the thought to settle within me. Acceptance spread along my bones like roots in the packed earth. The satisfaction, the personal debt I owed myself after being so torn for years, was soothing.

The choice to leave took back a piece of the person I'd lost. Built her back up. While I may miss the girl I used to be before my world was burned down, the woman who emerged from the ashes was a force ready to forge her broken shards back together, retake ownership of her life, and return stronger than before.

Each step away from Damenal lifted pressure from my shoulders. Like I'd been held beneath water, my air supply running out, and now life was slowly refilling my lungs. Maybe it was the distance from so many expectant eyes, maybe it was the proximity to my target, maybe it was being beneath the stars with only my horse for company, but if healing was a feeling, I think this lightness in my chest was a part of it.

With that strengthening my resolve, I walked to Sapphire and pulled my cloak from my bag, donning it. Though we were still in the Soulguider desert, the farther we got toward the Mindshaper Territory, the colder the wind turned.

"What do you say, girl?" I muttered to Sapphire. "Got a bit more left in you?"

I was grateful when she immediately turned, as if telling me to hurry up and get on. I wasn't ready to stop yet. Not until exhaustion dragged at our bones. Too much land still sat between me and Tol.

But as Sapphire carried me closer, I contemplated how I might find him. There was no guarantee he'd even made it into Mindshaper Territory, let alone the capital he aimed for. I knew the path he'd planned to take, though, and I followed it south, trusting the Spirits would guide me.

The constellations popped to life above us, and I smiled at them. At the deep spaces between the stars that made my darkest parts feel welcome.

Unfortunately, they did not smile back.

Titus saw darkness in my celestial future. The promise of destruction burned through me, a predator I couldn't fight—didn't know—lying in wait to wrap its claws around my life.

Oh Damien, I thought, for once wishing he would appear to answer my questions, *what waits for me?* He hadn't visited since his prophecy, and a piece of me wondered what kept him away.

Seeking out the most familiar constellation, the Mystique Sword, I inwardly cursed the Angel, but the moon's glow pulsed, and my heart lurched. I stopped myself from screaming my anger at the Angels.

There was too much at stake right now; I needed their guidance.

"Please, Damien," I whispered. Sapphire's ears twitched at my voice. "Please, if you have any kindness in that fucking eternal soul of yours…please. Let him be okay." A hollowness echoed through my chest. I bit my lips to keep them from trembling, clenched my hands around the reins. "I…I need him."

I didn't know if anyone heard the confession, but I repeated it under my breath, my mantra cast into the ethereal night, begging the clouds to carry it away.

"I need him. I need him. I won't survive without him."

I whispered it again and again as Sapphire marched across the moonlit dirt, hoping any Spirit or Angel listening might send him a sign that I was coming.

We hadn't been traveling for long when a wild roar cut through the still night.

Sapphire kicked into a gallop, not waiting for my instruction.

I swiveled atop her, looking over my shoulder to see a trio of mountain cats descending the rocky foothills above.

With long legs and lithe bodies, they leaped through the air and landed in pursuit of us. Bright green eyes, haunting and glowing, stood stark against dark brown coats.

Nemaxese, I realized. Large felines—larger than me if they stood on their hind legs—that prowled the mountain range in the dead of night, hunting.

A second high, scratchy growl echoed from the one in front, his scraggly mane shaking.

Jaw dripping.

Dread pooled within me.

"Come on, girl," I encouraged Sapphire, turning back around. There was nothing but empty land ahead of us, no towns in sight. I supposed that was good. No one else was in danger.

My heart pounded in time with Sapphire's hooves, the plain blurring around me. I peered over my shoulder again. They were close enough now that I could see the rabid hunger in their eyes.

"*Spirits*," I cursed under my breath. Something was wrong with them. Nemaxese weren't a threat to warriors; we weren't their natural prey. I'd heard of some even voluntarily settling in warrior homes, becoming domesticated.

Not these ones—these were tainted. It was in their unblinking stare and frothing mouths. In their relentless pursuit, homed in on us.

The journey to the Undertaking flashed behind my eyes in snips of red-coated terror.

The creature that attacked us in the forest, nearly taking my sister's life.

The animals that rifled through our food supply.

All wild. All unnatural. All hungry for more than their rightful prey.

Sapphire cleared a low hill, and a stretch of cypher trees came into sight. If we could make it there, we may be able to lose them among the sweeping branches. I didn't want to hurt them. Whatever had happened to them, these creatures were innocent. They were—

Compromised, I corrected myself as something flashed in my peripheral.

A sharp pain shot through my shoulder as the world flipped, sky and earth melting together.

I rolled across the dirt, the largest nemaxese bounding after me. Getting my arms beneath me, I pushed upright. I focused despite the spinning earth.

I pulled Starfire from my hip, but she'd be useless against one of these creatures if I wasn't smart. Jaw or eye—those were the only two places a blade could pierce a nemaxese, their skin impenetrable.

Long teeth flashed. I braced my stance.

Spirits, I didn't want to hurt an animal. I had no problem slicing a man's head from his body if attacked, but this felt wrong. Like I was breaking a sacred law. I almost dropped my sword. But as it circled me, the other two flanking it, no soul looked back....there was no hint of life left.

Their hearts may beat, blood may spill, but they were puppets to the rot within them.

I adjusted my sweaty grip on Starfire and gritted my teeth. My Angelborn necklace warmed, but I ignored it.

Instead, I watched that wide vibrant stare and shoved down any remorse crawling its way up my throat.

"I'm sorry," I whispered, chest heaving. I didn't know if it was to the creature itself or the Angels I may be upsetting. Maybe it was to the God of Mythical Beings for harming his ward, or to myself for the guilt I'd suffer.

The cat snapped its dripping jaw. It bent its legs, preparing to pounce.

I raised my sword higher, aiming for that exposed maw.

But then, a shadow reared up above me.

Two hooves planted firmly on the cat's side and threw it to the ground, unmoving. I blinked as the dust settled.

My grip tightened on my sword again as the second nemaxese leaped after its leader. But Sapphire reared up again, clouds fanning out on either side of Sapphire's body like a pair of luminous, swirling wings. She hit the second nemaxese square in the skull, then the third in the ribs. Each fell into a heap on rock-strewn dirt.

Almost laughing at the shock flooding my system, I jumped back into the saddle, and Sapphire galloped away, releasing a triumphant whinny into the night that echoed up to the stars.

As the adrenaline faded, though, anger slid into its place, a hot knife slipping into a waiting sheath.

Because there was something very wrong among the wild of Gallantia, and while most of the troubles among the warriors could be traced back to our former Revered and his wicked queen, I doubted even Lucidius and Kakias could be responsible for this corruption.

Sapphire whinnied a second time, and I shouted out with her.

The fates had been unfair to us all, and I poured my anger into that endless night.

For those who had suffered from the war, for those who were hurting now from the deep-rooted corruption, for every innocent soul being forced into a battle they never asked for, I roared my frustrations to the stars.

CHAPTER THIRTY-ONE

MALAKAI

I BIT BACK ON a roar that wanted to burst through my lips as I swiped my sword across my sparring partner's and sent his rattling to the ground.

"Good, Malakai!" Cypherion barked from the sidelines. His eyes had been burrowing into my back the whole time, tracking every move. With more warriors attempting their Undertakings, he'd grown more serious about training than ever. And with the additional sleeping tonic I'd gotten from Rina's stores, I was more rested. Working harder despite the fact that I fucking hated training now.

I nodded at him, bending to retrieve my opponent's weapon.

"Thanks," he said, smiling despite the fact that I'd beaten him.

I didn't know him well, but I knew his name was Gerad, originally from Turren, and he'd been hovering around the palace lately. Alvaron had recruited him as a member of his trainee program. He'd appeared sharp when I'd heard him conversing with the Master of Coin, quick and resourceful.

His sparring skills were no different. We were even in the count for the day. Two wins each. One match left.

"Ready?" I asked.

He brushed his dirty blonde hair back from his face and nodded, his eyes already intent on my stance. I gripped my sword, prepared to wait for his strike first. The weapon was foreign between my hands. It wasn't a sword I'd trained with all my life; I had no attachment to the thing at all.

There were a number of exquisite options in the vaults beneath the palace, adorned with precious gems and crafted of rare metals, forged directly from the fire of the volcano, but each was tainted by my father's hand. Being in this palace was hard enough, living where he lived, working where he worked…it ripped apart pieces of my soul each day. Using the weaponry he had deemed his most cherished was more than I could bear.

I'd stuck with the armory's supply of practice weapons, but none were right. Nothing fit in my hand the way a personal blade would.

If I could find a weapon of my own, maybe I'd be more eager for training. Not one I shared with others, not a symbol of my previous life.

But one forged for the present me—the one who was not meant to be the Revered. The man who had no destined future ahead of him.

Still, when Gerad lunged, I tried to beat his blow.

But the sun shone above, bouncing off his blade. It dragged me back to the Engrossian raid in the Southern Pass. The moon had looked down on us in the same way, casting their scarred skin in stark relief.

Warrior Prince, they'd called me. *We should have killed you.*

All I heard were chains. Scraping against rock. Snapping closed around my wrists. Rattling through my head as I was slammed back into the wall. Sharp and bruising. My flesh torn open, jagged edges pressing into scarred skin. The agony it had been—it was all I knew.

I stood frozen in the training yard, but I was really back in that place.

Isolated, alone, forgotten.

Knives dragging along my skin. Blood beading vicious and unremorseful. The scratch of blades being sharpened.

All of it taunting me as their threats did. Drowning me.

My sword nearly fell from my hands.

As much of a coward as his father.

No. I may have said it out loud; I couldn't be sure.

A burst of energy shot through me, and I pushed Gerad back.

I won't be a coward, I swore, surging forward. *I will not be my father.*

Another strike.

I'm stronger than him.

Another.

I—

A blade clattered to the floor, snapping me back to the present. I blinked, realizing I stood panting over the Turrenian warrior, his freckled skin darker than the pale Engrossian tone. His light brown eyes kinder than their vengeful glares.

"Take a break." Cyph patted Gerad on the back, coming to my side. He dropped his voice. "Are you okay?"

"Fine," I grumbled, stomping toward the stairs that led back to the palace. But I didn't want to be there either. At the last minute, I turned and stormed across the arena, out into the gardens. Cyph followed, instructing the others to continue their training circuits.

Once I was far enough away that I couldn't hear the clashing weapons, I stopped. Rows of vibrant flowers lined the earth, herbs and vegetables stretching out across the dirt. So much life.

"Gerad is a strong fighter," Cyph said, coming up behind me.

"Clearly," I mumbled.

"He's in the next group to complete the Undertaking. They'll be done before Daminius."

I cast a narrowed glance over my shoulder. "Good for them."

"They'll be in the ranks when the troops march out."

Because war was coming. We still didn't know when or how, but Kakias's army was marching through neutral land in Bodymelder Territory, skirting the Seawatchers' borders and heading toward Mystique land.

We would meet them.

Every day more warriors dove into the Spirit Volcano, and most returned. Those who were attempting the Undertaking after the last war were the most committed, the warriors who had been devastated they'd missed their chance.

A few hadn't made it, and Cyph shouldered those losses personally, but his determination was evident in the tenacity of his training regimen.

Our numbers were creeping up. We'd have over a thousand new recruits to pair with the four thousand across the territory who'd returned from the last war. It was nothing compared to the twenty thousand we'd been told Kakias was marching east, but if we were fierce enough fighters with strategic enough leaders, we could win. Especially if we could take out their queen. And with the small legions of the Soulguiders and Starsearchers plus a host of Seawatchers—it was something.

But only ascended warriors were allowed in our army.

And I would not be completing the Undertaking, despite Cypherion's gentle prodding. I may have been putting on a front in council meetings since Ophelia left, dragging up the dignified future Revered I was raised to be, but I didn't know how long I could keep it up. Every day was a battle, and I was being battered.

Still, I'd sworn to try.

"Warriors need weapons," I said without looking at Cyph.

"We have weapons."

"Their own weapons," I muttered. I was worn, my bones leaden. The scarring on my mind and body from my time imprisoned was pulling, tearing me apart. No part of me was intent on completing the ritual I'd once lived for…but a weapon…

That I could handle.

Cyph gently rested a hand on my shoulder. "We can take care of that."

"Have you had any luck with the readings?" I asked Vale as we strolled through the Ascended Quarter with Cyph, passing the tattoo parlor and leatherworkers.

"Not yet." She swallowed, lashes fluttering. "I'm trying, though. I know I'm getting closer, but the fates seem reluctant to share what I need. I think I'll have the answer soon." The words came out in a rush, as if reassuring us.

I avoided looking at Cyph to gauge his reaction and ignored a woman who almost walked straight into me as she exited a gem shop, keeping my gaze intent on the Starsearcher. "I appreciate you trying. We need the information." I clenched my hands at my side. "Ophelia needs it."

Spirits, my stomach churned to mention her, to think about how she'd raced off into the night and left us here.

To remember the fact that she wasn't mine to protect anymore, and I had to let her go.

Jezebel had been right—I'd done enough damage there. The best way I could make up for it was to stop trying and let time heal us both.

"I'm doing everything I can," Vale muttered, her chin ducked. The clang of a hammer against steel rang out, and she lifted her face, light returning to her eyes.

The blacksmith's shop was overwhelmed with work, every shelf and table covered with a menagerie of swords, spears, knives, and armor.

"What can I do for you?" A broad man stepped up to us, his short gray beard tinged black from the forge, small eyes looking over our trio. "Oh," he sighed upon recognizing me. "Hello, Malakai." There was no malice in his voice, but the tinge of disinterest stung.

I cleared my throat, biting my tongue. I was so fucking tired of the reactions to my reappearance into the world, but I supposed it was my own naivety for expecting otherwise.

"Malakai needs a weapon," Cyph interjected.

The blacksmith nodded. "Right, we have plenty." He wiped his hands on his apron and waved an arm around the shop. "All being prepared to be sent off with our army. Take your pick."

He turned to leave, but Cyph grabbed his wrist. "He needs a weapon made specially for him. Your best work. And we need it done quickly." The command in his voice had even me straightening my spine.

"That'll be a rushed order. Expensive." The blacksmith narrowed his eyes, assessing Cyph.

"That's fine." Cyph shifted his stance so the bag of coins at his hip jingled.

The blacksmith looked at the pouch then back at Cyph, ignoring my presence entirely. "Take a look around, tell me what you like, then we'll talk price." He returned to his station, picking up his hammer.

"Impressive," Vale muttered to Cyph, breezing past him. His eyes followed her as she rounded the corner.

"I hadn't realized you were such a strong negotiator," I joked, walking between the aisles of swords, all different sizes with various pommel decor and cuts. When Cypherion looked back at me and shrugged, his cheeks were flushed. I'd bet the most expensive weapon in my father's vault it had nothing to do with the heat in the shop.

Daggers lined the shelves, all exquisitely made. Had any been forged in the fire of the volcano? The tradition was meant to bring a warrior luck. According to legend, my spear—Ophelia's spear—had been made that way. I swallowed the lump that formed in my throat and picked up a knife, testing it.

Across Gallantia, each clan had their own superstitions when it came to forging. Not all Mystique weapons were given the volcanic honor, but if they were, it was considered a gift of the Spirits. It was said that blades forged of rare minerals and coated with a source of magic were the strongest of all, capable of severing the richest life forces.

I hoped to the Spirits that I would never find myself at the end of one of those sacred blades.

"Is there a certain kind of weapon you want?" Cypherion asked. He swung a sword, clearly trying not to push me too far.

Swords, spears, daggers…they all felt wrong in my hands now after years away, like I didn't belong with them.

"I want something new." I dragged a pair of twin knives off the shelf, but the balance didn't feel quite right.

"You could try the needles of the Bodymelders," Cyph suggested.

I considered, picturing the long, thin rapiers—nicknamed for their needlelike appearance—Esmond had shown us. He claimed that a well-trained Bodymelder knew exactly where to insert one between the muscles to do the most damage with a singular, nearly indiscernible prick. They were impressive. Subtle.

That wasn't my style.

"Maybe a scythe or hooked sword like the Soulguiders," Vale offered, popping up at my shoulder. She moved quietly, but her voice rang through the space like a bell. The Soulguider weapons were interesting, their blades nearly a half circle and deadly in multiple ways. "I've always liked those."

"Cyph uses a scythe," I commented.

She whirled toward him, and I grinned at him over her head. "I've noticed."

"Family heirloom" was all he said, throwing a broken dagger

handle at me when she turned away. "What's your weapon of choice?"

"I wasn't taught to fight until I came to Damenal." She may claim to have never held a blade before, but the muscle control and instincts she demonstrated said otherwise. "Most Starsearchers are trained with an extensive supply of weapons, though. Many tend toward three-pointed blades." She spoke as if in a dream, voice wandering as she disappeared down the aisle.

"I've never seen those used," I commented, following her.

"They're small and quick, easy to launch at an opponent." She picked up a small knife, no larger than her hand. "Like this, but with three blades instead of one. But not useful if you don't have exceptional aim."

"Malakai could use some work on his aim," Cyph taunted.

"Fuck off." I shoved his shoulder.

I was intrigued by the weapon, though, and made a note to see if I could find any to test.

For today, I settled on a sword. One with a moderate blade and simple detailing, crafted especially for me. No wings, no mountains, no aquamarines. Nothing like my old weapons.

The blacksmith didn't say a word of complaint when we handed him the first half of the overpriced fee and told him we'd be back in three days.

"I'll see you both back in the palace for dinner," Vale said when we stepped onto the crowded street. I'd forgotten how many residents were in Damenal now. "I have some errands to run." She didn't wait for a response as she bounded down the road toward the Sacred Quarter, her light brown curls catching the sun.

When her long skirt disappeared around a turn, I muttered to Cyph distastefully, "She's secretive."

"I can't figure her out," he agreed. But from the low tone of his voice, I guessed we had different reasons for wanting to.

CHAPTER THIRTY-TWO

MALAKAI

THERE WAS A KNOCK on my door as I was stepping out of the bath.

"Just a minute," I called, stretching my arms above my head and groaning at the burn of my muscles before reaching for a towel.

The past few days had been exhausting, my body aching from the extra work I'd been putting in to train the weapons and tactics of minor clans as well as adjust to my new sword. It was heavier than I was used to, but solid. And with Esmond and Erista helping me with needles and scythes, muscles I'd trained my entire life were learning how to work in different ways.

Even after an hour soaking in the hot water, massaging with whatever relaxing oil Rina had supplied, I moved slowly around the bathroom.

I was beaten down beyond my muscles, though. To my bones, my soul. The added pressure of the war council, of everyone looking to me, weighed heavily on my shoulders. But as much as I hated to admit it, Ophelia leaving was the space I needed. Participating in these meetings, I think I was beginning to understand the stress she'd been under.

You're not who they need, the ghosts inside my head echoed. *Warrior Prince, this is your fault.*

Those voices haunted me. I wasn't sure if it was my own inner demons, the boy who had died at the hands of those Engrossian guards, or something else speaking to me, but the guilt rocked my bones. I gripped the counter at the shock of it.

Was I really going to be able to reverse all of that pain by attending meetings? By playing a role? Was I going to make any difference on a battlefield?

Likely not. I wasn't enough—nothing I was doing could be enough.

Whoever was at the door pounded again, forcing me out of my spiral.

"I'm coming!" I yelled, stomping toward the door, my voice gravel in my throat. I locked the guilt and self-pity into my heart once again. Promised myself I wouldn't let it out this time.

A third knock, and I realized it wasn't from the entrance to my suite; it was directly on my bedchamber door. Whoever felt they could let themselves into my personal rooms was going to be in trouble.

My hair dripped water down my torso, leaving a trail across the wood floor of my new room. Smaller than the one I'd shared with Ophelia, with a less expansive set of rooms, it was set in one of the towers of the palace. The curved walls, large windows, and dark colors were comforting.

Wrenching the door from its frame, I opened my mouth to yell—and I froze.

"Lyria?" I sputtered.

"Well, that certainly is quite a welcome." She lifted a brow, gaze trailing over my body. "Two years locked away doesn't seem to have undone all the good things about you." She crossed her arms and leaned against the door frame.

"What—I didn't know you were coming." I gripped the towel at my waist, making sure it stayed in place.

"You wrote to me," she said, brow furrowed.

"You didn't respond."

"Luckily for you I was already on my way here. And once I got your message—" Her lips pulled into a tight line, all semblance of humor leaving. "I needed to get here as soon as possible."

I nodded, not wanting to crack open the grief she poorly hid.

"Have you heard anything?" she asked.

"No." Water droplets flew as I shook my head. "Ophelia went after him almost a week ago and that's all we know."

"She'll find him." It sounded like assurance for herself more than me, but I nodded in agreement. "It's good to see you, Malakai."

Then, Lyria Vincienzo swept forward and crushed me to her, resting her head against my shoulder. One hand on my towel, I held her as tightly as I could, instilling as much confidence as possible into that embrace. Lyria was as much a fighter as her brother. We'd all watched her complete the Undertaking a few years before the war. I still remembered the day she marched off with our troops—eyes bright and dark hair braided back. Clad in metal and leather, she'd seemed hopeful about the outcome of the war.

Until this moment, that was the last I'd seen of her. I tried not to think about the horrors she must have faced in the years since, only holding her tighter with a silent promise that we'd find Tolek.

Lifting my head, I looked over Lyria's shoulder and realized she wasn't alone.

Mystlight silhouetted a woman. When she took a step forward, I was certain she wasn't from Palerman. Those large blue eyes, high cheekbones, and hair so blonde it was almost white were memorable.

Full lips lifted into a smile that looked like she had something to hide, and goosebumps rose along my skin. Lyria composed herself, turning to see what had caught my attention.

"Oh, Malakai, this is my closest friend, Mila. We were traveling together when I received your note." They'd certainly been traveling, both women baring golden tans from the summer sun.

Mila came closer, her steps soundless—a warrior, then, to be that quiet. And her leathers, brown and threaded with hints of light blue—Mystique.

"Pleasure to meet you." Her voice was low but welcoming, the kind that makes you want to lean in to listen closer. A pair of wide gold wrist cuffs caught the light falling through my doorway as she lifted her hand, carved ivy detail glinting, and her eyes fell down my body.

I was suddenly very aware of the fact that I was naked and pulled my towel tighter.

"You, too." I slid my hand into hers, relishing how soft her skin was. Everything about her looked like a warrior. The sharp, assessing stare, the controlled movements, and pristine leathers that hugged her curves and thighs—but no calluses. Interesting.

"If you'd like to come in, I can call for tea. Or something stronger."

I stepped aside to leave room for Lyria and Mila, but the former said, "It's been a long journey and we're renting a property in the city. We should return to it, but we'll come back in the morning to be put to work." She spoke as if I was the one that would be assigning their tasks. With a jolt, I remembered I was. Inadequacy rattled the cage in my chest once again.

"You've already secured housing? How did you—" I paused, as Lyria held out a letter signed in a hand I recognized. "Danya. You're who she invited as her apprentice?"

I wasn't sure why I was surprised. Tales of Lyria's successes had reached Palerman during the war, as she made a name for herself despite her age.

Still, it almost felt surreal for Tolek's sister to be here, on our council. Like not much had changed in the last few years after all.

"She said she only wants the best." Lyria smirked at Mila, smug satisfaction passing between them. "It appears we'll all be spending more time together. Good night, Malakai."

"Good night," I said, nodding, though the shock lingered.

They walked away, and I watched them go, rubbing my chest to alleviate the unusual warmth that had settled there.

CHAPTER THIRTY-THREE

OPHELIA

"IT'S THE KINDA PLACE where people ain't gonna ask ya questions," the young waiter said, laying my bowl and glass of cheap rum in front of me.

"Hm?" I hummed, barely registering his words. My eyelids were drooping, the people in the room blurring. I was focusing all of my remaining energy on guarding my surroundings. I had learned my lesson after not stopping for proper sleep for nearly a week, but even the few hours I had managed to steal were fitful.

The barkeep gestured to his head. "Ya don't hafta hide yer face. No one cares here."

"If that's truly the case," I replied, pulling my hood down further to shadow my trademark eyes, "no one will ask why I'm choosing to remain hidden."

The boy flushed, and I almost felt bad. But there was a hot bowl of stew in front of me that smelled surprisingly tantalizing given the run-down state of the inn I'd found—*Wayward*, the sign on the door proclaimed. I'd passed others on the way, nicer establishments with finer dining and more comfortable beds, but this one had an air of privacy.

I was getting closer to the Mindshapers' capital. Once I arrived...I wasn't sure what I'd do. I tried not to fret over it as I dug into the meal, slow sips of rum washing away my nerves.

Forcing myself awake until I could disappear into my ramshackle room on the second floor, I cataloged the dining room's occupants. Wayward was truly an inn fit for those who *didn't* fit. Though we were on the border of Soulguider and Mindshaper Territories, warriors of every clan tucked into tables, the combination of different garb blending until you could barely differentiate between them.

With soft yellow mystlights gathered in the corners and laughter bursting through the steady hum of conversation, Wayward was cozy; the unguarded interactions of the menagerie lining the stocked bar were comforting.

A large man came clomping down the staircase, the banisters shivering with each step, and a slight woman with a low-cut dress followed. They claimed a table beside me, their bedraggled state not observed—or at least, not audibly commented on—by any patrons.

I scraped the bottom of the bowl, getting every last bit of hearty broth and potatoes, then pushed it across the table, standing.

But right as I did so, someone moved to the front of the room, and all eyes turned. A tall, curvy woman took the stage, her hip-length dark hair and her long brown dress seeming to flow with every breath.

"Good evening, children." Her voice enveloped the crowd like a wave rolling across a smooth shore. "I'm Aimee, a Storyteller."

My jaw nearly dropped open, and I sank back into my seat. Because in this obscure Wayward Inn, I'd happened upon a woman of an infamous cult. Claiming no clan, Storytellers were rare; centuries ago, they'd traveled the continent sharing lore that wasn't guarded in the temples. Telling tales known only on their lips and those of their ancestors.

Now, their numbers dwindled, their stories scattering.

"Gather, if you wish. Tonight, we have a legend that dates back to the Angels."

The hair on my arms rose beneath my cloak, and I thought of the Angel who had eluded me recently.

"Before warriors inhabited the earth, when magic was not segmented and we communed with our great friends across the seas, there were seven altruistic beings who roamed Gallantia. It was only them, the wild beasts—many of which are lost to us now—humans, and the magic cascading through the land. They were one people, the seven of them. Immortals, but more person than myth."

The picture unfolded in my mind as she spoke—blissful and uninhibited.

"Until Ambrisk's magic started eating away at them. After centuries owning this land, the undeniable ether within the earth acknowledged them. It spread up in tendrils as they slept, at first sprinkling itself upon them in dribbles so small, they were practically nonexistent, born of mist." Her voice lowered, a hush creeping across the room like those fine strands of magic. "But over time, it became *more*. The tendrils penetrated flesh, rooted themselves into their very beings, molded with their blood and bones. Until they transformed. The warriors were born."

A low gasp spread through the crowd. It was a rendition of a story many had heard, but it was laced with a truth only a Storyteller could confirm.

"It took decades," she continued, "for the seven to realize their newfound strength was manifesting in transitional ways between them. Of the seven, five received unique designations from their power. Tendencies, areas they fell toward, gifts they excelled at. And the other two…" Aimee's tone darkened. The mystlights dimmed. "They held undeniable strength. Something unheard of, something *unfelt* crawled out of the earth and wound its way around those two beings. It lifted them up. Made them exceedingly strong—threatening."

She paused, and her eyes landed on me, infinite knowledge shining through. I sank back against the bench, ignoring the spike of both of my pulses.

"In time, the variations in power became points of tension. Arguments rose—strong enough to shake the foundations of the continent itself. The seven divided the land, each staking a different claim on territory." Every noise in the room evaporated, some warriors shifting away from those of different clans instinctually. "But they were foolish. For in their isolation, they eroded. Their minds could not handle being so alone, having no other living being of their nature. They started talking to the magic, all seven of them treating their individual strengths as if they were alive. And while that nurtured those powers…it also gave the ether control. Magic took solid form—unnatural and raw. They were gifted mates to procreate with, and descendant warriors were born unto the earth, a reward for pleasing the power.

"But the magic around the seven prime became too much. Slowly, it leaked from their bodies, and it is this that was left behind when they ascended as Angels ten thousand years ago. For while they may have been warped by magic, the ascension process was clarifying. They entered into their eternal existence with clear eyes, able to view all of their faults and be plagued by them for eternity. With an unbreakable vow to the warriors that came after them.

"They were our first leaders, and they are now our Guardians, watching over us, guiding us. We act in their name, carry on the mission the magic gave them, and trust they will keep us from the impurities of the power that corrupted them."

I snapped back to the present, the noise within the room swelling again.

Slumping back against the bench, I pulled my glass toward me, eyeing the thin sip of rum lining the bottom. I tipped it back as the Storyteller's words flooded my mind. There had been scores of legends passed down about the ascension of the Angels, who they were before, where they had come from.

But Aimee's dripped with antiquity, words bolstered by unseen Spirits. A layer of validation wrapped around them.

The solidifying of magic within the Angels stood out to me, but I wasn't sure why. It was a tale I had yet to come across, the implication nagging at my brain. The notion that they left something behind when they turned from warrior to Angel…well, my pulse pounded with strands of that legend.

Angelblood.

But magic taking solid form? I'd never heard of such a thing.

Aimee's rendition of the Angels' lives stirred a dim sadness within me, though. It sounded…lonely. Did Damien feel isolated in his desolate existence?

"How did the Angels ascend?" asked a small woman wrapped in a draping blue cloak and silver jewelry, seated in the front of the room. A hush returned to the crowd.

"Ah, my star-searching child, it is through the power of that who surrounds us. The great creator of it all…"

I scoffed, tuning her out. There was no being above the Angels. The six gods and goddesses were their equals, and that was it. Thirteen sacred beings.

It seemed the Storyteller did not always have reliable information.

"You don't believe her either?" The man at the table next to me asked, lifting one dark, neatly trimmed brow.

"I enjoy the stories." I pulled my hood tighter around my face. "But sometimes that's all they are."

"I think she is full of tainted Spirits." The woman with him spoke in a lilting accent, her words lifting slightly at the ends. I couldn't tell which clan they belonged to. "But it certainly makes for a fun evening."

"I beg to differ." That voice. I knew that voice.

Though the stranger who had spoken kept his hood tightly drawn around his face as he pulled back a chair to join my table, I'd recognize the gruff tone anywhere—had heard it in my nightmares.

His hulking frame and commanding presence. The dagger at his hip.

He'd changed his clothes since I last saw him, the current leather pants and blue linen shirt blending in much better, but I didn't need to see the elongated canines or pointed ears shadowed beneath his cloak to remember the fae male that had held a knife to Santorina's throat—Lancaster.

"What are you doing here?" I ground out, hands already reaching toward my weapon.

But his brows lifted, eyes flitting about the room, challenging me to fight him here. Where so many would see. Where so many would realize who I was.

Once my hand fell back to the table, he said, "Looking for you," and fell into a seat beside me.

Me? Why me?

But I couldn't ask now—not with so many listening.

"Well, it is a pleasure to see you," I said with saccharine sweetness.

"Is it?" Lancaster smirked. Slipping a hand around my glass, he lifted it to his lips. Where it had been empty before, he now tossed back two fingers of liquor. The subtlety of the magic went unnoticed with the others, but I tucked away that little skill of his.

"You believe in this *great creator*, then?" the woman asked Lancaster, trying to peek beneath his hood.

He pulled it tighter. "I've studied many different denominations in my long lifetime. Which I succumb to is beyond the point. I believe it is foolish to rule any out."

Briefly, I wondered how fae texts conveyed the histories. Warped, I was certain, but curiosity still bloomed within me. And Lancaster couldn't lie, which made his theories on power even more intriguing.

The woman brushed her long brown curls behind her shoulder and leaned forward, her low-cut green dress shifting with the movement, but before she could respond, her partner interrupted, "It's a load of shit." His voice was less kind, but his attention dropped to the woman's breasts pressed against his arm.

I stifled a laugh, and it appeared Lancaster did, too. Some people were so easily distracted.

The man propped his arm on the back of his partner's chair, his sleeve rolling up to expose—

A silver cuff hung around his wrist, the chain connected to it dangling, broken. Lancaster stiffened.

Though he couldn't see my face, the man raised his brows as if he knew he'd caught my attention. "See something you like?"

"Certainly interested in whatever story deems that necessary," I intoned, waving a hand at his wrist.

"It's from my latest stint as a prisoner."

"Your latest?" I asked.

A smug smile lifted his weathered cheeks. "There's been a few."

"You can't take it off?"

"I could...but then women such as yourself wouldn't ask." His eyes were curious as they rested on my hood, like his attention alone could convince me to pull it back.

"I wouldn't get on her bad side," Lancaster scoffed, leaning back in his chair. I couldn't decide if that made me like him more or not. Though I'd agreed to a tentative peace with the faerie the last time I'd seen him, I would never forget his original intentions for Santorina.

"I'm Lessel, by the way. This is Mora." The former prisoner ignored Lancaster's advice.

"Pleasure," I deadpanned.

"What's your story?" Mora narrowed her eyes at me when I didn't offer my name.

"What's yours?" I asked. Out of the corner of my eye, I caught Lancaster's amused exhale. He waved a hand above his glass, and it refilled once again. *A handy trick.*

A smile cut between her high cheekbones, softening her features. "I ran away from a husband who gave me one too many bruises." My stomach lurched. Lancaster's fingers curled around the glass, and I thought a low growl escaped him. "Now I do what I must to get by." Which apparently included spending evenings with men like Lessel.

Part of me wanted to offer her money, to give her whatever she needed, but I clenched my hands within my cloak and pictured Tolek. I had to keep a low profile, and handing out money was certainly not the way to do that. It was bad enough I had a possibly untrustworthy fae to deal with now.

"Your turn," Mora said, pushing her bottle of rum across the table to me.

I ignored it. "I'm looking for someone."

"Descriptive."

Lessel narrowed his eyes at me. "You're awful cagey, the two of you." He shot a glance at Lancaster, face still shadowed beneath his hood. "You don't have anything to do with that strange, black-tented camp, do ya?" His words slurred slightly at the end. Mora refilled his glass again, winking at me.

"What camp?" Lancaster perked up.

"The one in the woods just north of the capitol. With the active guard. More weapons than I've seen since the war." I sat straighter, too. "They're silent. Didn't see 'em until we stumbled right into their line of defense. They sent us away right quick, they did."

"What clan were they?" I rushed, leaning forward. Lancaster mimicked the motion.

Lessel shrugged, but Mora answered, brow furrowed, "They wore all black armor. Not identifiable as any clan."

"Weapons?"

"Daggers, small swords, mostly. Some axes."

A variety, then. Maybe it wasn't Kakias. But maybe—

"Where?" I nearly spat, but scratched at my Curse scar beneath my cloak to temper myself.

"About a mile south of here. Like he said, it sprung up on us. Silent as the deepest night, and deadly as it, too." Mora's eyes widened as she remembered it, pale skin nearly gray. "I'd advise you not to look for it. But if you must...you'll know it when you're near."

I fought every instinct to tear out of the place, doing my best to remain calm. "Thank you for the information." I fished some coins out of my pack and dropped them on the table.

Before anyone could respond, I was outside, running through the brisk night to reach Sapphire at her post down the road.

"Warrior, wait!"

I spun to meet the faerie on my heels.

"*Wait?*" I snapped. "Why are you following me?"

"As I said, I was looking for you." He strode down the stairs, hood falling back. And I finally had a view of those pointed ears poking through his hair.

"And why is that?" I walked backward, unable to stand still for too long.

"I can't—" His voice stopped, whether because he was bound from telling a warrior of his mission or because what he'd been about to say was a lie, I didn't know. In the night, Lancaster's canines reflected the moonlight when he growled in frustration. "I wish to help you."

"*Why?*"

"Don't ask questions if you aren't prepared for the answers."

"Are you going to assist me, then, or threaten the life of someone else I care about?"

Those canines glinted again, frustration piercing his controlled immortal demeanor. "That was a misunderstanding. I swore not to hurt her."

He couldn't lie, so it had to be true.

"Excellent. Now if you don't mind, I have somewhere to be." I stepped into the dark street.

"You won't get in there without me."

I froze and turned back to the shadow watching me. I swept my eyes over his broad form, stopping on the blades strapped to his side.

I curled my hand around my own.

"Watch me."

Lancaster did, to my ire.

With that infuriating fae speed, he kept pace with Sapphire as we tracked the camp Mora and Lessel mentioned. Frost crept over bare tree limbs as we traveled deeper into Mindshaper Territory, but we were far enough north that we did not have to face snow or sleet.

Mora had been right. A slinking presence crawled to us while we were still a quarter mile out, like shadowed hands slithering around my muscles. Coaxed us through the trees, a misty voice on the wind, right to a clearing.

Four pointed tents were raised, dark as night with fabric that looked thick as leather, wide shielded pathways connecting them all. It didn't appear to be a camp that was easily collapsible, made for quick retreats or last-minute marches.

No, this was a base.

There were too many signs of permanent inhabitation for it to be anything else: stores of weapons and food being carted in, fires burning in the frigid Mindshaper air. Travelers concerned with being caught did not dare light fires.

The largest tent was in the center, the three smaller ones forming a guard around it. Based on the number of people traipsing in and out of the dim opening, it seemed the most secured.

The most likely place to keep a hostage.

Tolek was in there. He had to be.

"Something here isn't right." Lancaster's voice was barely a whisper as he crouched beside me. Though I'd suspected as much myself, the tone undulating through his words chilled even me—terror.

"What is it?"

The fae only shook his head. "I can't name it. Never felt anything like it. But there's a barrier here I can't pass." He extended a hand. At the edge of the shadowed tree line, his palm flattened.

Mimicking him, I tested the air, but my fingers passed straight through into the dim moonlight filtering through the branches woven atop the clearing.

I pulled my hand back quickly.

"Looks like you won't be any help to me, then. You can go." I needed this faerie to stop distracting me so I could form a plan.

He groaned, mumbling something under his breath.

Then, "Make a deal with me, Mystique."

I whipped my head toward him. "You have got to be out of your immortal mind."

251

"I can't enter that camp, but I can get you in. In turn, you help me."

It was reckless, making a bargain with a faerie. They were tricksters, enemies of the warriors.

But if he truly could get me into the camp...I looked at the array of guards surrounding the clearing. They swept around with the same unnatural, windy movements of the Engrossians we'd fought in the Southern Pass.

Tol was there; I knew it in my bones. And I'd do anything to reach him.

Without letting myself second guess it, I said, "This way."

We walked until we were far enough to not be overheard.

"What do I need to help you with?"

"When the time comes, I'll call on you." From the predatory curve of his lips, I had a sick feeling there was more he wasn't saying. A concrete reason he needed me.

"Absolutely not." I wouldn't make such a loose deal.

"Set your parameters, then," he agreed quickly, and I realized he'd known I wouldn't be so easy to sway. And that—that feeling of being a step behind this immortal being—had me reconsidering.

Conflict warred in my gut at the thought of trusting him, but I supposed I didn't have a choice. This damn fae was forcing help I very much needed upon me, and I wasn't sure what that meant for our history with them.

I did not want to offer this to him, to trust even a breath from his lungs, but...

"Parameters," I repeated. "If I make this deal, it cannot harm anyone I care for. It cannot touch them; you cannot use or manipulate them. I will do what is needed, but everyone else is left out of it. I will not come if I am in the middle of my own war, nor will I respond immediately if doing so will jeopardize any members of my clan."

His eyes flicked over my face, narrowing in his search for loopholes with that expert mind of his. I repeated my words, checking for any myself.

"Anything else?"

"Yes." Now my smiled turned wicked. "I want to be able to call

252

on you in the future, too. If a time comes when I need your help again, you come."

"An indefinite bargain?" He almost looked impressed. "I've never made one before. Not in the centuries I've lived."

I held my hand out. "Afraid of one small warrior?"

"Never." He looked at my hand. "But that is not how bargains are sealed with my kind."

"For the love of the Angels, Lancaster, what do you want?" I was growing impatient with his games.

"A kiss."

My stomach hollowed out. "A kiss?"

"I did not create the magic," he grumbled with an impatient eye roll. "It's the only way to seal our bargain."

The alternative to a kiss…possibly losing Tol. That thought nearly carved out my chest.

One kiss. That was all he asked. I could kiss an immortal faerie and sign over a piece of my loyalty indefinitely if it meant getting Tolek back.

"Fine."

Lancaster leaned over me, his hand grabbing the back of my neck. Then, his lips were on mine, and I jolted—it was the first time I had kissed anyone besides Malakai.

It was different, kissing this faerie. Wrong. Despite the magic that passed between us as I opened for him, there was an unnatural collision in the way our mouths moved. Though it was clear he was skilled, had probably spent centuries bedding females, I did not want him beyond this deal.

His magic twisted along my bones as the bargain solidified itself, tying us to each other *indefinitely*, until the day one of us broke our end of the bargain. It tasted ancient, made of secrets and the foundations of nature.

A bolt of lightning flashed between the trees, striking the frosty ground where we stood, and he backed away.

"Done."

His smile turned vengeful, ready to hunt. And fear flooded my gut at the gravity of what I may have just agreed to.

Lancaster lifted his hand, conjured a small charm out of nothing.

Gold and engraved with a symbol too worn to make out. "Add that to your necklace. Wish on it when you want to invoke our deal, and I'll know."

Shaking myself of the inexplicable sensation that bargain had wrought within me, I pushed every fear of what I'd just committed to from my mind.

"Can we get on with this now?" I asked once the charm was hanging beside my token from Angelborn.

"Give me five minutes," Lancaster said. "And your path into that camp will be clear."

I nodded, watching him disappear silently into the trees, unsure of what he was about to do but knowing there was a time we would meet again.

Creeping back to the edge of the camp, I tried to form a plan as if this was nothing more than one of Cyph's drills. Find the guards' weaknesses, look for those who seemed slowest, map a route in and out.

The seconds ticked by painfully as I waited for a signal. Doubt crept in. If that pointy-eared bastard had bailed on me, left me sitting here like patient prey through some loophole, next time I saw the faerie, I'd ensure he paid—

But a satisfied smile split my lips when an inhuman roar cut through the air.

Thank you, Lancaster.

The guards snapped to attention, running from the clearing toward the supposed threat.

I shot out of the brush, heading for the largest tent.

I peered inside. There was nothing—

A second scream froze me, this one guttural. Desperate and strained. And it was coming from the opposite direction of Lancaster's distraction.

From a voice I recognized all too well.

CHAPTER THIRTY-FOUR

OPHELIA

I DIDN'T STOP TO think. I ran.

Another echoing cry spurred me on, faster.

Tangled branches of the cypher trees whipped at my cheeks, a trickle of blood slipping down, but I was barely aware of anything besides my pounding heart and trying to keep my hands locked on Angelborn. One name repeated in my mind:

Tolek.

He screamed again—more ragged and closer this time—and I sped up.

My throat was raw by the time I saw a smaller tent through the gaps in the trees. Darker than the rest and tucked away from their crowd. Hidden.

Angelborn's second pulse beat through my body, the necklace heating. I shut off all emotion welling up within me and sank into that primal, fury-fueled instinct. Burned ice cold with the need to protect what was *mine.*

I burst into the clearing. Angelborn shot through the head of a guard, pinning him to the tent's leather wall. Crimson oozed down the side, shining death against the dark fabric.

Starfire sang as I pulled her free and easily knocked aside the jagged knife the second guard slashed at me.

Fool.

Even with their unnatural movements and silent approach, that knife was no more than a stick compared to my short sword.

She swiped across his throat, brutal and bloodthirsty.

A tingle traveled down the back of my neck, and I whirled. The third guard swung his ax. I crouched, pulling my dagger and sheathing it between his ribs as I stood.

Seconds—that was all it had taken.

I caught my breath, listening to make sure no other guards were coming. Then, I sheathed my dagger at my thigh and was ducking inside the tent. An orange glow from a woodstove illuminated a small space with a desk, a shelf lined with weapons, and—

I couldn't see much more before an arm looped around my neck, crushing my windpipe.

Starfire tumbled from my grip, pommel smacking my shin.

"Took you longer than we expected," the guard growled in my ear. His leathers pressed against my spine, vambrace hard against my throat.

A second guard lifted an ax. It hovered above me, small and sharp.

How many people had that weapon killed? Had it taken anyone I knew during the war? Did families now grieve because of the lethal blade and the sharp-eyed, remorseless warrior before me?

I didn't know the answers, but I knew no more would weep because of this man.

Kicking out, I drove the heel of my thick-soled boot into his groin, and the blade fell. I caught it before it could hit the ground and *swung*.

The warrior with his arm around my neck pulled me back. Too late.

It sliced cleanly into his comrade's skull.

But he kept pressing down on my throat, metal digging into my airway until breaths were nothing more than choked gasps.

Keeping my grip tight on the handle, I wrenched the ax out of the warrior's head and kept swinging true. Not caring where I hit, only that I hit *something*.

The impact jolted my bones as he screamed.

He released my throat and lurched forward, nearly crushing me.

Scrambling out of the way, I watched him tumble to the ground with that ax in his side. I braced my hands on my knees, catching my breath.

"By the fucking Angels," I panted.

"You're glorious." Though the voice was strained, laughter and utter adoration bubbled beneath it, and every strand of tension within me unknotted.

Across the tent, just on the outskirts of the fire's warmth, Tolek stood tied to a wooden post.

"Hey, Alabath." He grinned.

Despite the bruises on his torso and the exhaustion dimming his eyes, *he fucking grinned.*

I flew across the tent, throwing my arms around him. He grunted, but I held on tighter.

For a moment, the danger fell away. It was just me and Tol, his heart pounding against my chest, each beat tying me back down to sanity. My hand slid up his neck, running through his hair, pressing his head into my shoulder. He sighed, and the heat of that breath against my neck was the purest form of relief.

His hands were cuffed. A rope wrapped around him and the post, restraining his arms so he couldn't embrace me, but I didn't care.

That spicy citrus scent caressed me, and I sank into it, losing myself to a reprieve.

I have him back. I have him back.

The mantra brought tears to my eyes, my breaths turning shallow as I tried to stifle them. I must have repeated it out loud because Tolek whispered against my ear, low and soothing, "Easy there. I'm right here."

I pulled back, assessing him. Bruises littered his torso, a purple one dotting his cheek. I couldn't see any new scars, but as I ran my hands over his ribs, he winced.

My eyes snapped up to his. Where I expected to see the sting of physical pain, I instead found reluctant anguish.

"What is it?"

"Hell Spirits…" His head dropped. "You shouldn't have come."

I rolled my eyes. "That's not quite the gratitude I was hoping for," I teased, retrieving my dagger and sword and slicing through his ropes. I inspected his handcuffs but couldn't see a keyhole anywhere to pick.

"You know I'm always happy to see you, Alabath, but I've never been more frightened about it than I am now." His voice held none of his usual mirth. "Didn't you realize it's a trap?"

"Of course, I realized that." Didn't *he* realize I'd stop at nothing to save him?

"Then, why are you here?" Loathing snaked into his voice, and for a moment it stung. But then, his eyes fell to the cuffs around his wrists, and it hit me. That shame wasn't directed at me. Spirits, it wasn't even directed at Kakias.

It was at *himself* for getting caught.

Tolek had been raised with undeserved blame on his shoulders, and I was still learning to pick apart the pieces of him that he used to hide it from the world. Deep down he warred with the guilt his parents had shoved on him since birth.

Didn't he see he was more than that? He was the brightest source of light in my life. Teasing stares may mask how he really felt, but there was no hiding from me.

I gripped his chin, turning it toward me. "Because I don't care what you *think* you deserve, Vincienzo. I would never leave you here."

Saying those words aloud unlocked a latch within me, some small shard of my heart sliding back into place.

It seemed to do the same to him. For a moment, I watched my words sink in, lifting spots of that loathing, disbelief unfolding in its place. His face brightened beneath the bruises.

Tol's eyes dropped to my lips, and his own parted.

But he didn't get to speak, because boots thundered outside the tent.

"You know," a familiar voice scolded as the tent flap swept open, "I told her this plan would never work." Aird stepped into the dim space. My gut curled when I saw Angelborn in his hand. "But I suppose I overestimated your intelligence, Miss Alabath."

Tolek cursed beneath his breath, stepping closer to me.

I hadn't asked who was responsible for his capture. I'd assumed it was only Kakias. But I supposed the enemy you knew was not always the greatest threat. It was those lurking in the shadows who wielded the sharpest knives.

"Aird," I sneered, summoning my mask of Revered and stifling every other emotion. "It appears we both were victims of overestimation." Aird raised his brows. "I wasn't foolish enough to trust you after the Rapture, but I assumed you weren't dim-witted enough to fall prey to Kakias's scheming."

The Mindshaper chancellor laughed, meandering across the space. Tol tensed, reaching for me, but he realized with his hands cuffed he'd only be in my way and dropped them.

Still, the look on his face turned more murderous with each step Aird took.

"You think I'm the fool?" the chancellor asked. "I don't engage in deals unless I'm gaining more than the other. She's promised me things you can never imagine." Power emanated from him, practically blurring the space around his body.

I stood straighter to block Tolek, though both men towered over me.

"And what exactly has she promised you that made you turn against the rest of the continent so easily?"

A manic gleam entered his eye. He removed a small, jagged knife from his belt—the Mindshaper weapons, I finally realized. Kakias had them in her army, too.

Aird's movements were as windswept as the guards had been.

I narrowed my eyes. "What has she done to you?"

"Defeated my weaknesses." A breeze—uncannily inside the tent—lifted his hair from his shoulders.

"Everyone has weaknesses," I told him. "They help us appreciate our strengths and relate to others. Weaknesses balance us as individuals."

"Weaknesses get you killed. Without them, you're infallible." Aird sneered at me, eyes lifting over my head. Evaluating Tolek. "And we found yours." He straightened, and a conniving smile twisted his lips. "Did you truly think you could be Revered of the Mystique Warriors, the most powerful leader on the continent, and choose to save your lover over everyone else? You cannot have it both ways, Miss Alabath."

His threats lit a fire within me—one capable of burning the world to ashes, his words dancing among them.

Love was no weakness, except perhaps the love of power that he and the queen seemed to share. That kind of toxic ambition would kill you.

"Protecting someone you care for is not a weakness. Relying on others is not a weakness. To love is a strength, and it is that compassion which makes me fit for the position of Revered." The air in the room stretched taut, about to snap. "Maybe if Kakias would stop kidnapping the men I love, I wouldn't have to rescue them."

"Why would she when it has proven to get you to come running?" He laughed, but there was no humor in the sound—only corrupt glee.

Tol slid out from behind me, but Aird's manic stare remained locked on my face. Where his eyes had once been dove gray, they were as deep as roaring storm clouds.

"Why does she want you?" He seemed to be talking to himself as much as he was me.

"No clue," I said, keeping my hand at my side as I flipped my dagger around.

"What's in your blood that makes you so special? Makes her so *desperate—*"

Quick as a whip, my dagger flashed toward his thigh. His reaction was quicker, though. He swiveled, the blade only skimming his leg instead of disarming him.

Blood gushed, but the wound began healing over quickly.

His hand flashed out, gripping my shoulder before I could dodge and throwing me back. I collided with the wooden shelf, spine cracking against the edge.

Knives clattered to the floor around my boots. I stretched a hand out to stop myself from falling, and a blade sliced up my forearm.

I cried out. Aird grasped the wound, lifting it.

"You're speaking nonsense," I panted, wincing as he tightened his grip. "Whatever she's promised you has taken your wits in exchange."

"Oh no, your blood seems very precious to her. I was instructed not to spill it." He shook my arm in his grasp. I blinked against the sting, fighting a scream. "But accidents do happen."

A secret darkened his voice—and that confirmed it. He wasn't loyal to Kakias. Aird was devoted only to himself. Greed dripped over his words. It didn't matter that he didn't know why Kakias wanted me; only that she did, and that he claimed me first.

"Sorry to tell you, I'm nothing special," I hissed. I clenched my teeth, refusing to squirm for him.

Aird leaned over me, chest crushing me to the shelf. The rough edge dug deeper into my spine. Starfire was still at my hip, but Aird was too close for me to reach her.

"There's time before she returns. I'll find out what she wants from you." His rabid gaze switched from the blood on my arm to my eyes.

Face close enough to mine that his breath fanned across my cheeks, he murmured, "Luckily for us both, she was on her own mission when you arrived. I'm supposed to hold you for her." He dragged the blade across my throat, marking the spot. "But if you're being difficult, I have to defend my—"

Aird's words broke off with a gurgle as cuffed hands slipped around his head.

A chain tightened against his throat, crushing his windpipe. The Mindshaper's eyes bulged out.

"Hands off, *Chancellor*," Tolek growled in his ear.

My jaw hung open as Tol used his handcuffs to choke the man who had been trying to kill me. Aird struggled, his face purpling. All too quickly, his body relaxed, and Tol shoved him to the floor, kicking the unconscious chancellor in the ribs.

The murderous rage glowing in Tol's eyes awakened parts of my body it shouldn't have. When he looked at me, though, he softened back into himself. Hair in disarray, chest rising and falling rapidly.

"Seems I'm always saving your life, Alabath," he panted.

I looked pointedly at the post he'd been chained to. "Yes, that's clearly what's happening here, Vincienzo."

"So ungrateful…" he mused, shaking his head. "You can thank me later." He gave me a roguish wink, and I fought the smile that bloomed across my face.

Cradling my injured arm, I retrieved Angelborn. When I turned back to Tol, he was holding my dagger. Without dropping his gaze from mine, he slid the blade home. His hand lingered on my thigh, burning into me.

"You're okay?" he asked, fingers curling into my skin above the sheath like he'd never let go.

"I'm okay." My arm was already healing, another proud scar for my collection. "And you?"

"I'm fine now."

"The warriors who came with you…"

"Gone." His lips pulled into a line. That explained the blood Kakias and Aird had delivered to us, using whatever power the queen was manipulating to freeze it.

I scowled at the Mindshaper on the floor, considering ending his life now for his crimes against Mystiques, but Tol twisted my fingers between his. "It could incite more problems."

He was right. Though Aird was complicit in Tol's kidnapping and the murder of our warriors, killing a chancellor now could turn clans against us. But I did stomp over to him and punch him squarely in the face, his nose crunching under my knuckles.

Turning back to Tol, his eyes weren't on mine, but my necklace. "What's this?" He touched the new charm from Lancaster.

"I—um—" I stumbled, realizing how foolish I was about to sound.

"Alabath?"

"Do you remember the fae who attacked Rina?" Spirits, he was going to think I was careless.

"Yes…"

My next words were rushed. "He found me on my way here and offered a bargain in order to help me get you out, so I took it."

Tol's face went blank. "You made a deal with a faerie in order to rescue me?"

"An indefinite bargain." I supposed I would tell him everything now. "We can each call on the other when needed, so long as it doesn't harm anyone I care about. The camp was heavily guarded. It didn't seem like I'd be able to get in any other way. I was careful with my parameters, though."

I looked at my boots, awaiting the anger that would meet my reckless decision.

But Tol slipped a hand beneath my chin, lifting my gaze.

"You did that to rescue me?"

I nodded.

"You shouldn't have…" A beautiful, crooked smile bloomed across his face. "But thank you."

"What?" I tilted my head.

"I know that you wouldn't have wanted to do that, to hand over a piece of control in that way, but you did it for me. Thank you." Cuffed hands slipped around me, pulling me close, one cradling the back of my head against his chest. Bemused, I wrapped my arms around him. Because I'd barely been thinking of myself or what it might mean when I made that deal—

I'd thought of Tol, and what it would feel like to lose him.

"You have to kiss the fae to seal a bargain, don't you?" Tol asked, his voice rumbling in his chest beneath my ear.

I looked up at him. "Am I the only one who was unaware of that?"

"You kissed him?" His smile didn't falter—he was laughing.

"Why is me kissing someone so funny?" I ducked under his cuffed hands and stepped back, crossing my arms.

That shut up his laughter. "Believe me, Alabath. I think more about you kissing someone than I care to admit." My breath caught at the implication darkening his voice. "But next time you kiss a beautiful immortal, I'd like to be present."

"Sure, next time." Now that I was away from his warmth, our reality set back in—starting with the pressing need to get out of this camp. "Is there a key for the cuffs?"

Tol shook his head. "Sealed magically."

A shiver danced down my spine. "Kakias didn't—what did she do—"

"Not here." Shadows danced in his eyes. I was afraid to learn the cause of them, but he bent to press a kiss to my forehead, and a bit of the tension in my shoulders loosened. "Let's go."

Swallowing my questions and the agony burning through me at Tol's pain, I locked my fingers around the chain between his wrists and tugged him after me. He smirked but followed obediently.

"What?" I asked, heat rising to my cheeks.

"Nothing," he laughed.

"Come on." I jerked the chain forward, and he obliged.

Under the cover of night, we fled into the trees to meet Sapphire, my heart pounding but a bit fuller with Tolek breathing beside me.

Chapter Thirty-Five

Ophelia

Sapphire seemed to be walking at her slowest possible pace.

"Come on, girl." I flicked the reins, but she only ambled across the dirt. Once she'd gotten us far enough away from Aird and Kakias's camp that we weren't worried about being followed, she'd slowed to a stroll that she showed no sign of picking up.

With only one horse, Tol was forced to sit behind me, his legs braced on either side of my own, squeezing me to him, his cuffed hands looped around me.

"So impatient." Tol's arms flexed around my waist, and everything within me tightened in response.

"I want to get out of the open," I breathed.

He looked up at the tightly interwoven branches, then around at the packed trees, sweeping cypher branches forming curtains around the path. "Yes, we're very exposed here." His whisper was hot against my neck, his stubble brushing my shoulder. "Relax."

I sank into the low tenor of his voice, but I knew what he was doing. He was distracting me from every pressure that chased us through this forest. From the threats of the queen, the deals of the fae, and the chains still around his wrists. The links brushed against my stomach as he shifted, a jolt of unexpected chill shooting through my body. I hissed, leaning back into him.

"Sorry," he laughed, moving his locked wrists forward so they didn't touch my skin. But then his hands rested just between my legs, and I wished for the cold sweep of his chains to calm the heat budding within me. "Where are we going, anyway?"

"I know a place," I whispered, my voice barely audible.

Tol's bare chest brushed my back as I pressed further into him. How he still smelled good despite his time captured was truly a mystery to me. The spicy citrus scent mixed with the feeling of his muscular arms wrapped around me and his torso cushioning my back didn't help the desire flooding between my legs.

His Spirits-damned smirk radiated against my shoulder, like he knew exactly how my body reacted to him.

Angels, with how attuned he was to me, he probably did.

"I think you have something that belongs to me," he muttered.

He didn't so much as brush his lips against my neck, though my hair was thrown over one shoulder. Didn't even dare twitch his hands where they rested at the hem of my skirt.

No, Tolek Vincienzo was a tease.

"What's that?" I hummed.

Slowly, his hands drifted to the sheath on my thigh, brushing my skin next to the Vincienzo dagger and giving me goosebumps. "This?"

"I brought it for you," I admitted, reaching to give it back.

But Tol clamped a hand down, pressing the handle to my flesh. "Keep it," he instructed, squeezing once. There was a possessive edge to his voice. "I like seeing my blade on you."

He placed his hands back where they'd been resting between my legs, smiling smugly when I released a slow breath.

With everyone else Tol had been with he'd likely used this anticipation to his advantage—coaxing them to the point of no return until they threw themselves at him. If I was any other person, I'd be tilting my head to the side, begging him to press dangerously slow, open-mouthed kisses to my skin. To drag his teeth across my collarbone. Wanting his fingers to slip from where they rested against my thighs up beneath my skirt.

Angels, a part of me did want that. To feel his hands exploring my body, his lips claiming mine…the image ignited something within me.

But this was us. And as well as he knew me, I knew every tell he had.

He may be wrapped in promises of pleasure and teasing smiles, but it was all to distract from what he was really feeling. Beneath the surface he bubbled with want rivaling the heat coiled within me. It was in every near-silent hum of approval rumbling within his chest, every move laced with the tension vibrating off him.

As I allowed myself to relax further into Tolek, Malakai flashed through my mind. The Bind pulsed, and the memory brought a pang of the shame I'd grown accustomed to. Was I wrong for considering indulging this need within me? Even now, weeks later, thoughts of Malakai still echoed with sorrow, but it wasn't the deep grief I'd expected.

It was a reluctant understanding.

Malakai and I had been over long before I'd said those words to him—as over as we ever could be with the Bind marking our skin. Perhaps we'd ended the day he walked away from Palerman, hands tied and lies sealed, and it took us over two years of fighting and torment to see it.

Did that mean I should turn my back on what was before me now—on the choice I had to be happy? Though I was still repairing myself, I was whole enough to know the answer to that question.

So, I did my best to dismiss that guilt and lean into what I had here. The promise of feeling whole and happy. Of just *feeling*.

In the subtle shifts of our posture and tightening of limbs tangled atop Sapphire, this had become a game between Tolek and me. There was no way in the Spirit-guarded hell I was going to let him win.

I scooted back against him until I could feel everything. He bit back a groan, his desire impressively evident. But then, he laughed at the challenge.

"Okay, Alabath." His words caressed the shell of my ear.

It wasn't meant for me to respond to. Instead, I sat up straighter. And I didn't pretend not to like it when his arms tightened around me.

"What was that about?" I asked Sapphire when we dismounted, Wayward's warm windows glowing in the late hour. She exhaled, nudging my shoulder toward where Tol walked into the inn, my pack in hand.

If my damned horse could have chuckled, I swore that's what it was.

It had taken her longer than I anticipated to get us here, and all the while Tol's heat burned into my body. I eyed Sapphire, her crystalline stare bright and innocent.

"Was that pace on purpose?" I accused, hands on my hips.

My fucking horse walked away, sending herself to the stables down the block. I frowned at her swishing blue tail, sighing as I turned to follow Tolek inside.

A nice long bath, a warm meal, and perhaps a moment alone to calm the heat that coursed through my body on the ride—the list wrote itself as we climbed the rickety staircase to the room I'd rented in Wayward. We'd taken an indirect route to the inn, heading south first then looping back north. I prayed it was enough to avoid being followed.

The idea of a mattress—even a hard one—and a moment to breathe between four walls rather than looking over my shoulder at every crack of a stick was enticing.

But when I pushed the door to our room open, I quickly lost any hope of solitude. The room was small at best—a chest of drawers and a desk on one side, a bathing area without a proper door or partition on the other. And in the center, demanding attention like a star falling from the sky, one bed.

"They didn't say there was only one," I murmured, walking to the window and throwing it wide, inviting the crisp air into the stale room.

"I think it's the only option in a place like this." There was a smirk in Tol's voice.

"And what's so funny?" I spun toward him, but my jaw popped open when I saw his handcuffs now sitting on the bed. "How did you do that?"

"Don't worry about it, Alabath."

"You got out of them on your own?"

My favorite smirk curled his lips. "It's not my first time."

I shoved away every salacious image *that* comment brought to my mind, all involving Tolek handcuffed to various—

No, I could not go down that path.

I cleared my throat, ignoring the heat gathering low within me, like a trap ready to be sprung. "You could have done it earlier," I mumbled.

"We were a little busy." He shrugged, then started unbuttoning his pants.

"What are you doing now?" Exasperation rattled my voice, but I couldn't stop my eyes from dragging over his torso. Broad shoulders and lean, defined muscles tapered into a narrow waist and hips. Angels curse me, even beneath dirt and bruises his body was perfect.

Half of me itched to slaughter everyone who'd hurt him—for the second time—but the other half wanted to close the distance between us, grab a cloth from the shelf above the tub, and slowly, carefully, clean each stained piece of his skin until it was once again flawless. Then, kiss each mark to remind him of my promise of revenge.

Tolek grinned like he saw right through me. "I'd like to get this mess off before I go to bed."

"And how do you plan on doing that?" I crossed my arms, stifling every ripple of taut energy coursing through my body.

Without breaking eye contact, he backed toward the bathtub and turned on the tap. "Sorry, did you want to go first? I don't mind waiting." He leaned across the basin, reading the bottles lining the small shelf. "They have a lovely little assortment of scented soap. Oh! This one is jasmine—"

"Fine, Vincienzo." I hated that I couldn't stifle my laugh. "I don't think I'll be using that tub."

"I'd prefer you bathe if we're to share a bed."

I was certain I did not smell good after days of travel with only streams to wash in. Still...

"I won't be bathing in here." Spirits, why did I suddenly feel self-conscious? We had been riding together all night; we swam in the river wearing little more than our undergarments our entire lives. But as I watched him open one of the bottles and pour a healthy amount into the tub, clouds of bubbles foaming, my chest tightened.

I had never been this way with Tol—with anyone. I always dove into challenges headfirst, but every move around Tolek was a dance toward an unspoken future I didn't yet understand. I thought I might want it, but I was afraid.

Afraid of messing up. Could you do that twice in such a short time?

While I may have once climbed into the hot water without a second thought, now I shook my head. "Sorry if I *smell*."

Tol only laughed. "Suit yourself." He stripped off his clothes, giving me just enough time to turn away, and splashed into the water. The sigh he released was so overly dramatic—so typically Tolek—it eased some of the unwarranted tension within me.

My heart thudded as I picked his clothes up off the floor and folded them, fingers digging into the leather when his spicy citrus scent wafted to me. They were stained and torn, but they were here. He had not been a sacrifice in exchange for my blood.

"You know," Tol hummed, angling his head against the rim of the tub. Water dripped from his darkened hair to the floor. "I can easily leave the room if you'd like. Then you won't get dirt all over the sheets."

I exhaled a laugh. "Maybe you can get us food."

"Deal."

His eyes tracked my every move as I walked to the tub and crouched beside him. He had filled the water with so many bubbles that nothing was visible, but I kept my gaze locked on his face regardless.

"For what it's worth, Vincienzo. I wouldn't want to share a tiny room with anyone else."

"I couldn't agree more, Alabath." His eyes darkened, and it seemed like he was seeing all of me, every facet of my heart laid bare before him. Who was I kidding, Tol had always seen me, even the most fucked-up pieces.

"Are you scared?" I whispered, folding my arms on the edge of the tub and resting my chin on my hands.

"About what?" His brows pulled together, leaning toward me until we were only an inch apart.

I searched his face, questions hovering between us. Things I wanted to talk about but was unsure how to. Fear of the encroaching war, the threats around our necks, the taut string pulling between us even now. Any would suffice, all terrified me.

"About sharing a bed with a woman who notoriously steals blankets?"

He sighed. "If you steal my blankets, I'll shove you out of the bed."

"You wouldn't." I narrowed my eyes.

He did, too. "Try me."

"Maybe I'll keep the clothes I brought you as a bargaining chip," I threatened.

He fell silent, looking down at his hands drifting across the bubbles.

"What?"

"You brought me clothes?" A sheepish red bloomed in his cheeks.

I swallowed the emotion that blush dragged up within me. "Of course, I did."

"But you didn't know if—" His throat bobbed, and he finally met my eyes. "Thank you."

"There was no reality in which I let them take you from me, Tol. You have to know that. You're too important to me." That truth alone answered so many of the questions swarming through my mind. I brushed his wet hair back from his face and breathed, "I'm so fucking grateful you're okay."

He captured my hand, bringing it to his lips. Heat stung my palm where he kissed it, spreading out along my veins. It was once, not lingering more than a second, as if testing but not pushing any boundaries.

"I'm so fucking grateful for you." He whispered the words against my hand, a secret I was meant to wrap my fingers around and hold on to forever.

The longer we held gazes, the more I wanted to dive right into that water with him. I told myself it was for no other reason than to cool off.

"Now hurry up," I said, pushing to my feet. "I want a bath."

"You are more than welcome." He stretched his arms, tucking his hands behind his head like he had no intention of moving.

"I will drop your clothes in the water," I warned.

His eyes widened, and he splashed beneath the surface, bubbles pouring over the sides of the tub.

Once Tolek left, I filled the tub with clean water and the jasmine soap he threw at me on his way out the door—which I loved—and sank into the warm escape. For a few minutes, all of my problems faded away.

My hair floated around me, each strand letting loose a different plaguing worry.

This one flowing for the war mounting.

That one for the curse dancing in my blood.

One for the man I'd once loved.

And another for everything I'd just stepped into.

They glided along the surface, and I held my breath beneath the cloudy water. For a moment, it was blissful, hidden in my own haven where nothing could reach me, hurt me.

Until a hand grabbed my ankle and hoisted it out of the water.

I came up sputtering, hair plastered across my face and breasts barely concealed beneath the bubbles. "Vincienzo!"

"You sent me to get food." He gestured at the tray steaming on the dresser. "It will get cold if you float beneath the water all night."

I scowled, but the scent of hearty spices was enticing.

"Get me a towel, please." He handed me one, his stare lingering before turning away.

I dried off and slipped into the silk nightgown I'd packed—a hopeful inclusion that I would get one night of rest on this journey. A breeze danced through the open window, raising goosebumps along my arms. The outline of the moon shone against the pane, full with promises and hope.

Tolek leaned against the wall, hair still a bit damp but clothes clean, elbows braced on the windowsill. He swirled a glass of wine, lifting it to his lips, eyes intent on the sky. What was he thinking about?

But instead of interrupting to ask, I picked up a bowl of rice and vegetables from downstairs and moved to the bed. Settling against the pillows, I watched him. He was so at ease. Not simply content, but actually relaxed.

By the time he finally turned to me, I'd finished my food.

"Are you going to eat?" I asked.

For a moment, his eyes darkened, but he blinked away the illusion.

"I guess." Tol sat at the desk, finishing the entire serving in only a few minutes, picking up both of our bowls, and setting them on the tray.

Then, he moved toward me—toward the bed we were meant to share.

Every step he took rattled through my bones, a tingling awareness of *him* heightening. He reached behind his neck to tug his shirt off in one smooth motion. Without breaking eye contact with me, he unbuttoned his pants, dropping them down his legs so he stood in only his undershorts.

"More comfortable to sleep," he explained, voice husky.

"Mm-hmm," I hummed, hot beneath his stare. I scrambled to the pillow, scooting between the cool sheets, doing everything to avoid looking at the lower half of his body.

The bed dipped as he laid beside me, our arms barely brushing each other.

Every hair on my body stood up. Chirping crickets and hoots of owls drifted through the window, but my heartbeat drowned them out.

Tolek rolled onto his side, facing me. "What are you thinking about?"

I considered the storm of worries weighing down my bones, but picked one thread from memory that was truly the least of my concerns. "Are you sleeping with anyone?"

"That's what's on your mind right now?" His brows flicked up.

"Yes," I admitted, unashamed.

He searched my face for a hint of a joke before answering. "No, Ophelia, I'm not."

I turned onto my side, too, only a few inches separating us. "Not even someone casually?" He shook his head. "No one from Renaiss?" Another shake. "Honestly?"

Tol laughed, rolling onto his back. "Do you really not believe me?"

"I find it hard to believe with the women and men constantly throwing themselves at you." A knot tightened in my stomach.

"And have you seen me returning those affections?"

I thought back to Renaiss and every night we had spent in the city before. Spirits, I even cast my mind back to Palerman. Beyond the flirtatious remarks and friendly gestures, I could not recall Tol engaging in anything that could pass as romantic.

"What about Hylia?" She was always near him, clearly fawning over him. Something tightened around my stomach.

"Hylia?" Tol lifted a brow.

"Oh, please, Tol." I pushed myself up on my elbows. "She's only been throwing herself at you for years." Not that I could blame her. The grip around my gut curled tighter as I said it, familiar and burning, and I finally recognized it for what it was—jealousy. A protective instinct rose in me as I pictured unnamed hands on his body, lips on his.

"She's never tried anything." Tol tucked a hand behind his head, thoughtful as the moonlight fell across his chest, outlining the cut of his muscles.

"I thought—"

"Ophelia," he interrupted, pushing up onto one elbow and facing me. "You may ask me as many times as you wish, you may phrase the question however you like, but I have not slept with anyone in over a year. Before we left Palerman, I'd kissed warriors and humans alike. I'd gone home with some—there was even a wraith from the isles once— never mind." He cut off the story at my narrowed stare, face turning serious again. "I was never able to follow through with anything. And since we've been in Damenal, nothing so much as a kiss has occurred."

"Oh," I breathed, blinking past the implications of that truth and falling back against the pillow, turning to face him. Hearing him say it so plainly soothed the tension mounting in my gut.

Though, I had no right to feel any of those things. I'd been with another man for years. Tolek had only recently admitted his feelings for me, and I hadn't technically given him an answer, but the territorial instinct still settled within me.

"Now that we've exhausted my sexual escapades," Tol started, settling back down, and I rolled my eyes, certain we had *not* covered the expanse of that topic. Our faces were barely an inch apart, the air between us prickling like moments before a rainstorm. "Tell me what is actually worrying you."

He had always seen through me, since we were children playing games. Though the competition may have shifted, the world becoming heavier with every exhale, that ability to pierce me with only a gaze never faltered.

I desperately wanted to tell him. To unload the angelic prophecy burdening my shoulders. What was I meant to unite? What was happening with the wild creatures and the queen's hunt for me? Why did this emblem on my neck heat with my pulse?

I wanted to spill every theory between us so he could help me parse out the truth.

But Damien's warning throttled me as the words rose, so I said, "The journey ahead."

"We'll be back in time for Daminius festivities if we ride fast."

Daminius. My deadline to earn those final votes on my title.

"And what if I don't know how this journey ends?" The full moon outside the window burned out the stars as it faded toward dawn, casting shadows across Tol's face, but I still caught the way his eyes flicked over my expression, picking apart every twitch of my brow and roll of my lips until he knew what I truly meant.

He shifted closer, our foreheads nearly touching. "Listen to me," he whispered, breath hot against my lips. I was trapped in his gaze, captured by his voice. "You don't need to know what comes next, Ophelia. Whatever it is—I'm here for you. Whatever waits in that cursed fate, we will face it together. From now until the end of time, I am infinitely yours."

I nodded, my eyes falling closed against the emotion welling within them. "I'm scared." I whispered the two words I hadn't wanted to admit, let them hover between us, a secret I only wanted him to hold.

"Of what?"

I was certain he knew, but he wanted me to say it.

"Of failing everyone relying on me." Of failing him.

Because if I could not give him what he wanted, if I could not be what he deserved, I didn't know what would happen.

Slowly, he lifted his hand to my hip. When he dragged his fingers over my nightgown, heat rivaling the Spirit Volcano flooded my core. I almost squirmed against it, but I didn't want to move, afraid of shattering this moment.

"You could never fail your people. You care deeply and are willing to fight for them. With that guiding your heart, they will always be safe with you." His thumb dragged over my hip, scorching a line through the silk.

"I'm worried about more than them." Being Revered was the fact I was least afraid of. Moments of doubt in myself washed in like the tide, but deep down I knew the power lay within me.

"What are you afraid of, then?"

"Breaking the things I treasure most," I confessed, biting my bottom lip.

Tol's lashes drooped across his cheeks as he tracked the motion. He pushed onto one elbow, dragging his hand slowly from my hip up my body, watching its path like he had to commit every inch to memory. He scorched a trail over my ribcage which expanded with my sharp inhale, across my collarbone, and came to rest against my cheek. Gently, his thumb tugged my lip from beneath my teeth and rested there. With the touch, my body both relaxed and coiled, heart fluttering with the way his eyes traced my face, so familiar yet so new. Raw adoration and protectiveness burned in his gaze.

"You will never break me." He brushed his thumb over my lip. "There are many promises I cannot make in this world, but that's one I *will* stake my life against. So long as you make decisions following your own heart, *I* will never break."

Spirits bless him for always knowing what I was saying when I couldn't find the words.

I wanted to melt into this moment. Into his warm embraces and comforting words. Into the place I was the safest in the world. Even when I was crying beneath a moonlit night, he was there to guard me.

It was because of that soul-deep feeling of safety that I wrapped my hand around the back of his neck and pulled him down to me.

It was a soft kiss, but it shot through my body, lightning igniting my nerves. His hand tightened around my hip, and his breath hitched as I shifted closer to him. My fingers tangled in his hair.

I didn't think of Malakai or the ache that relationship still sent through me. In this moment, it was only Tolek. *Infinitely.*

When I opened my eyes, breathing heavy, the amber specks in his own were sparkling in the way I loved, wonder and lust staring back at me. He licked his bottom lip, as if savoring what I'd just done.

"Thank you, Tol."

I didn't know if it was for the kiss or the gentle touch, if it was for the reassurance or the reliability, the time or the temperament.

But I knew something that had been shattered within me sealed over in that moment.

For now that was enough.

CHAPTER THIRTY-SIX

MALAKAI

THE FIRST LEGION REACHED their outpost along the eastern side of the mountains, fortifying the borders. The smallest trickle of success worked through me. Though it had really been Danya and Lyria's execution with Ophelia's strategizing before she left, I'd been present for the decisions since then, and I hadn't fucked it up.

"I didn't realize you had such an instinct for battle," Cypherion commented to Lyria after she wrapped up her report with the Master of Weapons. We'd known Lyria had a number of personal victories against the Engrossians during the war—which were causing harsh prejudice between herself and Barrett and Dax—but her knowledge stretched far beyond physical skill, tactical planning surpassing even Cyph's. "Tolek never mentioned."

Tension snapped through the room, from where Vale, Jezebel, and Erista conversed beside Cyph all the way to Barrett and Dax across the table. Guilt over how I'd treated my friend rose in my throat, tasted acidic. I may have been angry, but as days passed and my head cleared, I was seeing that it was possible I'd overreacted. Of us all, Cypherion was the only one who freely used Tolek's name, as if he was only out for a stroll and would return shortly.

"You can learn a lot in a year if you pay attention." The Vincienzo heir tossed her hair behind her shoulder. The smirk she gave was so much like her brother's, it twisted my gut. "They tried to keep me off the front lines because I was young, but I didn't listen."

"Lyria is a sharp fighter and a sharper mind," Danya added with a wide smile.

"And what did you learn from the war?" I asked Mila where she stood beside Lyria, scrutinizing the maps we had spread before us. "Were you on the front lines, as well?"

Lyria stiffened, but Mila twirled her tight golden cuffs around her wrists.

"Briefly," she said, voice low. I leaned in to capture her words. "But I learned that not everything ends with a treaty."

The comment shot through me like a spear to the heart, tearing out the other side. Mila's ice-blue eyes bored into mine, but there wasn't venom in them. If I wasn't mistaken, I thought it was understanding.

I looked back to the maps, rolling the tension from my shoulders.

We'd gone over the numbers repeatedly, traced the routes through the mountains and the alternate ones the generals would lead if there was an obstacle. There were numerous fallback plans, and a last resort to retreat entirely and fortify Damenal if needed.

This could work.

But there were still key factors we didn't know. The most important of all—Kakias's motivations.

"Could this all truly be a ploy for control of the mountains?" I mused, dragging my fingers across the peaks printed on the map.

"I don't think that's it," Barrett claimed, stepping up beside me. Lyria and Mila went still as he grabbed my wrist, moving my hand to a region in the far southwest reaches of Gallantia. *The Dark Valleys.* "You forget that we have power, too."

The swirling whirlpools of tar had resided in those valleys since the time of the Angels. Foreboding corruption swarmed within the confines of their shores.

"But that's dark magic." My eyes flicked to the Engrossian heir. "It's unstable. The only usable power lies in the range." I pointed at the mountains again.

"That's where your Mystique education is lacking, dear brother. The pools in the Dark Valleys don't only contain magic. They aren't cases or guards the way your mountains are, channeling ether into the world and warriors." He was right. Dark power couldn't imbue us in the same way we channeled strength and agility from the raw source within the range.

But those pools weren't to be used, so why did it matter?

"The pools feed on power," Barrett finished, jaw clenched.

"How?" Cyph asked.

"After being contained for so long, the magic has germinated. They've become sentient." The prince ran a hand through his hair. "They barter with power."

The thought of a structure of the land developing a humanoid mind and the skill to wield it...cold terror gripped my gut.

"It's forbidden by Bant himself to go near the pools unless you're attaining your scars after the Endeavourance—our version of your Undertaking," Dax added, placing a hand around Barrett's waist. The prince leaned into him instinctually, the tension in his jaw slacking. "Engrossians are raised on tales of the pools taking lives. We're warned to stay away except on those rare circumstances."

"Banning something doesn't always keep warriors from what they want." I thought of my closest friends diving into the suspended Undertaking and the events that decision set in motion. "It often makes it more attractive."

Dax clarified, "After completing the Endeavourance, some Engrossians are stationed at posts around the valleys to guard them. To keep others out. No one gets in."

My eyes met Barrett's, and we both filled in the unsaid words. No one *without the queen's jurisdiction* gets in.

"How do the pools work?" I asked the heir and his consort.

The two exchanged grimaces, as if sharing this was against their laws, but whatever the prince saw in his consort's eyes must have been convincing. Dax's hand tightened on Barrett's waist.

"The pools' magic is stronger than any other source because it's been isolated. It's grown—thrived. Whatever exists in there feeds off of the dire, carnal need in warriors to make deals with them. The warrior sacrifices something to them. In exchange, they're given a kernel of the pools' power. Even a drop is said to be enthralling."

My breath caught in my throat.

"Consuming," Dax muttered, looking at the map but not truly seeing. "It ruins you. It's why no one can go near."

Magic that changes you. That takes a sacrifice and plants something in the one desperate enough. Rots their soul, their entire being. I saw my father's black eyes and sneer rabid with vengeance. Orders to kill, maim, torture…and I wondered—

No. I couldn't let myself hope for that explanation. I clenched my eyes, willed the thudding of my caged heart to slow, and counted to five.

Then, I banished the thought and focused on Barrett's drawn expression.

"Do you think your mother…"

"I once thought there was no chance she'd be so reckless." He swallowed, his voice grim. "But now…I'm not sure."

I recognized the clenched line of his jaw, the avoidance of his eyes. Misplaced guilt. For the first time, I stopped to consider that the Engrossian heir had taken on the burden of his mother's decisions as I had those of my father. They left us both with an undeserved weight we felt responsible to amend.

If Kakias had made a deal using dark magic, we were outmatched in worse ways than we'd imagined.

"Do you know what it would be?" I asked.

"No…I don't even know when it would have happened. There are no marked changes in her countenance that I can recall. She's always been cold, driven by bloodthirsty ambition."

Barrett and Dax had another moment of silent communication, and the heir hung his head.

"I think…" He sighed. "Bant's cock, Ophelia is going to kill me for what I'm about to say."

Everyone in the room perked up at her name.

"Why?" Jezebel's voice dripped with cold threat.

Nerves sent my heart pounding against my ribs.

"Because she knows more than she's told you all, and now I have to be the one to fucking reveal her secret." He leaned forward, bracing himself on his fists. "The reason I came to Damenal was because of the moving troops and the discovery of Mystique lore in my mother's possession. But there was more. My mother has an alarming interest in Ophelia."

"We knew that, though." My shoulders sagged. "Kakias wanted her before the war, wanted her for you. When I was imprisoned, she was originally planning to have you two take the Revered's power. Until…"

What changed her mind? Something made her decide to kill Ophelia in that cavern instead. I wracked my brain for any mention of it.

"Until she decided Ophelia was a bigger threat alive," Barrett finished my thought. "I don't know what, but there is some reason she needs Ophelia dead, and I think it ties back to the lore she's gathered on your people. She has a plan bigger than any of us can imagine."

Distantly, I heard Jezebel and Cypherion questioning the Engrossians about the deals made with the pools and how long Ophelia had known of Kakias's twisted interest in her, but I wasn't listening to any of the answers. My mind spun with all the information laid before us.

It connected—all of it did. The dark power, the obsession with Ophelia, Kakias's motivations. It was all here, poured between her sacrifices, but—

"By the fucking Spirits."

I tore from the room before anyone could answer and ran flat out for my father's study. The shining palace walls blurred around me, my heartbeat pounding a desperate rhythm.

Mystlight flared to life when I threw open the doors. Shattered glass and scraps of statues crunched beneath my boots.

I didn't stop when everyone hounded me. They gathered in the doorway, but no one commented on the state of the room. Not as I prowled among the wreckage, searching.

There. Stained brown with long-dried liquor and lying face up, as if waiting for me to find it.

Papers scribbled with my father's hand, theories smudged in corners and drawings I didn't understand.

But it was here.

I slumped to my knees, ignoring the lump his handwriting brought to my throat and scanning the documents.

One word stood out: *Sacrifice?*

It was circled, darkened as if traced over multiple times. I could picture him hunched over the desk, worrying at the end of his pen, dragging his hands through his hair as he struggled to piece it all together the way I did now.

One thing was clear from his repetitive theories: Kakias had not shared everything with my father.

She had indeed made a deal with the dark pools. What she offered them, I didn't know, but I had a suspicion it was tied to the plan she'd concocted with my father and the haphazard way her army now marched across the continent. She had sacrificed some part of herself to the secrets lurking within those tar pits.

And my father hadn't known.

He had suspected, based on the scrawl before me. He'd listed notes about the workings of dark power and the notable times it had been abused in history, but he hadn't solved it.

And…Ophelia.

Flipping through the pages, I stopped on two familiar words: *Chosen Child*. An arrow pointed to the top of the page, to the phrase *blood of the Chosen will grant the wish*. And below it, words that were quickly becoming my undoing: *sacrifice her*.

I stood and stumbled back a step.

It was all I could do to pull air into my lungs. Papers crumpled in my fists.

I had given myself over. I had signed that fucking treaty and submitted to torture, in large part to protect Ophelia, because she was supposed to live out her life unknowing and happy. And I'd realized the mistake I made in that, but what I hadn't realized was my error in thinking that with my father gone and his truths exposed, she was safe.

Ophelia was never safe, because Kakias had made a deal that involved the sacrifice of the *Chosen Child*. That's exactly how Damien had referred to her—and clearly the queen knew that.

And we'd been oblivious for months, allowing her edge on us to increase.

Hurried footsteps sounded in the corridor, and my head snapped up. Everyone was watching me, concern painting their expressions. Rina rounded the corner at top speed and came to a halt in the middle of the room, Esmond breathing heavily behind her.

"What the—" She looked around the catastrophe of the office, but shook her head. "I don't care. We have a problem."

"We have a lot of problems." I shook the papers I'd found. "It's—it's true. Kakias made a deal. And now, whatever she got from that deal, requires sacrificing the Chosen Child." I was panting, my chest tightening. "Sacrificing Ophelia."

Silence dropped over the room, ringing like the echoes of an explosion.

"What?" Santorina gasped.

But Jezebel ripped my father's papers from my hands, sharing them with Cyph.

The treaty, imprisonment, the war—Spirits we'd been in the dark about the true causes of it all. Pawns in a larger game that now threatened to crush me.

That night I'd been convinced to sign the contract came back to me, terror burning scarlet across my vision as my hand was forced. I rammed my fingers through my hair, gripping it at the scalp, my breathing rapid and shallow.

"Breathe in," someone said from my side, snapping me from the memory. I whipped around to see Mila. "Breathe in, count to four."

It was hard to calm myself enough to focus on counting, but I did as she said, watching the lashes flutter around her almond-shaped blue eyes.

"Now hold it for seven. Count down from eight on the exhale."

By the time I'd repeated the meditation three times, the rest of the room had skimmed my father's papers, conversation exploding among them.

"Rina, what's the other problem?" I asked, and they all fell silent.

Fingers fiddling with the corner of the thick book she held, Rina swallowed. "Ophelia asked me to research curses. She assured me the Undertaking had healed her, but there was something unsettling in her tone. She seemed particularly interested in those cast by higher powers, but I couldn't find any information here. So, I went to the Sacra Temple and dug into the Angels and the Undertaking. That led me to a tiny shop deep in the Ascended Quarter, the Reverent Tome. They carry everything from wards against haunted spirits to books with banned legends. And I found...well..."

She propped the book on the back of a chair and turned to a dog-eared page. "*Of all the curses that exist among warriors, the most infamous is the Angelcurse. Though it exists largely in folklore and there has not been suspicion of a case in hundreds of years, the most recent rumor was a Mystique Warrior tasked by the higher beings themselves. There is no cure but blood for seraphs kissed by the Angels. Death is the ultimate sacrifice."*

"Oh, fucking *Spirits*," Jezebel hissed, her face pale.

"What?"

"*Angelblood.* The Alabath line has Angelblood." When no one said anything, she continued, pacing around the room. "Don't you see? That Mystique Warrior in the book is Annellius and he died because he couldn't complete the task the Angelcurse required of him. Angelblood marked him as chosen, something ignited the curse, and he lost his life because of it.

"For whatever reason, the Angelblood is dormant in me, but it's active in Ophelia. She was told as much." Her voice rose, a mix of impatience and desperation. "And now she's stained with another curse—this Angelcurse. It's not a farce like the last. This one could truly kill her." Jezebel's face paled as she said it.

No cure but blood...death is the ultimate sacrifice.

"And somehow," Barrett continued, "it seems my mother knows what lurks in Ophelia's blood. And she wants it."

"Two forces, both threatening Ophelia's life..." Lyria mumbled. My Bind thudded once.

"The question is," Cyph said, looking up from my father's papers to meet my eyes, "which will kill her first?"

CHAPTER THIRTY-SEVEN

OPHELIA

AS I BLINKED MY eyes open, dusk cut harsh shadows across the room. A heavy weight settled across my hip. Tol's arm.

We'd slept all day—the most rest I'd had in weeks—and at some point, I had curled into him. I looked up at the relaxed lines of his face. His lips were set in a peaceful smile that even the bruise on his cheek couldn't mar.

My stomach flipped when I remembered kissing those lips just hours ago. Fear threatened to bubble inside me, the sharp edges of a heartbreak I was still healing from prodding against my mind.

No, I coached myself. *Don't retreat.* Because I didn't want to succumb to that fear with Tol. I wanted to allow him to soothe those jagged parts for me, rather than let them tear us apart.

"What are you looking at, Alabath?" he whispered.

"Nothing," I sighed, burrowing closer to him, telling fear to take a reprieve.

Before my eyes could close, voices rose from the dining room, feet stomping up the stairs, and our bubble of bliss burst. We both shot up.

"Window?" Tol asked.

"Window."

We threw our leathers back on, cramming the rest of our belongings in my pack and strapping on weapons.

I tossed the Vincienzo dagger to him as the door burst open and three Engrossians charged through.

"Nothing like a good wake-up call," Tol said, hopping over the bed and driving his dagger into the first warrior's neck before he could raise his ax. "Window, Alabath!"

I jumped to the ledge, but the second Engrossian was closer to me. He grabbed my boot, tugging me back.

Latching on to the top pane of the window, I swung my other leg up, toe catching him in the chin. He released me with a grunt, head cracking back as he fell.

"Go!" Tol shouted.

He fought off the third Engrossian, dagger to ax, backing toward me. In my mind, that ax landed on Tol again. The memory of his blood coated my cheeks and the air between us.

Looking around, I grabbed Tol's wineglass from the night before and threw it at the Engrossian. He ducked, the glass brushing his shoulder as it sailed past.

I climbed out the window, fingers digging into the greenery that grew up Wayward's facade, and scaled down. Tol was above me.

When my boots hit the ground, a fourth Engrossian rounded the side of the inn.

"You've got to be fucking kidding me," Tol cursed. His hair stood up on one side from sleep, but he had a white-knuckled grip on his dagger.

I ripped Angelborn from my back, launching her at the Engrossian. She stuck in his shoulder, and he fell with a thud.

"We've got to get out of here," Tol said, retrieving my spear. A crowd was forming around us—warriors of all clans whispering about the Engrossian dead before them.

I caught snippets of musings, "Is that the Revered Mystique?"

"What is she doing here?"

"It must be her."

I whirled toward Tolek. "*Now*," I ground out, a hint of pleading in my voice, and he whistled for Sapphire.

Tol wrapped his hand around my wrist and tugged me toward where she galloped around the corner. As he was hopping up behind me, the final Engrossian—the one I'd thrown a wineglass at—burst from Wayward's entrance. The door banged back against the wooden facade, the *boom* hushing the crowd.

"Alabath!" the warrior called after us.

"Fucking Angels," I cursed. How had they found us?

The Engrossian jumped on his horse, speeding after Tol and me, his black armor swallowing up the sunset streaming between the trees. They moved with a preternatural grace, sweeping beneath branches as smoothly as we did.

"My queen has need of you," he taunted.

Tolek's arms tightened around my waist. "Tell your queen to suck Bant's golden cock. Ophelia isn't hers."

In response, the Engrossian launched a knife that sailed inches above Tol's shoulder. Hot fury boiled within me at it all. The queen, her foot soldiers, and the uncanny ownership she felt over me. Spirits, even the claim the Angels had over me.

Ever since Damien's first appearance to me, I'd become a puppet, strings warred over by agents of fate.

"I'll kill her," I growled.

"I'll fight you for the honor," Tol responded. "How far are we from the mountains?"

"A few miles." Wayward's small town was hidden among the trees not too far from the rocky base of the Mystique Range.

Still energetic in his pursuit, the Engrossian released another knife in our direction. Sapphire zigzagged through the trees.

"Caves?" Tol asked.

I nodded, picturing the deep caverns cut into the mountains like burrows, like the one I'd seen on the raid with Barrett.

If we could get away from our attacker, we'd be able to hide there for the night and continue our trek home in the morning. Hopefully—

Another knife whistled behind us.

I ducked, but Tol pushed himself up behind me, nimble fingers snatching the dagger from the air. The blade sliced his bare hand, but he barely grunted. Without a breath, he flipped the weapon around and sent it flying back toward its owner. The *squelch* and echoing *thud* told me enough.

"Impressive," I panted, stressed nerves still tingling, ears perked for signs of pursuit.

"I know," he murmured, laughing and pulling me tighter against him with his uninjured hand.

No hooves rang out in the trees as we ran. It was only Sapphire, Tol, and me, hearts pounding in sync below a dusk fading into night.

"That one," I directed Sapphire after we'd been riding in silence for miles.

"Why that one?" Tol asked, curious.

We'd passed a few caves already, looming entrances spotting the base of the mountains, but at the nearest one, the second pulse beneath my skin sped. I couldn't put a name to it, that instinct twisting through my body.

"It feels right" was all I said, and Tol took it as explanation enough.

We dismounted, and he headed inside, taking Sapphire by the reins. I threw one last glance over my shoulder, sweeping my gaze across the trees, but all was quiet.

Tolek was already getting out the mystlight lantern when I entered, a pale sheen falling across the hard-packed dirt floor and gray walls. Using a bit of water from our canteen, he cleaned the blood from his hand, the cut already healing over. The tunnel stretched into the distance, my skin prickling as I looked toward that darkness.

"Don't set up yet."

"Why not?" Tol asked.

I couldn't explain the pounding of my pulses, the feeling that the walls breathed.

"I want to see what's back there."

Tol sprang to his feet and held out his hand. I looked at his fingers for a moment. Why did every movement between us suddenly feel weighted? He put no pressure on me, behaving as he always had. The only difference was I now knew what purpose lay beneath each gentle brush of his fingers and teasing hook of his lips.

Though, I think a part of me had always known—the part that dared to kiss him. The part that felt free, that relented to the wild abandon he encouraged of me. There was a passion within me that only came alive in Tolek's presence, muted when he wasn't around. The part that belonged to him—

No, it didn't belong to him.

Because Tol hadn't asked me to give any piece of myself up, especially not after everything I'd been through.

But the quickening of my heart when I looked between his outstretched hand and his carefully shuttered eyes told me that I might one day want to give it all to him. All of those broken pieces he'd so delicately held together, even when I hadn't realized he was.

I crossed to him, gravel crunching beneath my boots, and it felt utterly right when my fingers curled between his.

I'd unknowingly but willingly traded a piece of my heart for a piece of his years ago. For now, we'd share those, guard them between us, and see what happened.

He squeezed my hand, and that silent promise was sealed.

With a mischievous flick of my brows, I swiped up the lantern and pulled him farther into the tunnel, following Angelborn's pulse within my own. Sapphire treaded slowly at our backs.

For a long time, we walked in silence, listening to the Spirits breathe within the walls around us.

The tunnel narrowed, the ceiling dropping slightly, but a sense of power thickened the air, pressing down on us. We shuffled over dirt paths, winding deeper into the mountains, and the magic stirred my blood.

"How deep do you think these tunnels go?" Tol voiced the question I'd been avoiding answering myself.

"If I had to guess, I'd say they cover the expanse of the mountains." Snaking passages stretching from one territory to the next, weaving through our source of magic. My chest tightened, a cold sweat beading on the Bond at the back of my neck. The tattoo seemed to come alive in here, nearer to its purpose, but my skin prickled, like eyes bored into it.

I whipped my head toward Tol, but his gaze was roaming the tunnels, cataloging every inch. A wind rolled through the corridor. His hand twitched toward his dagger.

"They must have been used for something."

"Maybe trade routes? For things they didn't want to haul up the mountains?" Even as I suggested it, it felt wrong.

Unease sank in my stomach, but I forged ahead, glad to have Tol's steady support at my back as that second pulse pounded beneath my skin like a beast ready to be unleashed.

Every step we took, the pressure was more pointed.

Finally, the mystlight fell across a doorway in the rock ahead of us, wide and arching.

I hurried toward it, the pulse quickening, tugging my gut until I was practically lurching forward. I pushed past that feeling, burst into the dark cavern.

And froze.

Empty walls towered over us, hard to see through the darkness swallowing up the space outside the circumference of our lantern. Branches stretched off the circular room, deep pathways into the mountains.

As I walked, holding the lantern higher, I realized three walls were carved with wide steps, climbing to the top.

No, not steps.

Seats.

Aimed toward where I assumed a stage would have been.

A theater.

Lifting the lantern higher, I ran to the front of the room. Crumbling rocks were all that remained—no signs of pageantry or ornate decor. Only remnants of the mountains' past and the thudding of my second pulse.

"What's wrong?" Tol asked.

"There's nothing here," I mumbled, my shoulders dropping.

"What did you expect?" Tolek asked, roaming the stage space in the dark, running his hands over the walls.

"I...don't know. More than this, though."

Still, a theater within the mountains was curious.

"What's this?" he called.

As I got closer, mystlight spilled over a large pile of rocks—

"A statue?"

Seven weathered figures circled around an eighth, that larger one absorbing their attention like a beacon in the night. Some were broken—one appeared to be headless, another with black moss creeping across its body—but no features were discernible in any of them.

They all appeared to be either on the verge of bowing or rising, immortalized in this indiscernible moment in between. Goosebumps prickled across my skin, the second pulse racing faster than the first.

I stretched up to drag my finger along the edge of the closest figure. When flesh met stone, my skin seared. My necklace with it.

"Fucking Angels," I hissed, shaking my hand. Sapphire whinnied, nudging me.

"What happened?" Tol wrapped my hand in his, looking between the wall and my blistered finger. "It did that?"

Tenderly, he took the lantern from my other hand and inspected the burn. It was already healing, but the throbbing remained.

"It didn't do anything to me," he mused.

"I guess it chose me." I shrugged.

He wasn't fooled by my attempt to make light of the occurrence. His eyes narrowed at the rock as if he'd jump between me and it, but then he stepped back.

I took the lantern and swept it over the statue and surrounding area one more time, bending to inspect the base and circling it, looking for anything suspicious. Lips pursed, I turned to Tol. He stood with his hands clasped behind his back, watching me.

"What if—"

He tilted his head when I paused. "If?"

Theories swirled in my head, but none of them made sense. And none of them could be explained in full until I saw Damien again and asked what his warning meant.

"Never mind." I shook my head. "I don't know what it is."

"We can stay and figure it out, if you'd like."

Looking back at the statue, I knew. Staying would provide no answers. Whatever once lived here had long turned to dust.

"Let's continue," I conceded.

"Good." He sighed, relieved. "This place doesn't feel right."

There was a piece of me that longed to pick apart this cavern, but instead I grasped Tol's hand again and chose one of the tunnels on gut instinct.

The farther we marched away, the more my second pulse dulled. I allowed the darkness to swallow the statue and hopefully bury its heated presence in my memory.

Tolek was quiet as we settled in an offshoot of the main tunnel to get some rest. I hadn't a clue how deep we ventured into the mountains, but Sapphire had chosen our last few turns, and I trusted her instincts.

"What're you thinking?" I asked.

He seemed to consider his words for a minute. He pointed to the sleeping mat he set out, telling me to take it.

Knowing he wouldn't give me an answer unless I laid down, I did.

"I meant what I said, Ophelia." He settled on the dirt, using my cloak as a pillow. "Before I left."

The lantern flickered behind me, casting shadows on his face.

"Which part?" My heart fluttered against my chest, and I fidgeted under his gaze, hair falling over my shoulder and across my cheek.

As tentative as a frightened animal and with a hesitancy so unlike Tolek Vincenzo, he reached up, catching the strand and tucking it behind my ear. It was a question, one that lingered as his thumb gently grazed my jaw. The things we shared at Wayward, our kiss, had been full of racing emotions and fears.

Now, as we lay secluded from the world, we slowed down.

I hardly dared to move, unable to, allowing Tol's heavy stare to take all it wanted from me.

He must have found whatever he needed because he said, "All of it."

His hand slid from my face to the cave floor between us. Without a word, I moved to the edge of the sleeping mat, making room.

"I told you to take it," he said.

"I want you here."

He smiled at that, and though I didn't have an explicit answer for him, he understood.

Our faces were close enough now that I could see the amber specks in his eyes even in the lamplight. They were full of questions, but no demand for answers. The decisions, the control, were all mine.

It was different than the challenges while we rode Sapphire and the gentle kiss we exchanged. This was intimate. Real. Two people, breaking down their walls with small gestures and few words, waiting to see what happened. Sometimes, quiet moments spoke louder than words.

I wasn't ready to make decisions in this dim cave with enemies breathing down our necks. But Tol's hand lay between us, so I hooked my pinkie through his, returning the relieved smile that lifted his lips.

"Good night, Vincienzo."

"Good night, Alabath."

It seemed like I'd barely shut my eyes when my hand was tugged to the side, caught by something.

A deep shout dragged me from sleep.

Beside me, Tol thrashed, my hand still in his grip. "Stop, *stop*! They don't—"

His eyes clenched tighter, sweat beading across his brow.

"Tol!" I shook his shoulder.

"*Please*," he begged. "I'm—I promise—"

"Tol, wake up!" I pleaded, and his eyes popped open.

He shot upright, breath as wild as his eyes, searching the cavern.

When they landed on me, his shoulders relaxed slightly. He pulled me toward him, lips pressing to the top of my head, breathing me in.

"It's okay." I squeezed him tighter. He cradled me against his chest, his spicy citrus scent enveloping me, my ear filled with his racing heart. "I'm here. It's okay."

We stayed like that, his arms banded around me, one of my hands wrapped around his neck, until his breathing returned to normal.

"What was that?" I whispered finally, pushing back to look up into his eyes. The brown hues were dull, no dancing amber flecks winking at me. "Nightmares?"

He swallowed, voice shaking. "Since the Undertaking."

The shame coating his words made me sick, but I remembered his pain when receiving the Bond. How the needle was excruciating against his skin.

The truth clicked into place.

Where my Undertaking had been cleansing, his had challenged him in a different way entirely. Fear flashed behind his eyes—the pain

293

of whatever the ritual had put him through echoing in his mind and body as he relived it.

I haven't slept well since we've been here, he'd said to me in the kitchens the morning after Renaiss. Because of the Undertaking and whatever trauma the damn Spirits put on his soul. I couldn't understand it; how they found misguided tragedies to torture his innocent mind within a sacred test meant to prove your worth.

When he'd admitted his sleeping troubles to me, I hadn't assumed he meant *this*.

"Do you want to talk about it?" I asked, prodding him to slice open that wound and pour out some of the toxins between us so I could help him siphon them off.

"My experience wasn't as…positive as yours." His voice faltered over the end of his sentence.

"I'm sorry it was like that for you." I held my palm to his cheek, turning his gaze to me. Spirits, why would they beat him down like this? "It's so much less than you deserve. But if there comes a time when you want to share it, I'm here."

"I think that's against the rules." He attempted to joke, but it was dull.

"I don't much like following the rules," I whispered, dragging my thumb across his cheekbone.

A small smile quirked his lips. He scooted us back toward the wall, and—arms holding me firmly—we fell into a contemplative silence.

There was something I was more certain of now than ever—even if I didn't have Damien's warning in my head, I couldn't tell Tolek about the Angelcurse. He was already fighting so many silent battles, I wouldn't add mine to his conscience.

Once I knew what it meant, formulated a plan, and confirmed that Damien's threat was nothing but overbearing privacy, I'd tell him everything. Pour every secret between us so we weren't tainted by them.

But right now, sheltered in this cave in the safety of each other's arms, I wouldn't take away what little peace he was able to find.

He deserved all the happiness the Spirits could offer, and I promised myself I'd ensure it. I'd never again hear that jagged scream from his throat, as awful as the ones I'd heard—

"Is that what the Mindshapers did to you?" I asked.

He stilled, then hummed. "Hm?"

I pushed up to look into his eyes, dissect that stare I knew better than most.

"That's how I found you. I heard you scream, and it sounded like…" The terror echoed his nightmares. "When I found you, though, you weren't being harmed." Not recently, at least.

"I wasn't being tortured physically." His eyes closed, forehead dropped against mine. "They used their…tricks. Made me relive some of my most horrifying memories and things I fear might happen."

The fucking Mindshapers.

My stomach churned with his confession. I'd forgotten how the minor clan's power could manipulate magic within the mind. It was usually reserved for instilling peace, but they could drag up his terror, feed it to him. If one of those warriors was corrupt, their power became inhumane.

I was glad I'd killed them; if given the chance, I'd do it again.

Tol's hand shook against mine, calling me down from my carnal revenge and back to who needed me.

"It's all right." I ran a hand down his arm. "You're here. You survived."

He nodded, the tremors slowly stopping. "Thanks for saving me."

I didn't tell him he was wrong. While I may have been the one to ride to his rescue, Tolek had been saving me from myself for years.

Chapter Thirty-Eight

Ophelia

"A DEAD END?" I asked dully as we reached a wall. Sunlight filtered between cracks in the thick white stones.

We'd been wandering these tunnels for days now, and Sapphire had taken the lead. A piece of me trusted she knew where she was going. If I'd counted correctly, the Daminius festivities began tonight with the Sunquist Ball at the Revered's Palace. And tomorrow, after the holiday, my time to persuade the delegates of my aptitude was up. Failure slackened my frame.

"Wait," Tol whispered. "Do you hear that?"

He held his ear to the wall, and I mimicked him. A dull hum of activity slithered through the cracks; voices chatting merrily and grunting, as if lifting and moving supplies.

"What is—"

My words were drowned by the cracking of the wall in front of Tol, debris raining down at our feet. He held up a gray brick, a smile on his face—the wall hadn't cracked at all. Tol had pulled a loose stone from it.

I didn't know how, but my warrior horse had gotten us where we needed to be. We followed Sapphire through, the rest of the wall remaining stable, and exited onto a street in the Merchant Quarter of Damenal.

Home.

I hadn't realized how much the Revered's Palace had become a comfort to me. Walking through the arched doorway and hearing our boots echo against the marble floors wrapped a warm embrace of safety around my bones.

Relieved tears stung my eyes. I looked down at my feet as I wiped them away, the mud caked on my boots standing out against the pristine white speckled tiled and inlaid gold embellishments lining the foyer.

We'd made it.

Tolek was back and safe by my side where he belonged.

I barely had time to take a grateful inhale before a parade of footsteps pounded down the staircase. My head snapped up, a smile breaking across my cheeks. Our friends and the delegates surrounded Tolek and me, the relief I'd felt radiating off all of them, too.

But there was something else in their eyes—something sharp enough to puncture the bubble of safety that secured me moments ago.

They looked between each other, all daring someone else to speak first.

"We need to talk," Malakai finally said, eyes barely leaving mine. His assessing gaze sent me fidgeting, remembering the way I'd yelled at him over his decision not to rescue Tol.

I started to ask what was wrong, but before the words left my mouth, someone grabbed Malakai's shoulder and pushed him aside in a flash of long, dark curls and shining leathers.

"Lyria?" Tolek barely had time to ask before the eldest Vincienzo pulled her arm back and landed a punch to her brother's gut.

"That's for abandoning me in Palerman," she hissed as he doubled over. Before Tol could even stand fully upright, she raised her hand again and brought an open-palmed slap across his cheek. "And *that* is for getting yourself kidnapped."

Tolek rubbed a hand across his jaw, the other still holding his gut, and a piece of me wanted to laugh at the scene. His expression frozen in shock, both at seeing his sister and at being hit—twice.

"Good to see you've returned in one piece, brother." Lyria's dark brown eyes shone, and it was concern forming those tears, hidden beneath wrath.

"Not that I'm not *thrilled* to be assaulted, sister"—he worked his jaw back and forth, blinking away the pain—"but what in the Spirit-guarded hell are you doing here?"

"My little brother disappears—with my horse I might add." Santorina winced at that, having used Lyria's mare to get to the mountains. "Then, he *never* tells the family he's okay, until I receive a letter from Malakai saying he's been taken. Forgive me for rushing to the mountains to see how I may help."

I looked to Malakai where he stood behind Lyria, eyes downcast. He'd written to her; the realization soothed some of the agitation that had risen upon seeing him. He hadn't given up entirely when I'd left. No, Malakai had found a shred of forgiveness within himself, a lingering bead of hope that inspired action.

"You didn't tell her you were leaving?" I whispered to Tol.

"I left a note," he muttered.

"Ah, yes, the note. *Ria, Going on a journey. Mother and Father don't need to know. Not sure when I'll be back. TV.*" Lyria tried and failed to mask the hurt in her voice when she added, "Thanks for the information."

"Are Mother and Father here?" Tol asked, spine stiff. I couldn't tell if he'd seen his mistake with his sister or not; he was guarding his emotions.

Lyria crossed her arms. "No."

Tol's shoulders drooped, but he continued to run a hand along his jaw, showing no other sign of disappointment. "Thank you for coming," he whispered.

"Of course." Lyria's voice softened, so unlike her previous fire. Her eyes were mirrors of Tol's—deep, imploring, a wealth of emotion she didn't want seen. But it could barely be hidden as she hugged him to her, and I recognized that desperation to protect your younger siblings.

It seemed Tol did have a family member looking out for him after all.

The Vincienzo heir stepped back and looked between her brother and me, one corner of her lips quirking in a smirk that matched his. "I hear tonight will be the largest Daminius celebration in years. I couldn't let you all have fun without me." With the same ease her younger brother had perfected at a young age, Lyria flicked her hair over her shoulder and winked at me.

I grinned in return. "Welcome to Damenal."

I'd always admired Lyria—had been jealous of her when she rode off to join the war. As she stood back and whispered to a platinum-haired woman I didn't recognize, I was grateful to have another fierce female warrior among us.

"Reunions aside," my own sister said, wrapping her arm around my waist and dropping her head on my shoulder. "We need to get ready for the Sunquist Ball, but there are some things that must be addressed first." Jezebel turned to face me, expression somewhere between heartbroken and horrified. "A lot has happened."

My brows pulled together as I surveyed the room. They all wore indeterminable expressions, the initial elation from our return wearing off.

"What's happened?" I removed my arm from around Jez and stood up straighter. Had there been an attack? Spirits, if I was galivanting around the continent and Mystiques had suffered for it—

"We figured everything out while you were gone," Malakai said, teeth clenched.

"You've kept a number of secrets, sister," Jezebel scolded. There was none of her usual humor in her voice.

"What are you talking about?" I'd kept secrets, yes, but how was that important right now?

Malakai looked ready to snap, but Cyph placed a hand on his shoulder. Malakai took a breath. "The Angelcurse and Kakias's motivations. We know it all."

"What the fuck is an Angelcurse?" Tolek asked, but no one answered him.

I couldn't.

I was too busy falling into the pit opening up beneath my feet, breath escaping my lungs as I finally put names to the expressions of everyone before me: anger, betrayal, fear. Even Cypherion looked concerned with a tinge of disappointment.

"You found the Angelcurse?" I directed it at Rina. She nodded. It was what I'd hoped in asking her about curses. That she'd find out about the one from Damien's prophecy so we could discuss it. But I'd hoped she'd have come to me. Fate truly was playing with our timing. "And you told everyone?"

"Ophelia, I didn't have a choice." She placed a heavy book on the side table, worn leather creaking as she rifled through the pages to read a passage, ending with, "*There is no cure but blood for seraphs kissed by the Angels. Death is the ultimate sacrifice.*"

It didn't take long for me to piece together what they had. Suddenly, I was back on that balcony with Damien, the morning after Malakai and I had been reunited and Lucidius killed. *You were never at risk of suffering from* that *curse*, he'd said.

The former case on a Mystique Warrior hundreds of years ago— Annellius.

A task by the Angels—what killed my ancestor.

Unite them. But…*Death is the ultimate sacrifice.*

No cure.

No cure.

No cure.

Fucking Angels. I'd known I'd follow Annellius's fate if I failed, but what was success? Death? Was that the sacrifice the Angelcurse demanded?

A hand snaked around my shoulders, squeezing once and snapping me out of my spiral. Tol looked down at me, concern creasing his brow.

"Someone explain to me what the fuck is going on here," he demanded.

"What we know," Cyph began, "is that the Alabath line has Angelblood. It's dormant in Jezebel, but active in Ophelia. The active blood signals this Angelcurse, which is very vague in every mention of it Santorina has been able to find, but seemingly lethal, and explains why the Angel has appeared to Ophelia on multiple occasions."

"What does that mean?" Tol's voice rose. "She's cursed again? Is this why Kakias is after her? Is she—" His sentence trailed off, his arms tightening around me.

"We don't know yet," Santorina attempted to soothe him.

"No." Tol shook his head, looking down at me with frantic eyes that caused my heartbeat to falter. "No, we'll fix this. I'll figure something out. I won't let it take you."

"There's more she isn't telling us." Malakai's eyes were narrowed at me, at the horror I'd failed to mask as I'd worked it all out. A beat pressed against my Bind, but I didn't know what it meant.

Tolek's eyes dropped at the realization that I'd kept more secrets.

I supposed now that they figured out about the Angelcurse on their own, I could tell them.

"When Damien last appeared, he delivered a second prophecy." My voice rose with desperation. "It—it was a task. *Born again through the shade of heart, the Angelcurse claims its start. Seek the seven of ancient promise. Blood of fate, spilled in sacrifice. Strive, yield, unite, Or follow the last's lost fight,*" I repeated the words I'd memorized many nights ago. "He said I must *unite them,* but I'm still working out what *them* could be."

"And you didn't think to tell us?" Rina asked. Betrayal stared back at me from all around the room. Spirits, this was what I'd been trying to avoid.

"I wanted to." I was floundering, reaching desperately for their support, but I'd pushed it away and now, they were hurt. "Damien warned me not to. He said only I could know, that *fate will fight back.*"

"What fate?" Cyph asked.

"I don't know. Something stopped him from continuing. But it was a command from an Angel, and I didn't know what would happen if I told you."

Skepticism met me, and I knew what they were thinking. It was a fragile excuse, a loose enough threat that it probably would not have held.

But I hadn't been willing to gamble their lives until I knew something. Until I had control of the situation. And telling them made it all real.

"The seven of ancient promise...could it be the Angels?" Jez asked.

"No, I doubt she could seek them," Vale guessed. "They don't exactly come when called."

She had a point, and I latched on to it. "But I think that's on the right path."

"The shade of heart. We know what that must be," Lyria's friend said, and everyone turned to her. She stared back, surprised. "Look at her eyes. Pretty rare, no?"

I nodded. "That's what I guessed, too. Annellius's spirit had a similar color." For some reason, the Angelcurse had to be the cause of my oddly discolored eyes.

I pulled every piece of information I had on the Angels to the forefront of my mind, picking apart the lore and the rumors. Everything my father had told me over mystlight lanterns before bed as a girl. Everything I'd gathered on my own in recent months. Everything the Storyteller had said. The emblem necklace heated.

"There's also news on Kakias," Malakai said, making my heart stutter.

"Has she attacked?" My voice was barely a whisper, these revelations draining every ounce of power from me.

He shook his head, and I released a breath.

"We moved half of our troops to the eastern border of the mountains, though," Lyria explained. "It's where her army appears to be headed."

I nodded, remembering the plan I'd established with Danya weeks ago. With various alternatives, given that we didn't know what Kakias was planning. Everyone kept the defenses up while I was gone—kept us in motion. Thank the Spirits for the council around me.

"What of Kakias, then?" I asked.

Barrett took wary steps forward and explained the sacrificial nature of the pools in the Engrossian Valleys, the theory that his mother may have bartered with the dark magic at some point in the past, though they couldn't figure out why, and that they believed it tied into her expansive collection of Mystique lore and knowledge on myself.

"And why didn't you tell us of that tidbit, sister?" Jezebel nudged me.

"I think she found out about my Angelblood." For some reason, it was easiest to look at Malakai while I spoke. Maybe because we'd already thrown so many accusations at each other, admitting secrets I was ashamed of didn't change anything. Maybe because we'd both hidden things for the good of others, and I understood that decision a bit better now. "I think that's why she wants me. But I thought if I told you, it would lead to questions I couldn't answer about what it means. About the Angelcurse."

"Well, now we know everything." Malakai crossed his arms. "Right?"

"Everything that I know, you know. I haven't figured out what I'm meant to unite. But if Kakias knows anything of this, I'm running out of time."

And if they were right, and the queen had employed the use of such dark magic, then I didn't know how I'd ever defeat her.

Her sharp-toothed smile and lifeless eyes flashed through my mind, and I feared my friends' suspicion was right. There had been a lack about her—some quality missing that made her less humane. Her ambition heightened, tunnel vision on her goals driving her forward. Her thirst for *me* controlling every decision she made.

"But if that's right, and she truly only wants me," I thought out loud, remembering what Aird had claimed as he tried to kill me—Kakias wanted my blood shed. "Then I don't see why she's waging an entire war."

I was one person. My blood held power, but what could that mean to her?

There were too many holes in the theories. I had all the pieces but was working in a room too dark to see their shapes.

I needed someone to turn on the light. Looking around at the dejected faces before me, I realized we all did. The hurt and disappointment staring back at me dragged guilt up my throat.

I closed my eyes, inhaling once.

As I exhaled, the doors to the palace opened. Staff walked in, pausing to greet us and share their excitement for the Sunquist Ball in a few hours. The grounds beyond the entryway were dazzling in gold streamers and candles.

Amid the excitement, I shoved all my concerns from my mind. There may be a dark queen hovering over me and a prophecy to untangle, but the people surrounding me did not deserve the worry etched across their faces.

It was with that resolve that I forced a smile to my lips.

"We'll figure it out," I promised, dropping my voice so the staff didn't overhear. "In the meantime, let's set aside our concerns and enjoy Daminius."

One last holiday before the battle began. I turned away from the disappointed faces quickly.

There were enemies breathing down our necks at every turn—a

queen, a curse, a war, and an unknown task by the Angels. I wasn't sure how I'd meet them, but that was my burden to carry. My friends could help me find answers, help me prepare, but as the Chosen Child, as the Revered, I'd face it all.

On Renaiss, I'd presented myself as an image of light and promises, instilling hope in the future for my people. Walking into Daminius, I wouldn't fail them.

"Alabath, wait."

I turned at Tol's voice, my shoulders slumping at the stern set of his lips. "Yes?"

"You knew about this?" he whispered, pointing back toward the foyer. "You knew this entire time that you were at risk and you didn't tell me?" His jaw ticked as he spoke, heat permeating the air.

Anger.

"Damien warned me not to tell you all. I didn't know what was happening." The excuses rushed out of me. "I only had suspicions, and I didn't want to tell anyone until I knew for sure that nothing would happen to you."

If I had told Tolek, he would have jumped to my defense, consequences be damned, but we wouldn't have known what enemy we were facing, which weapons to raise. If we turned our force the wrong way, we could've been attacked from behind.

"I don't care if you didn't know the whole truth, or what the fucking Angel told you." His voice cracked with restraint from keeping it quiet. "You should have told me. That threat wasn't complete, you said he didn't even finish speaking it. You can trust me with anything, you know that."

I did know that. And after being fiercely burned by a lack of trust with Malakai, I should never have allowed that to fester between Tolek and me. But I had, and now, he was looking at me with a hurt that pierced my soul.

"Tol, I—"

"Not right now," he interrupted. "I...I'll see you later."

He left me in the hall, storming away with his hands flexing at his sides.

CHAPTER THIRTY-NINE

DAMIEN

SALVATION, THAT SATISFIED PURR from our master said, bright power swirling about him, begging to break free.

There had been a ripple. A subtle but rattling tremor through us all. There and gone so briefly, it could have been imagined had it not been for the glow of the Angelglass.

It was enough to sate our master as he prowled the chamber. Enough to weaken the walls around us so we could cast our presence deeper within them, use the magic we were once gifted in long forgotten ways.

We were all pushing boundaries now to see, to hear, to learn anything that went on beyond our terrain. And though I feared the moment he'd change his mind on our restraints, I had remembered something with that ripple of power: He needed me.

He needed the girl, and he could not get her without me.

I was a key.

Or perhaps she was the key, and I the lock.

Regardless, no matter my prior missteps, fate had given me a safety net. The old mist's wicked humor found loophole after loophole in this world of unbalanced magic, seeking to restore order, and I would thank her for this one if I ever met her.

I drew up to the Angelglass, running a golden hand over its cracked surface, promises pouring into me. It had not shone since the ripple, had not depicted any hint of what she was doing.

Locks and keys, the roles we were fated for, the multitudes of endings played out in my head. One thread of fate withdrawn from the loom meant a distorted tapestry. It would still fulfill a purpose, but at what cost? Who could say?

"Damien," our master muttered.

I pulled myself from my thoughts to see the fogged glass clearing slightly, wanting to show us something.

My brothers and sisters gasped, hushed questions filling the chamber.

Faces swarmed through. All faces that surrounded the Chosen Child. All holding answers to be pieced together. Hints as to what keys turned the locks.

This mirage wasn't a current moment—it was a prediction. I knew from the way the image rippled and pulled at the edges as though a veil was draped across what could be.

"He has—" Blood poured across the image, cutting off Bant's outburst.

"The stars can't tell her," Valyrie whispered unconvincingly as crimson faded to a lavender haze.

And that was replaced by a burst of light. A tangle of two opposing threads, warring within an iridescent ring and bouncing off marble. Statues shattered. Leaves and brush and petals whirled through the air. A dagger flashed in the middle of it all.

"Is she—"

The light refracted off the weapon, filtering through the glass to actually *touch* us.

And then, it went dark.

A low hiss filled the room as the Angelglass smoked. Tendrils wafted through the chamber, across faces that had only once before been stunned as they were now.

And I once again felt that fear. Perhaps we would be undone after all.

-PART THREE-
ATROPOS

CHAPTER FORTY

MALAKAI

FOR WEEKS, I'D TRIED not to think about how much I'd fucked up when fighting Tolek. His capture made the guilt worse, and I could only handle so much of that.

Now that he was back, that I'd seen Ophelia's plan had worked and they'd *both* returned safely, I felt like an even bigger fool for not trusting her or understanding why she had to go.

It was regret that warred within my stomach when I located him atop the highest turret in the palace, settled above the afters lounge. Alone and contemplating, his eyes flashed between the journal in his hand and the expansive world stretching before us.

Standing beside him, stomach in knots, I waited until he was done writing, wondering what conflict was causing his silence, as I figured out what to say. *I'm sorry* was too small for the way I'd acted. *I'm glad you're okay* too simple for what he'd been through. He stiffened as I shifted, and though the physical bruises from his time captured were gone, I imagined the imprints left beneath the skin. I knew better than anyone how deeply the real wounds would last. These scars were something we now shared. Maybe they'd form a bridge over my mistakes.

Finally, Tol closed his journal and set it on the floor beside his feet. "Are you going to hit me?" he asked, running his hand over the Vincienzo dagger that had been returned to his belt. He was dressed in formal pants and shirt, the sleeves cuffed at the elbow. We didn't have long before we were expected in the ballroom.

I exhaled, releasing a low laugh. "I think you've been through enough." I paused, chewing the inside of my cheek. "If you need to talk about it, I'm here."

"Thanks," he said, looking at his weapon for a moment. When he finally looked me in the eye, resolve hardened his stare. No more stalling, then. "Are you mad at me for how I feel?"

His question was simple, straightforward. It nearly knocked me off guard.

"No," I said, and it wasn't a lie. "How can I be when I felt the same?"

He tilted his head. "Then what caused that attack?"

I flinched at the word, but it was the truth of what I'd done. I'd considered the same question while he was gone, and I wasn't sure I had an easy answer. There were so many things twisted inside of me, I no longer knew how to handle my emotions. And that day, I'd snapped. The fight had been about Ophelia, but it also hadn't.

"It was about being lied to for so long by so many people I trusted, that I couldn't take it anymore."

"I never lied to you." He clenched the railing.

"I realized that after," I agreed, nodding. It only took that conversation with Ophelia to realize how much of an ass I'd been to the best friend I'd known my entire life. Tol may have averted some truths, but he had never lied. "If I'm mad at anyone, it's myself. Or maybe I'm mad at the twisted fate that landed us here." The beings that took our lives and treated them as their playthings. Pawns.

Tolek pushed off the rail and paced around the circular tower, hands behind his back.

"Things used to be easy," I muttered.

He froze at that, and the mountains seemed to hold their breath. "For you," he whispered. There wasn't malice in his voice, but recognition.

"What do you mean?"

"Mali," he exhaled, coming back to stand beside me and looking me square in the face, searching. Some shreds of understanding clicked together in his mind, and he sighed. "I've lived my entire life in your shadow. No, my life wasn't hard per se—I've been afforded a level of privilege from my family name—but I was always your sidekick, the second choice. *You* were the future Revered, partnered to the most incredible warrior, and I was…there, by your side."

"Ophelia—"

"No," he cut me off, eyes hardening. "I don't want to talk about her yet. I want to talk about us."

I clenched my jaw, teeth aching to grind the truth in his words to dust.

"You were the star all our lives, and I never resented you for it. Even my own parents didn't want me around, and maybe that's where most of this pain stems from, but that, paired with being second best to your closest friend and watching him love the girl you want…it *wasn't* easy, but I accepted that was what my reality was."

My brows pulled together as he bared the truth of his fucked-up life, and I realized not all scars were visible. Tolek may not have suffered as I had, but he *had* been struck.

"Everything changed when you left," he continued, shoulders tense. "I feel awful for even saying it, but I got a taste of life outside of your shadow. And then I felt guilty every day for enjoying it because I would have rather had you back with us than have any attention for myself.

"You were my brother, Mali. Had been since birth. And I thought you were dead." His voice cracked over the last word, but he blew out a frustrated breath and forged ahead, seeming like if he didn't, he'd lose the nerve. "I know why you did it, but it fucking *hurt* to find out the truth. And again, I cast my feelings aside because I knew you needed support assimilating back into our world more than you needed to feel guilty for hiding things from me."

I tried to think back to our childhood, to see it from his perspective. He was right that I—Ophelia and I—had been on a pedestal. We'd never asked for it. I refused to feel guilty for it. But that didn't make his feelings any less valid, and hearing how he'd felt for nearly two decades was a knife through my gut.

Hearing how he had been cast aside by his own parents twisted the blade.

And how he had put aside his feelings for my own upon my return…that was the final blow. Cyph was different—more practical. When he didn't puzzle out a way around the choices I'd made, he'd

311

accepted them. But Tolek had always been the more volatile of the two, driven by emotions, whatever they may be. Even while he was stifling them, they had been there, pain and resentment simmering.

He was wrong about one thing though.

"I deserve that guilt," I admitted. "I made mistakes. So many fucking mistakes. I thought I was doing the right thing in signing the treaty, but I didn't realize what it would cause. And I never realized how you felt."

About Ophelia, his family, or my leaving.

"That's my fault, and I'm sorry." He placed a hand to his chest. "If I wanted to resolve my own feelings, I should have spoken up."

"No." I shook my head. "I should have seen it." If I was truly a good friend, I should have understood how he'd been treated our entire lives. Should have dragged him out of the shadows and into the light where he belonged.

Tol shrugged. "It's all out in the open now."

"You're still my brother," I said, putting a hand on his shoulder. "You always will be." I set aside my own pain in order to be there for Tol in that moment, but I wasn't smothering it as I had. Instead, warmth spread throughout my chest, cracking open at bearing his pain before my own. A step toward healing.

Amicable silence surrounded us as we turned back to the mountains. Tol's confession repeated in my head, and I drew one conclusion: Maybe even those who seemed the strongest among us were broken in their own way. Maybe I didn't only need to heal myself but learn to be there for those I cared about.

"If I hadn't started that fight with you," I began, "would you have ever said anything to her?"

"Never," Tolek swore, laughing. "Not unless she asked."

Spirits, he truly was the most selfless bastard in existence. Honed through years of pushing aside his feelings. Tolek looked at everyone else's happiness first—it was time for a change.

"Ophelia and I couldn't be together. Despite how you feel or how she may feel toward you." The words hurt to push past my throat, but he needed to hear it from me. "I changed when I was imprisoned, and so did she. We grew into different people, and we aren't right for each other anymore." Instead of the flash of blades tearing my skin that I'd expected to feel, there was only an echo of longing through the Bind. Then, the tattoo fell silent. "She deserves someone who's able to love her the right way."

The way I chose not to.

Tolek wasn't looking at me. He was watching the sun slip toward the mountains, drawing closer to the end of another day, but when he spoke, his voice was laced with unabashed truth, despite who stood beside him.

"I'll always love her." His promise seeped into the world spread before us, bathing it as the sunset did the peaks. "It's up to her how."

CHAPTER FORTY-ONE

OPHELIA

JEZEBEL HAD NOT BEEN happy with me.

She had torn into my suite, hands braced on hips clad in cream silk and tulle. Her features were painted with rouge and liner, but beneath the beauty was a silent fury.

"You have a lot of explaining to do, sister," she'd scolded as she forced me onto the stool before my vanity and began combing my freshly washed hair.

I'd apologized profusely for my secrets as she applied cosmetics and set my locks in waves, hoping she'd find a twinge of understanding in her stubborn heart. Explained that it wasn't that I didn't trust her, it was that I didn't understand what Damien meant in his warning.

I still didn't, still carried that fear of what would happen now that everyone knew, but since they'd found out about the Angelcurse themselves, my priority was showing everyone how much I did trust them.

When she set the liner aside and perched on my vanity, looking down at me, shadows lined her face.

"I understand." She didn't meet my eye. "We all keep secrets, and you felt bound to yours. There are truths to each of our souls that cannot be divulged until the time is right."

I wanted to ask what she meant, but the noise in the palace was rising, and we were running out of time.

"Jezzie," I began, taking her hand. "If you listen to only one thing I say tonight, let it be this: You are destined for greatness. The youngest ascended warrior in Mystique history. And I am honored to be your sister."

She crushed me to her then, allowing for a moment of soft grace before yelling at me to get dressed. Then, she swept from the room, leaving an air of questions behind that I didn't understand.

Thirty minutes later, I stood on my balcony, preparing the rest of the apologies I wanted to make tonight. Damenal's beauty soothed me, sparkling as the sun started its descent.

The highest-ranked warriors entered the palace in their finest outfits and jewels, bearing the weapons they cherished most. Light gilded the terra-cotta roofs of the city atop the mountains, dancing across stacks of tapered rocks and tiers of stone buildings. Spires poked into the air from the temples in each quarter, gold adornments accenting the smaller buildings. Everywhere you looked, life was breathed back into Damenal. Even from my balcony, the revelry in the streets was contagious.

I watched it all, concern gnawing at my stomach. Jezebel had forgiven my secrets rather quickly because we were cut from the same cloth. For whatever reason—maybe it was an Alabath trait—my sister and I both tended to keep truths close.

I only hoped the rest of my apologies would be as smooth.

My fight with Tol twisted my gut. I had not seen him since we'd returned. He wanted space, and I gave him that, but every second I worried what he was thinking. If I'd hurt him like I'd feared I would, and after only a couple weeks of knowing how he felt...

"Daminius in Damenal is truly a special event," my father said, stepping onto my balcony. The vest beneath his dark jacket was nearly the same color as my champagne gown, but the fabric hugging my frame was thin and beaded. Shining.

"I've always hoped to experience it. A part of me thought we never would."

"Let's make it one to remember, then." His arm slid around my shoulder, squeezing me to his side. I wrapped my arms around his waist, hand grazing the large sword strapped on the opposite hip. It was an Alabath heirloom I once thought I would wield. Now, with Angelborn on my own back, the weapon held less promise. "May this holiday be the first of your long, fruitful reign as Revered."

A lump formed in my throat at his words. "And hopefully one day a peaceful one."

I contemplated telling him about the Angelcurse, but there wasn't time now. After the ball. I would tell him then. No more secrets.

"I believe you can handle whatever is thrown at you, *sorrida*. I'm very proud of the way you've conquered what you've faced so far."

"Even the rescue?" I looked up at him, expecting frustration for once again running off, but his eyes crinkled as he smiled down at me.

"Especially that." He placed a kiss to my head. "You were handed a tough decision, and you followed your instincts like a true leader. You'll find your heart and head will often be at war while you're forced to consider so many lives beyond your own, but place trust in yourself and your path will be clear. The Spirits bless you, may you always follow your heart and choose what you love."

His words were simple, boiling down my rule to intuition and choice, but they echoed through my mind as we watched the sun's rays spread across the mountains, piercing through the wisps of white clouds lingering from the summer day.

I was grateful to have him beside me, reminding me that no matter what happened with the council or my position, with my heart, I wasn't alone. There was another hand to guide me, to remind me why I was fit for this position when I sometimes forgot myself.

For there was a war on the horizon, and my heart and my head were caught on the brink of battle.

Tonight, I wouldn't think of it, though. I'd forget curses and queens and heartache. I'd remind myself of the power thrumming through my blood and the promise the Mystique Warriors wanted from me.

"They're almost ready for you," Danya said from the door. "We'll head to the temple shortly," she directed at my father.

The rest of the council would make their way to the Sacra Temple to wait for me while I completed one ritual in the ballroom with Missyneth. Then, I'd meet them to honor the Angel.

"Thank you, Danya," I said. Maybe it was the beauty of Daminius, maybe it was the swelling emotion overwhelming me from the conversation with my father, but I stepped up to the Master of Weapons and Warfare and took her hand. "And thank you for everything you did while I was gone. I truly don't know how we'd be faring without you."

Her answering smile was small, but her cheeks blushed as she looked up at me. "It is an honor to serve the Mystique Warriors. And you, Revered." She shook her dark hair back from her chin, straightening her muscular frame. "We will see our people through any approaching threats together."

"That we will." I grinned, warmth blossoming around my heart. "Go," I told her and my father, hugging him a little tighter one last time, hoping he understood every ounce of appreciation pouring from me. "I'll meet you down there."

Then, I turned to the window and stole one last moment to stare out over my sacred city, soaking in the golden sunlight and the joy buzzing through the crowd.

Missyneth would call for attention soon, but I had some atoning to do first.

Rushing into the ballroom, I ignored the hushed murmur of voices at my entrance and deposited Angelborn and Starfire on the rack waiting before the dance floor to hold the Revered's weapons. The scene was dazzling, thin golden streamers trailing from the chandeliers and dousing every surface in sparkles. My dress fit right in, but I barely appreciated Jezebel's fine design.

Instead, I found Santorina and Cypherion, pulling the latter away from a stunning Vale in her emerald gown. He protested, but followed when he saw the plea in my eyes.

"What's going on?" Cyph asked as I tucked us away into a corner. I hadn't seen Malakai or Tolek yet, but this was a start.

"I need to apologize." They stared at me, confusion in their eyes and protests on their lips, but the hurt expressions they'd worn when the Angelcurse was revealed haunted me. "I shouldn't have hid what I knew from you all. I should have found a way around Damien's warning. It wasn't fair to expect your help only to keep secrets."

"Ophelia, we understand—"

"No." I shook my head. "I wouldn't be here without you both. Without all of you. And…just let me finish." I took a breath. "I didn't

317

truly try to fight Damien on the warning because if I kept it to myself, it was easier to pretend it wasn't a threat. I thought telling everyone would be adding kindling to a fire we couldn't control. The truth is, though, I was the one who wasn't in control, and that only got worse by letting secrets pile up."

With my friends—my family—by my side, everything could be controlled. Every puzzle would find an answer.

As I admitted that to myself, those pieces I was given during the Undertaking—the riddles of truth and forgiveness—clicked together. I had seen them in my past, but now I knew how to take the steps forward. To work toward instituting them in my life.

Because the Undertaking may have made me a warrior, but it didn't ensure that I never made mistakes. I had to work for that. Every day, every word out of my mouth to these people I loved more than life itself, I would work for that.

"Santorina, you may be human, but you're fiercer than many warriors. You've always provided steadfast healing and even stronger friendship." I squeezed her hand, and silent understanding passed between us. "And Cyph, you may be the most aggravating trainer I've ever had the displeasure of working with and the biggest self-sacrificial martyr among us—"

"Is that supposed to be an apology?" he whispered to Rina.

"She doesn't do it often," Rina muttered back. "Maybe she needs practice."

"But," I said loudly, smiling at them. "My mind would have fled to dark places long ago without you. So, thank you. I promise to do better." Words didn't do justice to the love I held in my heart for them. For Jezebel and Tolek and Malakai. The five people who had gone to the ends of the earth to protect me, to fight for me—even in ways I didn't always understand.

One thing was certain—it was more than I deserved.

"You don't need to thank us, Ophelia," Cyph said.

"It doesn't hurt." Santorina shrugged, but her round eyes glinted. "You know we're always here, no matter how dark things become. And we know you were afraid, but think of how you felt when things were hidden from you."

"We know you thought Damien said not to," Cyph elaborated.

"But if the threat wasn't explicit, there was a way around it. Next time, let us help."

"No matter what that damn Angel says," Santorina finished.

I swallowed that truth, my skin tingling with premonition.

"We're honored to follow you, Revered." Cyph's sly smile tilted one corner of his lips at my title. "Just don't make us do so blindly."

The only resemblance I saw to the young boy who questioned his worth in our world was in the soft flicker of his eyes. He had grown exponentially, and I thought maybe I had an inkling of what the fates held in his future.

"Now, get back to the ball," I said, spotting a pair of familiar green eyes across the room. "I have a few more conversations to have."

CHAPTER FORTY-TWO

MALAKAI

THE SUNQUIST BALL WAS an image born of myth, worthy of the presence of an Angel. Fitting, given the purpose of the day. With our current predicament with their curses and blood, though, I didn't really want to revere any Angels tonight. They'd fucked up a lot of things for us.

Personally, while I was upset about Ophelia's lying, it had only clarified things for me. It was exactly what I did—hiding a truth about myself because I thought it would hurt others. Although, if she'd have asked, we'd have known Damien's threat wasn't complete. That was only rumors. But I had a feeling that wasn't really why she'd lied. It had been denial.

And in that, I understood her completely.

I think, based on the way she'd looked at me as she confessed, she understood me now, too.

Despite all of that, it was more proof that we couldn't be together. If we were, we'd continue to feed into each other's unhealthy behaviors instead of healing them. Perhaps we were too alike, sharing vices that only wanted to tear us down. What we both needed was a counter. Someone to pry those bad habits from us in the face of ancient curses plaguing us now. Not that I had any room left in me for that. Emotions only resulted in pain, a tool to be used against you.

But no matter how I felt about the Angels and their involvement in our lives, on our most sacred holiday, the concerns of mere warriors were obsolete.

Instead, we donned our finest clothes, jewels, and weapons—the most ostentatious we owned—and fluttered beneath the shining rays that symbolized Damien's almighty ascension from warrior to Angel. I'd considered wearing the sash my mother had given me, but I couldn't bring myself to.

Despite the festival's ridiculousness, I claimed a spot against the wall to watch the levity unfold before me. I held a glass of honeyed liquor in one hand, while the other rested on the pommel of my newly forged sword. Though its grip was slowly forming to me, its blade earning a few nicks between polishings, the weapon was still foreign. Absently, I trailed my fingers over the simple engravings and observed the crowd.

Members of the highest-ranking Mystique families had been twirling across the floor for nearly an hour now, since the doors first opened. Danya, Alvaron, and Larcen departed from the ballroom with boisterous waves, off to prepare the Sacra Temple.

My presence was required at Sunquist, but my participation was not. With Ophelia back, I was allowed to fall into the background as before, handing control back to her. My chest loosened with the prospect as I spotted her across the room, talking to Cypherion and Santorina.

Tolek still hadn't arrived, saying he'd needed a moment after our discussion. An unnamed conflict warred behind his eyes as we descended the staircase from the turret. He'd likely returned to his room to divulge the thoughts in his journal before sealing away whatever pain he was feeling and providing the celebratory side of himself for the evening.

The realization soured in my stomach, blending with the alcohol I downed.

Across the room, Cypherion hugged Ophelia and left their circle to join Vale. Santorina went next, and their expressions were all heavy. Tonight was meant to be revelrous. What had they been discussing?

I shook away the thought. It was likely nothing. Best if I stayed out of it.

Barrett and Dax were in attendance tonight, catching questioning looks from Mystiques around the floor, but I hovered at the edge, a ghost walking among the living. Isolating myself—punishing myself—it was instinct.

I inhaled, my head tipping back against the wall, squeezing my eyes shut against the influx of emotions tonight threatened to stir within me.

But when a soft laugh cut through the fog, my eyes snapped opened.

Not twenty feet in front of me, Mila and Lyria had entered the ballroom, the former laughing at something the Vincienzo heir whispered to her. Many eyes lingered on the pair. Lyria's skintight black velvet dress was a statement for the Sunquist Ball, but more stares rested on her friend. On the gold corset laced tightly to her body, etched with ivy to match her wrist braces and binding a sheer turquoise gown that rippled with each step, exposing long, lean legs and—

My heart thudded against its cage.

Scars.

Mila's skin—normally covered with leathers and boots—was peppered with scars. Some large, some small, all pale and shining in the mystlight. They carved a history of warfare and pain.

My own scars along my back throbbed as hers slid between the slits in her dress.

Gerad, the Turrenian warrior I'd been sparring with recently, approached Mila and Lyria with a friend, asking the two to dance. My fingers curled around my glass as he swept Mila across the floor, but I couldn't look away from those scars, each slicing against the memory of my own. They were a legacy of the war my father had caused, and Mila was a true warrior.

If I'd been inclined to dance, maybe I'd have asked after them. It was prying, my own selfish curiosity ignoring propriety, but a piece of me needed to know how she came to be marked.

I formed different scenarios in my mind until the Master of Rites, Missyneth, called attention to the front of the room. "It is time for the Revered's dance."

The crowd fell silent, a buzz of anticipation slinking through them. Heads turned toward the floor. Ophelia stood beneath the grand chandelier, chin high, magenta eyes on me as if she'd been on her way over here.

Now, she appeared caught.

It took me a moment to understand the flicker of uncertainty in her forced smile. Every warrior present was waiting to see what we'd do. The Revered's dance was an honor shared with their partner. It was a moment for the Mystiques to exalt the chosen leader and the one they deemed their equal.

The crowd waited to see whether we'd play the game for the evening and pretend that the golden children of the Mystique Warriors were still intent on their happily ever after.

Or if we'd publicly allow the illusion to slip away.

The sun's rays flashed against the chandeliers, casting drops of gold around the dance floor awaiting its main event. And a tug in my gut told me—that stage wasn't mine to take.

Ophelia blinked once, long and slow.

Then, sending what I hoped was reassurance through our malfunctioning tattoos, I lifted my glass to her and smiled. It wasn't a smile that said I'd be right there.

It was one to set her free.

CHAPTER FORTY-THREE

OPHELIA

I'D BEEN HALFWAY TO Malakai to make my next apology. We may have torn each other apart, but we had a deeper understanding when it came to secrets and lies, he and I. Now that I wasn't at the brunt of his, I saw that.

I'd wanted to tell him that.

Instead, lingering stares were burning into me, waiting to see whose hand I took.

A cowardly part of me considered turning to Cypherion, asking him to play the part so I wouldn't send a mistaken signal to the swarm of warriors lining the ballroom. But Cyph was oblivious to my current debate, his eyes on Vale. I would not be selfish enough to steal that chance from him.

I forced my smile not to falter. One more second. That was all I had to make my choice; image or heart, which should I choose?

I closed my eyes, inhaling the hot summer air rich with wine and flowers.

Why did it have to be one or the other? Choosing between the symbol of hope or what I desired. Malakai and I had been a promise our entire lives, a vision for the future of Mystiques, but I could still be one without him—I *was* still one.

I caught Malakai's gaze from the corner. He lifted his glass to me and a gentle nudge hit my Bind. That, combined with his smile—a genuine one for once—banished my uncertainty.

Dipping my chin, I focused my attention on the Bind and tried to send the words I'd planned to say to him. *Thank you for everything you've sacrificed. For fighting for us all and teaching me what love was. I understand. And I'm sorry.*

I'd never know if he felt it, but he nodded, and the leash around my heart snapped.

"May I have this dance?" a voice asked from behind me, coaxing my nerves off the edge. Tolek stood waiting, hair combed back, bowing slightly, a hand extended.

Relief unspooled within me, champagne bubbles fizzling away in my stomach.

He was here. Despite my secrets and omissions, he still held his hand out to me.

For a moment, I was taken back to my birthday. Before any visits from Damien, before the Undertaking and the fallout of Kakias and Lucidius's truth, when I was merely facing a cursed death in a matter of days, and Tol had extended his hand.

But this offer meant more, as it meant more when I slid my fingers between his and said, "Of course you may."

As he led me onto the floor, I caught my father's eye across the room. He gave me a soft smile, pride pouring from him as he watched his daughter choose her own happiness. He lifted a hand, waved goodbye, and disappeared out the door to make his way to the temple. For an unknown reason, tears lined my eyes.

But before I could indulge them, the music picked up, and we were turning about the room. Tol's chocolate irises burned with those amber specks, and my heart fluttered like an Angel's wings. His lips quirked up at one corner, as if he heard it.

"This is long overdue," I commented.

"What's that?" He slid his hand around my waist, pressing it gently into the small of my back.

"The dance. From my birthday."

He guided us effortlessly around the floor, without taking his eyes off me. "I would have danced with you all night."

"I know." I bit my lip, and his eyes flicked down to it.

As if on instinct, he pulled me closer until there was no space between us, the champagne fabric of my gown doing nothing to stifle his heat. The arches of beading throughout channeled it, and though the gown made me feel like a vision born of Angellight, I wasn't sure if I was grateful or furious with Jezebel for choosing such a thin material that every inch of his body scorched mine.

His gaze dropped for the briefest second. When it lifted, his eyes burned with need, tracing over the thin straps and low neckline.

"You're beautiful," Tol exhaled.

"You're not half bad yourself, Vincienzo." Unlike many, he'd gone without a jacket, wearing a white linen shirt with the sleeves rolled up. Leave it to Tolek to add his own take to even the most reverent of holidays.

I wouldn't have him any other way.

"I know," he replied with a wink. But then, his face fell slightly. "I'm sorry for how I reacted earlier."

"You had every right to be angry with me." I tilted my head up. "I'd placed a value on honesty and then didn't show it." He deserved better.

"Correct," he agreed. "I have a right to be upset." I was glad he didn't try to placate me. "But I shouldn't have walked away without an explanation. Why did you hide this prophecy from me, though?" *Me.* Not *us.* He understood why I didn't share all my secrets with the entire council, with all of our friends. But the pain rounding the edges of his question—it was personal. Tol's heart ached because I kept the threat from *him.* "I know it wasn't just the warning. That wouldn't be enough to stop you from doing what you wanted without an explanation."

"I wanted to tell you, Tol. So many times. But I was afraid of what it meant for you. Speaking it made it feel real. And then, once I thought maybe it would be okay—" I thought of those thrashing nightmares he fought off in the cave. "You already had enough to worry about. I didn't want to make it worse."

"I'll worry a lot less if I know what's going on." He lifted our clasped hands to brush a strand of hair out of my face. "You can share anything with me. I'm not going anywhere." As if to prove it, he squeezed me to him. "By your side, infinitely, remember?"

I had known that for a while—since the day he jumped in front of Victious's ax for me, and truthfully much longer than that. But the reminder that I wasn't alone settled in my chest, prying some of my headstrong habits from me.

I let them go, promising to myself—to Tol—to do better. To be worthy of his honest heart.

"I'm sorry," I whispered. "I'm still not used to someone carrying burdens with me." For years, I had shouldered my frustrations alone, refusing to acknowledge those who longed to help.

Tol spun me as the music whirled, and when I settled back in his arms, he promised, "Your curses aren't burdens. We'll conquer the Angels together, Alabath."

Together.

I wanted together with Tol. That truth slammed into me, enough to stop my feet from moving, but he continued to carry us across the floor.

"I told you I don't lie to you. I only ask that you do the same." The weight of that request gathered in the sliver of space between us. I moved closer, swallowing it.

"No lies," I swore to him. "And no omissions."

"No lies, and no omissions," he repeated, and it sealed like a promise. Like the thousands we'd exchanged in our short lives. The certainty that we would trust each other, be honest with each other no matter what, soldered a few of my broken pieces back together.

Tol's body was firm against mine, and the thoughts it dragged to the surface were enough to cause my cheeks to heat. He was giving me a questioning stare, one brow raised. His thumb dragged absent-minded circles around the base of my spine. Desire unlike anything I'd felt before burned through me, and I forgot what we were talking about. Every thought, every inch of awareness focused on those slow motions and where else I wanted to feel them.

The music faded, but neither of us pulled away.

I was distantly aware of Missyneth announcing that the council was ready for my promenade from the palace to the Sacra Temple. That everyone was to congregate in the streets to line the path. That I was needed.

"I should—"

"Wait," Tol interrupted. He looked at the crowd now filtering around us and the curious stares we were drawing. "Come with me first."

Grabbing Angelborn and Starfire awkwardly in one hand while Tolek clutched the other, I followed him unquestioningly.

He spun me into an empty bathing chamber, closing the door and shutting out the train of voices parading through the palace. Leaning against the dark wood, he lowered his chin and took a breath, his thumb brushing over my knuckles as he thought, collecting himself before me.

Slowly, I set my weapons down on the counter and sidled toward him, not stopping until I stood against him, our hands locked.

His forehead lowered to mine, and we remained like that, eyes closed, breathing each other in. For a moment, the threats on my shoulders fell away, the world fell away. It was only me and my tether to reality, holding me here to stop me from floating off into the clouded fear of what waited. To stop me from disappearing from myself and him.

With each exhale, the questions faded, my senses becoming overwhelmed with Tolek instead. The sound of his heart pounding, and the way it sent mine fluttering. The gentle drag of his fingertips down my arm, and the goosebumps left in their wake. The soft strands of his hair when I lifted my hand to the back of his neck, my fingers aching to dig in deeper.

I swallowed the feeling that we stood on the edge of something monumental.

Tol sighed when my nails grazed his skin, his breath ghosting over my lips. "Spirits, Alabath. The things you do to me." His hands snapped to my waist, tugging my hips flush against his so I felt every hard inch of what I did to him. Heat pooled low within me.

But it was more than the physical desire between us. That had been there for some time now, though I'd tried to say it was nothing.

With Tolek, there was so much more—a deeper connection built through years of steadfast friendship, endless support, and understanding. *Always* understanding when I was rash or fiery or teary-eyed, but without a fear of prodding me when I needed it.

That was what scared me.

Because there *was* so much more between us than the current moment. And if we took that step, that one final step, it would forever shatter what we had. I had seen enough ruins in recent years. I wasn't sure if my heart could face any more.

But sometimes things did not crash and burn—they soared.

Tol cupped my face, one thumb tracing my cheekbone. Hesitantly, he leaned in, kissing the space beneath my ear so gently I shivered. It was different than any reverent kiss he'd placed on my cheek before. This one was laced with the desire he'd hidden for years, and it awoke the one I was stifling.

His smile widened against my neck as he traced it with kisses. I let my eyes fall closed, relishing in how soft his lips were.

With each open-mouthed press of his mouth against my skin, I was becoming weaker beneath him. My body melting into every touch, every breath. That heat turning demanding.

Brushing my hair behind my ear and ghosting his lips up my neck, he whispered, "Tell me what you want."

The sentence—command—shot through me, and I struggled to rein in my breathing. I had even less control of my thoughts. I arched into him, fingers curling around his arms as I tried to remember how to speak and do what he said.

Tell him what I want.

There were many things I could think of—things that would undoubtedly be pleasurable—but what was it I wanted *after* this? Because I knew that while Tolek would do anything I needed right now, I wasn't willing to risk the aftermath without certainty.

My head dropped backward as his lips outlined my collarbone. Slowly. Torturously. Waiting for me to say the word.

My hands tangled in his hair, messing it into the disarray I loved so much.

I thought of how many times I had almost said goodbye to Tolek for good—the ax, the Undertaking, Aird…and the hole that always wedged itself into my stomach returned. The one only his presence could fill. Each touch flooded it now, sending sparks through my body. They landed on my heart, igniting it, and I knew without a doubt what I wanted.

I wanted my moonlight on the darkest night.

I wanted the tether that tied me to sanity.

I wanted *him*. My best friend and so much more.

I was too blind and broken to notice before, but now, as his lips worked their way back up my neck, my body and my heart knew.

I wanted Tolek Vincienzo, and I wouldn't let anything—no Angelcurse, no wicked queen, no shattered soul—stand in my way. My heart pounded wildly, heated desire and a bounty of adoration unfurling with each stuttered beat against my ribs.

Tol nipped my ear. "Tell me," he whispered, as breathless as I was. His hands trembled on my hips.

Restraint. He didn't dare explore my body further until he had permission.

I lifted my head, eyes opening to look directly into his heavy-lidded ones. The amber shone like embers buried in the dark hues. His hair drooped forward over his forehead, every inch of his appearance a sign of the control he was longing to lose with me.

Carefully, as if moving too quickly could shatter whatever precarious bridge we were daring to cross, I traced his jaw, the rough stubble soothing and familiar under my fingers. He exhaled, lids drooping.

"Eyes on me," I instructed.

He listened.

I dragged my thumb across his bottom lip, and the world went silent. Waiting for me to shatter the glass.

"There are a lot of things I'm unsure of right now." Walls snapped up behind his eyes, one hand pulling back from my hip.

I reached down, holding it in place, and he swallowed. A tangle of patience and lust burned in his gaze as he waited for me to finish, but his other hand fisted the fabric of my dress.

"But I know the only time I feel whole is when you're here." Jezebel's words from the night I left came back to me. How right she'd been. Tol was the source of my brightest beads of happiness, the receiver of my most genuine smiles—the ones I didn't even realize were sewing my heart back together. Through dark nights, he'd done that. A stitch for each laugh, steps toward a happier future.

"You want to know what I want, Vincienzo?" I pushed onto my toes, pressing him against the door until our bodies were flush, and slowly brushed my lips across his. "I want *you*—in every way."

My words snapped the restraint holding him back, embers in his eyes flaring to roaring flames. He spun us so quickly, I barely had time to take a breath before I was pressed firmly between the door and his body.

"Thank the fucking Angels," he breathed, and his lips crashed into mine. His hand cupped the back of my head as his tongue slipped into my mouth.

It was passionate and full of promises, speaking a language only we seemed to know. I wanted to memorize it, become fluent in Tolek in a way no one else could.

He ground his hips against me, every hard inch of him ready. Fucking Angels, I'd never wanted anything more, but I was also content to remain right here, exploring his mouth and his body slowly. It was a way I'd never thought I'd get to know him, but when my nails dragged through his hair, and he groaned into my mouth, it was the most enticing sound I'd ever heard. I wanted to own it, to make him *mine*.

He deepened the kiss, tilting my head back. Pressed against the door with his solid form shrouding me, I was completely consumed by him. He brushed a hand over my breast, down my side, coming around to grab my backside and pull me against him.

Our tongues explored each other in perfect tandem, as if we'd been doing this for years, each sweep of our lips like a match being struck within me. That fire was ready to burn the world down, forging my broken pieces back together as it went.

I bit down on his bottom lip, sucking gently, and my new favorite sound rumbled from the back of his throat again. Even the sheer fabric of this Spirits-damned dress was too heavy.

My hands ran up his chest and down his back, feeling the muscles through his shirt and wanting him even closer.

Tol's hands were firm—assured—as they slowly pulled down my dress.

"Fucking Angels," he muttered, ducking his head to kiss my neck. "You're devastating." One calloused finger dragged over my nipple, cruelly teasing me. His lips closed around the other, and now I was the one cursing the Angels, watching him through heavy-lidded eyes as he looked up at me.

Greedily, I reached for his shirt, undoing the buttons.

But Tolek shot up, grabbing my wrists and pinning them above my head.

"Undressing me, Alabath?" he said against my lips.

"Should I not be?" I hooked one leg around his hips and pulled him to me, eager for friction.

"I've waited years for this, Ophelia, and we don't have time for the kind of attention I want to give you." He kissed me roughly, hand gripping my neck, thumb tipping my chin up. "When I finally have you, it's not going to be up against a door with hundreds of warriors waiting outside. I'm going to take my time."

Heat gathered between my legs at those words, and I rolled my hips against him in argument. With a groan, Tolek's lips took mine again, one hand still holding my wrists above my head.

This felt right, like it was what we should have been doing all this time. Every breath, every touch, I wanted it all—

But before I could take it, the mountains beneath us shook with the force of the earth cracking in two.

CHAPTER FORTY-FOUR

OPHELIA

TOL'S HEAD SNAPPED UP, eyes burning into mine, but every drop of lust quickly faded into a fervent dread.

For a moment that stretched on, we remained frozen, catching our breath until the shaking ceased. Reality suspended in the stillness, fear coiling around my stomach like a snake ready to sink its fangs into this perfect escape we'd created.

The first screams echoing through the palace stiffened my muscles.

Tol was already moving, pulling my dress into place and straightening his shirt before my heart rate had calmed.

I grasped his wrists, nails digging into his flesh. His eyes met mine, the terror coursing through my body plain on my face.

One moment, that was all we had before we faced whatever was drawing screams from our people, and there would be no room for fear. Tucked away in our haven as we were, it was easier to let worries sweep in.

Gently, Tol removed my hands from his wrists and pushed my weapons into them. The leather and metal were reassuring against my palms. He wrapped my fingers around them and the familiarity of the motion pulled me back to the present.

"Let's go," he whispered, pressing his lips to my forehead for one last lingering, scorching kiss. Desperate desire poured into it.

Then, he reached around me to open the door, and we left the wanting behind.

I held my breath and shut out every emotion threatening to overcome me, slinging Angelborn across my back. The noise built as we fled through the high-ceilinged corridors of the palace.

We burst onto the entrance stairs to a world clouded with destruction. Gray smoke spiraled over our beautiful, hopeful city, darkening the lilac sky to a vengeful violet.

"Is it the volcano?" I asked as ash swirled onto my shoulders. The Spirit Volcano hadn't erupted in thousands of years.

Warriors poured across the palace lawn, thundering into the streets with aggrieved roars I didn't understand.

"It's not the volcano," Malakai said as he approached. Cyph and Rina stood with him.

"What—" Through the smoke billowing over the winding city of Damenal, between the buildings carved against rock, I could make out the swirling black armor of the new Engrossian army. They'd ambushed us, attacked when we were distracted. There was no time to organize our fighters as they poured into the streets to defend our capital.

"How did they get in? We have guards surrounding the city at all hours, stationed in the passes. How—" The second my gaze met Tol's horror-stricken eyes, I knew.

"The tunnels," he said.

"We didn't secure them." In the flurry of our arrival and what the others had revealed, in the rush of Daminius, we'd left entrances directly into our city unguarded. This attack—the warriors screaming and bloodied—was our fault.

"Where's the smoke coming from?" I growled, fingers tightening around Starfire, channeling that guilt into fury as best I could, trying to hold myself together.

I followed Malakai's line of sight to the Sacred Quarter. Perched on the palace steps, I could see the pillars of smoke. Tol's hand slid around my waist the moment before realization slammed into me.

And every scrap of control I had unraveled.

The cry that tore through my throat was piercing and raw, devastation wringing my bones until I could no longer hold myself up.

The smoke threatened to swallow me whole as I watched the space where the Sacra Temple used to stand swirl with dust.

The air suddenly didn't only sting with smoke—it reeked of

death. Because I'd been meant to promenade to that temple to present the offering to Damien. I'd been late, but within those pillars—

The Mystique Council. My father. They'd all been inside.

And Kakias had blown it up.

Danya, Larcen, Alvaron…all gone. The shoulders carrying the Mystiques through reconstruction blown to pieces.

And the ones that had supported me my entire life, the tawny eyes guiding my every move. I'd *just* seen them across the ballroom—the sheen of proud tears as he'd watched me.

Now, he was gone. Bacaran Alabath had been wiped from the world with the blast that rocked the mountains.

"No," I sobbed, tearing down the steps, across the lawn, and into the fray.

Voices yelled after me, but I charged through Engrossians. Starfire sliced where I needed her to, not stopping to see what carnage I left behind.

The temple had stood for centuries—millennia. It couldn't have fallen. *He* couldn't be gone.

My dress caught on rubble as I ran, one of my heels snapping with the force of my steps. I kicked them off and kept going. Ignored the rubble slicing into my feet.

The closer I got to the structure, the thicker the smoke. It stung my lungs, my breaths harsh through it. That pungent, ashy smell overwhelmed me as I charged into the haze, and the clashes of battle turned to a dull hum.

"Where is he—where—where…" I coughed over the pain in my chest and the ache in my heart.

Sobs wracked my body as I tore at debris. The echoes of the blast rang in my ears, the tumbling rock that followed it. I tossed crumbled marble and stone aside. Each clack of rock against rock made me flinch, the thought of what it sounded like on bone…

The temple was gone, only existing in chunks.

And even through my clouded eyes it was clear—there were no survivors.

My hand pressed against my chest; my lungs tightened.

He couldn't be—he couldn't be—

I was vaguely aware of a hand cupping my cheek, forcing me away from the columns of gray smoke that rose above the spot my father had last stood.

Around the corner, down an alley, into a shop with the windows blown out. Shelves turned over, bottles of oils and incense spilled across the floor. But I was surrounded by a safe huddle.

A steady thumb brushed the tears from my cheeks.

"Breathe. Breathe," a voice repeated softly. Through my panicked sobs, chocolate eyes swam into view. He inhaled slowly, waiting for me to match it. Once I forced my lungs to cooperate, he exhaled. I mimicked the motion, ignoring the tears gathering in Tol's eyes, as well.

The rest of the battle through the city dimmed as I looked at him and let his presence tether me down to this bloodied reality.

"She'll pay," I finally sputtered, voice thick. "They will all pay."

"I promise," he whispered, wiping away the last of my tears.

"Jez," I gasped, spinning to find my sister clutching Erista's arm. Still as a sculpture, she stared out the window at the smoke-streaked sky. Silent tears streamed down her face, but when I placed a hand on her shoulder, she looked at me with nothing but molten resolve, dark and agonizing and ready to burn the world down.

She didn't speak—she didn't need to.

My sister blinked her tawny eyes—our father's eyes—and transformed into a weapon ready to be wielded against those who took him.

The pain we were feeling wasn't the only loss that would come from this attack. The battle was raging through the streets already, and some of the strongest warriors we had to offer stood in this shop, ensuring Jezebel and I were okay.

I shoved away the ache stemming through my heart and turned to my friends. My family. Tolek, Jez, Cyph, Rina, and Malakai. Lyria and Mila. The delegates and even our two Engrossian guests.

They'd all come.

"This is an act of war." I bent and sliced Starfire through my skirt, leaving the fabric in an uneven trim around my thighs. Tiny beads fell like golden raindrops through the ash. "And it ends tonight."

I straightened to find everyone preparing as I had. There was no time to run for our leathers, to don any kind of armor. I was barefoot, relying on the mountains to heal those small cuts as I went.

Tonight, we'd fight with the honed skill flowing through our blood, the desire to protect our home, and the desperate need for vengeance.

Lyria fell into the role she'd been trained for, quickly assessing the damage that could be seen from here and working with Cyph and Dax to predict what the Engrossians' next tactic might be. Figure out a way to spread a strategy through the city.

I didn't let myself think of how Danya should have been at her side. That Danya would never stand here again.

Once they'd set a plan, Lyria fled out the damaged door with Mila.

Before turning the corner, she stopped. "Baby brother!" The black velvet of her fitted dress was spotted with ash, but the jagged edge she'd cut with her sword flared around her thighs.

Tol was already watching her. "Yes?"

"I'm proud of you." She flashed the classic Vincienzo grin that carried more than her words.

"If you win this for us, maybe I'll return the sentiment." Tol grinned right back. She rolled her eyes, and Tol watched the only family member who had ever bothered to show him love charge into a fray of singing blades and bloodshed.

Santorina pulled her hair into a ponytail, saying she and Esmond would prepare the infirmary for the imminent influx of patients. Before they ran off, though, I grabbed my friend's hand. She turned her dark, concerned eyes on me.

"Wait," I said, needing one more moment with the people I loved most in the world. I tugged her back to the small huddle we'd formed. "No matter what happens tonight, I am grateful to have you all fighting by my side."

My sister was quiet beneath Erista's arm as my gaze met hers, but she managed to crack a smile of encouragement. She'd seen and survived horrors that no seventeen-year-old warrior should have to face. Though it went against my very nature to admit it, I couldn't protect her from the battle below. From the heartbreak we'd both face when this was over.

I took a breath, eyes flashing over Jezebel and Santorina,

Cypherion and Malakai. Tol's warmth pressed into my back, his hand supporting my waist. I looked up at him over my shoulder, barely able to breathe past the emotion in my throat. Quickly, I faced the group.

"I am grateful the Angels placed us in each other's lives. Though they seem to think I am a pawn for their schemes and curses, they blessed me by gifting me your love."

Weapons clashed in the city, and it was all I could do to force away images of my friends beneath them. Nothing could happen to them. I'd lost too much, fought for too long, defended those I loved with every breath in my exhausted body…I didn't think I could rebuild myself again. I'd lost enough in this life, and no more names would be added to the list I mourned.

"We're grateful to follow you, Revered," Cyph swore, drawing his weapons.

"Believe in the Angels," Tol began, squeezing my hip.

"Be guided by the Spirits," Jezebel added, and my chest tightened.

"And align with the stars," Malakai finished, bringing the tears in my eyes dangerously close to spilling over again.

"Stay true," I muttered.

One by one, the group around me dissolved, scampering into the bloodshed, weapons raised to the heavens.

Before joining them, I turned to Barrett and Dax where they'd been lingering on the outskirts of our goodbye. "You have to choose."

"We chose long ago," the heir answered without missing a beat.

"You know what this means."

The Engrossians exchanged a glance. "We're on the side of life, Ophelia," Barrett said, expression tight. And I understood. They weren't choosing between Engrossian and Mystique—their people or mine. They were choosing to fight for everyone that deserved to live.

The two charged after the others and were swallowed up by smoke.

Then, it was me and Tol. His hands came up to cup my cheeks.

"Be careful," I whispered, biting down on my lip to stop it from trembling. Why was I always forced to say goodbye to him?

"You don't need to worry about me, Alabath." He tugged my lip from between my teeth and ran his thumb across it.

"I know, but—"

He pressed his mouth to mine, drowning my concerns. "I'm not going anywhere," he whispered against my lips. "We have unfinished business."

I pulled back to see a familiar, taunting glint in his eye. Even amid the fighting, my stomach swooped.

"In the mood for revenge, Vincienzo?"

Tolek grinned. "There she is."

CHAPTER FORTY-FIVE

OPHELIA

SMOKE STUNG MY EYES as I charged through the streets, ash clinging to my skin along with the gore that sprayed through the air.

The death-and-iron scent of the battle was gut-churning, but I sank into the mind of a predator and blocked out the screams, the echoes of clashing blades.

It was only me, my weapons, and the dark-armored enemies charging through my home. Begging to fall at my hands.

I lost track of the lives I took as we fought down a street packed with looming apartment buildings and innocent lives, my fury a storm unleashed.

One for every tear I would shed over my father.

One for every scar they put on Malakai's skin.

One for every breath they silenced from my people.

The streets were overwhelmed, bodies falling as quickly as the ash coating them. The Engrossians—and likely Mindshapers if Aird's agreement stood—moved as swiftly and quietly as I remembered, some unknown magic masking any clinks of armor.

Tolek and I fought back-to-back. Starfire met the blade of a long, jagged knife. Shoving the Mindshaper back, I brought my short sword up, swiping cleanly through his leathers from hip to neck.

I spun to meet the next opponent, but amid the shouts, a gravelly voice stood out. "Behave, girl." A slap of flesh on flesh sounded.

A child's scream followed.

Gritting my teeth, I ducked my attacker's blade and ran down the nearest alley. I was vaguely aware of Tol taking out that warrior behind me. Following me, he guarded the entrance.

My eyes locked on the tear-streaked face of the young girl. On the hand locked around her throat, pinning her to the wall.

The Engrossian didn't even hear me approach. Didn't have time to fight back as my spear shot through his neck.

Crimson arced through the air with his tumble sideways, his body falling with a thud. The girl nearly collapsed with him—from relief or terror, I wasn't sure.

"It's okay," I soothed, bending down to her level. My blood-streaked and tattered appearance was likely no comfort, but I placed a hand on her trembling shoulder regardless.

Her arms wrapped around her small body, holding her up—she couldn't have been more than ten.

When she finally looked at me, recognition dawned in her round green eyes.

"He can't hurt you now," I muttered. Tentatively, I tucked a piece of hair that had pulled free from her braid behind her ear, fingers grazing the bright red spot on her cheek where the Engrossian had hit her. "What's your name?"

"Anabeth—Anni," she whimpered.

"Do you live nearby, Anni?"

Tol's sword rang loudly behind me, but I couldn't pull my attention away from this child. The way she stubbornly set her jaw and lifted her chin reminded me so much of my sister.

"Just there." She pointed to a tall, narrow building at the dead end of the alley. "I only—I left my training sword outside. I thought I should get it. To protect my little brother and sister." The apology in her round cheeks—the way her small lips trembled despite her forced confidence—twisted my gut.

She may resemble Jezzie's courage, but that protective gleam in her eye was one I knew well.

"That's okay, you didn't do anything wrong. You're so strong to defend your family. But you have to protect yourself, too, okay?"

Her lips twitched upward, cheeks flushing. "My mom and dad said they'd be back soon."

"They will, I'm sure." The uncertain words tasted like tar. "But grab your sword and stay inside. Promise me?"

"I promise, Revered."

I watched until she disappeared through the dark doorway, a small wreath of daisies swinging as it closed.

The moment the lock slid home, the roars of battle crashed back down on me.

Forcing myself to tear my gaze away from the apartment and the vulnerable children inside, I gritted my teeth and ran back toward Tol. There would be more children like Anni at risk if we didn't win.

Adrenaline kept my body moving quickly through the crowded cobblestone streets, coming closer to Angentia Plaza. My weapons sang as they clashed with opponents', each strike I landed adding to the two mounting pulses in my blood.

We wove between dueling warriors, the Mystiques recognizable in their finery.

On both sides, fighters fell. Scarlet painted the stones, glass shattering in windows and bodies crashing to the brick.

We'd been so focused on the troops they were moving, we'd left Damenal as our last resort. But as I watched a Mystique at least two centuries old take a knife through his chest, I wasn't sure we'd made the right choice.

I should have foreseen this. Guilt weighed heavily on my shoulders as I swung my sword into the arm of an Engrossian.

His ax fell from his hand, and I swiped my blade across his throat, relishing the way his screams were silenced by my steel.

I didn't stop to watch him die, instead slipping my spear between the metal plates of another's armor and hearing him collapse beside his comrade as I moved on.

With each kill, the pressure in my chest tightened.

It was clear even from this one small spot of the battle that they outnumbered us. Each warrior Tol and I took out was quickly replaced by another, with soulless eyes and swirling armor.

Swinging beneath the outstretched blade of an Engrossian with a grunt, I grabbed her long braid and tugged her to the ground. My spear was in her throat before she could scream.

The blood that burst from her reminded me of Kakias's red lips.

I wished it was the queen squirming beneath my weapon, now. I imagined her face on the warrior.

"Very smooth, Alabath," Tol called as I swung Angelborn onto my back.

Shaking the vision of the queen's face from my mind, I whirled to see him ram his dagger into the thigh of an opponent, then sweep his sword upward to finish the job.

"Speak for yourself," I panted.

He smiled at me, wide and brilliant beneath the blood and dirt. With his shirt torn, chest heaving from the thrill and panic of battle, a victorious grin split his lips—

A second deafening rumble shook my bones.

Tol's hand pressed against my chest, shoving me backward. Out of the way of the explosion.

Dust and debris engulfed me. The roar of glass shattering and brick tumbling was deafening.

And then, only silence filled my head. Because—

"Tol!" I coughed over the smoke.

I couldn't see him. Couldn't see—

Rubble rained where he'd stood a moment ago—where he'd stepped to push me out of the way.

Buried him.

"No, no, no." The word left my lips, a repeated prayer. My entire body shook as I stumbled forward, falling over rock until my knees were cut.

Clawing, climbing, digging. Others joined the search, throwing aside ruins to find those buried.

My nails cracked and bled. Chest seized.

"Please, Damien, please…" I begged.

I tried to channel that place of calm Tol would instill in me, willed my body to stop shaking, but I couldn't do it.

It was only panic and fear and emptiness without him.

He was alive. *He was.*

I just needed to find him, needed to see him smile and tell me my fear was unwarranted. To hear a sarcastic remark fall from his lips. To feel—

An arm wrapped around my shoulders.

A blade pressed into my throat.

"I've been looking everywhere for you," a familiar, cruel voice snarled.

"*Aird*," I gasped. "No, I have to…I need to find…"

My breathing turned ragged, limbs thrashing and neck arching into the blade. The cool sting passed through my flesh, a bead of blood forming. As the chancellor of the Mindshapers dragged me roughly away from the rubble, I watched that spot I'd seen Tolek disappear.

He's okay. I told myself. *He's alive.* Half of my heart was in my throat, the other half buried beneath that rubble—*please, Spirits, let him be okay.*

Aird tugged me so quickly around corners that I lost track of where we went through the curtain of smoke. Lost track of where Tol had been.

He threw me up against a wall. Angelborn dug into my shoulder blades. The cool kiss of his jagged knife was still at my throat, above my emblem necklace.

That roaring silence echoed in my head. But Aird gripped my wrist, twisting until Starfire fell from my grip.

"The queen wants you," he sneered.

The queen…Tolek…the queen.

It snapped into place in my mind, then.

Kakias was here. She'd evaded our search for weeks, only to deliver herself to our doorstep.

And I shoved aside all fear for my best friend, assured myself that there was no way he'd leave me, and looked into the steel-gray eyes of the Mindshaper chancellor.

"She had the decency to show up?" I growled.

"She does what she wants when it serves her," he spat. His rancid breath was hot against my skin. Spirits, the smoke was preferable to this.

But I considered what he said. Kakias refused to be controlled. Refused to share her plans with those around her. She may be a corrupted, bloodthirsty ruler, but she was also cunning and meticulous.

If she was here, it meant this attack was more than an unprecedented advantage against us. She had a reason for the explosion in Damenal tonight—for her disturbing presence—and I was willing to bet it stretched further than disrupting our most sacred holiday.

I was willing to bet it ended with me.

"Where is she?" I hissed as his knife pressed deeper.

Aird's face faltered ever so slightly, but I caught the moment of hesitation. The belief that I'd hand myself over.

A cruel smile split my lips. "I only ask so I can repay her for the surprise she's gifted us tonight." I blinked innocently, sarcasm thick in my voice.

With a growl, he gripped my shoulder and threw me to the ground. My head snapped back into the cobblestone, vision blurring for a moment.

"Ugh," I groaned. "I really should have killed you."

But my hand stretched out. Fingers grazed Starfire.

And Aird's eyes were only on me.

"You'll come quietly to the queen," Aird snarled, prowling toward me. "Or this battle will end with everyone you care about suffering slow, torturous deaths."

His eyes roamed over my body, sneering, from the neckline of my sheer gown to where the hem had ridden up my thighs, and that was when I realized—he knew who I was, my legacy, my position, yet he still saw me as nothing more than a young girl.

A toy, incapable and unworthy of power.

But I was so much more.

I'd honed my strength and agility for years; I'd studied politics and warfare to give my people the best chance at survival.

I was the damned *Revered* for Spirits' sake, chosen by the Angels and confirmed in the Undertaking. Power ran through my blood just as the Angelcurse did, and the two tangled together now, dual pulses synchronizing into one as the emblem around my neck heated.

I'd bow to no one. Go forth on no one's terms but my own.

When the first war broke out, I'd lost everything, but I'd be damned to a Spirit-guarded hell if I'd let these enemies take anything—anyone—else from me tonight.

Underestimating me was the last mistake Aird would make.

Swinging my legs, I knocked his out from underneath him. He hit the cobblestones with a rattling thud.

Then, I was on him. Short sword at his neck.

My necklace seared my skin with a heat I relished.

"Where. Is. She?" I hissed, each word punctuated.

He stared back at me with a manic gleam in his eyes. "She's looking over us. She sees all, and she waits for you."

I gasped. There was only one place in the city where you could see all of Damenal laid before you.

"Pleasure working with you, Chancellor."

The Mindshaper's blood was hot over my fingers as I sliced my sword across his neck.

I sheathed my weapons, turning back in the direction where Tolek had fallen, but I didn't even know my way back through the debris.

And Aird's threat rang in my ears.

Every part of me wanted to crawl through that bloodshed. To find Tol. To fight side by side with my family.

I tried to dig into the roots of the Bond on my neck, but it was impossible with the amount of warriors in the city. These tattoos weren't meant to form a bridge like the Bind.

I had to trust that the other Mystiques would take care of Tolek. Because the only true way to end this was with Kakias, and I was the only one who could see to her. As long as she was alive, the people I loved weren't safe. I'd throw myself into the Spirit Volcano before I dragged any of my family into her vile presence.

Clamping down on the taint of fear stinging my throat, shoving aside the images of my family bloodied and dying, I turned my back on the battle and fled, off to bring a cursed end to a wicked queen.

Chapter Forty-Six

Malakai

ANOTHER WALL HAD COLLAPSED moments ago, only a few blocks over.

The dust in the air was so thick, everything blurred. Screams were nothing more than ghostly echoes.

How the fuck are they doing this? I charged down a side street, following Cyph away from the latest explosion, through dueling warriors and toward the plaza.

Cyph swiped his scythe through the air. An Engrossian's masked head tumbled across the stone.

I hopped over the body, boots sticking in puddles of blood, and tightened my hand on my sword. We rounded the corner into the plaza and—

It became harder to breathe.

The Engrossian army moved like wraiths across the wide-open space. Charging from alleys and banging down shop doors. Cries rang from upstairs windows as they ransacked homes.

And in the square…blood. Flashing steel and bodies. My lungs tightened with every weapon I saw, my throat closing.

Mystiques were strong fighters—once the most powerful across the continent—but they were falling to the unpredictable strikes.

A scream pulled our attention. An Engrossian towered over a Mystique woman, an ax swinging down. Cyph threw himself at the warrior, grabbed the back of his neck, and chucked him to the stone.

The ax went flying as Cyph swiped a dagger from his belt and sliced it across the man's throat.

Then, a small, black-armored figure swiveled below the fray. Darting around two warriors, she charged. A dagger aimed at Cyph's back.

I tried to yell for him, but it was drowned out.

Instead, I ran. Held my breath and swung.

The grind of metal through flesh and bone was gratifying. Her arm severed above her metal vambrace. I blocked out her agonized scream and indulged in the satisfaction warming my blood.

Maybe I could do this. I *could* fight.

She fell at my feet, and that tortured side of myself took over. "That's nothing compared to what you did to me." She continued to scream, not hearing me.

I lifted my sword, prepared to silence her for good. But a scar on the side of her neck froze me.

An ax.

Purple against pale skin, her commitment to the cause of the Engrossian Warriors—so fucking similar to the white scar on my own chest.

The echo of the constellation heated as I stared at her, and everything slammed into me. Every minute in that cell. Every drop of blood. Everything, all of it and all at once, a cascade.

Fuck, I couldn't—this—

Axes flashed through the square, suddenly all I could see.

My arm fell, sword scraping the ground as I stumbled back. My muscles weakened, my knees buckling. Harsh screeches of blades on stone, on bone, were all I heard.

I stumbled to a halt on the outskirts of the battle, slamming up against a brick wall to catch my breath.

But I forced my eyes open. I may be a mess, but I wouldn't be that stupid.

One breath in—count to four—hold seven—release eight.

Watching the massacre before me, I repeated the meditation. My hand shook, sweaty on the grip of my sword.

This is ridiculous, I scolded myself, still panting. *You're being a fucking child.*

All I could smell was blood and terror. All I could feel was the sting of blades carving my flesh.

Warrior Prince, the taunting voice echoed. *You're not even a real fucking warrior. You don't deserve to be.*

Fear gripped the bars of my heart, rattling until the organ shrank away like a lashed creature, my chest hollow and empty. Dark shame unfurled before my eyes. It slid into that void space, becoming my master, and I its vessel.

I hadn't completed the Undertaking. Couldn't even find it within myself to attempt it, overridden with disgrace and the secret fear that I may not be worthy of true ascension. After all, I'd been sired by the Spirits-damned man whose despicable, selfish actions caused the horrors now playing out before my eyes.

Maybe it would be best if I let fear take me—

Then, a young warrior took an ax to the gut only feet away, and I shouted out with him—desperate and pained.

Blood bloomed across his white shirt, my stomach contracting as it spread.

I stumbled forward.

As his last hope, he swung out with a dagger.

It landed in the enemy's neck just before the boy's arm dropped. The Engrossian's ax hit the stones, and both warriors fell.

The Mystique couldn't even have been eighteen; there was no chance he'd completed the Undertaking either. Yet, as blood bubbled through his lips, and his eyes found mine, there was no fear in his stare. That boy died with nothing but a fortified strength, taking out one last threat as he went. The heart of a true warrior burned through his gaze, searing my ravaged soul.

He was braver than I.

As his life drained unjustly, I didn't move from my position on the outskirts of the battle. But something raw—something jagged— stirred in my chest. *Anger.* Hot and vivid, it soared through me, not alleviating my fear, not shrouding it, but *igniting it.* Melting it. Instilling the durability and immortality of volcanic fire that could only be a strength.

Gripping my sword tighter, I summoned every ounce of my dying strength and convinced one foot to step forward.

Then, the other.

Until I was shoving through crowds, dodging blows and debris, the only place I looked was at the ax that ended that young boy's life.

That Spirits-damned weapon, it's curved blade stained crimson.

Through the clouds, moonlight hit the edge. My muscles locked, remembering precisely how that thick, sharpened edge tore through flesh.

But I am no longer captive. Chains and secrets didn't dictate my life.

I wasn't a fucking animal to be caged, a toy to be used as they desired.

I swiped that ax up and flipped it in my hand, ignoring the twisting of my gut. They'd tried to wreck me with this weapon—instead, I'd become its master, using it to slay the shadows around my heart.

With that promise sealing itself in my mind, I rejoined the battle and lost count of the Engrossians I took down. My sword settled into my hand as if it had always been there, waiting for me to realize it, and the ax warmed in the other.

I transformed in that battle, ripping through enemies. No compassion broke through the iron bars around my heart, no guilt plagued me. They wanted to torture me? Fine. I'd turn that pain into a weapon, desensitized and thirsty for blood.

Death rose around me, the endless swirl rivaling my blackened heart.

I fought back-to-back with Cypherion, my brother before all else, and smiled as the black-armored warriors piled up around us.

The fight lulled, allowing us a moment to catch our breath. Cyph and I looked at each other. Blood trickled from his lip, a cut of my own stinging at my collarbone, but we exchanged devious grins.

"Good to have you back," he panted.

"I'm not—"

A hand closed around my wrist. I whirled, ready to strike, but instead of the dark, inhuman eyes of the enemy, I met Vale's harsh stare.

"What the fuck?" I started, trying to throw off her grip.

A fresh flood of Engrossians charged in across the square, weapons raised and cries echoing. But Vale tightened her fingers, digging into my skin.

"I need to speak with you," she said over the din of battle, her usual chiming tone higher than the bloodshed. She was bruised, ash coating her hair, but her tight expression was determined. Her other hand latched on to the fabric of Cyph's shredded shirt.

"What are you doing here?" Cyph growled, no doubt having told her to shelter in the palace. But he was a fool if he was trying to protect her. She was no safer there, not with the way the Engrossians were driving through the city.

Cyph opened his mouth, most likely to insist she retreat, but without an explanation, she dragged us both from the square.

CHAPTER FORTY-SEVEN

OPHELIA

"I'M DISAPPOINTED IN HOW long it took you." Kakias's voice was chilled, slithering over the marble floors of the Rapture Chamber and up my body.

She'd pulled the Revered's chair—*my chair*—to the open wall, facing the drop over the mountains. The queen didn't even deign to look at me. She only watched the city below, her tainted troops ravaging ours.

The Rapture Chamber—the one place where you could see all of Damenal, spread out before you like a map teeming with life.

"I'd have been here sooner, but your lackey deterred me." I clenched my bloodied hands around Starfire and Angelborn, forcing my body to retain its calm, and wandered to the pillared wall.

The sight below tightened my chest. As a girl, Damenal had been a glorious playground, a future just out of reach. Lately, it had become winding pathways of hope, promises for glory once lost. Tonight, as I looked down upon my home, lives slipped away, blood blotting out those dreams.

From here, the sound of the battle was dim, but the dull hum of roars and groans—of encroaching death—remained. Smoke spiraled away into the night-dark sky, grays tarnished in the burning light of the moon and stars. It thinned where it skimmed the tops of buildings. Fewer explosions were detonating, providing a clearer sight into the carnage below.

Each death prickled my skin like a fine blade. I breathed in those losses.

Then, exhaled them, and turned to face Kakias.

The queen's sharp-toothed smile sent me back to the night, months ago, when everything I thought I knew had been turned upside down. Except here, poised to destroy everyone I loved, with moonlight gilding her profile, she was more fearsome than I could have imagined. Those soulless eyes turned on me, and they threatened to swallow me whole.

"And where is Aird?"

"I killed him."

"Pity," she deadpanned.

"Don't hide your devastation on my account."

"When will you learn, Ophelia?" Kakias drummed her knife-sharp nails on the arm of my chair, each tap burrowing into my mind. "*Sacrifices* are vital."

"No," I spat. "I won't sacrifice anything else to you."

A smile. "We'll see."

"This ends here, Kakias. With you and me—no more loss of life." I pointed to the city below. "Call off your legions and face me like a true warrior."

"Where would the fun be in that? I'm winning." The queen stood from my chair, circling until she was in front of me. That power—that unnatural, stirring, pool-granted magic—wrapped itself around my bones. My breathing shallowed. "Perhaps if you hadn't stolen my last toy, I'd be more open to negotiating."

I swallowed my outrage at her referring to Tol as *her toy*, focusing on fighting the dark power trying to steal my autonomy. Tol's life had never belonged to her—

I couldn't think about him now. Couldn't lose focus.

It took everything in me not to explode on the queen as she had on our city. Instead, I pulled the Revered mask I'd come to know intimately into place, sliding it between her influence and my resolve.

"Oh, corrupt queen," I scoffed, trying to move. Her power locked my muscles. "Do you truly expect me to believe my cooperation would have deterred you? Your hands are bathed in the blood of centuries of sins."

She narrowed her eyes at my choice of words. At the smug smile on my face.

Then, she returned it—hers full of secrets and twisted truths.

Regardless of whether I'd rescued Tol or not, Kakias would have blown up the mountains. This was her game.

"You're correct about one thing, vicious child. This ends tonight." She took a step back, her train shuffling behind her, swallowing the light. Long and skin-tight, the dress was an insulting confirmation that she never intended to partake in the fight below. "When the sun rises, there will be nothing left of you to love."

We stared at each other. Two warriors. Two queens. Two hearts staked on revenge.

From behind her back, Kakias removed a dagger, the fine blade catching the moonlight. Her power still held my bones, circled me like a python's mighty body.

It slipped along my spine, slithering around my shoulders and down my arms.

And then, it encircled my wrist. Pulled it out and flipped my hand palm up, open to the ceiling.

The rest of my body became free, but that power remained concentrated on my hand, warping and prying with an aching pressure.

My lip curled, fingers flexing around Starfire. Kakias balanced her dagger against the pad of her finger, smile growing as she pushed her blade in. I gasped as something sharp pinched my own and—

A warmth gathered in my hand. *Blood.*

I hissed as it flowed faster.

When Kakias pierced her own flesh, it drew my blood. How in the realm of the fucking Angels had she done that?

I masked the shock chilling my blood, spewing, "Clever."

"Only the beginning."

My blood dripped to the floor, more than I'd expected from the small slice.

Around my neck, the emblem of the spear flared with a burst of heat, but I didn't yell out against it. The fire melded into my chest, soothing instead of searing. Bolstering instead of scarring.

"What's the purpose of it? Why do you need this power?" I asked as the warmth faded into my skin, making the second pulse pound faster through my body.

Then, that power, too, crawled along my veins, toward the hand

Kakias's magic held. Like fingers prying open a fist, it picked through the darkness until it released me, and I smiled.

The queen glared.

"Next?" I asked, as if I wasn't as shocked as she was by what just happened.

But I only had half a second to consider it before Kakias raised her arm, palm open toward me.

With a twist of her hand, I was flying back.

The Rapture Chamber was a whirl of marble and moonlight as my weapons flew from my hands, leaving me defenseless except for the dagger strapped to my thigh.

I collided with the statue of Damien, my bones cracking and breath leaving my lungs. The Angel fell with a piercing shatter, and I crumpled to the ground atop the rubble, shards digging into my skin. My tattered dress tore further.

But above it all, dread shredded my gut—harsh and undiluted.

Because no warrior should have been able to do what the queen just did.

"That's a new trick." I staggered to my feet, ignoring the ringing in my ears.

I shuffled forward, nearly tripping.

When I looked down, my heart stuttered. A large square marble tile had been removed from its spot in the floor, revealing a dark cavern beneath.

"The tunnels?" I breathed, eyes flashing back to the queen. "They lead here?" The maze through the mountains burrowed into the Rapture Chamber itself—and who else knew where.

That ancient network of pathways handed over the key to our home.

Damien, I cursed, frustrated.

The Angel who built this house couldn't have revealed this little weakness? The invasion stung, even more personal now.

"That's why Aird was here after the Rapture, isn't it? He was searching for an entrance." I clenched my hands at my sides, remembering the chancellor's unsettling responses when I found him in the palace.

I've found what I needed.

Spirits, I'd been too caught up in Malakai and the prophecy to see the threat right before me.

"Good work, Chosen Child." Kakias's bloodred lips parted around razor-sharp teeth.

"Again with your false titles." I stifled the violation, the treachery and fury, and stepped forward, feigning a limp. Angelborn only lay a few feet away.

"Have you still not figured it out?" Kakias tutted, hungry eyes flicking between me and my spear. She curled her fingers and Angelborn shot toward her, rolling to a stop at her feet. I growled when she slammed a heeled foot across the hilt. "You're smarter than that, Ophelia."

Kakias tilted her head, studying me—and I surveyed her in return. The creeping silence of her movements. The swirling secrets behind her dark eyes. The power that seemed to have multiplied in the months since I last saw her. How she seemed to know I was chosen. What Barrett had revealed about the source of dark power in the Engrossian Territories. The intricacies of how those pools worked, what they took...

"What did you offer them, Kakias?" I asked, voice light.

"Did my son enlighten you?" The moon cast shadows on her high cheekbones, a wide grin splitting her lips.

"We worked together."

Those words hit her, her eyes flaring wide for a brief second. "He was always too weak for my plans, wasn't he?"

I wasn't sure if it was a question for me or for herself.

"Barrett is stronger than you are." I held her gaze. My arms fell to my side, body indulging in the magic of the mountains to heal where it had been battered. "He saw the atrocities you were planning and sacrificed his standing—his title and birthright—to save his people from unnecessary bloodshed. That is a sacrifice you would *never* have made, for you are *far* too selfish, Kakias."

"Don't you dare speak to me of sacrifices." Her voice was sharp and jagged, lips pulling back from her teeth.

"Why? You're forcing them on my people tonight. On your own." I thrust a hand toward the city, the movement jarring my aching body. "You may be after *me*, but those are not only Mystiques screaming below."

"And yet, here we are." She gazed wistfully over Damenal. "Things set in motion centuries ago finally falling into place."

"All blood spilled tonight is on your hands." I set my feet, fingers finding the cool leather at my thigh. "Except this."

The dagger flashed from my hand, but instead of nesting in her heart where I'd aimed, it grazed her collarbone, tearing black lace and flesh. Only a thin line of crimson showed that she was even hurt.

Her expression didn't flinch as she lifted a hand to the spot. Carefully, she caught the drop beading on her skin, lifting it to eye level.

Fear—that was what flashed behind her stare, quickly replaced by frenzy.

The blood was swallowed up by her ebony gown. She lifted an arm, hand aimed at me. Kakias squeezed her fist, and invisible fingers clenched around my throat, cutting off my airway.

I clawed at my neck, trying to tear them off, to get air back into my lungs, but nothing was there.

"Don't fight, Ophelia." She stalked toward me. "This—the bloodshed—it will all be over much quicker if you simply let me win. Think of all the lives you'd save with your noble *sacrifice*."

She drove my back into the wall, lifting me against the cool marble and artwork. The corner of a frame dug into my spine.

"What—" I wheezed. I kicked the air fruitlessly. "What—did you—"

"That thing you think makes my son stronger than me?" She pressed closer, nearly nose to nose with me. "That thing that aches for the people dying below. *That* is what I traded."

My...strength...what—I couldn't make sense of it, not with the spots clouding my vision. The riddle she presented of her sacrifice to the pools swam through my mind.

My head was cemented against the painting. Needles drove themselves into my lungs.

Life slipped from my body, darkness begging to take me in its gentle embrace, and I forgot why I was even fighting the queen.

Chilled numbness wrapped itself around my limbs, soothing the sparking pain in my lungs and removing the needles one by one. It tempted me to succumb to the release of oblivion.

And so I did.

CHAPTER FORTY-EIGHT

MALAKAI

VALE'S GRIP REMAINED FIRM as she dragged us away from the battle and into an empty market. The door hung on a hinge, dim mystlights filtering through dark aisles lined with wooden fruit boxes and bottles of liquor.

How the fuck she thought this was a good idea right now, I didn't know. Did she not see the Engrossians infiltrating our city? Outnumbering our own. She wasn't Mystique, but I'd thought she was an ally.

Whatever she needed had to be very fucking important to justify pulling the two of us from the plaza.

When she set her olive-green eyes on me, mystlight flickered over her resolved expression. Hesitant eyes and lips pressed together, considering.

"What is it?" I hissed. I barely kept my stare on her, casting looks back toward the window, the new wave of warriors slinging axes and jagged swords toward our people.

"I need to get to a temple," Vale said.

I turned to her, jaw dropping open. A warrior—I couldn't tell if it was a woman or man, friend or foe—slammed into the window, the pane cracking.

"And why does that matter right now?" I barked, waving an arm at the spiderweb crack through the glass. The body slumping before it. "We're in the middle of a *war*, Vale."

She stepped up to me. "Because if I can conduct a session, I may be able to see how we win this war, Malakai."

My heart skipped a beat at the promise in her voice, but I shook my head, stamping out the hope that threatened to spark. I shoved my newfound rage into its place. "No offense, but you've been trying to read for weeks now and haven't gotten any results. Why didn't you see this invasion coming? Why didn't you warn us?"

"Malakai—" Cyph warned.

"You know that isn't how it works!" Vale shouted over him. "I can't choose what I see."

"Then what will be any different if you get to the temple this time? How can you ensure that you'll get us out of this in one piece?" I waited for her answer, but when she said nothing, the spark of hope burned away entirely. She gritted her teeth, eyeing me with a conflicted look I didn't understand.

I scoffed, turning on my heel.

"Wait, Malakai." Cyph put a hand on my shoulder.

"No," I snapped, ramming my palm into his chest. "We don't have time for this right now." Ash wafted in the door on a wind, carrying the tangled scents of iron and smoke with it. *That* was where I needed to be—fighting, killing, burning while this rage flowed through me because I couldn't say when it would snuff out.

"Maybe she's right," Cyph proposed, faith lifting his words.

"The only thing that's right is defending our city." I barely recognized the resolve in my own voice. I'd spent so long forcing away these ties to my people, the duty I was bound to, but now I wanted to fight.

And I wanted to do it with my brother by my side, but Cyph was looking from me to Vale, clearly wanting answers, and that choice pierced me.

"Do whatever you want," I grumbled, striding toward the door, adjusting my grip on my sword as I went.

"I've been sabotaging my readings," Vale blurted right before I pushed through the swinging door.

Cypherion and I both whipped our heads toward her.

"You what?" he hissed. I pretended not to hear the edge of hurt in his voice.

Uncertainty tangled with my already peaked aggression as I took in the Starsearcher with new, less trustful eyes. I'd suspected for a while that she was hiding something, but this? Telling us she wanted to ally with us, telling us she'd given Titus her recommendation for Ophelia's appointment, then sabotaging the advantage we had through her magic…

Traitor, a voice in my head snarled, and I almost snarled with it.

She'd been fooling us worse than I'd imagined.

Vale's spine straightened. "As you said, we don't have time for the drawn-out story right now." She looked us each in the eye, unashamed, and my apprehension deepened.

"You're going to have to tell us something, Vale," I threatened. There was no way I'd help her without at least a sliver of an explanation. I'd been burned enough by lies.

She groaned, words coming out in a rush. "Titus told me I must not conduct any full sessions or hand over pertinent information while residing with you. I've been using tinctures to cloud my connection to the stars. That's all I know."

My brain ticked through her words, searching for holes in the story. From his stoic silence, I guessed Cyph was doing the same.

Titus had been skeptical of Ophelia since his initial destruction reading, but it had been his idea to begin the delegate program. He'd been the one who suggested Vale stay with us initially…only to sabotage us, stop any advantage we may have gained through her abilities. It undermined the entire compromise he'd negotiated, diminished the alliances we'd been working to build across the continent.

He was a rat.

Had he planted Vale as a spy? Had she been reporting on our movements all this time? And if so, why?

Vale didn't know much that could hurt us, anyway. Titus couldn't be working with Kakias—he'd sent troops to our side.

There was something, though…something Vale could have read that he didn't want us to know. But she was only an apprentice. How powerful could her communication with the stars be to provide any pertinent information that could spin the tide of Titus's agenda?

Spirits, my head was pounding. None of it added up, but it hit me with the familiar sting of betrayal.

Two things were true—we couldn't trust Titus, and we certainly couldn't trust Vale.

"Why not conduct the sessions and lie?" Cyph finally asked. His eyes narrowed, and I wished I could communicate with him without her hearing, figure this out together.

"I didn't want to see something tragic and have to hide it." She shook her head, eyes wide and pleading.

"What tragedy could you have seen that Titus wouldn't have?" The venom in my voice was palpable, the atmosphere icy.

Vale sucked in a breath, eyes flicking between us. After a moment of contemplation, she exhaled. Beyond the market, the city shuddered through another blast. Voices rose, swords clashed, and these new lies wrapped around me like my former chains, using their iron will to pull me back. To drown me once again.

"We don't have time for explanations now," Vale snapped. She shoved past us, pulling a Mystique short sword from her side and marching toward the door. "Get me to the temple and I'll ask the celestial powers for a way your people can survive this battle."

CHAPTER FORTY-NINE

OPHELIA

DARKNESS LEFT ME AS it had come—first in spots that grew into columns of moonlight piercing the clouds. Then as pricks of feeling returning to my limbs. And finally, a sharp burst of air down my lungs.

I fumbled upright, gasping the crisp night down greedily. But something closed around my throat, quickly forcing me down again.

Kakias's power pressed my wrists to the cold floor beside my head.

The truth of what she'd done—the deal, the magic she abused—came rushing back to me.

"This is—against all natural—balances—in the world," I panted, still regaining breath, and kept my eyes on the queen.

"Some things are worth upsetting the precious balance." Her back was to me, her form blurred, but her voice was high and clear. "If you'd been more coldhearted like I'd advised, you'd have learned that."

"What's worth this?" I asked. "What could have been worth the sacrifice that turned you into a heartless monster?"

She froze. "If I am a monster because I sought internal peace and revenge, then you are, too."

"No," I spat. She went to lengths I would never consider. Killed thousands, enslaved her armies to whatever cursed magic she wrought from those pools, and laid her vengeance upon the land. I'd never fall to those twisted levels. "There are lines that I'd never dare to cross."

"Everything in this life costs something, Ophelia," the queen mused. "Sacrifice is unavoidable."

"Just because you're desperate, doesn't mean your actions are necessary." I tugged against her hold, but my hands were locked beside my head. The statue of Damien lay in pieces at my side. "You can choose what you're willing to sacrifice."

"And I did." Her voice carried around the chamber as she walked toward me, bouncing off the marble and into the blood-soaked night as she prowled toward me. "I chose what I was willing to lose in order to hang on to what I wasn't."

The manic flare in her eyes deepened, her chest rising and falling with the memory of her pain. Dark curls flowed around her shoulders, rising in time with her breaths as she exhaled a phantom power.

"What did you feed it?" I whispered.

"I traded my soul."

My heart clenched behind my ribs. I didn't know it was possible to bargain a soul, but it was time I stopped underestimating dark magic. When combined with a ruined heart, corrupted power was the most deadly of poisons. My own weathered soul knew the lengths it would go to in order to obtain its greatest desires. In that, Kakias and I were not that different.

"The thing that ripped me to shreds after I lost what mattered most," the queen continued. "In exchange, I won secrets to ward off my greatest enemy."

Fear trickled down my spine. "Who is your enemy?"

"Death." Her tone went cold with the word—the entire night chilled. The bonds on my wrists tightened. "When I was younger than you are now, I had a child. I was practically still one myself, only eighteen, but it was with a man I *truly* loved. I thought he truly loved me in return—but I was wrong. To him, I was nothing but a means to an end. He knew the power in my heritage; he wanted to use it."

"He wanted your crown?" It was not uncommon for suitors to appear around heirs, thirsty for a taste of rule. I didn't see how that ended with us here.

"No." Her voice was nothing but venom as she tumbled back into her haunted memories. "He wanted my child. To raise without me, feeding it nothing but darkness to survive."

I stilled, horror and disgust wrenching through my gut as I began to understand. "He—"

"Children cannot survive the influence of power so bleak." Her voice faltered, jagged breaths cutting through. It was the most vulnerable I'd seen her—true pain over the child she'd wanted tearing the words to shreds.

For a moment, I was sad for the queen. For the teenage girl who had not meant to bear a child yet loved it fiercely. And had it ripped from her.

"He claimed he didn't know, didn't understand the magic he sought to usurp. I told him he was a fool for toying with things he did not grasp. Then, I killed him. And with the swinging of that blade, I *swore* I would never feel such pain again." She prowled above where I lay, the press of her power weighing down further on me with each step.

"I promised to take back everything I lost and more. In my distraught state, I went to the dark pools and offered up a piece of my own soul—the mortal piece capable of feeling agony. I asked the magic to give my child a second chance at life in exchange, but the pools insisted it was impossible. Death could not be undone." She grimaced, a flash of distrust passing through her eyes, but continued, "They offered an alternative. A way that I would never suffer pain again. Never love that way again. Never be swept away into the darkness that took over my life when my child was stolen from me. Never fall to the cruel hands of Mistress Death."

Realization struck me—the power emanating from her, the vacancy in her eyes, the way she extended her control over her army— and I gasped. "You're immortal?"

It was wrong among warriors—it was unnatural for us to live forever since our power grew over time. She had gone so far as to break the magic binding our lives to mortality out of pain from her loss and the agony it rooted within her soul. Escaping that terror—that had been all she'd wanted.

Though it was a vile decision that led us here, and I could never begin to grasp the exact pain she had experienced in losing her child, a piece of me understood the desperation that consumed her.

And I understood—Kakias was composed of fear and grief.

Every decision she had made in her war with mortality was staked in one or the other. She had once been a girl in love, and the betrayals of a greedy man had tainted her future, her heart, her soul. Set us all on this bloody trajectory where no one could truly win. Kakias could be immortal, but she'd never return the broken pieces of herself. And if she died—if I killed her tonight—I would be bathed in her grief, my hands stained with what her life could have been had fate not cursed it centuries ago.

Had she even wanted this future? Or had the sentience in the pools recognized an opportunity to manipulate her? She'd been willing to sacrifice herself, but without the influence of darkness warping her, maybe she wouldn't have chosen this. Her autonomy was compromised the moment she stepped foot into those pools.

It didn't redeem the decisions she made, the lives she took, but dammit, the Angels were cruel at times.

Kakias stalked toward me, stopping near my head and leaning down, winding her fist into my hair. "I am not immortal yet, dear girl." She yanked me upright, crouching down to look me in the eyes. "But after tonight I will be."

"What—" My question faded into a scream as Kakias sliced my arm open.

Blood gushed from the wound. She lifted a chalice I hadn't noticed and held it to my wrist, the cut burning. My blood trickled into the silver basin.

I waited for the flow to stanch. For the wound to stitch itself up.

But the rivulets continued down my arm, dripping over my fingers until the silver rim was nearly overflowing.

Kakias tossed me aside, pain ricocheting through my bones. I could only stare at the gash, trying to make sense of why the mountains had not yet begun to heal it.

Nausea washed over me as I realized.

Kakias's blade was laced with power, too.

Not only had the queen been gifted—she'd gone as far as to ensure her weapons were unstoppable. Her army, unnaturally skilled and moving like the wind, was the first defense.

The dagger the second, creating wounds that magic alone could not heal.

My gaze snapped to her shadowed form as I struggled, still in her power.

With slow, careful movements, she moved to the edge of the Rapture Chamber and lowered the chalice to the ground, directly in the center of a ring of moonlight. She circled it, bending to drag her fingers along the marble, smearing some kind of oil on the ground.

"Tonight," Kakias's voice echoed, "you help me finish what was promised to me centuries ago." She continued her lap. "The blood of the Chosen, transformed under the light of midnight, stirred with elements of sacred land, and spelled with the dark power of the Fallen." Her words chilled my bones, the pool of blood growing beneath me.

"Tonight"—Kakias stopped walking, turning to face me—"you make me immortal."

White light flared from the oil she'd drawn, burning a ring through the pillars and shooting into the heavens, dimming the stars. Kakias stepped into the circle.

I blinked against the light, my eyelids growing heavy, but I could just make out the movement of her lips as she recited the words the dark pools had given her for this ritual.

Quickly, she sprinkled whatever ingredients were demanded into the chalice. *Elements of sacred land.* I'd bet my last breath that those items were what she'd been after these months, traveling the continent to obtain the ritual's puzzle pieces. Waiting to attack until she had them.

With the third one, a blue glow burst from the cup, transforming my blood into her potion. I was cold with dread as she lifted the cup to her lips and drained it.

Kakias turned toward me, and her sight pinned me to the ground. Nothing human swam behind those eyes.

That was the sacrifice, I supposed. To live forever, one must relinquish their ties to the mortal world.

It was the result of years of mourning. A desire born of fear, terror at having the person she loved most ripped away from her.

Even now, as I writhed beneath her clutches, I understood that pain. I'd clawed my way back from it, dragging myself through darkness and flame to escape. It was an all-consuming, blinding fear.

Barrett once said his mother and I had more in common than I realized. Though I doubted he knew the extent of that claim, he'd been right. We were two women ripped to shreds by the turns of fate, left to repair ourselves after being broken beyond recognition.

I'd found my own solace in my family, but Kakias had been alone. She'd turned to oblivion to heal herself, and now, she'd given up any feeling that remained in her body in order to outlast death itself.

The power that had planted itself in her using *my* blood swirled around her as she stalked toward me. Her power loosened enough for me to sit up.

"There's one more step to hand over my mortal soul for eternity and make my transition complete."

"What is that?" I panted, chest tightening.

Bloodred lips split into a grin, sharp teeth still impossibly white. "Now, you die."

CHAPTER FIFTY

MALAKAI

THE SAFEST TEMPLE TO reach was a round stone building in the western sector of the Sacred Quarter. Small and abandoned, its copper-plated facade was tucked away from the heart of the battle. Though I wanted to tear back toward that chaos, I led Cyph and Vale there.

The Starsearcher didn't stop as it loomed into sight, its tarnished door glinting green in the smoky night, the pillars framing the door cracked but standing.

Vale soared past us, up the small flight of stairs and through the creaking door.

Ripping open cabinets along the curved wall, she piled supplies in her arms. Tinctures and herbs, jars and candles, muttering under her breath the entire time. She carried them up the short aisle to the front of the room, striking matches, igniting pipes and rolled herbs. Smoke of various floral scents filled the air, mingling around her frame and shrouding her in a cloud of lavender fog.

"Go outside," she hissed through the veil. The smoke drifting around her thinned so we could make out her actions.

"Why?" I snapped.

"Because you need to stay present in case someone comes, and I don't know how the tinctures will affect you." She poured a few drops of oil onto her hands within her cocoon of incensed smoke and pressed her fingers to her temples.

I was weary of leaving her alone, but Cyph's hand was on my shoulder already.

With a reluctant snarl, I followed him outside, leaving the door open to keep an eye on the Starsearcher.

We took up spots on either side of the entrance, shadowed by the thick columns lining the wrap-around walkway. Cypherion was stoic beside me, eyes flicking inside every other second. There was an unfamiliar hardness behind his gaze—hurt and mistrust I normally saw within myself or Ophelia, but not in him.

Despite the distance from the fight, the clash of destruction echoed to us. I flinched as each cry hit my ears, both guilty I wasn't there and grateful for a moment to rest. Still, the shame that washed through me knowing warriors were falling in my stead was icy.

That anger, that courage I'd found, seemed so far gone already. It wasn't Vale's deceit exactly—I'd had a feeling she was hiding something. It was the fact that the moment I dared to fight, another lie had come along and rip the rug out from under me. Old wounds tore open. I'd fucking bleed out if this kept happening.

"Can we trust her?" I whispered.

Cyph stiffened, hands flexing. "She told us her secret—one that could make her our enemy."

In my eyes, that didn't make her trustworthy. It only showed that she now thought she gained a bigger advantage by being more honest with us than she once had. Or maybe she truly hadn't had a choice, but now was forced into one.

Spirits, betrayal was never black and white, was it?

"Why do you think Titus instructed her to lie?" I asked, running a hand through my hair. Specks of ash shook from the strands, floating around me. I caught one on my finger and looked at it—this tiny speck of my city that had once been beautiful but was now tainted.

"I'm not sure." Cyph made a noise somewhere between a snarl and a sigh. "He has an abnormal hold on her. I'm going to find out why." His gaze lingered on the cloud of smoke that Vale sat cross-legged within, and his hands tightened on his scythe. Vale's wavy hair frizzed from whatever was in the incense, but her spine remained straight as she communed with the Angel and Celestial Goddess.

Cyph's lips lifted at the corners despite the hurt still echoing in his stare. That small smile was a promise, I realized. Whether to himself to find answers or to her, I wasn't sure, but I hoped the former.

I smiled, too. While I may be wrecked beyond fucking repair, maybe my friend could find it within himself to hold faith.

"You're a good man, Cypherion." It was important he knew that. For months, I'd watched him fall into this new role among the warriors in the palace, grasping leadership, providing insight and strength. He'd shouldered each misstep of those he trained as his own, but he grew more confident each day. Cyph had fought to prove himself for so much of his damn life, and while we'd always believed in him, maybe he was starting to, as well.

He turned to me, cheeks slightly red. "Thanks, Mali."

Then, something shot between us.

And Cyph was screaming. A roar that took with it every fragile wall I'd built back up. Snuffed out my last shreds of confidence.

I lunged, catching him around his ribs before he could fall and—

There was a spear through his Angel-damned shoulder.

His screams echoed through my head. Spirits, I'd never forget that cry as long as I lived.

Gently, I lowered him to the ground as he groaned, his blood quickly turning the sandstone red. I tried to apply pressure to the wound, but the spear remained lodged in his shoulder, protruding through his back. My stomach turned, heart rattling.

Footsteps sounded. Hands painted with my best friend's blood, I looked up.

Three masked Engrossians stalked toward the temple from one of the narrow alleys.

Fucking Spirits, they'd followed us. We were stupid to drop our guard. And now—

The red seeping into Cyph's white shirt was growing too quickly, the color draining from his face. He groaned as he rolled on his side, taking the weight off the wounded shoulder.

"Look at me," I snapped, bracing my hands on the ground that was rapidly becoming a sticky puddle. I lowered myself to look into his eyes.

"Don't—give me—a fucking—pep talk." His words were labored, thick breaths between each. "Go!"

I spun, lifting my sword, but froze at the axes trained on me.

"Shit," I breathed, fingers shaking.

No, I couldn't do this. I couldn't freeze again. Not now. Not with my best friend bleeding out beside me. But my mind was tunneling back into my past as those axes shone.

My eyes flashed to Cyph—

He was crawling through the temple, inching up the aisle with his good arm. Agonized cries left his lips with each pull. A thick red trail of blood painted the stones behind him.

"Vale," he panted. "Vale, you need to snap out of it."

I turned back to the approaching Engrossians, their weapons ready. Three against one.

"Vale, you need to run." Cyph shook her shoulder.

My vision blurred around their forms. He was trying to get her to flee. Leave him here.

Memories flashed before my eyes. A knife carving an ax into my chest. A sword being sharpened. The scars stung.

"No," I whispered. Sweat beaded on my skin. "Stop it, stop it, not now."

Blood pounded in my ears. My flesh tore beneath a whip. Cyph's broken pleas.

"Please, Vale. Come back. You need to run, *please*." But the Starsearcher was lost to her session, taken by the celestial beings that controlled fate.

And Cyph was hanging on to consciousness for the sake of saving her.

And I was…I was…failing. Being the weak, inadequate man they'd turned me into.

I'd made amends. Made so many fucking amends to those around me in recent months. But this…everything going on inside my head…I'd avoided it.

And now it was undoing me.

The Engrossians stalked up the stairs, almost close enough to reach me.

Cowardly, I stepped backward. My foot landed in the puddle of Cyph's blood, deep red and once so full of life, now death beneath me. It tainted the stones, so much of it. And yet he fought. He wouldn't give up until Vale was safe, because Cyph was a true warrior. Despite his past, despite his views of himself, he was resilient.

My sword was raised toward the Engrossians, but the blade shook in my hands. I adjusted my stance, and the ax I'd stuck in my belt swung against my thigh.

I jolted but looked down at it for a moment.

I am no longer a captive.

Cyph fought—he fought for someone he cared about. Who was I to stop myself from doing the same?

The axes were only objects. These opponents were only warriors. I sheathed my sword and pulled the enemy weapon from my hip. It was a blade like any other—it could hurt me if I allowed it to, or I could end its reign.

Stepping forward, leaving a bloody footprint, I tightened my grip around the foreign handle.

"You chose the wrong fucking time to mess with me," I snarled. Determination was igniting within me. The anger I'd tasted before returned with each plea that left my friend's lips, with each drop of blood that spilled from his body.

I lunged at one of the Engrossians. The ax was top heavy, a balance I wasn't used to, but I ducked his first blow and used the momentum to swing around.

I was quick. The weapon lodged in his ribs. With a grunt, I wrenched it free and he tumbled down the stairs. He landed flat on his back with an echoing crunch and didn't move again.

Then, there was a grunt behind me.

I whirled. The other two Engrossians were circling me, cornering me against the temple wall.

I looked between them. They were both larger than I was, both their weapons heavier, too. Nerves clawed up my throat as I looked between their axes, the knives strapped to their belts.

One raised his weapon, swinging downward in a perfect arc to swipe my head from my body.

I spun to the side at the last moment, tucking against the wall. The blade clashed against stone. He struck again, and this time I met it with my ax. The force rocked up my arm, jarring my shoulder.

I gritted my teeth for a third swing, seeing the last Engrossian raise her own weapon.

Then, a flash of platinum hair streamed up the steps, and a small knife rammed into the woman's back. Blood bubbled up her lips as she swayed. The Engrossian fell at my feet, and Mila stood in her place, both of us turning to the final warrior.

"Need help?" Mila flashed a wry smile.

"Holy fucking Spirits," I breathed. "I've never been more relieved to see someone." I didn't care where she'd come from or how she knew to find us here, I was simply glad to not be alone.

"I thought you might give up for a second there," she joked, as if we hadn't killed two opponents and now faced down a third.

"Would you have saved me if I had?" A smirk actually lifted my lips.

Mila laughed, a sound like cruel death. She was a huntress stalking her prey, and some part of me enjoyed the feral spark in her eye. "Yes, but I would have been really fucking angry that I had to."

"Glad I saved you the trouble, then," I answered.

We both raised swords. Blood dripped from our weapons, creating a steady tune to carve out life.

The final Engrossian was smart to look scared as I swung. Our weapons clashed, the blunt force of his ax against the fine precision of my sword.

Though he moved with the inexplicable grace of their army, I was fighting for the life of my best friend. It was with little effort that I ducked beneath his weapon, catching his wrist and twisting it behind his back.

Swift as a bird, Mila swiped up the ax I'd dropped and dragged its heavy blade across the Engrossian's throat. His gargled scream swallowed the screeches of battle.

I threw him forward, his body falling in a lifeless heap on the temple ground. In the silence, his eyes stared out toward the city. I wondered what his final thoughts had been. Was he proud to have fought, or was he wishing he'd made the weaker choice?

Perhaps if he had, he'd still have his life, though no path that followed Kakias would end well.

Chest heaving and blood-soaked, I looked up at Mila. Her lips were pursed as if evaluating me, eyes assessing as always. But an appreciative smile bloomed across her face.

For half a second, I returned it.

Then, the adrenaline of the fight drained from me and reality settled back onto my shoulders.

I tore into the temple, falling by Cyph's side.

"Cyph...Cypherion," I begged him to focus on me.

He kept muttering pleas to Vale, unaware our fight had ended. His vision swam out of focus, color leaving his cheeks. The mountains couldn't begin to heal his shoulder—not with the spear still piercing it.

Finally, Vale's head snapped up. She sprang to her feet, swaying slightly. Her eyes widened for a moment, her dazed stare not truly seeing as she looked at the blood around us.

"I know what it means," she said dreamily before collapsing to the ground beside Cypherion.

CHAPTER FIFTY-ONE

MALAKAI

"FOR THE LOVE OF the fucking Angels," Mila hissed, diving to check Vale's pulse.

Cyph groaned—the only sound he was able to make to ask if she was okay. He tried to push himself up, but I pressed a hand to his good shoulder to keep him down.

Mila pulled Vale clear of the fading fog, lying her where we could both see the shallow rise and fall of her chest. The herbal scents still clung to the Starsearcher's silk dress and skin, rich even from here.

She'd figured it out—whatever *it* was. An answer to surviving this battle, hopefully. I chewed the inside of my cheek nervously as Mila assessed her, needing that knowledge from Vale.

"She's fine," Mila finally declared. "She probably just overdid it with those tinctures. She should wake soon."

Cyph sighed, his bloodstained body relaxing.

Mila stood, turning her crystal blue eyes to meet mine, reading the panic written across my face as I held my bleeding friend in my arms.

Distantly, I was aware of the battle still raging and the possibility that we could be found here again. Of how many others were dying. But right now, all I could do was look at the wound darkening Cyph's skin and clothes, his blood on my hands. It was so much, too much. Hysteria rose in my chest, clouding my mind. I had to do something—

Then, quick, small hands were there. Clearing away the scraps of his clothing, Mila ripped the already-torn hem of her own dress into pieces.

"Look at me," Mila instructed, her voice much softer than the assured movements of her fingers. I tore my eyes away from Cyph to meet hers. We both breathed heavily, watching each other, and I tried to match her determination. "You can't freeze now, do you hear me? He needs you."

The last sentence rocked through me. It had been so long since I thought someone needed me in any way, yet here was this clear-eyed warrior claiming so.

I nodded fervently. "What can I do?"

"For starters, we need to get that spear out so it can start to heal. That will take both of us." She spoke slowly. I absorbed every word as she surveyed the weapon, careful not to prod it. "It doesn't look poisoned like some of their weapons were, so once we remove it, the mountains should begin to work, but we'll want to stop the bleeding as quickly as possible, rather than waiting for only the magic. Once the spear is removed, I need you to search the cabinets for anything that may help us."

The ground shuddered with a distant blast. Cyph groaned, and I flinched, but Mila remained steady.

"Got it."

She guided my hands to where she needed them to support removing the spear, her fingers sure and warm. She had me brace Cyph's body, holding both him and the weapon as still as possible. Fucking Spirits, his dead weight was heavy to maneuver.

"This is going to hurt," she told him, not sugar-coating a single second of it. Cyph would have appreciated her straightforward attitude if he had the energy to tell her so.

Then, with precise, steady movements, she used a dagger to saw through the shaft of the weapon. Sweat coated Cyph's body, cutting paths in the blood across his shoulders and chest. He passed out but kept breathing. The knife dragged through wood, splintering the spear.

Finally, it snapped.

Mila cleared away the splinters as much as possible.

"Here we go," she murmured. In one motion, she drew the weapon free and threw it aside. Then, she took my place supporting him, and pressed the strips of her dress to the wound.

"Go," she spat, not even looking at me, focused on her patient.

I dug through cabinets and drawers, finding mostly candle stubs and matches. Tinctures and herbs. Stacks of old notebooks and—there. My fingers locked around a small box. Flipping it open, I found thread, needles, and a number of other tools that were clearly once used for repairing the robes of the temple acolytes. It wasn't Bodymelder quality, but it would do. It had to.

Flying back up the aisle, I skidded to a stop next to Mila and dumped the supplies on the floor. "I don't know how long it's been there. If it's clean."

"They'll be able to get rid of any infection later. What matters now is stopping the blood."

My stomach sank at the implication. With our quick healing and proximity to our source of magic, the only true way for a warrior to die in Damenal was through loss of blood. Major injuries—slitting the throat, loss of limb, blade to the heart—those usually sufficed. Decapitation was quickest. If a warrior bled out before their wounds could heal…

"It's not—I don't know how—" I looked between the thread and Cyph's bloodied flesh. Mila had cleared away the worst of it, and now mangled skin and muscle stared up at me.

For what seemed the hundredth time, uselessness drained the fight from me.

"I do." Without looking at me, she threaded the needle. Her hands didn't even shake as she pushed it through Cypherion's skin, the stitches ragged but efficient.

At some point, my breathing evened out. As I watched Mila tie off the thread and the bleeding stopped, I sank to my knees. Tears stung my eyes, but I barely dared to blink as I watched Cyph. He was so still, but he was alive. His eyes fluttered beneath their lids, and his chest rose with shallow breaths.

Finally, once I was sure he was no longer dying, I lifted my head. "How did you know how to do that?"

"You learn a lot on a battlefield," Mila said dully. She sat back, wiping her hands on scraps of fabric. "It's the only way to keep yourself going. You have to distract yourself, or you'll be lost."

"It's easy to lose yourself," I said.

Mila's eyes were piercing when she looked at me and whispered, "You have to retain a belief in your cause, in yourself. Without that, you're nothing."

The sentiment settled in my chest like a weight. Not for the first time, I considered what her life was like during the war. Out there with Lyria, fighting the battles my father had caused. Watching warriors die—comrades she knew and those she may not have had a chance to meet. Likely taking an abundance of life herself if the skill I'd seen from her so far was any indication.

How many wounds had she delivered? How many had she stitched? Had she saved lives as well as taken them? Had she scrambled desperately to cling to those she was about to lose, to buy them one more moment, one more breath? Did her hands shake then or had she always been as steady as she was now? Maybe that part came with time, or maybe her confidence and ability were natural-born talents.

I wanted to ask her; I wanted to know what it was like. I wanted to ask how she'd received each scar—the ones I'd seen on her legs, and the ones I was sure she hid. But a part of me knew this wasn't the time.

Clearing my throat of the lump that had formed, I said, "Thank you."

I meant it for so much more than saving Cyph's life. Based on the smile she gave me, she understood.

"Anytime," she sighed.

It was a bit of an unfair reprieve from the battle, hiding in that temple as we waited for Cyph to gain strength. I'd considered asking Mila to watch over him and going back out to join the fight, but I couldn't bring myself to abandon my friend.

Finally, Vale stirred. I'd almost forgotten about her—the traitor she'd become in my eyes.

But the second she was seated upright, she looked directly at me. "I figured it out."

"You know how we'll defeat Kakias?"

Her lips pulled into a tight line. Whatever she saw of the queen, it couldn't have been good. "I know a lot more than that."

CHAPTER FIFTY-TWO

OPHELIA

KAKIAS'S THREAT HUNG IN the air between us. *Now, you die.*

Her words had been calm—the power she'd adapted engulfing her until her countenance was lethal ice.

And those serenely bloodthirsty eyes had one goal: *me.*

The only way to ensure her immortality stuck was to eliminate the key to her unnatural existence. Because all magic had a loophole, a scale to balance, and I was hers.

Her power released its hold on me, and I staggered to my feet. Black spots were starting to cloud my vision, speckling the sides.

My body was wrung out, exhausted.

But a small, curious piece of me was in awe of the impossible ritual I'd witnessed. A queen halfway to immortality thanks to some thread of power that I hadn't even known resided in me.

It finally made sense. Her motivation for the war—it wasn't only to grasp the Revered's power, though that was what she'd told Lucidius. It was to isolate the *Chosen*—the blood she needed for her ritual—and steal that power for her own. She'd oppress the entire Mystique population if that was what it took, all because she'd traded the shred of herself that would feel remorse for such a thing.

The dark power built within her, ebbing off her body like trails of ghostly shadow. The twining black tendrils reached around her like roots, reminding me of—

"You planted the Curse in the Mystiques, didn't you?" I gasped, lungs clenching as they fought to keep sucking down air.

Kakias's wicked smile was answer enough. There was no sorcia. The sorceresses in the Northern Isles didn't interfere as we'd been told. That was only another one of her lies to sow discord.

"You learned how to cast it through your deals with the dark pools."

I'd always wondered what the Engrossians had offered the impartial sorcias in order to lure them to their side, but it had been a cover for Kakias's schemes.

"There are endless possibilities if you're willing to sacrifice, Ophelia." Her sneer twisted my gut.

"Was there more of a reason to it, though?" I cradled my injured arm against my chest. The warm crimson stained my dress, pooling in the crook of my elbow. "The Curse—it—"

"It was created to target Mystique blood and would not touch those who contained what I needed. When your family was never tainted, I had my suspicions."

"But I *was* Cursed." Or at least to her—and everyone around me—it looked real.

"I admit, that did give me doubts. I knew it couldn't be my own, though. I'd lifted it after the treaty. After Malakai handed himself over, and I knew it was you I needed." She crossed closer to me, tipping my chin back. I was too weak to fight her. "And once I saw you for myself, I was certain. Those eyes of yours are rather distinct…"

"Mother!" A voice carried clear across the chamber, a shadow appearing in the doorway.

Barrett.

Chest heaving slightly as though he'd run here, the Engrossian prince strode into the room. His curls were tame, his clothes not too battle worn. Only a small cut lined his high cheekbone, already healing over.

As he approached, the rings on his fingers reflected the moonlight. His eyes, though—those were darkened aggression.

The queen stiffened as her son came closer, but she quickly fell back into her facade of disinterest. Her lip curled when she spoke. "The rat has come out of his gilded cage."

Barrett barked a laugh. "Please, Mother. The only cage I've ever been kept in was the one you held the key to." His eyes flitted over me, over the blood still trickling from my wound. Catching the heaviness of my eyelids. "Let her go."

"Why would I do such a thing?" Her gaze shifted between us.

"Killing Ophelia will not give you what you want." Barrett stepped closer to me. Though my heart pounded behind my ribs, there was a twinge of comfort now that I wasn't alone. The spots in my vision expanded.

"You know nothing of what's going on here. Killing her"— Kakias grasped my jaw—"will give me *everything* I have ever wanted."

"Do you hear that battle raging down below?" He paused, the echoes trailing up to us. "I've been living here for over a month now, Mother. I've seen how these people respect her. How they honor her. If you kill Ophelia Alabath, the entire Mystique population will rise up against you. And I promise you, their vengeance will be your downfall."

Warmth bloomed in my chest at the certainty behind Barrett's words. At his steadfast belief in me, his mother's greatest enemy.

It was quickly replaced by an icy dread as Kakias's grip tightened.

"I should have known you didn't have what this required," she spat at her son. "You were never strong enough to support my cause, to serve in my house."

"Because I didn't let you sink your claws into me as you tried to for twenty years?"

As he said it, her nails curled further into my skin, but I remained silent. It was all I could manage to stay upright at this point, my knees trembling.

Barrett needed this. To confront her for the invisible chains she'd put around his wrists all his life and the future she tried to force him into. Tried to wring the good from his heart.

"No," the queen hissed at her heir. "Because you speak of things like respect. You never learned that in our position, we don't need such a thing. Power was born in us, strengthened through the deals *I* made. It *belongs* to us. Yet you were born without the ability to remove your emotions from our goals."

"Your goals. Not mine. You speak of sacrifice as if it's a solution to all of fate's challenges." He sighed, reaching out slowly to grip his mother's wrist. "No one else has to die."

His fingers and jaw tightened, throat bobbing as he swallowed. Nerves slipped through his tense body.

But Kakias had frozen, seeming to actually listen to her son's words. The son who had come after the child she lost savagely. Though her soul had already been given to darkness, maybe she could find a sliver that retained compassion.

Barrett's other hand twitched, and for the first time, I noticed the sword at his hip.

Sword. Not an ax.

A Mystique sword, set with aquamarine stones that shimmered in the moonlight. Kakias's eyes flicked to it, her sharp teeth bared, and any hint of softness left her.

"Not everyone gets to live," she snarled.

"Where does this end, then?" Barrett's voice was soft.

"With her death, and my eternal existence."

Her words hit Barrett like a storm, and I realized he hadn't seen the ritual. Hadn't known precisely how far his mother dove into this ambition, this fear.

"What have you done?" the heir gasped, voice dripping with disgust. He shoved her wrist as if it burned him and stepped back, wrapping a hand around my waist and tugging me against him gently. Every facet of his body, from his hard stare to his hasty retreat, screamed with loathing.

But Kakias jerked me back toward her. My trembling knees gave out, and I crashed to the marble.

"I won't lose anything else." For a moment, she truly seemed a woman with an aching hole in her heart. It was the only sign that a sliver of humanity still existed within her. A desperate, small piece, barely acknowledged, but a piece all the same.

One my death would wipe from her, sealing her immortal fate.

As if hearing that thought, Kakias tugged me upward, her blade balanced below my chin.

The gash in my arm throbbed as I thrashed my weak limbs. Blood painted the marble, and I clutched it tighter to my chest.

That red warmth seeped over my skin, though, coating the emblem hanging from my necklace.

And a flare of golden light burst forth. Hot and burning and tinged with ancient power.

The queen shouted as it singed her, shielding her eyes and pushing me away. Two strong arms wrapped around me. Barrett tugged me toward the door, toward safety.

The blinding light continued to pour from my necklace—warm and protecting. Burning Kakias, but not me.

No, this blast soothed, its energy familiar and comforting. *Emboldening.*

It filled the room. I'd only ever experienced one presence like it. Ancient and all-encompassing, it pushed Barrett and I backward.

Sheltering me, he slid an arm around my waist. I latched on to his wrist, and when the blood from my arm fell freely onto his hand—onto his sigil ring—the power of the rays doubled, shooting out between the pillars and clearing the smoke.

Kakias screamed again.

Then, she was gone. Tumbling over the edge of the marble floor, tilting toward the mountains below, tendrils of ghostly shadows fluttering in her wake.

When the light finally faded, Barrett and I rushed to the ledge.

There was no body. The queen had vanished.

My knees gave out, the ground hard beneath them as I crashed to it.

"What the hell was that?" Barrett asked, kneeling next to me. He picked up my arm, looking over the wound without touching it. The world was becoming fuzzy, but the concern and hurt were clear in the prince's voice.

"I—I don't..." My voice trailed off, the words tasting funny on my tongue. I had a theory, but the details were slipping away as my vision narrowed.

Barrett dragged me into his arms and stood, striding for the door.

I shuddered into the warmth. In the gaps between my heavy breaths, clashes of battle echoed up to us. Those were my people down there—dying for me.

My father, the council...their deaths all stained my hands. I couldn't let anyone else suffer a fate meant for me.

Looking over Barrett's shoulder through heavy lids, my eyes fell on the burnt ring of oil from Kakias's ritual as it glowed—a physical confirmation of the impossible that had occurred tonight. A mortal warrior becoming immortal and disappearing into thin air.

I didn't know what it meant for the rest of us, but the chill lingering in my bones promised darkness.

CHAPTER FIFTY-THREE

OPHELIA

THE FARTHER BARRETT CARRIED me, the more my thoughts scattered. The entire night melted together.

I told him of the ritual and his mother's dagger as best I could, hoping he could pass along the information. We swept down the palace steps, toward Santorina's workshop.

Storms of battle mounted again as we passed the entryway, and something like a roll of thunder echoed in my blood. My eyes snapped open fully.

That was where I was needed. Not in a sickbed.

"Put me down." I swatted Barrett's arm, a lazy brush of a slap he likely barely felt. Screeches reached my ears; iron coated the air.

"You can barely open your eyes," he argued, arms tightening beneath my back and legs.

But a *boom* echoed in the distance. It sounded like one I'd heard earlier. I wracked my wrung-out brain. It sounded like—

"Tol!" I burst, summoning all of my strength to push out of Barrett's arms.

When I staggered on my feet, he gripped my good wrist. "Where in the damned Spirits are you going?"

"Tol," I muttered again, the only word I was able to form. I tugged out of his grip. Blood spotted the floor as I reached for my weapons, and I cradled my injured arm to my chest again. Barrett held them out of my reach.

My head cleared a bit more as another explosion rattled. Though the queen was gone, the Engrossians didn't relent.

I looked over my shoulder, out toward the grounds. Night was quickly shifting into dawn, and through my hazy gaze I could make out the spikes of the golden gates against a pale sky.

My heart twisted at the thought of Tol somewhere out there, broken and bleeding.

Please let him be okay, I begged.

But Barrett lifted my weapons farther out of my reach.

"Listen, Your Royal Highness," I snapped with as much strength as I could muster. Though I was standing through force of will alone, I'd been through worse and survived. "Hand me my damn weapons and get out of my way or send the Revered of the Mystique Warriors into a battle defenseless, but I have someone I need to find."

He sighed, but handed over my spear, switching it from his back to mine. I slid my dagger into its holster at my thigh and gripped my sword in my hand.

I charged down the stairs on wobbling legs and across the grounds, swaying slightly when I reached the gates.

Gripping the gold bars, I squeezed my eyes tight for a moment. Deep breaths in through my nose, out through my mouth. Three times, until my head stopped spinning. Screams rang in the distance, the cries of Mystiques in need bolstering me.

When I opened my eyes, I looked at Barrett. "You're being ridiculous," he chastised. "Let's go to the infirmary."

"Okay." But I darted down the hill toward the center of the city, ignoring the ringing in my ears and the swimming of my vision.

"Dammit, Ophelia!" Barrett called, chasing after me. His footsteps hounded mine as I ducked between buildings and through streets littered with debris, but I didn't slow.

Adrenaline mounted in my veins the closer I got to battle, my heart tearing for the warriors who depended on me and the one I couldn't bear to lose.

"Where was it, where was he..." I panted, turning down alleys at random. The world was spinning quicker.

But as my people fell, I had to at least try to fight with them, die with them, rather than remaining locked up in the palace. I stumbled over rocks, knees still weak. My bare feet sliced open again, but I forged on.

We rounded a corner and nearly ran into the backs of a pair of Engrossians.

Lifting my sword with all the strength I could muster, I stabbed an unaware warrior. He fell hard and fast, eyes flickering with recognition as I slayed him. The half-second of shock in his widened stare was satisfying.

Beside me, Barrett used his Mystique sword to cut down one of his own men, fighting with me, though the tension bunching his muscles said it was the last thing he wanted.

He grimaced as the man died. "That was a better end than a life without honor." There was a squelch as he removed his sword. "My mother ensured that he had none when she corrupted her army with dark magic," he reassured himself.

I swallowed, not knowing what words to offer the exiled heir who readily chose honor at the expense of his own blood.

"Barrett," I breathed, extending a hand.

But the thin layer of clouds blocking the moon shifted, and there was a flash behind him.

"Duck!"

I groaned as I ripped my dagger from my thigh with my injured arm and sent it spinning at the warrior sneaking behind Barrett.

It lodged itself in his throat, blood spurting from the artery. Barrett whirled, barely stepping out of the way as the warrior fell.

"Thanks," he panted, retrieving my dagger.

I nodded, energy fading quicker now.

Lifting my gaze to the street, I froze. A wave of black-armored warriors were rushing toward us. They injured and killed Mystiques still dressed in their Daminius finery—one by one.

I was too late, I realized with a devastated slice through my heart. The Mystiques were losing. I hadn't found Tol.

It didn't matter that Kakias had fled; she'd left her army behind to take us out in her wake. If I managed to survive with the poisoned slice to my arm, she'd be back for me. To finish what she started.

And we'd spread ourselves too thin. We'd fallen for her trap, stationing warriors at points around the mountains instead of fortifying the city.

We had thought Damenal was safe.

We had underestimated her desperate schemes. What she'd been doing all these months. We hadn't accounted for the tunnels through the mountains. Her plan had been to throw us off—and we had fallen for it.

And now, blood splashed across the streets. Screams tore through the air. We were dying.

My vision darkened for a full second. Holding my head up was difficult.

When it returned, a slight Engrossian woman was charging at me. Forcing my sword arm up for one last fight, I landed my blade against hers.

The impact rocked through my bones, but I gritted my teeth against the pain. My injured arm throbbed, the rest of my battered body echoing it.

I met her weapon again. The steel sparked a third time, Starfire slipping sideways.

I dropped, rolling away as her ax swung where, a moment before, I'd been standing. The Engrossian grunted, spinning to face me.

Her dark hair was chopped at the shoulders, her eyes endless pools of black ink. With Starfire raised weakly, arm shaking, I feared those eyes might be the last thing I saw.

But then, an arrow shot through one of them, jutting out the back of her skull. Blood burst between us. She swayed.

Her ax fell first, then her armored body tumbled to the ground.

More arrows rained down across the streets. Across the city.

They arced through the air, shot from the highest points of the mountains, finding homes again and again.

Not a single one missed.

And—I realized with a wildly hopeful beat of my heart—not a single one hit a Mystique.

Seawatchers. I nearly sobbed as they emerged atop buildings and cliffs, their light tan leathers bright against a sky fading from navy to pale yellow, stars slipping away with the night. They'd come to our aid.

One by one, Engrossians fell across the stone streets.

The Mystiques fought back, finishing off those who became distracted by the sudden appearance of the archers.

Hope bloomed across the faces of my people, even as bloody and defeated as they were. Their fire ignited once again, setting a peace burning through my chest, and I collapsed to the cobblestone.

CHAPTER FIFTY-FOUR

MALAKAI

THE STREETS WERE QUIET by the time we left the temple. While the battle I'd feared still echoed in my head, there was no clang of swords around us. Smoke drifted through the brightening dawn, clouds thinning into a yellow haze, pink rounding the edges. No buildings rumbled as they collapsed. No screams echoed as lives were taken.

But the moans of the dying could be heard across the city. They were being tended to, though, so we didn't stop. Not with Cyph finally awake but stumbling between me and Mila, and Vale still weak on our heels. Mystiques lay in the streets, comrades tending to them and—Bodymelders, I noticed with a drawn brow. A small host of them walked through the city, healing where they could.

The number of Mystiques I saw upright was encouraging. How they'd defeated the Engrossians, I didn't know.

But when we reached the palace, I found out.

I left Cypherion, Mila, and Vale to walk to the infirmary when I saw Ezalia, the Seawatcher chancellor, and her sandy mare. One look at the few arrows remaining in the quiver on her back, and I understood who we had to thank for this victory.

"They crossed through our territory while the queen led their diversion east," she explained when I asked after her appearance here. "The moment one of their less obedient warriors killed a Seawatcher, I declared it an act of war. We left two weeks ago to travel here with some Bodymelders. It appears our timing could have been slightly better." She frowned, looking at the warriors spread across the lawn.

The less severely injured had been given sleeping tonics, unconsciousness taking over as their wounds were healed by the mountains.

"Your timing was magnificent," I thanked her.

Her lips pulled into a thin line. "This is our fight now, too."

"What about the coasts? Who will guard them?" I asked. Their posts were a defense of the entire continent, never to be abandoned.

"We will always monitor the seas as guided by the Angel." She lifted her chin, sea-glass eyes blazing. "But avenging our own is our priority."

I understood that sentiment all too well.

"Malakai!" a deep voice shouted.

Barrett charged up the hill to the palace, a nearly unconscious Ophelia draped in his arms. The sight knocked the wind out of me.

"What the fuck happened?" I stormed up to Barrett. "What did you do?"

Ophelia looked up at me as I shifted her weight into my arms. At this proximity, I noticed an echo of a beat in the Bind.

Dull magenta eyes blinked up at me, lids heavy and irises fogged over as life seeped out of them. Crimson stained the front of her dress, spread across her chest, and matted the long strands of her hair. I looked for the source of it, only finding one slice to her arm. It didn't appear deep, but—there was too much blood.

"Not him," she exhaled.

Gently, I turned her face toward me. "What?" I whispered, but her eyes slipped shut again.

"Kakias."

I glared at Barrett for only a second, spinning to carry Ophelia toward the palace. I called for Santorina, and someone yelled that she was in her workshop. The prince followed, eyes half-crazed and dirt smeared on his cheeks, like he'd actually been fighting. We tore down the steps, my heart rattling its cage as loudly as ever.

"Tell me everything," I barked.

Barrett recounted an absurd tale of seeing a flash of bright light that led him to the Rapture Chamber, where apparently his mother was completing a ritual he didn't fully understand. He claimed she'd used Ophelia's blood to become immortal and tried to kill the woman in my arms. I ground my teeth together at his lack of detail.

He saved her, I reminded myself. That much was clear. And if Santorina could heal her now, I'd have to thank the bastard.

We burst into Rina's workshop, the place overrun by frenzied warriors tending to the injured. The door to the garden was thrown open and people ran in and out, carrying blankets, bandages, tonics.

"Santorina," I barely breathed. Desperation cracked my voice.

Rina's head snapped up. Her gaze fell to Ophelia, who rolled her eyes to the side and tried to crack a smile.

"Hi, Rina," she wheezed before her lids fell shut again.

"Fucking hell," Rina gasped, horror dropping her jaw. "Put her there." She pointed to a cot in the corner and asked Barrett to recount everything again. He rushed through it, giving only the necessary details of his mother's magic and the wound on Ophelia's arm.

Now that I'd gotten Ophelia into Rina's care, hearing the explanation a second time made me nauseous. *Immortality.* We'd never considered anything of the sort. It changed everything.

But we'd worry about that later.

First, we needed to heal the weakened woman before us. Seeing her on the brink of death, not knowing if she'd survive it—Spirits, anger flared through me. She may not be mine anymore, but I would always protect her. I made a promise to whatever hands of fate controlled us that I'd never see her like this again.

When Barrett finished speaking, Rina promptly told everyone to leave, wanting quiet as she worked.

As I stood, I brushed Ophelia's hair back from her face. *Until the stars stop shining*, I whispered to the Spirits, begging them to bring her back.

A weak hand grazed my wrist, her attempt to grab me barely a flutter.

"Where's Tol?" She blinked up at me, fighting to keep her eyes open.

My heart broke in that moment. Not because I was jealous that I wasn't the one she wanted, but because I didn't have an answer for her.

From my perch on the edge of the balcony of my father's ruined office, legs swinging above the land below, the afternoon looked peaceful. On this side of the palace, overlooking empty mountains, you'd never guess the destruction the city had faced only days ago.

Boots thudded behind me, but I didn't expect to see Barrett emerge from the doorway.

"Are you responsible for the redecorating?" He raised a brow.

I looked over his shoulder, at the papers and fragments of glass and marble still littering the ground, and laughed. It was a sound I hadn't made in a long time, but I'd been feeling lighter since sneaking sleeping tonics from the Bodymelders' store. In the aftermath of the battle, they hadn't noticed.

"I'll clean it up eventually." I shrugged.

"Don't do it on my account." The prince—no, I supposed he no longer had that title now that he'd cut ties with his mother. The former Engrossian heir walked up to the stone ledge and swung his legs over beside me.

We sat in silence for a while, and I considered everything that tied us together. From the tangible fact of our shared blood to the invisible scars of betrayal and abandonment left on our hearts. We'd both been wrecked by our father, and Barrett had been—well, the woman who birthed him was hardly a mother.

"Do you think she ever truly loved him?" The words burst from me before I could stop them. They'd been plaguing me for days. After Vale had told us of her scattered vision of Kakias and her inhumane ritual, what she'd wanted from Ophelia, gathering ingredients from around the continent, and Barrett told us what he'd seen, we'd pieced together Kakias's repugnant plan. Since then, I'd been wondering how my father had agreed to it, what she said or did to convince him.

Absently, I ran my fingers over his dagger where it hung on my belt. He may have been a warped man at his end, but there had once been good in him—or so I liked to believe. I didn't want to consider what it said about me if only soiled blood ran through his veins.

Barrett contemplated my question. "I think she cared in her own way, yes. But I don't think she was capable of love as we know it."

Love as we know it. That was a concept I needed to relearn. I'd seen Barrett with Dax after the battle, tangled together upon their reunion. While he certainly knew love, I'd been too destroyed by my father and his mother to know what love truly felt like anymore. I tried to hang on to the memory of it—the way I'd felt with Ophelia before we'd changed—but even the bright moments I could recall were fleeting, overshadowed.

"I don't think he knew her plan," I stated, curiosity bubbling in my gut. "At least, not all of it."

"Really?" Barrett raised a brow.

"I think they both had secrets." I looked over my shoulder at the ruined office and swore to myself I'd find out what my father's were. "Thank you for saving Ophelia," I added after a beat of silence.

I knew he didn't do it for me, but if he'd wanted to spite me as badly as I once had him, he could have let her suffer more. But no, while he may be an Engrossian, sired by the wicked queen herself, Barrett was undoubtedly good.

"Of course." He waved me off, but his expression turned pensive. He ran a hand through his black curls, similar to my own. "You truly love her, don't you?"

A sharp pang went through my chest, heart rattling. I inhaled around it, looking over the expanse of mountains. Peaks jutted into the clear blue sky of the summer day and reached hopeful hands toward the heavens. I waited for the Bind to ache, but nothing came.

"I always will," I admitted. I think he understood that it was in a different way than before. A piece of me would always belong to Ophelia. It would live with the boy and girl we used to be, in the future they should have had.

And it was inked in the promise of our Bind, unbreakable yet faulty. Our souls were connected whether we wanted to be or not.

"She's our best hope," Barrett said.

"Hope," I scoffed. Another thing I didn't have. But inadvertently, I remembered crystal blue eyes and a whispered conversation in a decrepit temple, and I thought maybe I could find it.

CHAPTER FIFTY-FIVE

OPHELIA

I SCRATCHED AT THE Curse mark on the inside of my wrist and gritted my teeth, eyes locked on the dark wood door. The slice on my arm from Kakias's blade still ached. Though the stitches holding my flesh together had faded into my skin and the wound was healed, an echo of dark power pulsed within the scar.

And I hated it.

The way it burned, like my blood was revolting against it, twisted my gut. Rina had leached the venom from that blade out of me using a slow process of needles and tonics. Or at least, that's what she'd said when I woke. I'd slept through the entirety of it, waking two days ago in a fierce sweat, thinking Kakias was standing over me.

It had been Jezebel, though.

"Thank the fucking Spirits," she'd sobbed, throwing herself at me, holding tight. I'd blinked as my head caught up to what was happening. We'd sat like that for an hour, tears silently streaming together, soothing whispers exchanged, sinking into the realization of our father's death.

Once Santorina had assessed me, Barrett and Malakai filled me in on the spotty parts of my memory—told me what had happened while I was off fighting Kakias and how the city was fairing since.

"Not well, but it could be worse," Cyph had said from his seat across from my cot. His expression was vacant. A fresh white bandage was wrapped around his shoulder, his broad chest bare beneath it.

I'd decided to take the wins we were given in that moment, cherishing the life still around me, but one person was missing.

"Tolek?" I'd asked, voice as small as could be.

"He's the same," Cyph had said, as he had every time I asked. Alive but the same.

But I wasn't allowed to think about him now. I couldn't lose myself to that pain when my attention was needed elsewhere.

Instead, I threw myself into reconstruction. Mystiques had rebuilt before. We'd do it again, and this time would be the last. I swore Kakias wouldn't have another chance at destroying my people. Not now that I knew her deepest secrets.

But she hadn't been the only surprise of Daminius, and now, it was time to deal with the traitor in our midst.

I swallowed, uncurling my fingers from the webbed curse on my arm.

"Ready?" I asked. My heart was heavy, but I forced away the ache in my chest, and didn't allow my mind to wander to the infirmary upstairs.

"Yes," Malakai answered.

Cyph only grunted.

Taking a deep breath, I sank into the presence of the Revered and threw the cell door wide.

Vale sat on her bed, chin resting on the windowsill, observing the clouds drifting through the blue sky. When we entered, she turned, spine straightening as she took in our trio.

Gone was the demure girl who looked at her feet during the Rapture, who averted her eyes when spoken to. Before us sat a woman dripping with confidence, albeit with a tinge of guilt coloring her eyes. Still, she locked her stare to mine, and for long silent moments, we stood like that.

Finally, I said, "The truth, Vale."

"If I talk to you, I'm betraying the man who has given me everything." She sniffed, lifting her chin—but she hadn't denied me.

"You've already started to talk," I reminded her.

"It won't take us much effort to figure out the rest," Malakai added.

"Or at least to create a story we find plausible." I tilted my head, my voice fading to a heartless taunt. "Rumors spread like wildfire once given a little kindling."

"Are you threatening me, *Revered*?" she sneered my title. A part of me wanted to remove the dagger from my thigh and remind her who she spoke to, but I didn't think threats would convince her.

No, I'd collected pieces of Vale's character for months now. Seen her for the secrets she'd tried to hide and the truths she'd let slip as she got comfortable in our presence. Vale was clever and unafraid. She'd faced horrors and risen above them. Threats would not frighten her into handing over information.

"I would if that would work, but it won't. Not with you." I crossed the room and sat on the bed beside her. Malakai followed, his disapproval dripping from his slow gait. He'd advocated for punishing Vale in ways I wasn't comfortable with, but in the end, I'd convinced him that it wouldn't be necessary. "You'll tell me because it's the smart thing to do. For us…and for you."

"And why would I think that?" Vale toyed with the ends of her hair, crossing her arms then uncrossing them.

"Because I know it was you that conducted the session in which Titus claimed to see my destruction." A smug smile spread across my face when she stiffened.

"How did you figure that out?" Reluctant approval glinted in her eye.

"I suspected for a while. Once my friends informed me you'd been lying to us, I was nearly certain. You confirmed it just now." I relaxed against the wall, crossing my feet on her bed. It was comfortable to be in my leathers after fighting a battle in a dress. These garments were a luxury I'd never take for granted again. I ran my hands over the skirt, the material cool beneath my fingers, and waited for Vale to form her response.

"I suppose it was only a matter of time until you threw me in this cell, then."

"For the love of the fucking Angels, Vale, tell us what this is about," Cyph snapped, speaking for the first time since we'd gathered upstairs.

Vale flinched, pursing her lips. I flicked my eyes between Cyph and the door, silently telling him if he could not control himself, he would have to leave. He nodded back.

I made a mental note to tell him I was proud of him for standing up to her, though. He deserved answers for being lied to—we all did.

"What Cypherion means to say is we know there is more to your story. And we have ideas of where it begins and ends, but it would be a cleaner process for you to share the truth."

"A cleaner process?" And there was a sliver of fear shaking her voice as she looked at the sword on Malakai's hip. The small ax beside it.

I gripped her chin, turning it toward me. "Not like that...at least not yet. I can't promise it will never come to that." Searching her eyes and not finding any hint of weakness, I added, "You've seen what I will do for my people, Vale. Do not become a threat to us."

Her lips quivered for a fraction of a second. "I can't tell you. I'll lose my home."

"A cage is not a home," Cyph said, much more collected than before. His eyes were on her shoulder—the spot where the tattoo covered the brand marking her as a slave.

Vale turned narrowed eyes on him, her chin still in my hand. "It is if it's all you know."

Realization snapped into me. I dropped the girl's face, standing from the bed. "Is there anything else you'd like to share today?"

She bit her lips, but her eyes landed on the emblem hanging from my necklace. "You figured it out, didn't you?" Her voice was low.

I nodded once, not needing her visions to confirm the truth my bones already screamed at me.

"I can honestly tell you that I haven't figured out what that vision meant. I've tried, ever since I've stopped suppressing them, I've attempted to recreate it. There's been no explanation—just darkness and you, Ophelia. But if I had to guess, I'd say it's all connected. The emblems, the queen, the Angelblood...and the reading."

"That's all for today." I spun toward the door. "Send word for us if you think of anything you'd like to share."

Malakai followed me from the room with one last threatening look over his shoulder. Cyph lingered for only a moment, a conflicted look in his eye.

We shut the door to her cell, locking it from the outside. As the heavy iron key hung in my hand, I couldn't help but feel bad for trading one of Vale's prisons for another. She'd only ever known cages. Was born to keep secrets.

Perhaps she needed to taste freedom.

The Mystique Council Chamber was stoic when I entered, marching to my seat at the head of the table. Malakai and Cyph followed, sliding into their places.

I tried not to think about the council members that were no longer here. Instead, I focused on those who *were* with me and the treacherous path awaiting us.

I didn't waste words on introductions, not when a heaviness pressed on my shoulders, my heart twisting in my chest. Truthfully, I didn't want to be here at all. My heart was elsewhere…

But I'd put this meeting off for two days already, allowing my council to grieve and dispose of bodies. To plan funerals, my father's included. My eyes stung, but I banished the thought, instead focusing on the pride he'd felt in me. I needed it to carry me through this.

My hands shook as I raised them behind my neck, flicking open the clasp on my necklace. I tossed the thin gold chain and emblem onto the table.

"This is the answer to Damien's prophecy," I clipped.

"A necklace?" Jezebel asked, perching on the edge of the table. Erista stood next to her, rubbing a hand over her brow in thought.

"A shard of metal that came from Angelborn." I remembered the first time I picked it up and how the scrap burned my skin—only *my* skin. "It has always reacted to me unlike any other warrior, creating a second pulse in my veins. The false curse was awakened by it to drive me here, to complete the Undertaking and start this whole journey. Given to me by the Angels. I believe this token is it."

"But what exactly is *it*?" Malakai asked.

"It's my theory that a crystallized piece of Damien's power lives within this shard of metal." Both pulses quickened within me as I remember the Storyteller's tale of fossilized power being left behind from the Angels. It wasn't just a legend, though. This emblem held the power of Angels.

"There are seven of these, then?" Cyph asked. Picking up the necklace and flipping it over, he held it to the light. Undiluted golden sun bounced off of it.

"One for each Angel," I confirmed. "If my guess is correct, every

Angel left one of these tokens behind. For the Chosen—the warrior with active Angelblood—to find and unite them. Based on how the metal ignited during my fight with Kakias, I think my blood activates it somehow. These shards are a part of me."

"It certainly burned with the radiance of the revered bastards," Barrett recalled. Reaching out a hand for Cypherion to pass the emblem, he and Dax looked it over together.

"And if I'm right, we have a second, too." I held my hand out to the Engrossians. "Your sigil ring, Barrett?"

Understanding spread across his face like the dawn. He removed his family heirloom and placed it in my hand. My pulses quickened again, a promise this time. The ring rolled over, the stone pressing into my palm, and I hissed in recognition of the heat singeing my skin, quickly dropping it to the table.

It bounced, landing face up, looking at me.

"The Engrossian emblem," I grunted. "When Barrett helped me against his mother, my blood spilled on his ring. More Angellight. Another token."

"Shame there isn't a less painful way of identifying them," Rina mused. I shrugged, not caring much about what pain I had to endure if it meant being certain.

"Okay, assuming your theories are correct," Erista started, "what are these tokens for?"

I shook my head. I had no answer for that. Since I'd woken up and started piecing together the scraps of information I had—the Storyteller's tale, Annellius's history, and Damien's cryptic words— I'd been struggling to decipher the *why*.

"Damien said to unite them." I shrugged. "I suppose that's a reasonable place to start."

A golden glow bathed the room, the maps lining the wall shining. While many of my companions gasped, I raised my brows. There were mutters and curses around the room, including Barrett's exclamation of "Bant's cock," to which the Angel smirked.

"I will tell him you inquired about it," Damien joked, turning from the Engrossian to me. "As requested, I have worked on my timing." He floated along the windows. With his large wings extended at either side, the sun haloing his figure, he brought legends to life. My pulses stirred, wanting to write them with him.

"It's appreciated."

The guests in the room watched me converse with the Angel, awe radiating from them, but nerves flitted through my body at Damien's sudden appearance. Based on my friends' tense stances and keen attention, they felt it, too.

"To what do we owe the honor?" I asked.

Damien raised his eyes, looking around the room, likely cataloging every person around me. When he finally turned fully toward me, I gasped.

"What happened?"

A jagged scar cut down the left side of his face. From his hairline, across his sculpted golden features, disappearing down his neck. Damien usually appeared unmovable—an ancient statue against our mortal forces.

But even marble could crack.

For a moment, his purple eyes showed something I didn't recognize in him. *Sorrow.*

"My own actions," he drawled, shoulders tense. A tic in his jaw. Then, eyes sweeping about the room and landing on the necklace, he proclaimed, "You've figured it out."

A proud smile split the Angel's lips and—was that relief I detected? It pulled against that fresh scar he wouldn't explain.

"Seven Angels. Seven emblems," I answered, basking in that pride, allowing it to warm a bit of the chilled uncertainty within me. "I'm meant to unite them."

"Good work," he said. "This does not end here, though." The warning crept around the room like a silent fog.

"What does all of this mean, Damien? What's the purpose of it?"

He opened his mouth, gaped, then shut it tight, wings ruffling behind him.

"There are things you can't tell me, aren't there?"

Everyone else in the room remained silent, as if only the Angel and I existed. Perhaps in this moment we did, our own reality where prophecies were spun.

He nodded tightly.

"Like the warning you gave? Why I couldn't tell anyone about the prophecy?"

"It didn't mean what you thought," he muttered, as though pained, searching for another thought he *could* speak on. "Beware the warped queen."

My gut sank, and I exchanged a look with Barrett. "She's alive, then?" he asked.

Damien nodded.

I'd been toiling over Kakias's confession for days now, and one question stood out to me: *Who* had given her the puzzle to achieve immortality?

The dark pools may be sentient, but Barrett and I agreed the ritual seemed too precise, the path too knowledgeable.

But I didn't ask Damien. From the way his wings flared and jaw clenched, I knew he was at the end of whatever leash it was that held him. Knew he must have something he was meant to share if he was still present.

"Why are you here?" Exhaustion weighed my voice, my bones, my being.

"Your curse runs true," he confirmed. Then, as I'd seen him do twice now, Damien swelled. Purple eyes swarmed with power, and the archaic voice that haunted me was cast over the mountains, "*The time is near, Cursed Child. Paint the shards with vengeance. Awaken the answering presence.*"

Angellight coated the room in a pulse of heated gold.

We stared at each other, two promised beings, two sources of indefinite power.

After a moment of prolonged silence, I muttered, "It will be done," as if I had a Spirits-damned clue what he meant, and the Angel vanished.

The truth hung heavily between our group. I swept my gaze around the table, the loss of the previous Mystique Council a gaping chasm.

This was our reality now; time for us to step into the roles we'd been training for. The last generation was gone. It was our turn to rise up.

We'd been preparing for our rule, we'd earned the positions, but this was not how any of us had wished they would fall onto us.

And I was formally claiming my position as Revered. The Soulguiders, Seawatchers, and Bodymelders all gave their blessing. Regardless, after the recent betrayals that were exposed, I was done waiting. I'd proven my loyalty to the Mystiques through strength on the battlefield and purity of heart in my defenses. Not only that, but I was chosen by the fucking Spirits, had been prophesied and cursed by an Angel.

When I'd first been told of my right to the position, I'd been shocked, but a deep recognition stirred awake within me. A spark ignited at the purpose I'd lacked for so long.

I'd been broken, my heart existing in only shards. In the months since, though, that spark had been nurtured, raised to a roaring fire that forged those shards into a formidable strength. It wasn't the future I'd ever envisioned for myself; I wasn't the girl I'd once been. This was something new—something beautiful, learning to heal, striving to fight.

While this meager, battered group around the room may be all the continent was left with in this mission, I swore it would be enough.

"Looks like we're following you into the unknown, Revered," Mila chirped from her seat at the end of the table.

Beside her, a red-eyed Lyria smiled softly, fighting off a worry I shared. It was an effort to meet her chocolate eyes that reminded me so much of Tolek's. She didn't have to speak, only nodded to tell me she'd be with me.

"And so your hunt begins," Cyph muttered, holding my necklace before me.

I wrapped my hand around the emblem. The heat burned through me, greeting my cursed blood like an old friend.

EPILOGUE

OPHELIA

MY LIPS TREMBLED AS I looked at Tolek Vincienzo lying in that bed. White sheets tucked around him, gore cleaned away, and bruises fading, but too still. Not his usual vibrant self, coaxing laughs out of me with a mere glance. Color was leached from his hollow cheeks, his lips set in a line.

Smirk, I wanted to yell. To drive one of those infuriatingly charming smiles from his lips that I loved so much, it was imprinted in my mind.

He'd been found beneath the rubble of the building he pushed me away from. Bones on the right side of his body shattered, lungs full of dust, bleeding internally—but still alive.

It had been days of meetings and burials and tears since the Battle of Damenal ended—and he had not woken. Though I'd spent each night at his bedside watching the moon rise through the high-arched windows lining the infirmary and listening to the steady beat of his heart that became my own lifeline, the hours were long. Every second was agonizing, waiting for his eyes to open.

"He'll wake," Esmond had assured me, the Bodymelder keeping a steady eye on Tol and the remaining patients in the infirmary.

They'd given Tol his own room, separating him from the conscious warriors who alternated between groaning and taunting each other at all hours of the day. I'd almost told them to move him. To place him with the others in hopes that their jeering would rouse him, but a piece of me had secretly wanted this privacy.

"How can you be sure?" I'd asked, tracing circles on the back of Tol's hand lightly, almost too scared to touch him. The entire right side of his body had been spotted with dark purple bruises when they found him. They were stubborn to vanish, even with the aid of magic. Fresh scars wove through them.

I'd torn my eyes away from Tol and looked to the healer. He didn't hide his flash of doubt quickly enough. My world tilted at the thought that I might actually lose Tol.

"The same way Vale consults the stars," Esmond had finally explained. "The way you direct that spear like a limb. It's my gift."

I'd sighed but relented, and allowed Esmond to guide me into a chair where I could remain through the night. The extra legion of Bodymelders that arrived with the Seawatchers had stayed to assist in healing, but only Esmond, Lyria, and my brigade of closest friends came in this room.

Esmond had walked toward the door, leaving just me, Tol, and the moonlight casting on his still features.

"Talk to him," the Bodymelder had advised right before he left. "Let him know you're here." The door snicked shut with a sound as hollow as my heart.

I did as he said.

I told Tol of everything that had happened after he shoved me aside, and how angry I was at him for doing it. I told him of the queen's ritual and imagined his outrage over her spilling my blood, of the Seawatchers riding valiantly into Damenal and taking out the Engrossian and Mindshaper forces when we were on the verge of death.

"You would have loved it, Vincienzo. The arrows were soaring across the sky. You would have stolen a few for sure, maybe had a chance to learn to use them for once." I'd stopped as a breath caught in my throat. "Once you're better, we'll learn together. Maybe take a trip to the Seawatchers' Western Outposts to train. Then, I'll beat you in an archery competition."

I'd smiled at the thought of him beaming beside me, taunting remarks and suggestive looks.

That had been days ago.

Tol still hadn't stirred.

I watched him from the doorway, tracking the rise and fall of his chest. Even from across the room, I could pick out his heartbeat as if it spoke to me.

Still here, it seemed to say. And I was almost furious with him for keeping me waiting, but at least he was alive. His heart still beat.

Fidgeting with my own leathers, straightening the journals I'd left at his bedside, I searched for anything he might want. There were more books than he'd need when he woke, but in case no one was here when his eyes opened, I wanted him to know he'd been thought of. Cyph had been polishing the Vincienzo dagger daily, leaving it on the table, and Lyria brought flowers. Next to me, she was here the most. Whenever I saw her, her eyes were red and guilty.

I wasn't supposed to come here today—I had only a few minutes to spare between meetings—but I needed his steady presence. I needed to tell him what had been on my mind.

"Hi," I said, sliding my fingers between his as I had numerous times before. His didn't tighten back.

Spirits, this was a conversation I didn't want to have, but I'd been talking to him every day and night, and I'd run out of updates and nonsense to spew. It was time I got the heavy words off my chest. I took a deep breath and watched the rumpled strands of his hair catch the light, smoothing them out.

"I don't really know how to begin this. I hope you can hear me, though." I waited, biting my bottom lip, but he didn't so much as twitch. "Maybe it's better that you can't interrupt me." I tried to laugh, but the sound was as lifeless as the cavern his injury had opened in my chest.

"You've been by my side through more than I could have asked, and you never thought to leave me. You pushed me when I tried to run, carried me when I couldn't stand, and somehow always knew the difference between the two, even when I didn't." A tear tracked down my cheek as every warm memory of the two of us cascaded through my mind, our own personal story.

I was not done writing it.

"But beyond that, you're strong, you've got the deepest soul of anyone I've ever known, and you're a *damn* impressive warrior. I've never been more sure of anything than I am of you, Tolek."

A steadying breath.

"I meant everything that I said to you before the Battle of Damenal. None of it was brought on by the lust of the moment, none of it was influenced by what we were doing—I need you to know that I was not coerced at all. I'd thought about it—you—for weeks, and it was what I wanted. What I want."

I thought of his hands warm against my body, his lips pressed fervently to mine, so much life poured into those moments. And I didn't regret any of it. Not a single kiss or touch.

But I'd gotten lost in the passion of *us*, all the while forgetting the broken pieces of *me* floating through the world, leaves caught on the wind. Tol was my own gift from the Angels, but his true power was in repairing me. This time, I could not rely on him for that.

It was not fair to either of us.

"It's you and me, Vincienzo. From here on out, there will be no one else. But..." I inhaled, almost too afraid to finish the speech I'd rehearsed, but waking or sleeping he deserved to know where I stood. He deserved more than half of a person, and I deserved to become whole again.

"I'm not sure what I can give yet. I need to take my time. To move slowly. I'm not sure what my heart can handle, but...I'd like to find out with you." In my memory, his thumb dragged slowly along my hip, his lips pressed softly to my forehead, and I remembered the way my heart stitched back together in his presence.

"You told me no matter what I decided, you'd be here forever. And I decided, Tolek Vincienzo—I want you. So, I need you to wake up." My voice turned pleading, breaking on sobs timed to his heartbeat. "I *need* you to come back to me so we can have that infinity you promised."

My chest seized with the tears trying to break free, each a splinter in my lungs. Tol was lodged there with them, a part of me I would never feel right without. He was woven into my life, my being, nestled between my bones. *My infinite tether.*

"Please, Tol. Please, you can't leave me. Life is so much darker without you in it. And you've had so much darkness yourself, you deserve to see the light."

I brushed his hair back from his brow, tangling my fingers in the soft strands. Bending forward, I pressed a firm kiss to his forehead, closed my eyes for a few seconds, and breathed in the spicy citrus scent that was my home.

Then, I left.

But at the door, I turned back one last time and whispered, "Don't keep me waiting, Vincienzo. Infinitely mine, remember?"

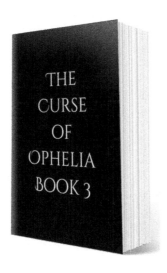

COMING SPRING 2024

Did you enjoy *The Shards of Ophelia*? Please consider leaving a review on Goodreads, Amazon, your favorite retailers, or social media.

I'd also love to have you join my newsletter for updates, my Discord Readers Group, or my Patreon for monthly bonus content.

Newsletter: https://nicoleplatania.com/
Discord: https://discord.gg/SVAaW2757D
Patreon: https://www.patreon.com/nicoleplatania

Cast of Characters

CHARACTERS WHO ARE CROSSED OUT WERE DECEASED
PRIOR TO THE BEGINNING OF THE SHARDS OF OPHELIA.

Mystique Warriors

Ophelia Alabath
Malakai Blastwood
Tolek Vincienzo
Cypherion Kastroff
Jezebel Alabath
Bacaran Alabath, Second to the Revered
Akalain Blastwood
Alvaron, Master of Coin
Collins
Danya, Master of Weapons & Warfare
Gerad
Hylia
Larcen, Master of Trade
Lyria Vincienzo
Marxian
Mila
Missyneth, Master of Rites
~~Lucidius Blastwood, former Revered~~

Engrossian Warriors

Kakias, Engrossian Queen
Barrett, Engrossian Prince
Dax, Lieutenant

Mindshapers

Aird, Mindshaper Chancellor

BODYMELDERS

Brigiet, Bodymelder Chancellor
Esmond, apprentice

STARSEARCHERS

Titus, Seawatcher Chancellor
Vale, apprentice

SEAWATCHERS

Ezalia, Seawatcher Chancellor

SOULGUIDERS

Meridat, Soulguider Chancellor
Erista, apprentice

NON-WARRIOR CHARACTERS

Santorina Cordelian, human
Sapphire, horse
Ombratta, horse
Astania, horse
Calista, horse
Erini, horse
Elektra, horse
Aimee, Storyteller
Lancaster, fae
Mora, not specified
Lessel, not specified

Acknowledgements

I learned a lot both about myself and about writing in general through this book. I think it's taught me about different kinds of love and helped me see when you need to be comfortable with uncomfortable situations. But writing a sequel had a world of challenges that book one didn't. There's a different kind of pressure, a lot of which is often self-inflicted, and I wouldn't have made it through without an army behind me.

First of all, thank you to my family for their endless support. This indie author venture is terrifying and eye-opening. To my parents and my brother for being a constant source of encouragement. Whenever I start to doubt myself, you make sure I keep going. Thank you. And thank you, Chris, for forcing everyone you know to buy this book. To the rest of my family (*cough, Uncle Anthony, cough*), thank you for your support no matter how far away we may all be.

To my friends—both "real life" ones and those met through the internet. To those I get to see every week, thank you for constantly getting me out of my head and understanding the "sorry I have to work" texts I send way too often. Your patience and excitement do not go unnoticed. Here's to trivia nights forever. To those who aren't as close, your support means everything.

And to those friendships made through the online book communities—I don't know where I'd be without you. It's mind blowing to me that some of the people I talk to the most are spread across the country. To Carm, Lynn, and Chey—thank you for helping me reach this book's potential and always making sure I'm taking care of myself. To Liz for being my permanent sounding board, the first to read the messiest drafts, and the reminder that there's gold in there. To Liv for understanding how hard this all is and never failing to hype me up when I need it most. To every author friend who has been there this past year. The indie author community is the most supportive group of individuals I've had the pleasure of meeting, and we're bonded through this very unique experience.

This book would have been a huge mess without the professionals who helped me turn it around. To my fabulous editor Kelley Frodel–you saw the potential in this story and consistently understand these characters. To my proofreader, Megan Sanders, for being passionate about this series. And to Franziska Stern for another jaw dropping cover. Your talent is unmatched. I can't wait to keep cooking up designs with you.

To my team of alpha and beta readers: Liz, Carmen, Lynn, Madi, Max, Mick, Taylor, Kira, Katie, and Jessica. Thank you for offering up your time and wonderful minds. To the artists who have brought these characters to life. To the ARC readers who helped launch this sequel, and to any bookstagrammer or booktoker who has shared this book with others. You're the reason this series is finding new hearts. Thank you for reading and for loving these characters as much as I do.

To Kelsea Ballerini (who won't ever see this) but the Spotify gods are probably concerned about me for how often I listened to Penthouse while writing this book.

Finally, to Ophelia and crew for stumbling through this journey and allowing me to tell it. You have made my life so much better.

ABOUT THE AUTHOR

Nicole Platania was born and raised in Los Angeles and completed her B.A. in Communications at the University of California, Santa Barbara. After two years of working in social media marketing, she traded Santa Barbara beaches for the rainy magic of London, where she completed her Masters in Creative Writing at Birkbeck, University of London. Nicole harbors a love for broken and twisty characters, stories that feel like puzzles, and all things romance. She can always be found with a cup of coffee or glass of wine in hand, ready to discuss everything from celebrity gossip to your latest book theories.

Connect with her on Instagram and TikTok as @bynicoleplatania or on **nicoleplatania.com**.

Printed in Great Britain
by Amazon

38388440R00249